ALSO BY E L JAMES

The Mister

Fifty Shades of Grey
Fifty Shades Darker
Fifty Shades Freed

Grey
Darker
Freed

The MISSUS

E L James

Bloom books

Published by Bloom Books, an imprint of Sourcebooks
P.O. Box 4410, Naperville, Illinois 60567-4410
(630) 961-3900
sourcebooks.com

Cataloging-in-Publication Data is on file with the Library of Congress.

Printed and bound in the United States of America.
LSC 10 9 8 7 6 5 4 3 2 1

For D with love.

Chapter One

My footsteps echo an urgent beat on the hard reflective floor, and I squint beneath the unremitting light of the fluorescents.

"This way." The A&E consultant stops, and she ushers me into a cool, stark room that is the hospital mortuary.

On a table, beneath a sheet is the fractured, lifeless body of my brother.

My shock is seismic, pressing on my chest and squeezing the last of my breath from my lungs. Nothing could have prepared me for this.

Kit, my big brother.

My touchstone.

Kit, the twelfth Earl of Trevethick.

Dead.

"Yes. This is him." The words are like cotton in my mouth.

"Thank you, Lord Trevethick," the doctor murmurs.

Shit. That's me now!

I look down at Kit.

Except it's not him. *I'm* on the table—lying bruised and broken… cold… dead.

Me? How?

From my prostrate position, I watch Kit lean over and kiss my forehead. "Goodbye, you fucker," he rasps, the strain of unshed tears heavy in his throat. "You've got this. This is what you were born to do." He smiles his crooked, sincere smile that's reserved for those rare moments when he's fucked up.

Kit! No! You've got this wrong.

Wait!

"You've got this, Spare," he says. "You're lucky number thirteen." His smile slips, and he disappears. And I'm looking down at him once more, leaning over him while he sleeps. Except his battered body belies that—he's not asleep—he's… dead.

No! Kit! No! My words stay stuck in a throat that's crowded with too much sorrow.

No! No!

I wake, my heart pounding.

Where am I?

It takes a nanosecond to orient myself as my eyes adjust to the half-light. Alessia is curled around me, her head on my chest, her hand splayed on my stomach. As I take a deep, cleansing breath, my panic recedes like the gentle wash of a tideless sea.

I'm in Kukës in Northern Albania, at her parents' place, and across the lake, dawn is a whisper in the sky.

Alessia's here. With me. She's safe, and she's fast asleep. Carefully, I tighten my arm around her shoulders and kiss her hair, breathing in her scent. The faint balm of lavender, roses, and my sweet, sweet girl soothes and stirs my senses.

My body rouses; desire, hot and heavy, flowing south.

I want her. Again.

This is new—this need, but it's become ingrained, a part of who I am, and it's heightened when I'm with her. She's so enticing and lovely that I crave her like an addict. But I resist waking her—she's been through nine circles of hell.

Again.

Fuck.

I bring my body under control and close my eyes as my anger and regret resurface. I let her slip through my fingers. I let that violent arsehole, her "betrothed," steal her away. What she's endured, I don't want to know, but her cuts and bruises tell their own awful tale.

I'm never going to let that happen again.

Thank God she's safe.

Let her sleep.

Gently, I toy with a strand of her hair, marveling as ever at its softness. Drawing it to my mouth, I brush it against my lips in a tender kiss.

My love. My beautiful, brave girl.

She's overcome so much in such a short time: trafficking, homelessness, finding paid employment… and falling in love with me.

My sweet daily.

Soon to be my bride.

Closing my eyes once more, I snuggle closer, seeking her warmth, and doze.

I wake suddenly, prompted by—something, an external source.

What was that?

It's later—the light in the room is brighter.

"Alessia!"

Her mother is calling her.

Shit! We've overslept!

"Alessia! Wake up. Your mother's calling." I kiss her forehead, and she grumbles as I extract myself from her arms and sit up. "Alessia! Come on! If your dad finds us, he'll shoot us both."

The memory of her father, and his pump-action shotgun from last night, rises unwelcome in my mind.

You're going to marry my daughter.

Her mother calls again, and Alessia opens her eyes, blinking the sleep away. She looks up at me, all tousled and sleepy and arousing, and beams her brightest smile. For a moment, I forget the grim threat of her father with his trigger finger on that shotgun.

"Good morning, beautiful." I stroke her cheek, avoiding the scrape that's still there. Closing her eyes, she leans into my touch. "Your mother is calling you."

Her eyes spring open, and her smile disappears, replaced with an expression of wide-eyed alarm. She sits upright, wearing nothing but her little gold cross. "O Zot! O Zot!"

"Yeah. O Zot!"

"My nightdress!"

There's a muffled but urgent knock on the door. "Alessia!" Mrs. Demachi hisses.

"Shit! Hide! I'll get this." My heart is beating a frantic tattoo.

Alessia bounces out of bed, all naked limbs and loveliness, while I jump up and slide on my jeans. Honestly, I want to laugh—it's like we're in some ridiculous British farce. It's insane. We're both consenting adults, and we're soon to be married. With a quick glance at Alessia, who is wrestling into her gothic nightdress, I pad over to the door, open it a crack, and feign sleepiness. Her mother is on the other side. "Mrs. Demachi, good morning."

"Good morning, Count Maxim. Alessia?" she asks.

"Has she gone again?" I try to look concerned.

"She is not in her bed."

Alessia's feet patter over the cold tiled floor, and she slips her arms about my waist as she peeks around me. "Mama, I'm here," she whispers in English for my benefit, I think.

Bloody hell.

We've been discovered, and now I'm framed as a liar to my future mother-in-law. I give Shpresa an apologetic shrug, and she frowns without a trace of humor in her expression.

Shit.

"Alessia!" she hisses and looks nervously over her shoulder. "Po të gjeti yt atë këtu!"

"E di. E di," Alessia replies and in answer to my scowl, she gives me a sweet, contrite look and raises her lips to mine, offering me a chaste kiss. She slips out of the door, shrouded in her Victorian nightdress, and regards me with a heated over-the-shoulder look as she follows her mother up the stairs. I forgive her for outing me as a liar to her mother, and stand and listen as they hiss at each other in Albanian. I don't hear her father.

I think we got away with it.

Well, he did say she's my problem now. I shake my head as I shut the door, angered by the thought. Alessia is not *my problem*, for fuck's sake. She's a woman who knows her own mind. How could he even think that? It grinds my gears. Culturally, her dad and I are poles apart, and as much as I want to be respectful to him, he needs dragging into the twenty-first century. It's obvious why Alessia is wary of him. She obliquely alluded to his volatile nature when she mentioned him during our time in Cornwall. She said then that she didn't miss him—only her mother.

Hell. The sooner we leave here, the better.

How long will it take to get married?

Perhaps we should make a break for it.

Elope?

We could hole up at the Plaza Hotel in Tirana while we wait for her new passport and discover the delights of the capital together. How long will it take to get a passport anyway? Long enough for her father to come after us with his shotgun? I don't know, and somehow, I don't think Alessia would like the idea.

But this furtive running around like we're kids—it's crazy. It's as if we've traveled back several centuries, and I'm not sure I'll be able to tolerate this for long.

I check the time, and it's still early, so I strip out of my jeans and lie down. As I stare at the ceiling and reflect on the last few days, thoughts of my most recent dream drift into my consciousness.

What the hell was that about?

Kit?

He approves of me inheriting the earldom.

Is that it?

Would he approve of my hasty proposal and this shotgun wedding?

No, I don't think he would. Perhaps that's what it meant. Come to think of it—I'm not sure anyone in my family will approve. I close my eyes, imagining my mother's response to the news. Maybe she'll be happy to see me married… finally.

No. She'll be furious. I know it.

Perhaps my dream meant Kit is offering his solidarity.

Could be…

Yes.

That's what the dream was about.

Her mother is angry, and Alessia doesn't know what to say to pacify her.

"What do you think you were doing?" Shpresa growls.

Alessia raises a brow in answer.

"Alessia!" her mother snaps, knowing full well what Alessia is trying to convey. "Just because that man has had a bite of your cherry doesn't mean you shouldn't wait until after you're married!"

Mama!

"If your father catches you!" She sighs. "I think he's gone out, maybe to look for you. He would probably have a heart attack if he knew what you were doing." She tuts in exasperation as they make their way down the hall, but her expression softens when they reach the living room. "I suppose you're pregnant already, so…" She lifts her shoulders, resigned.

A slow flush creeps over Alessia's face. Should she tell her mother it was a lie?

"So, your handsome count, he's in good shape." Shpresa eyes her daughter with a teasing smile.

"Mama!" Alessia exclaims.

"He has a tattoo."

"Yes. It's his family's coat of arms."

"I see." She sounds disapproving and she purses her lips.

Alessia shrugs. She likes his tattoo.

Her mother smiles. "He is good to you… in bed?"

"Mama!" Alessia's voice rises several octaves in shock.

"It's important. I want you to be happy, and you must keep him happy. And it won't be long before the child arrives, and, well…" Her mother huffs, her disappointment rolling off her in waves while Alessia stares back at her blankly.

What can she say? That she lied to her parents?

And is this how it was for her mother after Alessia was born?

Alessia doesn't want to think about that. Besides, it's too early in the morning to be having this conversation.

"I think he's happy," she says eventually.

"Good. We can talk more on this."

"I don't want to talk more on this," Alessia retorts, mortified.

"Don't you have questions?"

Alessia pales at the thought. "No!"

"I suppose it's a bit late for that now. But if you have questions, your father and I—"

"Mama! Stop!" Alessia puts her hands over her ears. "I don't want to know."

Her mother laughs good-naturedly. "It is good to have you back, my heart. I have missed you so much." Her laughter fades, and her eyes narrow, her expression shifting—becoming serious. "Last night, I tossed and turned in bed. I was thinking about the ramifications of something that Lord Maxim said. I couldn't sleep with worry." Her voice fades away.

"What is it, Mama?"

She takes a deep breath as if what she's about to say is particularly unpalatable. "He said something about sex trafficking."

Alessia gasps. "Oh, Mama, I have so much to tell you, but first I'll have a shower."

Her mother gathers her into her arms. "Sweet child of my heart," she says softly in her ear. "I'm so glad you are home. And safe."

"Me too, Mama. And no more Anatoli."

Shpresa nods. "And your fiancé, does he have a violent temper?"

"No. No. He doesn't. Quite the opposite."

Her mother beams. "You light up like summer when you talk about him." She takes Alessia's hand and, raising a brow, admires the beautiful engagement ring. "He has money and taste."

Alessia nods and stares at the sparkling diamond on her finger.

This beautiful ring is now hers.

She can hardly believe it.

"Go shower. I will make bread and coffee."

Alessia stands beneath the shower in the family bathroom, reveling in the hot water. It's not as fast flowing as the showers in Cornwall, but she welcomes the warmth as she scrubs her skin clean. This is the first moment she's allowed herself to reflect on all that's happened over the last few days.

Anatoli. Her kidnapping. The long journey here. His brutality.

She shudders. He's out of her life now, and for that, she's grateful.

And she was welcomed home; even her father admitted he missed her.

Alessia closes her eyes as she vigorously rubs the shampoo into her hair, trying to erase her guilt. She's lied to her parents, and her dishonesty chafes like a burr on her conscience.

She's not pregnant, but should she tell them the truth?

What would her father say if he knew? What would he do?

She raises her face to the cascade and lets it wash over her.

And then there's Maxim.

She grins into the stream of water. He crossed a continent to find her and brought a ring with him to propose. It's far more than she could ever have dreamed of or hoped for. Now, she needs to find out how Maxim really feels about having an Albanian wedding forced on him.

He didn't object last night.

But she wishes her father were less insistent.

Alessia would be happier back in London and worries Maxim will feel the same. How long will it be before he becomes bored of being in Kukës? He's used to a very different life, and there's not much to entertain him here. Perhaps they should flee Kukës together. They could marry in England.

Would Maxim consider this idea? Alessia rinses her hair and stops.

No. Mama!

Alessia cannot leave her mother at the mercy of her father. She must bring her mother with her. *Could she? Would Maxim object?* After all, Shpresa speaks fluent English. *Her* mother, Alessia's beloved grandmother Virginia, was English. She must have family in England. Alessia doesn't know. Her Nana never spoke of her English family because they disapproved of her marriage to an Albanian man.

Will it be the same with Maxim's family?

Will they disapprove of her?

A shiver skitters down her spine. Maxim's marrying his cleaner, a penniless foreigner. Of course they won't approve. Alessia's mood sours.

What can she do?

Perhaps they shouldn't marry until she's met his family, and she'll know if they accept her, or not, because in the depths of her heart—she wants their blessing.

But first, she must navigate her father and his expectations, and he's a stubborn, temperamental, proud man. He said he wanted them married by the end of the week.

Is that even possible?

She scrubs her face. There is much to think about and much to be done.

When Alessia enters the kitchen, her mother looks up from kneading dough and studies her. "You look different," she says, setting the dough aside to rise.

"Is it the clothes?" Alessia does a twirl. She's wearing a skirt, top, and cardigan from the collection that Maxim bought her in Padstow.

"Yes, maybe. But you look more worldly." Her mother moves to the sink to wash her hands.

"I am," Alessia replies quietly. She's been trafficked through Europe, been homeless, lived in one of the busiest cities in the world, and she's fallen in love… then had that all snatched away from her as she was kidnapped, and nearly raped, by her betrothed. Alessia shudders.

Don't think of him.

"Coffee?" her mother asks.

"No sugar for me," she says as she sits at the table.

Shpresa peers at her in surprise. "It tastes okay?"

"You get used to it."

Shpresa places a full cup on the table for Alessia and sits opposite her with a cup of her own. "Tell me. What happened after I put you on that minibus on the road to Shkodër?"

"Oh, Mama." Alessia's lip quivers as the enormity of what she's experienced since she left Albania rises in her chest like a tidal wave. Haltingly, between her tears, she tells her mother the whole story.

I wake feeling refreshed. The sun is higher in the sky, and when I check the time, it's 9:30 a.m. It's late. Hurriedly, I drag on my jeans, T-shirt, and sweater. At some point, I'll need to head back to the hotel and collect my stuff. But more importantly, I need to know what's happening with our shotgun wedding.

In the family room, I find Alessia and her mother quietly sobbing at the table.

What the hell?

"What's wrong?" I startle them both as my anxiety rockets.

Alessia dashes the tears from her eyes and leaps up from her chair into my arms.

"Hey. What is it?"

"Nothing. I'm glad you are here." She hugs me.

I kiss the top of her head. "So am I."

Shpresa rises too and wipes her eyes. "Good morning, Lord Maxim."

"Good morning. Um… Maxim is fine. It's my name."

She gives me a tight smile. "Coffee?"

"Please."

"No sugar, Mama," Alessia interjects.

I tilt her chin up and gaze into sad, dark eyes that have seen and experienced too much. My heart clenches.

My love.

"Why are you so upset?"

"I was telling Mama about everything that happened after I left Kukës."

I tighten my hold on her as a surge of protective energy constricts my chest. "I see." Kissing her hair, I cradle her against me, grateful once more that she's survived her harrowing ordeal. "I've got you now, and I'm not going to let you out of my sight."

Ever.

I frown, surprised at the ferocity of my feelings. I really *don't* want to let her out of my sight. She's been through too much already. "I mean it," I add. She runs her fingertips over my stubble, and her touch reverberates… everywhere. "I need a shave." I sound gruff.

She grins. "I would like to watch."

"Would you now?" I raise a brow.

Alessia's eyes are no longer despondent but sparkling with amusement and an emotion that speaks directly to my groin.

Mrs. Demachi busies herself preparing coffee, noisily banging the small pot, so the spell between Alessia and me is broken. I kiss Alessia's nose, and grinning like a fool, I turn my attention to her mother. Alessia nuzzles my chest as I watch the elaborate process that includes a small tin pot, a long teaspoon, and studious stirring at the stove.

Mrs. Demachi gives me a brief smile. "Sit," she says, so I release my fiancée and, with a glance at the shotgun on the wall, take a seat at the table.

Alessia retrieves a cup and saucer from the dresser. She's wearing the dark denim skirt we bought in Padstow, which clings enticingly to her perfectly formed arse.

She's gorgeous.

I shift in my chair, and Alessia fills my cup from the tin pot. "Your coffee," she says, her dark eyes gleaming with delight, and she places the cup in front of me. She knows I'm ogling her, and she likes it. I grin and, with my eyes on hers, purse my lips together to blow gently over the rim of the cup. Her lips part as she inhales sharply, and my grin widens.

Two can play this game.

Her mother clears her throat, and we're both brought back into the kitchen. Alessia laughs and says something in Albanian to Mrs. Demachi, who nods in quiet disapproval at her daughter.

I attempt a sip of coffee. It's scalding hot, aromatic, and bitter but warming. Alessia's mother lights the oven and then starts rolling out some dough. She's quick and efficient, and before long, she's cut them into strips, then squares. The speed is impressive. No wonder Alessia cooks so well. Alessia joins her, and I watch, fascinated, as they each form little round dough balls in their hands. Their ease in the kitchen reminds me of Jessie and Danny at Tresyllian Hall in Cornwall. Her mother arranges them close together on a baking tray, and Alessia paints them with milk using a little plastic brush. Their competence, their ease with each other—their domesticity is comforting to watch.

Hell. Where are my manners?

C an I do anything to help?" Maxim asks.
  Alessia carefully shakes her head while her mother nods.

"No, Mama. The nodding means yes."

Shpresa laughs. "We are not used to help from men in the kitchen." Her eyes are alight with humor as she places the baking tray in the oven.

Alessia starts laying the table. "I told you. Only women cook here."

B reakfast is a delicious fresh-from-the-oven feast. I'm on my fourth bubble bread roll with butter and berry jam and my second coffee when we hear the front door slam. A few moments later, Mr. Demachi appears wearing a somber suit and matching expression that gives nothing away. Shpresa leaps up from the table and starts to fill the coffeepot with water.

Perhaps she needs a larger pot.

Alessia rises from the table, reaches for a plate, and lays it at the head of the table with a knife. Demachi sits down, and it's obvious this is normal—he's been waited on, hand and foot, for his entire life.

Um… So have I. But not by my mother—or my sister for that matter.

"Mirëmëngjes," he grunts, looking directly at me as inscrutable as ever.

"My father is wishing you a good morning," Alessia translates and looks amused.

Why does she find this funny?

"Good morning." I give my future father-in-law a nod.

He starts speaking, and Alessia and her mother listen,

enthralled by his deep melodious voice as he explains something to them. I just wish I knew what he was saying.

Eventually, Alessia turns to me, her eyes wide as if she doesn't quite believe what she's about to tell me. "My father, he has arranged our marriage."

Already?

It's my turn to look incredulous. "Tell me."

"All you need is your passport."

We gaze at each other, and I think the same thought runs through her head and mine.

This sounds too easy.

My eyes meet his, and he raises his chin in an arrogant don't-fuck-with-me glare as if he's daring me to argue.

"He met the clerk of the, um…civil status…office. I don't know the precise translation," Alessia says. "They met for coffee this morning. They agreed on everything."

On a Sunday? Is it that simple?

"Okay. When?" I keep my voice measured, as I don't want to rile the old goat. He has a short fuse—almost as bad as my friend Tom's.

"Saturday."

A frisson of doubt trickles down my spine. "Okay," I answer, and my hesitancy must give me away. Mrs. Demachi glances anxiously from me to her husband, then to her daughter.

Alessia says something to her dad, and he shouts back at her, startling us all. She pales and hangs her head but peeks at me as I push back my chair.

He shouldn't speak to her like that.

"The clerk and he are good friends," Alessia says hurriedly. "Old friends. I think I know him. I've met him before. My father says it's all arranged." She's obviously used to his outbursts, but she, too, seems uncertain.

As am I. This arrangement seems far too convenient.

Perplexed, I settle in my chair once more, not wanting to provoke him. "What do I need to do?"

"We must meet with the clerk tomorrow at the bashkia—I mean, town hall—to answer some questions and complete some paperwork." She shrugs, looking as troubled as I feel.

Okay. Let's talk to the clerk.

As I stand under the rather rudimentary shower and wash my hair, I have a complete crisis of conscience. A quick internet search on my phone has told me that it's far more complicated to marry as a foreign national in Albania than Alessia's father seems to think. There are forms to be completed, then translated and notarized—and that's just a quick and dirty glance of what's required.

What has her father organized?

How has he managed to circumvent the usual protocols?

If he has, are they legal?

And if they're not, how can I go ahead with a wedding that's probably not legal to appease a proud, impatient old man? I know he'll be my father-in-law, but what he's asking is too much. All his talk of honor yesterday accounts for nothing if he treats his daughter this way.

And I'm in a bind. I can't leave without Alessia, and I know the old bastard won't let me take her with me. She needs a passport and a visa to return to the UK, and I have no idea where or how we get one. Probably somewhere in Tirana. I don't know.

Though he did say she was my problem now.

Maybe I should take him at his word.

I switch off the shower, resentful and bewildered by the situation I've found myself in—and by the large puddle of water I've left on the bathroom floor. It does not speak well of Albanian plumbing. I snatch a towel and quickly dry myself, then drag on my clothes and open the door.

Alessia is standing outside, brandishing what looks like a high-tech shower-cleaning device. I laugh, surprised and pleased to see her, and I'm transported back to a time when she was in my flat, wearing her frightful nylon housecoat, and I was surreptitiously watching her… and falling in love.

She grins and places her fingers against her lips.

"Does he know you're here?" I whisper.

She shakes her head, places her hand squarely on my chest, and pushes me back into the bathroom. She drops the mop and promptly locks the door.

"Alessia," I warn, but she cups my face and pulls my lips to hers. Her kiss is soft and sweet but demanding—surprisingly demanding. As her tongue finds mine, she presses her body against me, and I close my eyes and wrap my arms around her, delighting in her kiss. Her fingers slide into my wet hair, and her lips become more insistent as she tugs. It's a wake-up call to my impatient dick.

Hell. We're going to fuck.

In an Albanian bathroom with poor plumbing.

I pull away so we can catch our breath, and Alessia's eyes are dark and full of promise but also uncertainty.

"What is it?" I ask.

She shakes her head.

"No." I clasp her face and gaze into her eyes. "God, as much as I want you, we're not fucking in this bathroom. Your parents aren't far away, and I don't have a condom. Now tell me, what's wrong? Is it the wedding?"

"Yes."

I blow out a breath in relief and release her. "Yeah. What your father's arranged—I don't know if it's… legitimate."

"I know. My parents want to discuss the, um…arrangements with us in the afternoon. I don't know what to do. I think it's because my father thinks I am with child. He's managed to pull the strings."

An image of her dad as an evil puppet master with Alessia and me as his marionettes comes to mind, making me chuckle. "We say 'pull some strings.'"

She repeats the saying and gives me a shy smirk.

"You still don't mind that I correct your English?"

"Never."

Okay. Let's go with Plan A. Here goes.

"Let's leave. You don't have to stay here. You're an adult. You're not beholden to your father—whatever he thinks. We can go to Tirana. Get a passport for you and arrange a visa. Then we can fly back to the UK. We'll get married there. And your parents can join us for the wedding."

Alessia's eyes widen as several emotions flit across her face. Hope seems to win, and I think she's been considering this possibility herself.

But then her face falls, so I draw her into my arms and hold her. "We'll figure this out." I kiss her hair.

She peers up at me, and I think she's inwardly debating whether to ask me something.

"What?"

"No. It's okay."

"What?" I insist.

She swallows. "My mother."

"What about your mother?"

"I can't leave her here with him."

"You want to bring her with you?"

"Yes."

Fuck. "Okay. If that's what you want."

Alessia looks stunned. "You are saying yes?"

"Yes."

She lights up like Christmas, as if she's finally unburdened of all her woes. She flings her arms around my neck. "Thank you. Thank you. Thank you," she gasps between kisses and starts to laugh and cry.

Oh, baby.

"Don't cry. I'd do anything for you. You should know that. I love you." I wipe her tears away with my thumbs as I caress her face. "And like I said, we'll figure this out. We'll make a plan."

Her eyes, dark with adoration, peek up at me as if I have all the answers to the eternal questions of the universe and a welcome warmth spreads through my chest. Her trust and faith in me are bewildering, but damn, it feels good.

And I know, for her, I'd do anything.

Chapter Two

It's dark outside as I stumble toward the bed and attempt to peel off my sweater, but it fights back and finally gets the better of me. "Shit!" I fall on the bed and stare blindly at the blurred ceiling.

Oh God. Why did I drink so much?

After an afternoon of wedding planning and trying not to lose my temper, the raki was a mistake. The room swims, and I shut my eyes, praying for sleep.

I surface from a dreamless sleep. It's quiet. And bright.

No. Dazzling.

I scrunch my eyes closed, then open them cautiously as pain slices with a laser's precision through my brain. I shut them again quickly.

Hell. I feel like shit.

Pulling the covers over my head to shut out the light, I try to remember where I am, who I am, and what happened last night.

There was raki.

Shots and shots of raki.

Alessia's father was exceedingly generous with his lethal, local intoxicant. I groan and flex my fingers and toes and am pleased to find that they still work. I reach out beside me, but the bed is empty.

No Alessia.

Drawing down the covers, I slowly open my eyes and ignore the sharp jab to my frontal lobe as I survey the room. I'm on my own, but my tired gaze rests on the little dragon nightlight on the table beside the bed. Alessia must have brought it back from London. The thought is touching.

Also, was she here? Last night?

Vaguely, I remember her joining me, and maybe undressing me. I lift the covers. I'm naked except for my underwear. She must have undressed me.

Damn. I passed out and have no memory of her in here at all.

Why did I let him ply me with so much alcohol?

Was it his revenge because I've bedded his daughter?

And what happened?

Snippets from yesterday sneak past the pain in my head. Alessia and I had sat down and discussed wedding plans with her parents. I close my eyes and try to recall the details.

From what I understand, we're departing from the Albanian tradition by celebrating on one day only—rather than several days. Firstly, because I'm British and have no family or home here, and secondly, we're doing all this at such short notice as Alessia is "with child." Demachi gave me a sour look as he sputtered this, and Alessia, blushing furiously, had to translate.

I sigh. Perhaps we should confess to the lie. Maybe he'll back off.

Maybe he'll let me take her back to the UK and get married there.

The ceremony and celebration will be on Saturday and will start at lunchtime—not in the evening. It's another break with tradition, but because I'm staying with the bride's family, it makes sense, or so they told me. Besides, the registrar has another wedding to conduct in the evening.

The Demachis will host the wedding themselves, and Mr. Demachi asked if my family would attend. I set him right on that score. My mother will no doubt be in New York, and she wouldn't get here in time, and my sister, as a doctor, won't be able to get the time off at such short notice. I reassured them that we will celebrate in London when we're back in the UK. My excuses seemed to pacify the old goat. I don't think my family will approve of a shotgun wedding, and I don't want to give them the opportunity to object, or question the legitimacy of our marriage. However, I'm hoping my sparring partner, Joe Diallo, will join us so I'll have him and Tom Alexander with me. They are my oldest friends.

That counts for something, surely.

I had offered to pay for everything but was shot down by my father-in-law, with his most wounded expression.

Boy, is he proud.

He would hear of no such thing. I suspect he likes a little drama; he's a melodramatic man. I suggested a compromise, and we agreed that I'll supply the alcohol. But it chafes that he'll be out of pocket if Alessia and I decide not to go through with it.

Hell. That's his problem.

There's also something about the rings, which I can't remember.

Rings! I need to buy rings.

Shall I buy them here?

I sit up and my head swims, but once it settles, I stagger out of bed and drag on my jeans to go in search of my future wife. What I do remember is that today we implement our plan. Alessia and I will visit the police station to apply for her new passport and then on to the town hall to keep our appointment with the clerk officiating the marriage and find out if what Demachi has organized is indeed legitimate.

Yeah. That's the plan.

I reach for my phone and notice a couple of texts from Caroline left last night.

Where are you? Did you find her?
Call me. I'm worried about you.

Surprised that my thumbs are cooperating, I send her a quick text, knowing she'll probably send out a search party if I don't respond.

All good. Found her. Will call later.

She'll lose her shit over this wedding; I know it in my bones. Perhaps I shouldn't tell her until I see her.

Coward.

My head throbs, and I rub my temples, trying to calm the squall that rages between them. If I tell Caroline, I'll have to tell Maryanne and my mother, and that's a conversation I'm actively avoiding, especially with a hangover. I'm not ready for that yet. I need to know where Alessia and I stand legally, then, maybe, I'll tell the Mothership, but perhaps I'll leave telling her until the day before we do the deed.

I drag on a T-shirt and pocket my phone. All that can wait; I need pain relief and coffee, preferably in that order.

Alessia and her mother are sitting at the dining table, drinking coffee.

"Mama, do you have my ID card?"

"Of course, my heart. I've treasured it since you left."

Alessia is taken aback at her mother's words, and an aching void forms in her throat as she reaches across to squeeze Shpresa's hand. "I thought of you often while I was gone," she says, her voice husky with emotion. "I didn't have any of my photographs or my phone. The men… They took everything. Including my passport. I'm glad I left my ID with you. I need to get another passport."

"I'll fetch it for you shortly. I'm glad that the scrape on your face has almost healed. And the bruises. They look much better."

Her mouth thins as she examines her daughter. "I would like to box Anatoli Thaçi's ears."

Alessia smiles. "I would like to watch you do that." She releases her and stares anxiously across at her mother. Alessia realizes this is her opportunity. She's been trying to bring up this subject since she and Maxim discussed it yesterday. "I have to ask you something."

"Yes, child?"

Alessia swallows, and the thoughtful speech she'd rehearsed so many times in her head dries on her tongue.

"Alessia, what is it?"

"Come with us," Alessia blurts, suddenly incapable of saying what she'd planned.

"What?"

"Come with me and Maxim to England. Please. You don't have to stay with him."

Shpresa gasps, her dark eyes widening. "Leave Jak?"

Alessia hears the dismay in her mother's voice. "Yes."

Her mother sits back in the chair and gapes at Alessia. "He's my husband, child. I'm not going to leave him."

This is not what Alessia is expecting to hear. "But he's not kind to you," she protests. "He's violent. Like Anatoli. You cannot stay."

"Alessia, he's not like Anatoli. I love your father."

"What?" Alessia's world shifts on its axis.

"My place is with him," Shpresa says with steel in her voice.

"But you told me love is for fools."

Her mother's eyes soften, and she lifts her lips in a rueful smile. "I am a fool, my heart. We have our ups and downs, I know. Like all couples—"

"I've seen the bruises, Mama! Please. Come with us."

"My place is with him. This is my home. I have a life here. There's nothing for me in a land I don't know. Besides, since you left, he's been more considerate. Contrite, I think. He believes he drove you away. He was so relieved when we got word of you."

Alessia is shocked. This is not how she viewed her father or, indeed, her parents' relationship at all.

"You see, my heart," her mother continues, and she reaches across the table to grasp Alessia's hand. "This is the life I know. Your father loves me. Baba loves you too. He may not show it like we see in the American television programs—and I see it's different with your betrothed, but that's how it is in *our* house. This is my home, and he's my husband." She shrugs and then squeezes Alessia's hand as if trying to convey the truth of her words through the pressure of her fingers, but Alessia is reeling. She'd always thought her mother was miserable with her father.

Was she wrong?

Did she misread the situation between them?

I stand unseen on the threshold of the family room and observe Alessia's mother speaking in urgent, hushed tones to her daughter. They're sitting at the dining table—the location of Mr. Demachi's raki attack last night—and their conversation is intense. But the pounding in my brain needs therapeutic drugs, so I stagger in, surprising them both, and slump into one of the chairs.

Shpresa releases Alessia's hand. "We can talk more on this later. But my mind is made up, sweet girl. I'm not leaving my husband. I love him. In my own way. And he loves and needs me." She smiles benevolently at Alessia, then turns her attention to Maxim. "Your count, he had too much to drink last night. Fetch him a couple of painkillers. I'll make him some coffee."

Alessia looks anxiously at her mother, surprised and confused by her reaction. "Yes, Mama. We'll talk later." She's bewildered by her mother's response, but she turns to Maxim, who holds his head in his hands, and her stance softens. "I don't think my fiancé is used to raki."

"I understood raki," Maxim groans, husky-voiced, and he peers at her, bleary-eyed.

Alessia smiles. "I will fetch some tablets for your head."

I lean toward her. "Thank you for putting me to bed last night." I keep my voice low as her mother busies herself with the coffeepot.

"It was interesting." She stops and checks that Shpresa is out of hearing range. "It was fun undressing you."

I take a quick, sharp breath as she rises and retrieves a first-aid kit from the pantry, and when she turns back, her dark, provocative eyes dart to mine, her face illuminated with a shy, secret smile.

My heart lurches in my chest.

My girl undressed me, and I was unconscious with drink.

Hell. An opportunity wasted.

But more than the wasted opportunity, she's not judged me for being inebriated, and now she's taking care of me. It's a new and wholly enlightening experience, and I love her for it. I can't remember anyone doing that for me as an adult—except Alessia when she put me to bed after that crazy drive from Cornwall. She's kind, caring, and… hot, especially in tight jeans.

I'm a lucky guy.

I attempt a broad smile but my head throbs, and I'm reminded that it was her father who inflicted this damage—and I was only drinking the ghastly beverage to be polite. Alessia places two tablets and a glass of water in front of me. "It was my father who did this to you. I know. And it was our local raki. Made here in Kukës."

"I see." *It was his revenge!* "Thank you," I offer.

"You are most welcome." She gives me a coquettish smile, and I wonder if she's talking about the tablets or undressing me. Grinning, I down the painkillers and wonder if Tom and Thanas will be in a similar state to me.

Following our lengthy discussions yesterday, and with the marriage formalities supposedly settled, Mrs. Demachi and Alessia had prepared a lavish meal and kindly invited my friend Tom, our translator Thanas, and Drita, his girlfriend. While they prepared the meal, Alessia taught me some Albanian words—my pleases and thank yous.

She laughed.

A lot.

At my pronunciation.

But it's always a joy to hear her laugh.

Alessia's mother had been in her element, happy to have a house full of guests, even though she didn't say much. She left that to her husband, who regaled us with stories of the turbulent 1990s as Albania transitioned from Communism to a democratic republic. It was fascinating—his family was caught up in a terrible pyramid scheme, and they'd lost what money they had. It's how they'd found themselves in Kukës during those dark times. While he talked, his generous but heavy hand poured and poured the raki. Tom and Thanas matched me shot for shot, I'm sure. They'll be meeting us at the town hall, provided they've survived the Ordeal by Raki. I check my watch. I have an hour to get it together.

The town hall is a nondescript modern building a stone's throw from Hotel Amerika where Tom and Thanas are staying. Hand-in-hand, Alessia and I stand in the reception area waiting for them to join us, and despite the dull ache in my head from my hangover, I cannot help my smile. Alessia's so buoyant since our earlier stop at the police station that she lights up the dreary foyer. Her new passport will be ready to collect on Friday—I paid for it to be expedited—and one would think I lassoed the moon she's so jubilant, but Alessia having a passport gives us options.

"Just the sight of your joy is easing my hangover." I try to contain my smile, but I fail. She *is* a joy.

"I think it is the tablets I gave you."

"No. It's you."

She laughs, peering at me through her lashes, and I lift her hand and skim her knuckles with my lips.

God, I wish I could whisk her away from this drab little town.

Soon, dude. Soon.

Tom and Thanas appear, Thanas looking how I feel—disheveled and hungover.

"Well, Trevethick, you look like hell. What are we doing here?" Tom asks, bright as a fucking button. Raki appears to agree with him.

"I am sorry we're late," Thanas mumbles. "I took Drita to board the bus to Tirana. She has to get back to her studies."

"We're here to visit the clerk who will officiate our wedding."

"The registrar. I'll go check where we must go," Thanas says and wanders toward the reception desk to wait in line. Alessia joins him.

"So," Tom hisses, keeping his voice low and sounding conspiratorial. "I never congratulated you about the baby."

The baby?

It takes me a moment in my befuddled state to realize what he's talking about. I laugh and stop suddenly as my head throbs. "Alessia's not pregnant. She told her father she was so she wouldn't be forced to marry that wanker Antonelli or whatever his name is."

"Ah." Tom looks relieved. "Well, I suppose that's good. Too early in a relationship for sprogs." He leans into me while watching Thanas and Alessia and hisses, "But you know you don't have to marry her, old boy."

For fuck's sake.

"Tom." My voice warns him off the subject. "We've had this conversation already. For the last time, I love Alessia and want her to be my wife. Understand?"

"Frankly, no. She's a beautiful girl, I'll give you that, but I can't imagine you've got much in common. But the heart wants what the heart wants."

I'm in no mood for an argument, so when he holds a conciliatory hand up at my scowl, I blow out a breath. "Should I humor the old goat, marry her here? Or wait until we return to the UK? I'm stuck here until she gets her passport and a visa, and I'm not leaving her on her own." I glance over to where she's standing patiently beside Thanas, who's talking to the receptionist.

"Well," Tom says. "If it's what you want, I think you should go along with it. It's a civil ceremony at the town hall. You'll keep the old chap happy, and then you can abscond with his daughter and do it properly in London, Cornwall, or Oxfordshire. Wherever." He frowns. "If you can."

"What do you mean?"

"I don't know if you can get married more than once to the same woman, old boy. I'm sure there are rules. What do you have to do here?"

"I have to show my passport, and apparently that's it, though that's not what the official government website says."

Tom's brow furrows once more. "You think something's off?"

I nod. "But we'll find out with Thanas. Will you stick around until then? And… you know, help out?"

"Of course, Trevethick. Wouldn't miss this high drama for the world."

"High drama?" My scalp itches. Has he guessed we might abscond?

"You've traveled to the back of beyond to save your lady. If that's not the definition of drama, I don't know what is."

I laugh. He has a point. "And, um… will you be my best man?"

Tom is momentarily speechless, and when he finds his voice, it's gruff. "I'd be honored, Maxim." He pats me on the back, and we turn to find Thanas and Alessia heading over to us.

"This way," Thanas says, and we follow him up the stairs to the next floor.

The brass nameplate on his desk reads F. TABAKU. He's the registrar who will officiate at our civil ceremony. He's a similar age to Demachi and wears the same dark suit and impenetrable expression. He rises as we enter his office, greets Alessia cordially, gives me a curt nod, then waves us to the small table where the five of us take our seats.

Thanas translates as we quickly establish that he needs to see a copy of Alessia's birth certificate and ID card, and my passport. I fish mine out of my coat and open it up to the correct page, realizing that I, too, will have to get a new passport. At present, mine is in the name The Hon Maximillian John Frederick Xavier Trevelyan.

We hand over our documents, and he gives Alessia's a cursory glance. My passport receives a more thorough examination. Tabaku frowns and says something to Thanas. Alessia interjects. "Vëllai i Maksimit ishte Konti. Ai vdiq në fillim të janarit. Maksimi trashëgoi titullin, po nuk ka pasur ende mundësi të ndryshojë pasaportën."

Tabaku seems satisfied with whatever Alessia has said and rises from the table to a small desktop photocopier. While he makes copies, I ask Alessia, "What did you say?"

"I told him that you have only recently…um…inherited your title."

He turns and addresses us both. Thanas translates. "Spouses, when entering into marriage, have the right to choose to keep one of their surnames as a common surname or you keep your own. You need to decide."

I turn to Alessia. "What do you want to do?"

"I would like to take your name."

I smile, pleased. "Good. For your purposes, Alessia's name is Alessia Trevelyan. Her formal title will be Alessia, The Right Honorable the Countess of Trevethick."

"Please write that down," Thanas translates.

I oblige on the notepaper provided and hand my scribble to Tabaku.

Tabaku responds, and Thanas says, "I will name Alessia as Alessia Demachi-Trevelyan; your passport says nothing about Trevethick."

"That's fine," I grumble and turn to Thanas. "Ask him about the certificate of no-impediment that I'm supposed to provide."

Thanas does, and Alessia glances anxiously at me.

The registrar's eyes widen, and he spits an answer back at Thanas, who turns to me as he reels off Tabaku's response. "He says that because time is an issue," his eyes dart to Alessia, "he is expediting your marriage. He has the power to do so in special circumstances. Alessia's father is a close and trusted friend, and that's why he's offering this service."

The registrar continues in his low voice, his eyes not leaving mine, and it dawns on me that he's doing Demachi, and thereby us, an enormous favor.

"He says the marriage will be legal. It's all you need," Thanas translates. "You will have a marriage certificate."

"And if we want to do it with all the correct paperwork?" I ask.

Tabaku retakes his seat, hands our documents back, and responds to Thanas's question. "That will take between two to three months."

"Okay. I see. Thank you." Even though he's doing us a favor, I'm still uncomfortable. It feels like a sham and that thought is unsettling.

The registrar says something to Alessia and Thanas. Alessia nods and starts speaking to him in Albanian. I look hopefully at Thanas. "He's asking for your profession, place of residence, and where you'll live once you're married."

Profession!

I give Thanas my address in Chelsea and tell him that's where we'll live when we're married. Alessia glances at me with a shy smile.

"And profession?" Thanas inquires as the words my father used to adopt when asked this drift conveniently into my head.

"Farmer and photographer," I state quickly, though it's not the entire truth. Now, I'm a landowner and a landlord—the CEO of the Trevethick Estate.

"And DJ," Tom interjects rather unhelpfully, and when I glare at him, adds, "You know, spin the decks." He mimes the action. "And peer of the realm, of course. Heavy is the head and all that."

"Thanks, Tom." I ignore Alessia's stifled giggle while Tabaku finishes scribbling his notes. He places his biro on his notepad and, leaning back into his chair, says something to Alessia and me.

"He has all he needs to write the contract," Alessia says.

Reaching over, I squeeze her hand. "That's it?"

"Yes."

"Good. Let's go back to the hotel and decide what to do next."

She nods, and I rise from my seat and give Tabaku a brief nod. "Thank you."

Thanas translates his response. "I will see you on Saturday in the afternoon. And you must choose two people to be witnesses."

Witnesses? More like accomplices.

A lessia does not know how to gauge Maxim's mood—or what he'll do. He was quiet and brooding as he stalked back to the hotel. Is he angry? Does he still want to flee? They're sitting in the Hotel Amerika bar, a first for her in her home country, and she wonders what he's thinking.

Tom and Thanas have returned to their rooms, so she's alone with him. He looks pensive as he reaches over and takes her hand. "I'm somewhat aggrieved that we're jumping through all these hoops to appease your father's ego."

"I know. I am sorry." She stares at the table, not knowing what to say and unable to escape the feeling that she's responsible for their predicament. If only she hadn't lied about the pregnancy. But then her father might have insisted she marry Anatoli.

"Hey. It's not *your* fault, for heaven's sake." Maxim gives her hand a reassuring squeeze. She returns her gaze to his and is relieved to see nothing but his concern. "I don't want to fight with your father, but I wish he hadn't put us in this position. I know he thinks he's doing the right thing."

Alessia nods, surprised at how seriously he's taking their situation. He wants their marriage to be authentic. His jaw is tense, his expression serious, and his eyes a glowing green. She hates that he looks so troubled. "What do you think we should do?" she asks.

Maxim shakes his head but then smiles; he's dazzling, stealing her breath away.

He really is the most attractive man.

"Well, we're stuck here until you get your passport and visa—I'm not leaving without you. So, if you have no objection, I think we should do it."

Alessia considers his words. He's resigned to the wedding. Is that what she wants?

"Do you feel trapped?" she whispers.

"No. Yes. But not in the way you think. I came here to ask you to marry me. You said yes, and fundamentally your father is fulfilling that wish for me."

Alessia nods. "I see that. Also, I think it will help my mother if we stay here and go through with the wedding."

"Oh?"

"She doesn't want to come to England with us. She wants to stay with him. I don't understand why. But I think he'll be angry if we leave, and he might—" She doesn't finish the sentence, too ashamed of what her father might do to her mother.

Maxim studies her, his expression full of resolve. "That's a compelling argument to go through with it. For her sake as well as ours."

Alessia breathes a sigh of relief. "I agree."

He smiles. "That makes me feel better."

"Yes. Me too. I think it's the right decision for her."

"And the right decision for you?" he asks.

"Yes," she answers emphatically. "It will mean that my family will not lose…um…the face in the community."

Maxim blows out a breath and looks relieved. "Good. Okay. Decision made."

And Alessia feels lighter—the weight of her father's expectation lifted. How easy it was for them to reach a consensus—her fiancé and her.

Is this what their marriage will be like?

She hopes so.

"And now, I have much to do," Alessia says.

"Yeah. I'll grab the rest of my things from Tom's room, and let's head back. I have something for you."

"Oh?"

He grins. "Yes."

There are several cars in the drive when we arrive at the house.

"O Zot," Alessia says as she turns to me. "My family. The women. They are here."

"Ah…" It's all I can think of to say.

"Yes. They will all want to meet you." She pouts. "And I wanted to…um…set up this phone." She holds up the iPhone box I handed her at the hotel, and I give her a sympathetic smile. She sighs. "I'll do it later. The women gather. We always do when there's a wedding. And they will want to check you up."

"Check me up?" I chuckle. "Well, I hope I don't disappoint them." But despite our levity, I feel a rising sense of panic, though I'm not sure why.

"Don't worry, you will not disappoint them." Alessia's lips quirk in a shy grin.

"Oh yeah?"

"Yeah. And I'll protect you from them. I've got you."

I laugh once more, and we climb out of the Dacia. Alessia takes my hand, and together we enter the house. I slip off my shoes, as does Alessia, and they join the many shoes scattered beside the shoe rack.

"Ready?" Alessia asks.

I nod and take a deep breath as we stride down the hall toward the buzz coming from the family room.

When she sees us in the doorway, Shpresa announces what I assume is our arrival rather loudly, and several pairs of eyes turn to stare at us as the noise level rises exponentially. There must be at least a dozen women, aged from fifteen to fifty, gathered in the room, and they surge toward us. The older women look a little like Mrs. Demachi and are dressed more traditionally with scarves on their heads and full skirts. The younger women are in more casual contemporary clothes. Alessia squeezes my hand and starts to make introductions as her relatives kiss and hug her. She manages to keep hold of my hand throughout as they kiss and hug me too. By all accounts, they are delighted to meet me. None of the older women speak English, but the youngest two are pretty fluent.

After fifteen minutes of continuous smiling to the point I might get rictus in my cheeks, I manage to extricate myself with the excuse that I have calls to make, and I head down to the guest room.

Alessia is overwhelmed with the attention of her aunts and cousins. *He's so handsome. Where have you been? What happened to you? We thought you were marrying Anatoli Thaçi. He's a count! Let us see the ring. So European. Is he rich?* The questions come thick and fast, and Alessia fends them off with the help of her mother.

"I did not wish to marry Anatoli," she says as the women hang on her every word.

There are gasps of dismay.

"But your father's besa?" Her father's sister tuts.

"He was not for me." Alessia raises her chin in defiance.

"Alessia has captured the heart of a fine man. She's in love. She will be happy," her mother declares. "And what's more, he's come all the way from England to claim her."

I place my luggage on the bed and withdraw my phone from my jacket, pleased to be out of the limelight and the rapt attention of so many curious women—though I can still hear them chattering and laughing above me through the ceiling. Ignoring them, I switch on the phone.

First, I call Oliver, the chief operating officer of the Trevethick Estate.

"My lord—I mean Maxim. How are you? Where are you?"

I quickly fill him in on all he needs to know. "…And we'll need to press on with a visa for Alessia. Let Rajah know. Alessia and I are getting married."

"Oh! And, um—congratulations. When?"

"Thank you. Saturday."

I hear Oliver's gasp and then his silence. It speaks volumes.

"Yes. Sudden, I know." I break the awkward silence.

"Do you want to place an announcement in *The Times?*"

"People still do that?" I'm unable to keep the incredulity from my voice.

"Yes, my lord. Especially as a peer of the realm." He sounds disapproving.

"I think under the circumstances, we'll draw a veil over that. No announcement. Can you give the keys to my flat to Joe Diallo? He'll come round and collect them from the office."

Well, I hope he will.

"Of course," Oliver breathes. I think he's still in shock. "I'll chase Rajah about visas."

"Thanks."

"I've also had news today from the Met Police. Alessia's assailants have been charged with trafficking offenses."

Fuck. Good.

"They've not been granted bail. They're a flight risk, and I believe other individuals have been charged too."

"I'm glad. That's a relief." I hope Alessia's not called upon to be a witness in court. That could get tricky. But she'll be my wife by then.

Don't dwell, dude.

Cross that bridge as and when.

"Any estate business I need to know?" I ask to change the subject.

Oliver fills me in on what's been happening back home. Fortunately, not much. "I've sent you a couple of emails that need attention, but nothing serious."

"Thanks, Oliver."

"My lord… um… is everything okay?"

I run a hand through my hair, feeling that same sense of panic

I felt when we arrived back at the house. I tamp it down. I don't want to tell him that my marriage might be illegitimate. I'll deal with that later once we're back in the UK. "Yes. Everything's fine."

"Righto. I'll report back on where Rajah is with visas."

Next, I call my friend and sparring partner Joe Diallo.

"Bruv," he says. "Where you at?"

"Albania. I'm getting married. On Saturday."

"What the fuck! This Saturday?"

"Yeah. Can you come?"

"Mate. Wait. Really?"

"Yes."

"Your daily?" he squeaks, several octaves above his normal voice and I roll my eyes.

"Yes," I hiss with exasperation.

"You're sure. She's the one?"

I sigh. "Yes, Joe."

"Okay," he says, his uncertainty ringing in his voice. "I'll look into flights."

"Can you be here on Friday? And bring one of my suits?"

He sighs. "Only for you, mate."

"I'm going to need you to go to Boodles too."

There's a loud knock on the front door, and as Alessia is near the doorway, she extracts herself from the crowd to find out who's calling. She's delighted to see her relatives but is grateful for the distraction and a moment of peace as she strolls down the hall. She's forgotten what it's like to be surrounded by her noisy and inquisitive family.

She skips up to the door and opens it.

And stops. Shocked.

"Hello, Alessia."

The blood drains from her face as she stares at the man standing on the doorstep. "Anatoli," she whispers as fear clogs her throat.

Chapter Three

Alessia cannot believe he's audacious enough to return to her father's home dressed in his fine Italian coat and expensive brogues. Yet Anatoli makes no move to come in. He just stares at her with eyes that blaze an icy blue. Then he swallows, as if he's going to say something, or from nerves; Alessia doesn't know. Instinctively, she takes a step back as her heart begins to pound and a shiver skitters up her spine, either from his presence or the chilly February air.

What does he want?

"Don't go. Please." He puts his foot on the threshold so she cannot close the door, his eyes beseeching her.

"What do you want?" she snaps as her outrage fuels her courage.

How dare he show up here!

She doesn't want to engage with him on any level. She glances behind her to see if anyone has come to see what's going on—but there's no one. She's on her own.

"I want to talk to you."

"We said all we needed to say on Saturday."

"Alessia. Please. I came to… apologize. For everything."

"What?" Alessia feels like the air's being sucked from her lungs. She's stunned.

"Can we talk? Please. You owe me that. I brought you back here."

A surge of anger rises from deep within her chest. "No, Anatoli! You kidnapped me," she snarls. "I was happy in London, and you took me away from all that. And put me in a difficult situation. You must go. I have nothing to say to you."

"I mishandled everything. So badly. I see that. I have had time to think. Let me plead my case. Please. I won't touch you."

"No! Go!"

"Alessia. We're betrothed! You are the most beautiful, maddening, and talented woman I have ever known. I love you."

"No. No. No!" Alessia closes her eyes, trying to contain her shock and outrage. "You don't know how to love. Please go." She tries to close the door, but his foot prevents her, and he splays his hand on the door, holding it steady.

"How can you marry someone that will take you away from your homeland? Our homeland? You are an Albanian woman to your soul. You will miss your mother. You'll never belong in England. The English are such terrible snobs. They'll despise you. They'll look down on you. You'll never be accepted there."

His words slice through her, their weight stirring her darkest fears.

Is he right? Will Maxim's family and friends despise her?

Anatoli's gaze intensifies as he senses her doubts. "I speak your language, carissima. I understand you. I acted stupidly. Badly. I can change. You've been in the West. You expect more, and you deserve more. I get that, and I can give you more. So much more. I will accept your child. Treat him or her as my own. Alessia, please. I love you." He steps forward and boldly takes her hand between each of his, imploring her and staring into her eyes. "You will make me a better man. I need you," he whispers, his desperation evident in every syllable.

Alessia tugs her hand free and meets his intense gaze. "Let me go, Anatoli." She takes a deep breath, her heart in her mouth, and finding a courage she didn't know she possessed, she reaches up and caresses his cheek. He leans his face into her hand as his eyes sear hers. "If you love me, let me go. I won't make you happy. I'm not the woman for you." He opens his mouth to speak—she suspects to contradict her—but she places her finger over his mouth. "No, I'm not."

"You are," he whispers, his breath warm on her finger.

She drops her hand. "No. You want to find someone who will light up when you walk into a room."

"I have," he whispers.

"No! That's not me."

"You did once."

"An age ago. But you…you hurt me. So much so, I had to get away. There's no coming back from that."

He blanches.

"You're not that person for me," Alessia continues. "You'll never make me happy."

"I could work at being that person."

"I've already met him, Anatoli. I love him. We're to be married this week."

"What?" His mouth drops open—he's stunned.

"Please. Go. There's nothing for you here," Alessia whispers.

He steps back in disbelief, his expression desolate.

"I hope you find your person," she says.

"Carissima…"

"Goodbye, Anatoli." Alessia, her heart still in her mouth, closes the door as her mother calls her.

"Alessia? What's keeping you?" Shpresa appears in the hallway.

"It's okay. I'll be there in a minute."

"Who was it?"

"Mama, I need a minute."

Frowning, Shpresa studies her daughter, then nods and returns to the family room. Alessia blows out a breath, trying to expel the frenzied fear and emotion that's choking her. She peers through the spy hole in the door and watches as Anatoli trudges with long strides up the driveway to where his car is parked. His shoulders are squared, a picture of a man determined, not defeated. It's a chilling sight.

No!

Alessia turns and slumps against the door.

That was most unexpected. But his words—*they'll despise you*—have struck home. She clutches her throat as it seems to constrict against the truth, and she suddenly has an overwhelming urge to cry.

What if he's right?

I've unpacked the few belongings that I threw, panicked, into my duffel when I thought I'd never see Alessia again. I've arranged them, rearranged them, and I know I'm actively avoiding my next call.

Coward. Call her.

I stare out at the still, quiet waters of the lake, the gray skies reflected in its depths, the scene mirroring my mood. The women upstairs are still in conference, and by their loud laughter and chatter, I know they're enjoying themselves. Taking a deep breath and figuratively girding my loins, I press Call on my phone and wait for Caroline to answer.

Shall I tell her?

Shall I not?

"Maxim!" she exclaims, gushing and concerned at once. "How are you? Where are you?"

"Caro. Hi. I'm in Kukës, staying at Alessia's parents' place."

"You're still there? I don't get it. If you've found her, why aren't you either back here or on your way?"

"It's not that simple."

"Her fiancé?"

The Arsehole. "Um… no."

She's silent for a moment, waiting for me to elucidate. She sighs. "What are you not telling me?"

Inspiration hits me, and it's the truth. "We have to wait for a passport for Alessia."

"Ah. I see." She sounds uncertain but continues, "You don't want to come home and go back for her?"

"Definitely not. I'm not letting her out of my sight."

"Oh, how protective!" she scoffs. "Your white knight is showing."

I chuckle, relieved she's her usual caustic self. "Yes. It's been showing for a while, much to my surprise."

"Surely she's safe with her parents."

"It was her mother who handed her over to the traffickers, albeit unwittingly."

She gasps. "I didn't know. That's awful."

"Yeah. Hence my need to be protective. Anyway—enough of this. What have you been doing?"

"Oh," she breathes, and I almost hear her fold in on herself.

"What is it?"

"I've finally found the strength to go through Kit's things."

My grief surfaces, unexpected, raw and vicious, winding me. *Kit.* My dear brother.

"I see," I whisper.

"I have a few things of his that you might like." Her tone is soft—laced with regret. "The rest… I don't know what to do with yet."

"We can go through it all when I'm home," I offer.

"Yes. Let's do that. I'm going to tackle some of his papers tomorrow."

"Good luck."

"I miss him." Her quiet sorrow is ingrained in her voice.

"I know. I do too."

"When will you be back?"

"Next week, I hope."

"Good. Okay. Thanks for calling. I'm glad you found her."

Feeling guilty as hell, I hang up.

Guilty by omission.

I should have told her.

Hell!

I'm tempted to call her back and confess that I'm getting married, but she'd want to get on a plane and come here, and frankly, I don't want the hassle.

I decide not to tell my mother for precisely the same reason. The Mothership will lose her shit, and I'm not sure Kukës or the Demachis are ready for the *Dowager* Countess in all her glory because I'm certainly not.

Better to ask for forgiveness than permission. My father's oft-repeated phrase comes to mind. He'd say it with a twinkle in his eye as he caught me about to do something I shouldn't.

I brush off the thought, and there's a knock on my door. Before I can say anything, Alessia hurries in, closes the door, and leans against it. She raises anxious eyes to mine. She's ashen.

"What's happened?" I ask.

She takes a deep breath, moves forward, and surprises me by wrapping her arms around my waist. I fold her into my embrace, alarmed, and kiss her hair.

"Alessia, what is it?"

She tightens her hold on me. "Anatoli. He was here." Her voice is barely audible.

"What?" My world shifts, and I tense as anger flares in my gut.

She looks up, her eyes wide with fear. "He came to the door."

Horrified, I cup her head in my hands and study her face. "That fucking animal. Why didn't you call me? Did he touch you? Are you okay?"

"I'm okay." She places her palms on my chest. "And no, he didn't. He wanted me to reconsider."

My breath catches in my throat. "And are you?"

That's why she didn't call me.

She frowns, not understanding.

"Are you reconsidering?"

"No!" she exclaims.

Thank God.

"Why would you think that?" She draws back, looking very much affronted, and I have no choice but to release her. "Do you think like this because you are reconsidering?" she asks, lifting her chin in that haughty way she does, and I laugh at the absurdity. The absurdity of the two of us…

How could she think that?

"No. Of course not. Though I wish we were doing this at our own speed. But you know that. Why do you doubt me? I'm thoroughly, indubitably… muchly in love with you." I open my arms, and after a beat, she steps back into them with a shy forgiving smile.

"That is many adverbs," she says. "Muchly?"

"My favorite word." I smile. "I want to marry you. Properly." Feeling a little calmer, I kiss her hair once more. "What did you say to him?"

"I told him no. I told him we were getting married. He left."

"I hope that's the last we see of him." Gently, I fist my hand in her hair, tugging her head back and planting a soft kiss on her lips. "I'm sorry you had to deal with that arsehole. I'm glad you stood up to him, my courageous girl."

Alessia stares into his glittering green eyes and sees her love reflected in the depths of his. She skims her hands up his muscled arms, his shoulders, his face, and into his chestnut hair. His scent is so achingly familiar—Maxim and sandalwood. She guides his mouth back to hers, driven by a desperate longing as she coaxes his lips with her own and opens her mouth to him. Maxim groans as her tongue pleads with his. She wants to climb inside his skin and obliterate the memory of her encounter with Anatoli. He tightens his hold on her, one hand traveling to and gripping her backside, the other grasping her hair at the nape and holding her fast as he takes what she so freely gives. He moves, steering them backward while they consume each other until Alessia feels the wall at her back. Desire pulses through her body and pools deep inside her, feeding her need.

Maxim breaks the kiss, his breathing accelerated. "Alessia, it's okay. I've got you." He leans his forehead against hers. "We can't do this right now."

"Please," she whispers. She wants him.

"With your extended family upstairs? Any one of whom could come looking for you?"

Alessia trails a finger down his throat to the collar of his sweater, making her intention clear.

"Baby, I don't think this is a good idea." He places his hand over hers, his eyes dark emerald and, if she's not mistaken, conflicted… yet he's saying *no*.

Alessia doesn't understand. Her first instinct is to withdraw.

It is not her place to question him. But this is her future husband, and his words, spoken on a winter's afternoon at the big house in Cornwall, come back to her.

Talk to me. Ask me questions. About anything. I'm here. I'll listen. Argue with me. Shout at me. I'll argue with you. I'll shout at you. I'll get it wrong. You'll get it wrong. That's all okay. But to resolve our differences, we have to communicate.

*W*hat the hell, dude?

I'm having a crisis of conscience or something. I don't want to get caught *in flagrante delicto* by a member of the Demachi clan. Frankly, it's just so weird when I can hear the gaggle of women laughing and joking above us with her mother, and knowing that her mad dad isn't far away with his shotgun.

I've stepped into the wrong century, and it's messing with my head.

Alessia's eyes widen. "You don't want to?"

"Oh, baby, nothing could be further than the truth. Here." I take her hand and press it against my rigid dick.

"Oh," she says, her cheeks pinking, and her fingers start exploring.

Fuck.

"Alessia," I growl, not knowing if it's a warning or an entreaty.

She peeks at me, all dark, dark eyes full of longing, and I can take no more. I haul her into my arms and start kissing her. Properly. Fervently, like a starving man. My fingers are in her hair, holding her in place while our tongues explore. Desire, hot and molten, fires my blood, and I think I'll explode. She matches my passion, pushing me back toward the bed, yanking the hem of my shirt from my jeans and tugging at my sweater. I cradle the back of her head with one hand, my mouth on hers, reveling in the taste of her, my other hand on her fine, fine arse.

"*Alessia!*"

There's a knock at the door.

Fuck.

We spring apart—each of us breathless and dark-eyed and panting and slack-jawed.

I run my hands through my hair. "Fuck!" I whisper, and Alessia giggles.

Blowing out a breath, I pull her into my arms and kiss the top of her head. "Come in," I call, my voice hoarse. "We never have long together, do we?" I say to Alessia.

"Except at night." Her eyes flash with a needy carnality.

Oh. It's like she's directly addressing my over-interested dick.

Shpresa comes into the room and frowns at Alessia in Maxim's embrace. "There you are, my heart." Her mother addresses her in Albanian. "We have guests."

"I know, Mama," Alessia replies, sounding out of breath.

"Put that man down, and let's continue with our plans. They'll be going soon."

Alessia smiles at Maxim.

"Are you going back to your relatives?" Maxim asks.

"Yes, I must. We were discussing food and decorations for the wedding," Alessia responds with a sigh. "Don't worry; they won't be here long. And then we start cleaning." Alessia huffs out a breath.

"I have some emails that need my attention."

"Mama. I will be a minute."

Shpresa frowns, then holds up her forefinger. "A minute. That's it."

She turns and leaves Alessia and Maxim, both still trying to find their equilibrium.

I watch her mother leave, grateful we were still clothed when she interrupted us. I kiss the top of Alessia's head again. "Baby, I will always want you. But let's wait until we're out of here."

"But that is days away!"

Alessia's protests widen my smile.

"And I don't have any condoms," I mutter into her hair.

"You should buy some."

"I should. But don't you think it will be odd if people think you're pregnant and I'm buying condoms?"

"Oh."

"I'll ask Tom to get me some."

Alessia gasps, flushes beet red, and buries her face in my Aran sweater.

I grin and tighten my hold on her. "I told him you're not pregnant."

"I… I…um…could go to the clinic. And get the contraceptive pill," she says, the sound muffled by my knitwear.

"That's a brilliant idea."

She chances a cautious look at me, and I smile.

Sex without condoms will be a first!

"Okay. I will do that. I should tell my parents that I am not pregnant."

"Yes. We should."

"I have a plan." Hesitantly, she looks up at me.

"You do?"

"Tomorrow." She buries her head in my sweater once more. "Is the date. I bleed."

Ah.

"Okay. So you'll tell your mother you're not pregnant?"

"Yes. I will find a time to tell her." She can't look at me, and I think it's because she's embarrassed. Taking her head in my hands again, I stare into her beautiful dark eyes.

"We should be able to talk about this—you and your body. It's okay. I think it's a good plan." I kiss her forehead. "Maybe tell her Saturday."

Reassured, I think, she nods. "I'd better go."

Reluctantly, I release her, and with a lingering, thirsty look at me, she exits the bedroom, leaving me with a hard-on and a severe case of blue balls.

Like I had when I first made her acquaintance.

I smirk at the memory and take a deep, cleansing breath. As predicted, her mother made an untimely appearance. And it's a fucking problem. The proximity and the constant monitoring from her parentals is driving me crazy. Being here has given me a valuable insight into Alessia's upbringing and makes me admire her all the more for escaping to London. She's grown up and lived in this stifling atmosphere, controlled by her mother and father her whole life. I've been here two nights, and I'm missing my freedom. I feel like a teenager back in school.

I'm a grown man, for fuck's sake.

Well, most of the time.

But I'm not leaving here, especially if that arsehole thinks he can turn up and have another chance with her.

I snort at the irony. *Man, you're keeping an eye on her.*

I rub the last of my hangover away from my temples and make

a mental note of where her father keeps his shotgun… just in case Anatoli the Arsehole makes another unwelcome appearance. I'd be more than happy to put a bullet through him.

Hell.

The sooner we're out of here, the better; I'm contemplating murder.

Chapter Four

Under the glow of the little dragon nightlight, Alessia lies in bed staring at the ceiling while her fingers worry the gold cross at her neck. She's exhausted, but her mind refuses to settle as it churns through the day's events and her to-do list.

This morning, Tom had driven Alessia and her mother to Prizren in Kosovo to buy a wedding dress. Her mother wouldn't let her fiancé take them because it was "bad luck" and would "spoil the surprise," so Maxim had insisted Tom drive. Her father had shrugged. "Like I said, you're his problem now. If that's what Maxim wants, then so be it. Besides, he and I have work to do here."

Alessia scowls in the dark and turns on her side toward the nightlight.

She is not a problem!

She directs her thoughts back to their trip. It had been a success. They'd been lucky to find a beautiful dress, and she'd discovered a softer side to Maxim's gruff friend. He'd been courteous,

kind, and vigilant while with them. He'd also given his begrudg-
ing approval of her dress as he'd sat quietly and discreetly near
the door of the bridal store.

"Yes. Yes. That's the one. Jolly nice. You look… um… lovely,"
he'd blustered and flushed the same color as his hair; then, to hide
his embarrassment he'd turned to scan the passersby through the
shop window. Alessia had suspected he was looking for Anatoli.

On the drive to Kosovo, Tom had told her about the security
company he owned where he could put the skills he'd learned
in the British army to good use. He'd been delighted to have
a captive and attentive audience. Alessia had been fascinated,
asking questions about his work, and grateful that he was with
them, as Maxim had been hypervigilant since Anatoli's untimely
reappearance.

She shudders, still shaken by her encounter with Anatoli.

What had he been thinking?

While out in the streets of Prizren, she'd found herself glancing over her shoulder several times, a sense of unease settling in
her stomach.

Was she being watched?

No. It was just her imagination.

She shuts down that idea, and her mind flits to happier
thoughts—her fiancé, recalling him in his shirtsleeves earlier this
afternoon. While she'd been in Kosovo, and much to her surprise, Maxim and Thanas had helped her father clear the garage
where the Demachis were to host the wedding celebrations. Her
dad, with Maxim's help, had driven the three Mercedes he usually kept locked in there to his repair shop in town. When he'd
returned, he and Maxim and Thanas had continued to empty and
tidy the garage in preparation for the tent that will arrive in the
morning. The plan is to erect it in front of the garage, making a
larger entertainment space.

When Alessia and her escort had returned from Kosovo,
Tom had rolled up his sleeves too and joined the men. While
they cleared the outside, Alessia and her mother had begun

the mammoth task inside of cleaning, cleaning, and yet more cleaning.

Alessia had managed to slip out in the late afternoon to the local clinic. After a brief conversation, she had persuaded the doctor to prescribe the contraceptive pill. She'd only just made it to the pharmacy with her prescription before it closed, and she'd been relieved not to recognize anyone there. She'd rushed home to continue cleaning, and no one asked where she'd been. Later, when her period started, she'd been able to sneak upstairs and take her first pill.

Early evening, Maxim had appeared in the kitchen, his shirt-sleeves rolled up despite the cold; he was dirty, his color heightened, and his hair damp with sweat. He looked… hot.

Manual work suits him.

He'd given her a quick kiss that made her long for more before heading to the shower.

Maxim in the shower.

Closing her eyes, Alessia turns onto her side, and her mind conjures a fantasy that she's in the shower with him. They're in Cornwall, at the Hideout, and Maxim is soaping her body while they stand beneath the cascade, getting wetter and wetter. Her hand travels down her body, becoming his in her thoughts as she hears his voice.

Do you want me to wash you all over?

Her breath quickens, and she tugs at her nightdress so the hem glides up her thighs. As her hand slips between them and starts to move, she rolls onto her back.

She remembers his skilled hands slick with soap on her breasts, then sliding over her belly and slipping down to the apex of her thighs. Her desire unfurls in a rush that stiffens her nipples against the soft cotton, but she imagines them hardening between his lips and against his stubble, then teased by his teeth.

She groans.

In her mind, he kisses her neck, a sound of approval resonating deep in his throat.

Mmm-hmm.

His words fill her head.

You're so beautiful.

She gasps as her hand picks up speed.

Faster. Faster.

You like?

And she's hanging.

Nearly there.

I want to try something new. Turn over, he purrs in her ear.

Alessia comes. Hard. Fast. And she gulps in a lungful of air.

And as her equilibrium returns, she thinks perhaps now she'll sleep. She curls up as her lingering sense of pleasure and well-being starts to fade, and her thoughts intrude once more.

Tomorrow the garage setup will be finished, but there's more cleaning and cooking to be done. So much cooking. And the party favors to put together: sugared almonds in tiny cloth bags. Fortunately, her extended family are eager to help—the menu and who is making what were set when they visited yesterday. A chef will be on hand to assist them on the day.

Will Maxim be happy with the arrangements?

O Zot! She hopes so.

She knows this isn't the wedding he wants.

But he's still here, he hasn't left, and he's proceeding with the ceremony for her sake—but also for her mother's. Alessia opens her eyes and stares at the ceiling again, her fingers finding her gold cross once more as her anxiety flares like a flame.

Her mother, who wants to stay with her father.

Will she be okay?

Having observed them for the last few days, her mother and father seem to have reached some kind of accord. It's strange to witness. Maybe her mother was right—he seems… kinder. Maybe Alessia leaving was what they had needed. Perhaps she had been the object of strife between them.

After all, she's not a boy.

The thought brings a lump to her throat.

All this time, had she been the one who stood in the way of her mother's happiness?

She's your problem now…

A tear trickles down the side of her face and into her ear.

This idea is too much to bear alone.

She tosses her sheets aside and climbs out of bed. Hastily grabbing the little dragon, she makes her way to the door. She thinks it's about two in the morning, but she doesn't know for sure. She tiptoes out of the room, silently closes the door, and stands in the hallway where all is quiet, as her parents went to bed hours ago. She moves noiselessly to the stairs and heads down two floors. Alessia doesn't care that she might wake him when she steals into this room, because right now, all she wants, all she needs, is Maxim.

I cannot sleep, and yet I don't think I've ever labored as hard as I did today. Well, not since my father had us helping with the harvests at the Home Farm on the Trevethick Estate. I was in my early teens then and had boundless energy.

Now? Not so much.

I didn't even begrudge the shot of raki I had this evening to ease my aching muscles. Tomorrow morning, I'm going for a run before I do anything else, and I'm grateful I packed my running gear.

Weirdly, it felt good helping my soon-to-be father-in-law. He's gruff and sullen, and I have no idea what he's thinking, but he's decisive, hard-working, and organized. He has a plan, which is a relief because I'm out of my depth here. And at the end of a long day, he'd clapped me on the back and given me the keys to one of his cars—an old Mercedes C Class. Thanas had translated. "For you. When you are here. Your car. You can give the Dacia to your friend. Collect it later. And for now, park it up on the road."

"Faleminderit," I'd replied. *Thank you* in Albanian.

He'd grinned then, and it was the first time I'd seen him smile properly. His acceptance and generosity had lifted my spirits.

Perhaps he's not so bad.

He's only doing what he thinks is right for his daughter.

But now I'm finding it hard to sleep. Did I ever imagine I'd get married in a garage? In Albania? Did I ever imagine I'd get married before I was thirty? Thank God my mother doesn't know. But the thought does bring a wry smile to my face… if she knew, she'd flip.

Alessia and her mother went shopping with Tom. I was forbidden to go as they were buying The Dress. I'd just handed her my credit card and winked. And she'd accepted it with a quick word of thanks and a kiss on the cheek.

They returned triumphant, and Tom was quite enamored of my wife-to-be.

"She's a gem, Trevethick. I get it," he'd said when he joined us in our quest to clear the garage.

Alessia and her mother spent most of the afternoon cleaning. By this evening, the entire place was spotless. She must be exhausted, and I hope she's sleeping soundly and dreaming of me. When all this is over, and after all this hard work, we're going to need a holiday.

A honeymoon.

I could take Alessia somewhere beautiful. The Caribbean, maybe. We could sit on a quiet beach beneath swaying palms, drink cocktails and read books and make love beneath the stars. My body stirs at the thought.

Fuck. I was in Cuba and then Bequia at Christmas with my brother and Caroline, his wife.

That seems like yesterday.

It was only eight weeks ago.

Hell.

So much has happened since then.

Earlier this evening, I spoke with Oliver. As well as updating me on estate business, he's arranged for us to collect a visa for Alessia from the British embassy in Tirana. It's been expedited by the ambassador himself—because he knew my father—so at least Alessia will be able to come to the UK as a visitor until we can get her settled status or a spousal visa. The embassy will also organize a notary to apostille our marriage certificate, which makes everything official.

I'll be meeting a lawyer that Rajah has recommended on our return to London. He's warned me that we have much more work to do before Alessia can stay in the UK.

The door creaks open, startling me, and Alessia creeps inside, wearing her ridiculous nightgown and carrying the little nightlight. My heart rate jumps.

She's here. My girl.

I grin into the darkness as she makes her way toward the bed.

"Hello," I whisper in the dark, my joy ringing out loud in my greeting. I draw back the covers for her to join me.

"Hi," she replies, and she sounds a little hoarse.

"You okay?"

In the glow of the little dragon, she nods once, places him on the bedside table, and climbs into bed beside me. I kiss her cheek, then wrap her in my arms and hold her close as she rests her head on my chest.

"I couldn't sleep. And I am so tired," she mutters.

"Me too. You can sleep now." I kiss her hair, inhale her fragrance, and shut my eyes. This is where she should be... with me.

Forever.

I drift.

A lessia closes her eyes in the arms of the man she loves. This is where she belongs. Being here, in his embrace, feels like home. She doesn't care if her father or mother catches her; she and Maxim are only sleeping. She sighs as her mind finally quiets, and she falls into a dreamless sleep.

~

It's early afternoon on Friday, and I can't stop checking my watch. Joe is due here around 3:20 p.m. Tom, who has done more than his fair share of driving over the last few days, has collected him from Tirana International Airport. Joe has texted me that they're on their way and he has a surprise for me.

I'm not sure I like surprises.

The front yard at the Demachis is pristine and wedding-worthy. There's a marquee of sorts up against the garage, and tables and chairs are arranged inside. The place has scrubbed up well. Yesterday, we'd all had a hand in putting up the white netting that was donated by one of Alessia's aunts. The ceiling of the garage is now swathed in gossamer and fairy lights. And it looks quite lovely. Romantic even. There are fairy lights on the walls and clusters of lights at each of the plastic tables, which are all covered in linen. The Demachis have done well—given the time. They've hired a few patio heaters for the marquee, and there's a sizeable wood-burning stove at one end of the garage, which I'm assured will be lit, so hopefully, our guests won't freeze.

The DJ, Kreshnik, one of Alessia's cousins, has set up a little booth in the corner of the garage. His gear is old school: a laptop and humble Numark Mixtrack pro DJ decks. I haven't seen one of those for years. He's plugged them into a couple of speakers, and the sound is surprisingly warm and crisp.

"Great sound." I give him a thumbs-up and a broad smile. He grins back, and I know he hasn't understood a word I've said.

"Maxim!" Alessia calls.

I smile. She probably wants me to taste something delicious. The aroma from the kitchen has been enticing all day. Demachi turns from piling wood in the corner of the garage, ready for the wood-burning stove and flashes a quick grin. "Ajo do të të shëndoshë!" he calls, laughing, but I have no idea what he's said.

Thanas joins me, chuckling. "He says, 'She's going to make you fat.'"

Amused by the banter, I begin to jog backward. "Tell him 'I hope so.'" Turning, I hurry back into the house, take off my shoes, and head to the kitchen. I lean against the arch and quietly admire my future wife. She's standing over the stove, stirring a large pot and swaying her hips to the music blaring via a speaker from her new phone. Her hair is tied back in a swinging ponytail, and she's wearing tight jeans with one of the tops we bought in Padstow and a pretty, flowery apron. She looks young, beautiful, and in her element—every bit the domestic goddess. All trace of her trauma has disappeared. No bruises. No grazes, and I'm beyond grateful she looks so well.

Shpresa is also jigging about in time to the music and kneads a large mound of dough.

Man, she has such energy.

The song they're dancing to is Albanian pop. It's a *tune*. A female vocalist with a great voice.

Alessia grins when she sees me. "Here." She holds up a wooden spoon dripping with an aromatic meaty concoction. When I reach her, she flashes me a smoldering look and eases it between my lips, watching me closely—her eyes darkening as the spicy morsel melts in my mouth.

It's succulent and with a hint of garlic and something piquant. *Delicious.*

"Mmm," I respond as I swallow.

"You like?"

"You know I do. Very much. And I like you."

She grins, and I give her a swift peck on her lips.

"Tavë kosi?"

"You remembered! My special recipe." She's delighted and swings her hips in time to the music, her dark eyes full of promise as she stirs the pot.

Oh, baby.

Soon.

She now has a brand-new passport, so we can leave whenever we want.

Thank heavens.

"*Hey!*" There's a call from near the front door.

"Joe!" I exclaim to Alessia and dash in my socks out of the family room into the hallway.

Joe stands on the threshold, looking his usual dapper self in a tailored dark blue suit and navy overcoat. As soon as he sees me, he opens his arms. "Trevelyan! Mate."

I run into them and hug him.

Fuck, it's good to see him.

"Mate." I sound hoarse as a sudden swell of emotion chokes my throat. He hugs me hard, then leans back, studying me.

"You okay?" he asks.

And I'm too emotional to do anything but nod.

Fuck. I do not want to break down right now. I'll never live it down.

"You look good, Maxim," he says with a wide grin. "Luggage is in the car. Brought your suits, the rings, and…" He turns, and behind him, standing by the car, is my sister.

Maryanne.

Shit.

Behind her, wearing an expression that may turn me to stone, is my brother's widow.

Caroline.

Fuck a duck.

Chapter Five

I glance at Joe, who shrugs apologetically as Maryanne steps over the threshold and throws her arms around me.

"Maxie," she whispers. "You found her then."

"I did."

"Something you want to tell us?" she adds, sarcasm dripping off every word as she cocks her head to the side—and I know she's apoplectic but keeping a taut rein on her temper.

Oh no.

Caroline waltzes in behind her and offers me a cheek to peck. No hug. "We had to fly economy," she snaps.

Shit.

I'm in more trouble than I thought. Tom and Thanas follow her inside.

"Come and meet the family," I say, ignoring her frostiness. "And shoes off."

Shpresa and Alessia are standing at the stove as I usher Joe and our surprise guests into the family room. They stare blankly at us as we crowd into the space. Alessia abandons the pot on the stove, wipes her hands on her apron, and switches off the music on her phone. I introduce Joe first, as we've been expecting him, and he's at the head of the queue. Ever the gentleman, he bounds forward, hand outstretched. "Mrs. Demachi, how do you do?" he says with a dazzling smile. "I'm delighted to meet you."

Smooth, mate. Smooth.

Shpresa, even in her state of shock, takes his hand. "Hello. You are welcome here," she says. He grins and turns to Alessia, who is wide-eyed and pale as if caught in the crosshairs.

Oh no.

"Alessia, how lovely to see you again."

"Hello," she responds. "And this time, you are wearing clothes," she adds.

He laughs out loud, and a little color returns to her cheeks as she breaks into a smile. He hugs her and kisses her on both cheeks.

Both!

Mate!

Her mother frowns at their exchange but keeps her counsel.

"Mrs. Demachi, this is my sister and my sister-in-law, Maryanne and Caroline." They shake hands in turn.

"And this is my fiancée, Alessia. Caroline you've met."

Caroline gives her a brief, but I think sincere, smile. "Hello again," she says.

Alessia offers her hand, and they shake. "Hello… Caroline." Her voice is tremulous, betraying her nerves, but before I can say anything, Maryanne offers her hand.

"How do you do?" she says. Alessia takes her hand and looks from her to me.

Yes. We look alike.

"How do you do?" she responds, and Maryanne's eyes widen slightly in surprise, and she smiles.

"I can see what all the fuss has been about," she says in her no-nonsense way.

Alessia's brow creases, presumably not understanding that it's a compliment.

"Yes. Well." I flounder for words.

This is awkward.

"Now we've all said hello—" I manage.

"Please sit." Shpresa saves me and waves to the dining table. "We are in preparations for the wedding."

"Actually, before we sit," Maryanne says, using her strident doctor's voice. "Could I possibly have a word with my brother? In private." Maryanne turns her brilliant green eyes on me, and I know I'm in deep, deep shit.

"You can use the front room," Alessia says, eyeing me anxiously.

"Lead the way," Maryanne says, and because I know what she's going to say, and I don't want her saying it in front of Alessia and her mother, I take her hand and practically drag her out of the room. In stiff silence, we stalk down the hallway.

A lessia watches Maxim leave with his sister. She thinks he's angry but doesn't understand why.

Does he not want his family here?

Is he ashamed of his relatives?

Or is he ashamed of her and her family?

Alessia doesn't dwell on this as she fears this may be the reason. She turns her attention to Tom and Thanas, who have walked into the room. She watches Tom fist bump Joe. "I'm so glad you've joined us, old boy." Joe flashes bright white teeth and slaps Tom on the back. It's obvious they're good friends. Tom offers Caroline a polite smile. He's more reserved with her. Alessia thinks Tom is happier in the company of men rather than women.

Like an Albanian man.

Tom introduces Thanas to Joe and Caroline.

"We were not expecting these women," her mother says in their tongue, distracting her.

"I know. I don't think Maxim is pleased."

"They will have to sleep in the room we had set aside for Maxim's friend."

"Yes. We should offer them tea or something stronger."

At that moment, her father enters, and the introductions begin again. He appears delighted to meet a beautiful, fragrant woman, and Alessia cannot blame him. She cannot take her eyes off Caroline. She's the most elegant woman Alessia has ever seen. In camel slacks and a cream sweater, a simple silk scarf with an understated camel-and-cream pattern at her neck, Caroline radiates wealth and good breeding. Even down to the pearls at her ears and her glossy hair, cut in a sleek bob.

Next to her, Alessia feels dowdy and unkempt in her jeans and soiled apron.

She looks every bit like Maxim's cleaner.

And the last time she saw Caroline, she was in Maxim's arms.

As I close the door, Maryanne whirls around, hair flying. "What the hell do you think you're playing at? Marrying your daily? Really? What the fuck has gotten into you?"

I gape at her, stunned by her attack and momentarily lost for words at her ferocity.

"Well?" she demands.

"I didn't take you for a snob, Maryanne," I respond, my anger rising.

"I'm not. I'm just being practical. What the hell can a slip of a girl from… here"—she waves her arms around the room—"offer you?"

"Love, for starters."

"Oh, for God's sake, Maxim. Have you lost your mind? What do you even have in common?"

"Music, for one thing."

She ignores me; she's on a roll. "And doing this just weeks after Kit's death? This is your grief—you know that, don't you? We've not had enough time to mourn. Have you no respect?"

"Well, the timing's not great, but—"

"Not great! Why the alacrity?" Her eyes widen. "Oh no." Her voice drops. "Don't tell me she's preggers."

I grit my teeth, barely holding on to my temper. "No. She isn't. It's—" I sigh and run a hand through my hair as I struggle to find an explanation that will satisfy her.

"It's what!"

"It's complicated."

She glares at me, and I swear if I were dry tinder, I'd be a pile of burnt ashes. She's livid, but suddenly her face falls. "And to think you would go ahead with this farce without even inviting us!" Her voice cracks, and tears well in her eyes.

Shit. M.A.!

She's hurt.

"That's what's most wounding," she whispers.

Her words are a gut punch.

Hell. I had no idea she'd feel this way.

"Is that the problem?" My tone is softer. "My marrying Alessia, or you not getting an invite?"

"The problem is you thinking that we wouldn't want to be here. Even in the back of beyond! Or it's that you didn't want us here. Either of those options is hurtful. What's wrong with you, Maxie? I've already lost one brother this year. You're all I have. You are my family." Her tears are flowing now. "And that you'd go through this without us." She sniffles and drags a handkerchief from her sleeve to wipe her nose.

Fuck.

"I'm sorry." I open my arms, and she walks straight into them without hesitating and hugs me hard.

"And I had to find out from Caro," she splutters.

"M.A., I didn't think," I whisper into her hair. "This has all happened so quickly. And we'll celebrate in London or Cornwall and do it again there. And just so you know, this isn't a fucking farce.

"I'm getting married because I've met a woman I'm passionately in love with, and I want to grow old with her. Alessia is everything to me, and I've come alive since I met her. She's supportive, caring, and compassionate. She's amazing. I've never met anyone like her, and I've never felt like this about anyone. I need her, and what's more, she needs me."

Dude, quite the speech.

She lets out a long, shaky breath and examines me with red-rimmed eyes. "You have fallen hard, haven't you?"

I nod.

"You know it's going to be hard for her, stepping into the role that's expected of her."

"I know. But she has us to help. Doesn't she?"

She studies me once more and sighs. "If she makes you happy, because that's all I want for you, Maxim, then yes, she does."

I smile. "Thank you. She makes me more than happy. And I hope I do the same for her."

"She's beautiful."

"She is. And funny and sweet and loving."

Maryanne's eyes soften.

"And she's extremely talented."

"In what?" Maryanne cocks a brow.

I laugh. "Alessia's a pianist."

"Oh." She's surprised and glances at the old upright piano that has pride of place in the drawing room. "I can't wait to hear."

"Um… did you tell the Mothership?"

Maryanne narrows her eyes. "No. I didn't want to hurt her feelings."

"She has feelings?"

"Maxim!"

"We should get back."

Everyone, bar Shpresa, is seated at the table. Alessia glances at me as Maryanne and I enter. She frowns and looks down at her nails, even though I try to telepathically reassure her that everything is okay. Caroline's eyes narrow as I hold out a chair for Maryanne to sit upon, and I know that in the not-too-distant future, I will face the same conversation that I've just had with my sister, with my sister-in-law.

Shpresa is bringing over a pot of tea, some cups, and a bottle of raki with several glasses.

Raki. Already? Oh boy.

A lessia twists the apron between her fingers. Maxim's sister is as elegant as Caroline. She's tall and beautiful, with vibrant red hair, and she's dressed as smartly as her sister-in-law.

How can Alessia hope to fit in with these women?

The English are such terrible snobs. They'll despise you. They'll look down on you. Anatoli's words return to haunt her and put Alessia on her guard.

Shpresa offers the women tea and the men raki.

"These women must stay here," her father says to her mother.

"Yes," her mother agrees. "Alessia, tell them."

"I can help," Thanas says as he skeptically eyes his glass of raki.

"It's okay," Alessia says in English. "Caroline, Maryanne, you are welcome to stay here. You will have to share a room."

"That's very kind of you, Alessia. We had thought we'd check into a local hotel," Caroline responds.

"You are welcome here," Shpresa says.

"We'd be delighted to stay if it's not too much trouble," Maryanne says.

"Great. That's settled," says Tom, and he turns to Maxim. "Now, as your best man, it is incumbent on me to organize your stag night. It's traditional."

"What?" says Maxim as he sits beside Alessia and reaches for her hand. He gives it a reassuring squeeze.

"Trevethick, may I remind you: you're getting hitched tomorrow."

"How could I forget?"

Maryanne and Caroline exchange glances.

"So tonight," Tom continues, "we're going to hit Kukës with all we've got."

"Bruv," Joe says. "I'm game."

"Thanas?" Tom asks.

"I wouldn't miss this for the world!"

"What is this?" Jak asks, looking toward his daughter for an explanation.

"The men are going out tonight in Kukës. I think it is a Western tradition," Alessia informs him.

"Out where?"

"To the bars."

"I must go with them. I know the best places." Her father beams at Maxim.

"I will tell him." Alessia looks uncertainly at Thanas, then at Maxim.

"Your father wants to join us," Maxim guesses.

"Yes."

"Oh boy." Maxim smiles and shakes his head. "Okay."

"I will let my brothers know. And my cousins and uncles," her father says.

"What about us? Maryanne and I?" Caroline asks, staring at Maxim with huge blue eyes. She cannot seem to tear her gaze away from him.

Oh.

"Stags only!" Tom insists.

"Maybe we should take Alessia out," Maryanne offers.

"I have too much to do," Alessia says quickly.

"Well, in that case, we'll help you. Won't we, Caro?"

"Oh, no. You are guests," Alessia protests.

"We'd be honored to help if we can," Caroline responds, but she gives Maxim a lingering look of anxiety, or is it devotion? Then Alessia remembers she's not long lost her husband—and Maryanne, her brother; they are bonded in their grief.

J oe and I are now sharing the guest room. It's not the first time we've bunked together. We've done it at school and on school trips, and more recently when utterly hammered at the end of a good night.

He's unpacking his bag, and I'm hanging the two suits he brought with him.

"Mate, how have you been, really?" he asks.

"Okay. A little stir-crazy if you want the truth."

"Maxim. I need to ask you. This marriage. Is it you? Is it what you want?"

"What do you mean?"

"You're a player. Are you ready to saddle yourself with one woman?"

I gape at him. "I wouldn't be going through all this fucking grief if I wasn't!"

"Mate. I'm just asking."

I blow out a breath, keeping a rein on my temper. "It's what I want. It's what she wants. Why is that so hard to believe?"

He raises his hands. "Okay, okay. I believe you."

"But enough of that. What happened?"

"I thought I'd bring two suits. Give you a choice."

"No. I mean about my family, whom you've brought along for a jolly."

"Yeah. Sorry about that. I met Caro as I was coming out of your building. I had your suits."

"Ah."

"I was dead in the water. She wanted to know what the hell I was doing."

"I see."

"She's pissed, bro. At you."

"I know. I didn't tell them. I didn't want the fuss. But I've managed to talk Maryanne down and round. Caro will have to wait."

"Does Alessia know about you and her?"

"What do you mean?"

"Before Kit."

"Um… No." And, of course, there was the grief-fucking after Kit's death.

Hell.

"Do you think I should tell her?" I ask.

He shrugs. "I have no idea."

"We've not talked about... any of that."

"Save it for the honeymoon."

I laugh a little nervously. "Yeah. Good idea."

"Have you planned to go away?"

"Yeah. Arrangements have been made. It's a surprise for Alessia."

"Cool. Here are the rings." He hands me a small bag, within which are two pink gift-wrapped boxes.

"Great. Thanks." I sit on the bed and start unraveling the ribbon.

Joe sits beside me. "So tell me how a wedding works here."

Later Maxim and Joe step into the kitchen. Alessia looks up from the worktop where she's beating eggs and inhales sharply, drinking in the sight of her fiancé. His green eyes gleam with a seductive promise and his hair shines, the golden high-lights glinting beneath the overhead lights. She still finds it aston-ishing that this attractive man will be her husband. In his jacket, white shirt, and jeans, he looks edible. His gaze finds hers, and he smiles and saunters over to her.

"How are you doing?" he asks so only she can hear.

"I'm good. You?"

"Good." He kisses her forehead, and she inhales a trace of his scent—soap and shaving foam—and her favorite fragrance, Maxim. He tucks a stray hair behind her ear. "You look delectable."

She laughs, basking in his attention. "I look like your cleaner."

He takes her chin between his thumb and forefinger, gently tilts her head up, and drops a lingering kiss on her lips. "No. You look like a countess."

She gasps at his shimmering, intense expression, but her mother clears her throat, interrupting them both. He turns and grins at Shpresa, then at the two women sitting at the table.

"I see you've been set to work," he says to Caroline and Maryanne, who are slicing spinach and sorrel at the table.

"We want to help," says Maryanne with a bright smile.

"This is surprisingly therapeutic," says Caroline, looking up at Maxim with her bluest of blue eyes.

"There's wine somewhere," he says, ignoring her look. "We bought a load for the celebration on Saturday. I think it's out back."

"I could murder a glass of wine," Caroline exclaims, and Alessia's not sure if she's expressing her desperation or relief.

"I will fetch a bottle," Shpresa says, and she disappears into the utility room.

"So, how's the nightlife here, Alessia?" Joe asks.

She shrugs, a little embarrassed. "I don't know. I've not been out at night much." All the English turn to stare at her, and she flushes. "My parents are protective," she explains in a rush but notices Caroline glance at Maryanne with a furrowed brow. Her mother returns, brandishing a bottle of white wine.

"I'll open that," Joe offers, and Shpresa hands him the bottle and a corkscrew and brings two glasses to the table.

"Two?" Joe says in consternation.

Alessia and her mother exchange a look. Then her mother's gaze passes over the English as they stare at the Albanians and lands back on Alessia, her eyes twinkling with a devilry that Alessia's not seen before. She grins and fetches two more glasses.

Mama!

Joe pours four glasses as Baba enters the room. He's freshly shaved and wearing a tie and a clean shirt. He looks quite dashing. "Is everyone ready?" he asks Alessia in their tongue; his tone is buoyant.

"I think so, Babë."

His eyes drift to his wife. "Are you drinking?" he asks, shocked.

"Yes. We have all eaten. I should be fine." She raises the glass to him. And Maryanne, Caroline, and Alessia follow suit.

"Gëzuar, Babë," Alessia says.

He gapes at his wife and daughter and then glances at Maxim, nodding. "Like I said, she's your problem now." But Maxim doesn't understand.

"Gëzuar, Zonja," he says to the women, then turns to Joe and Maxim. "We go."

What!

Alessia gapes at her equally awestruck mother. It's the first time they've ever heard her father speak English. She takes a quick gulp of wine and watches as the men file out of the room.

"What is it?" Maryanne asks Alessia.

"My father. He never speaks English."

Maryanne laughs. "There's always a first time. And this wine's not bad."

"It is Albanian," Alessia says and cannot keep the pride out of her voice.

"Cheers, Alessia, Mrs. Demachi, and congratulations." Maryanne raises her glass. Caroline follows suit, and they all take a sip. The wine is delicious, though not quite as tasty as the wine she had in the library in Cornwall. Still, Caroline and Maryanne seem to appreciate it, which, as a proud Albanian, pleases Alessia.

"That's the last of the spinach. What shall we do now?" Caroline asks.

Alessia has placed the two large dishes of Tavë kosi in the oven to bake, and she takes a seat beside her mother as the women make byrek rolls. Shpresa rolls out the dough while Alessia, Maryanne, and Caroline fill them with the spinach, sorrel, and feta cheese mix, which Shpresa has prepared with eggs, onion, and garlic. In between rolls, they each sip their wine.

The conversation ebbs and flows, but the banter between Caroline and Maryanne is entertaining.

"I can't believe you've fallen for an American," Caroline teases Maryanne.

"Fallen?"

"Darling, you've had an uncharacteristic smitten look since he called you at the airport."

"I have not!"

"Methinks she doth protest too much. When are we going to meet him?"

"I don't know. Ethan may come to the UK at Easter. We'll see. He's hard to read." Maryanne gives her a pointed look, and Caroline purses her lips in feigned contempt.

"How long have the two of you known each other?" Alessia asks. She's feeling a little light-headed from the wine, especially as they're on their second bottle.

"I was friends with Maxim at school," Caroline says. "Well, more than friends. But that was a long time ago." She frowns at the spinach mix, pats it down on the dough, then twists it efficiently into a roll.

More than friends!

"I think *we* met at one of Rowena's summer parties. The annual Trevethick cricket match at the Hall," Caroline says to Maryanne.

"Yes. Back in the day. You came down from London with Maxim. I have to say, those are still so much fun. I do love a man in cricket whites."

"Yes." Caroline sounds wistful. "Kit looked great in whites and was a skilled batsman too." She stares down into her glass.

"He was," Maryanne says, and the atmosphere among the women nosedives.

"I am sorry for your loss," Alessia says quietly.

"Yes. Well. Thank you." Caroline swallows and tosses her glossy hair as if shaking off a nasty thought. "It will be down to you to host the annual village cricket match next summer, Alessia, among many other events."

Alessia stares at her. She knows nothing of cricket.

"You really don't know what will be expected of you, do you?" Caroline states.

"Not now," Maryanne warns Caroline.

"No," Alessia whispers.

Caroline sighs. "Well…" She gives Maryanne a reassuring glance. "We'll be there to help you."

"Let's get these byrek finished," Maryanne chirps, and Alessia knows she's trying to lighten the mood.

The bar is crowded and noisy, but the atmosphere is sociable and celebratory, despite the spartan surroundings. This is the third bar we've been in, and it's as functional as the first two, though not quite as austere because there are several FK Kukësi football scarves and shirts on the walls. Football is big in Kukës. Tonight the men, all of whom seem to be related in some way to Jak Demachi, are drowning their sorrows as their team lost to Teuta, the team from Durrës.

Our love of football is an icebreaker—Joe and I, who are Arsenal and Chelsea supporters respectively, share their sorrow. Tom, on the other hand, is a rugby man, as are we—but he's no time or love for the beautiful game.

I'm on my fourth beer and feeling the buzz. I cannot remember anyone's name, but Tom and Joe are holding forth.

Joe, as a good-looking guy, is undoubtedly an attraction. I've not seen any Black people in Albania, though I'm sure they exist, so he's an object of curiosity. He doesn't seem uncomfortable—quite the opposite. He's lapping up the attention, and we're all treated as honored guests. The Albanians are delighted that we're here.

Frankly, it's touching.

There are only two flies in the proverbial ointment: One is Caroline and facing her wrath at some point—I've not been lulled into a false sense of security about that. She's probably hurt too, and I need to make it up to her. The second is the uneasy feeling that I'm being watched. I know that we're curiosities here in this small town, but every so often, an unsettling itch skitters down my back as if someone has me in their sights.

Is it him?

Her *"betrothed."*

Is he watching? I don't know.

It could be my overactive imagination.

"Urdhëro!" Jak hands me another beer. "Më pas raki!" He clinks my bottle with his.

Oh God, raki. The devil's brew!

I't's late. The food is cooling and ready to go into the refrigerators in the utility room. Alessia sits with Caroline and Maryanne at the table, and they're on their third bottle of wine. Alessia, feeling more light-headed than before, has stopped drinking. Her mother has been sensible and retired for the night. After all, they have a big day tomorrow.

She yawns. There is no sign of the men, and she suspects Maxim will be as drunk as he was that night of the raki. She'd like to go to bed, but Caroline and Maryanne are talking about men, and it's fascinating.

"Men are confounding," Maryanne says.

"Emotionally unavailable more like," Caroline responds. "But, all they really want is someone to suck their dick." She laughs, but her laughter sounds forced and hollow.

"Caro. Enough," Maryanne scolds, glancing at Alessia, who is trying to absorb this arresting insight. She's shocked at the turn in the conversation but keeps her face neutral, she hopes, as she struggles with how to respond.

Is this how English women talk to each other?

Caroline turns her attention to Alessia, narrowing her eyes as if assessing her anew now that they're all tipsy. "You really are very pretty," she says, slurring her words slightly.

Alessia suspects she's more than a little tipsy.

"I'm not surprised he's fallen for you… but… I've not seen it before. Him. In love. You know, he's my best friend."

Best friend, now.

Alessia seizes her chance.

The phrase *more than friends* has been rattling around her brain, tormenting her since Caroline blurted it out earlier. "You and he were… lovers?" she asks.

"I should say so. We popped each other's cherries." Caroline quirks her lips up as if it's a fond memory. "He's a better fuck than my husband."

"Oh." Alessia is now completely lost for words, as a vision of Caroline wearing nothing but Maxim's shirt and making coffee in his kitchen comes unwelcome to mind.

"Caroline!" Maryanne exclaims, shocked.

"It's true. I know he's your brother. They're both your brothers," she slurs. "But you know Maxim's a complete player." She turns her unfocused gaze on Alessia. "Darling, he's slept with most of London." Her face falls. "And after Kit… Well, we— Ow!"

"Enough," Maryanne growls, her voice much firmer, and Alessia suspects she's kicked Caroline under the table.

Caroline shrugs. "It's true. Promiscuous doesn't cover it. He's proof of the adage: Practice makes perfect."

"I think it's time we got you to bed, Caro." Maryanne stands. "Forgive her; she's grieving and had too much to drink," Maryanne says to Alessia. "Don't pay any attention."

Caroline frowns as she stands as if she's just realized what she's said. "Yes. Of course. I'm sorry. I don't know what I'm talking about. Do forgive me."

"Good night, Alessia," Maryanne says, and she drags a staggering Caroline out of the room, leaving Alessia reeling.

He's a better fuck than my husband.

Present tense.

Chapter Six

Mrs. Demachi has cooked a monumental breakfast for us all. From her huge smile and the little song she's humming as she makes coffee and busies herself around the kitchen, I know she's in her element and loving every moment. It's heartening that we're not too much of a burden on her.

"Good morning, Maxim." She greets me, radiating happiness.

I give her a quick kiss on the cheek.

"Good morning, Shpresa. Thank you for feeding my friends and family."

"Dear boy." She places her hand on my cheek. "It is my pleasure. I know you bring great happiness to my Alessia."

"And she to me."

She grins. "Sit. Eat. Big day, today. And the weather has been kind to us." She directs my gaze to the window, and outside the sky is glorious—a bright February blue. I hope it's not too cold.

Maryanne and Joe are already seated at the table. They're in high spirits as they tuck into omelets and Mama Demachi's delicious bubble bread. There is cheese, olives, local honey, and stuffed vine leaves too. Jak sits at the head of the table, slathering butter and berry jam on his bubble bread. He is the definition of bright-eyed and bushy-tailed. He's been positively upbeat since last night. There's a smudge of soot on his hand, and I know he's been outside to light the stove in the garage to warm up our wedding venue.

The Demachis are the most excellent hosts.

Apart from the cockblocking, of course.

The only person not full of the joys of the day is Caroline, who sits quietly, looking pale and morose as she nurses a cup of coffee. I suspect she's hungover. Maryanne casts an occasional anxious glance at her and then at me.

What? What's happened?

Maryanne gives me a quick, subtle shake of her head.

Leave it, she's saying.

Of course, missing from the table is my beautiful bride. Alessia is being prepped for the wedding, and I've not seen her since we left for my stag night. And what a night it was—Kukës can party. Well, the men of Kukës can. And it ended happily—meaning I wasn't handcuffed to any street furniture without my trousers, which Tom threatened at one point during the night.

You don't have any handcuffs.

I'll improvise, old boy.

And I feel fine this morning. That's probably because I ditched the raki. Now, I'm excited and a little anxious to get on with the day, and I'll be glad when it's over.

"Can I talk to you?" Caroline asks as I take my seat. I glance at her, sensing she's on edge. And Maryanne is being evasive. Has something happened? If so, what?

My stomach churns.

"Of course." My tone is brusque.

This is it. The moment of reckoning I've been dreading.

"In private?"

"After breakfast. You should eat something."

She grimaces, and I know she has a Grade A hangover.

A lessia stares unseeing at her reflection in the bedroom mirror. She's seated at her dressing table as Agnesa, her cousin, who's a hairdresser and makeup artist, curls her hair with a styling iron. Agnesa chatters away, excited to be involved in all the preparations and eager to see Maxim, the handsome fiancé, again.

Alessia tunes her out. She's numb, and she's not sure if it's her nerves or if she's still reeling from Caroline's drunken revelations.

Darling, he's slept with most of London.

This is not news to Alessia. She used to empty his bin of condoms every time she cleaned for him. She wrinkles her nose in disgust at the recollection—sometimes, there were *many* discarded condoms.

And then they suddenly stopped appearing.

She rubs her forehead, trying to remember when that happened. So much has occurred since then, and her memory of the timeline is confused. She attempted to figure it out last night while trying to sleep but couldn't because Caroline's thoughtless words echoed through her brain, taunting her.

He's a better fuck than my husband.

So, they *were* together.

Maxim and Caroline.

But when? When did this *fucking* happen? It sounds recent, and an unwelcome image of Caroline in Maxim's arms in the street outside his apartment forms in her mind.

No.

Her imagination is choking her and making her doubt herself. Making her doubt him—her man. Her Mister. On her wedding day.

She feels like she's going to suffocate under the weight of these awful thoughts.

"I need a minute," she says.

"Okay," Agnesa responds, a little surprised, but she steps aside. As only half her hair is curled, Alessia finds a scarf and ties it around her head, concealing it all. She grabs a robe, hastily wraps it over the slip she's wearing, and leaves the room. She needs the one thing that will bring her solace.

She reaches the bottom of the stairs and hears everyone at breakfast. Ignoring them, she hurries to the front room and sits at the piano.

She takes a deep breath and places her fingers on the keys, feeling immediately more grounded as her fingers touch the cool ivory. She closes her eyes, then launches into Beethoven's *Moonlight Sonata*, the tricky third movement. In C-sharp minor. It's the most fitting piece, in the correct key to reflect her anger. The music flows. Loudly. Easily. Blistering off the walls, through the room. Her anger and resentment pour into the keys, emphasizing the loud accents of the sonata in brilliant oranges and reds until there's nothing but her and the colors of the music.

The frantic, fast arpeggios of Beethoven's third movement echo furiously off the hallway into the family room with such ferocity and passion that the entire table is momentarily silenced and paralyzed.

I look up at Shpresa, who looks anxiously at Jak. He shrugs.

"Alessia?" Maryanne asks, and I hear the breathless wonder in her voice.

I nod and turn to her parents. "Has something happened?"

"I do not know," Shpresa responds, and her eyes widen in astonishment. "You know?"

"That she's angry. Yes. But I don't know why." I frantically rack my brain, trying to think if I could have done something to upset her.

Hell. Is she having doubts about the wedding?

"That's Alessia?" asks Joe with a forkful of omelet raised midair.

"Yes."

"Dude!"

"I know."

"She's extraordinary," Joe murmurs.

"Yeah. But she's pissed off. At something or someone." I turn my attention to Maryanne and Caroline, who saw her last night. Maryanne's lips thin, and Caroline avoids my eyes, and I have my culprit. "What did you do?" I ask quietly as my scalp tenses.

What the fuck? Did you say something?

"Caroline?"

She pales and shakes her head, still avoiding my gaze.

Shit.

"I'll go." Shpresa wipes her hands on a dishcloth and heads out of the room.

"How do you know she's angry?" Maryanne asks.

"This is in C-sharp minor."

She frowns.

"C-sharp minor. Angry music. In reds and oranges. She told me. Sad and angry. E flat."

"Wow."

"Yeah. Music. I told you."

"She's brilliant."

"Yes. She has synesthesia. She's playing this from memory." I can't hide the pride and awe in my voice.

"She's amazing." Joe is stunned.

"She is," I agree. "In every way."

Alessia reaches the end of the piece, and I listen acutely, wanting to hear if that's the end or if she'll play something else.

A lessia is breathing hard when she finishes. Her thoughts clear as the colors fade, and she takes a deep breath. She turns to find her mother in the room. She'd been so lost in the music she didn't hear her come in.

"That was beautiful, my heart. What's wrong?"

Alessia shakes her head. She doesn't want to admit her fears. If she speaks them aloud, she makes them more tangible—more real. She's at a crossroads. Does she believe the man she loves or… not?

"He knows," Shpresa says.

"Knows what?"

"That you are upset."

"He's heard me play."

"Often, I think," her mother says.

Alessia nods.

"He's so proud of you. I can tell."

"I must go and get ready." Alessia stands and faces her mother.

"He loves you."

"I know." But her voice wavers, betraying her true feelings.

Why is she so suddenly unsure? Of everything.

Shpresa's expression softens. "Oh, my heart. Go and get ready. You're making the right decision. These past few days, I've never seen you so happy. And he's glowing."

"Is he?" Alessia hears the breathless hope in her own voice.

"Of course he is." She caresses her daughter's face. "You have made us so proud, Alessia. Me and your father. Go conquer the world. Like you always wanted to. And with that man by your side, you won't fail."

Alessia's spirits lift. This is the most robust affirmation she's ever heard from her mother. "Thank you, Mama." Alessia clasps her mother tightly, and they stand hugging each other in the front room.

"I know about the baby," Mama whispers.

Alessia gasps.

"I know you're not pregnant."

"How?"

"The number of painkillers you've been taking over the last few days. And I found your contraceptive pills while I was cleaning your dressing table."

Alessia flushes. "I'm sorry to… mislead you."

"I understand. And I'll find a way to break it to your father. Does Maxim know?"

"Thank you. And yes, Maxim knew from the beginning."

"And he still went along with all this?"

"Yes. For me… and for you."

"For me?"

Alessia nods.

"I don't understand."

Alessia kisses her mother's forehead. "One day, I will tell you."

*F*uck this!

I've been stewing in my own juices, trying to figure out what's wrong with Alessia, and I can't bear it a moment longer. I leave the table, and disregarding the many pairs of eyes I feel burning into my back, I stalk down the corridor toward the front room.

"Alessia," I call through the door and hold my breath.

"Yes," she says eventually.

I exhale sharply. "Are you okay?"

"Yes." She sounds uncertain.

"Do you want to talk about anything?"

"No."

It's not enough. I don't believe her.

"I don't care about this superstitious nonsense, but you and your mother do. That's why I'm staying out here. I don't know what's upsetting you, but I want you to know, I love you. I want to marry you. Today. If you need to speak to me…I'm here."

Shpresa eyes her daughter.

"Mama, I need to talk to him," Alessia says.

"I will leave you. It is your decision whether you invite him into this room or not. Nothing about this wedding is conventional… so…" Her mother waves her hand in resignation, kisses her forehead, and leaves.

"Can I come in?" Maxim asks from outside the room.

"Yes."

Maxim peeks around the door and smiles when he sees her. It's impossible not to return his smile, and her heart rate spikes at the sight of him. She's missed him. He enters and comes to stand beside her, green eyes ablaze. He's in a T-shirt and jeans, the black ones with the rip at the knee... and he looks concerned and *hot*.

Especially hot.

"What's wrong?" he asks.

A lessia is wearing a blue scarf around her head that conceals her hair and a blue robe, reminding me of when she was in my flat.

What a time that was... Me lusting after her while she ignored me.

She's as lovely now as she was then. More so, and I'm still lusting after her. She gazes at me, a mountain of hurt in her eyes.

"What is it?"

She pales a little.

Shit. It's bad.

"Tell me, please."

"It was... just words."

"Tell me," I insist.

"Your sister-in-law." Her voice is barely audible.

"Caroline?"

She nods.

"Ah." *I knew it.* "What's she said?"

She seems to be debating whether to tell me. I watch her inner struggle play out on her expressive face. Finally, she swallows. "She said that you are a better...*fuck*"—she whispers the word—"than her husband."

I inhale sharply as my temper flares. I've never heard Alessia use crude language before, and hearing that word come out of her mouth has shocked me more than it should.

What Caroline said is more shocking and *un-fucking-becoming*. No wonder she's at breakfast, hanging her head in shame.

So she should be.

Caro's come here to cause trouble. And she's succeeded. I bridle my anger, knowing I can deal with her later. "I'm sure she was drunk," I mutter charitably.

"I could not stop thinking about that last night. As I was trying to sleep."

Shit. We're having this discussion now—on the day of our wedding?

"Do you love her?" Alessia asks.

I gape at her, stunned into silence. *What? How can she think that?*

"You are not answering my question. In Cornwall, you said, 'talk to me,' 'ask me questions.' I am asking you now."

"No, I don't love her like that." I'm emphatic. "I used to, a long time ago. But I was fifteen. She's family. My brother's wife."

"And physically?"

I frown, not entirely understanding what she's trying to ask.

"Did you have sexual intercourse with your brother's wife?"

Hell.

"Um… no. But I had sex with his widow."

Alessia winces and closes her eyes, and her expression slices me to the bone.

Shit. And I've never felt quite as ashamed as I do now.

"When I last saw her," Alessia says as she opens dark, dark wounded eyes, "she was in your arms, on the sidewalk outside your apartment building."

"In my arms?" I frown, desperately trying to remember, feeling like I've been caught on the back foot.

"I was in Anatoli's Mercedes."

A chill grips my heart, and I'm transported back to that dreadful night. "Oh, yes. She was apologizing, and she ran into me. We would have fallen had I not caught her." I swallow. "We had a fight. A big fight."

"It makes sense. You and her. You are the same. The same class." Her voice gets quieter and quieter.

"No! I don't want Caroline. I want you, Alessia. When I went to see her, I told her I was in love with you. She threw me out of the house and then came running to apologize. And it was just as Anatoli was getting into the car. I didn't listen to what Caroline was saying. I knew something was wrong. I recognized the Albanian plates on his car, and I cannot tell you how harrowing it was to watch in complete helplessness as it drove off into the distance." I close my eyes and remember the feeling of utter impotence and despair as the Mercedes disappeared from view. "It was one of the worst days of my life."

Her fingers find mine, and I open my eyes as she squeezes my hand.

"What's going on, Alessia?" I return the squeeze.

"Are you sure you want to do this?" she asks. "She loves you too."

I pull her into my arms and hold her. "It's you I love, not her. It's you I want to marry. Not her. Please don't let her ruin our day."

I can't believe we're having this discussion.

Alessia lets out a sigh, her dark eyes on mine.

"Baby, let's do this." I stroke my thumb over her lip. "I want to grow old with you. And I don't want my family to be in any doubt about how I feel about you, Alessia Demachi—you are the love of my life."

I hear her small gasp. "You are the love of mine." And she presses her lips against the pad of my thumb.

"Thank God." I exhale with relief. "I'm not going to kiss you. I want to save that for tonight." As the words leave my mouth, a frisson of desire skates over my skin, lifting the hairs on my body.

Wow.

Alessia inhales sharply. "Okay." She sounds a little breathless.

"Okay." I grin.

Her answering smile is shy, and I know I've won her back.

"That was a stunning piece you played. Knocked the socks off my friends and family."

"I was angry."

"I could tell. I'm sorry."

She shuts her eyes and quickly shakes her head as if ridding herself of a terrible thought.

"Are you packed?"

She opens her eyes and nods. After the wedding, we are out of here.

"Good. Please, go and get ready." I lean forward and kiss her forehead, closing my eyes.

I do not want to lose you. Again.

I return to the breakfast table, where the conversation is more muted, and I know all eyes are on me. I cannot bring myself to even look at Caro. She's really crossed a fucking line, and I'm furious.

No. Raging.

How dare she?

Right now, I don't trust my temper, and for fuck's sake—it's my wedding day.

There's a knock at the front door, and Jak springs up from the table as if he's expecting the caller.

"Okay, mate?" Joe asks me.

"Yeah." I glance at my watch. I have time. "I'm going for a run."

When I come back upstairs in my running gear, it's a hive of activity. There are more people in the house, presumably to help with the catering and set up. I manage to avoid them; I'm glad I'm leaving for a run. I've left Joe in the room to shower, and I've no idea where M.A. or Caro are, and frankly, I don't want to know and I don't care. I need some time with my own thoughts to calm down.

I step outside into the bright but chilly day to see sunlight bouncing off the glittering green lake. But just at the bottom of the driveway, Demachi is in a full and intense conversation with *him*!

Demachi and the Arsehole turn to stare as I stand immobilized, glaring at them.

What the fuck is he *doing here?*

My hands fist, and I'm ready. Nothing would give me greater pleasure than beating this man to a pulp—especially the way I'm feeling at this minute.

"This is not what you think, Englishman," Anatoli sneers.

Demachi holds up his hands. "Po flasim për punë, asgjë më shumë."

I have no idea what he says.

"Ha!" Anatoli says, his scorn evident in that one syllable. "If you knew the language, you'd know what he's said. We're discussing business. Nothing more. Nothing to do with you." The Arsehole's English is impeccable, which is bloody irritating. "We're not discussing Alessia," he continues, and his voice catches as he says her name.

What! Does he care for her?

"Mos e zër në gojë Alesian," Demachi snaps at him.

"I'll be here, Englishman, waiting, in her homeland, with her family. When you fuck up," Anatoli scoffs.

"You'll wait a long bloody time, mate," I mutter, more to myself than to him. "I hope."

Fuck this.

"Farewell, Arsehole," I call, knowing full well my father-in-law won't understand, and turn and sprint up the driveway, leaving them standing. To my great satisfaction, I see Anatoli's mouth pressed in a hard line, and I know my gibe has provoked him.

Yes!

Out on the road, I dodge past his Mercedes, stretch my legs, and run.

Run like I've never run before.

"You look great, mate," Joe says as he straightens my tie.

"I'm glad you brought the Dior. It's my favorite."

"French navy is your color. Goes with your blood."

"Very funny, Joe."

"I'm pissed you didn't give me time to make you a bespoke suit."

"You'll get a chance."

"For a wedding?" Joe's brow furrows.

"We'll do this again in London, or Cornwall. Or Oxfordshire," I reassure him.

"You and Alessia?"

I laugh. "Yes. Don't look so alarmed. It's complicated. But I'll probably be in full morning dress."

"Dove gray? Black? Stripes?" Joe's eyes light up.

"Mate. Let's get this wedding out of the way first."

"Buttonhole," he says and pins the white rose to my lapel. He places his hands on my biceps. "You look like a groom."

"Thanks, bro." And I'm suddenly overwhelmed by all that's happened, by what I'm about to do. I hug him. Hard. "I'm so glad you're here, mate."

Joe slaps me on the back. "Me too, Max. Me too."

I clear my throat. "Now. You know what we have to do."

"Yep."

Albanian tradition dictates that the groom should collect his bride and take her to his home for a feast. That's impossible for us as I don't have a home here. But I'm to escort Alessia from her front door to the wedding party. It's the closest we can get to this tradition.

Outside, by the front door, Joe, Tom, and I wait for my bride. Joe's also in a navy suit, and as ever, he looks sharp and stylish. Tom is in a black dinner suit with a black tie.

It's all I brought with me, Trevethick.

Both have buttonholes, and I'm relieved they're here with me. Their friendship and support over the last few years has been everything. And they scrub up well.

Wedding guests are milling around in the driveway, and some are coming out of the house. I think they're immediate family who have been greeting Alessia inside, as is traditional. Some are filing into the tent beside the garage as it's warmer in there, and I know the registrar is already inside and set up. Beside this stunning lake and mountain setting, there's a convivial, festive feeling of a community coming together.

It's moving and I swallow down my emotion.

I'm definitely not in Kansas anymore.

The colored lights on the fir trees that Jak hung yesterday add to the atmosphere, as do the few children running and laughing in the yard, holding and waving Albanian flags.

People greet me with a handshake or kisses. Many of the men I met on our impromptu stag do address me as "*Chelsea*" after my football team. It's a nickname I rather like—but I'm still finding it impossible to keep up with all their names.

A photographer is documenting our day with a Canon EOS. I think she's one of Alessia's cousins. But I'm not sure.

I'm a world away from home.

Maryanne and Caroline exit the house to make their way to the venue. They're both in winter wedding finery. Maryanne's in a navy trouser suit, and Caro, a navy velvet dress—and I know Joe has tipped them off as to what I'm wearing.

Maryanne hugs me. "Maxie, you look splendid. So does your bride." She sniffs and walks hastily away before I have a chance to say anything.

Caro still can't look me in the eye. "You've been avoiding me," she says quietly.

"What did you expect? This isn't the time, Caro. I'm still so fucking angry with you."

"I'm sorry."

"I'm not the one you need to apologize to."

"I needed to tell you something." And she peers at me, her blue eyes wide and a little teary. "And you're going to be angry about this too, but I did it for you and her," she whispers.

"What did you do?"

"I told your mother. She'll be here shortly."

"What?" The word is almost inaudible, and I can hardly breathe.

Fuck.

Chapter Seven

"Darling, I'm here already," a clipped, mid-Atlantic voice drawls over the light breeze toward us. We whirl around as my heart sinks, and my mother is making her way down the drive through the crowd. She's dressed in a heavy black coat—probably from Chanel's upcoming collection for next winter—oversized Chanel sunglasses, a faux fur hat, and Louboutin boots.

Accompanying her is a young man about my age, dressed in black Moncler. He has model-good looks, American teeth, and I suspect he's her latest fuck. Her hand rests in the crook of his arm.

"Mother, what a pleasant surprise," I say, retreating into the detached persona I reserve exclusively for the woman who birthed me. "You should have told me you were coming."

"Maxim." She offers her cheek, and I give her a quick peck, inhaling the expensive scent of Creed, her perfume of choice.

"Joe and Tom, you know. And Judas Iscariot, my sister-in-law." I take a small amount of pleasure in Caroline's ashen face as she gives her mother-in-law a quick kiss.

"Thank you for letting me know, Caroline. Short notice, I know. But it looks like we made it here in time. This is my friend, Heath." Rowena introduces the blond on her arm.

"How do you do?" I respond, plastering a smile on my face.

Before he can reply, she releases him. "Might I have a word, darling?"

"I'm afraid it's not convenient at this time. I'm about to get married. Please make your way into the venue." I wave her in the direction of the marquee. "Judas will find a seat for you."

Caro flushes and stares down at her Manolos.

"I'm not here to prevent your wedding, Maxim. That would be a little vulgar, don't you think? But we will talk afterwards. And you will explain to me why you are marrying the help and why the fuck you haven't invited your grieving mother to this... event. Are you ashamed of your bride and her family? Because, frankly, that's how this looks."

I can't see her eyes, but she purses her scarlet lips, and I know that beneath her cool disdain, she's seething.

Well, that makes two of us.

No, I'm not seething. I'm apoplectic with rage.

But I hide it well. "I didn't invite you, Rowena dearest"—I lean down and whisper in her ear—"because you're doing exactly what I thought you'd do. Projecting your pretentious privileged shit onto my situation. Now, if you'll excuse me, I'm about to marry the woman I love."

She stiffens. "I know that marrying this girl is a way to get back at me, but let me warn you—"

"It's not about *you*, for fuck's sake," I hiss. "Not everything is about you, Rowena. I fell in love. Deal with it."

Tom clears his throat, a flush at his neck—did he hear us? Behind him, Jak and Shpresa have appeared at the front door. I turn to greet them. Shpresa is almost unrecognizable. She's wearing a pale pink shift dress and a matching chiffon wrap. Her hair is coiffed and sleek and dark, like Alessia's. And she's wearing a little makeup.

She looks stunning.

"Mama Demachi, you look lovely," I murmur, and she smiles, showing us where Alessia gets her looks.

Chin up, dude. Here goes.

I turn and make the introductions. "Jak, Shpresa, my mother has decided to grace us with her presence. May I present Rowena, Dowager Countess of Trevethick." I stress the word *dowager*, and Rowena's lips tighten—because it's rude and also incorrect—but she doesn't miss a beat, and graciously, she holds out her hand.

"Mr. and Mrs. Demachi, what a pleasure to meet you and under such happy circumstances." She sounds sincere, but her statement is tinged with condescending sarcasm for my benefit, I'm sure.

It's infuriating, but I ignore it and wrap my arms around my in-laws as they shake hands with my mother. "Jak and Shpresa have done an incredible job of pulling this event together at such short notice." I kiss Shpresa's cheek, and she flushes and quickly translates everything for her husband.

"Konteshë?" Jak says.

"Yes."

"How do you do?" Shpresa says. "Please. Come." Shpresa casts a curious glance at me and directs Jak to accompany my mother and her lover into the house.

"That was a bit rough." Tom states the bloody obvious. "You okay, old boy?" He pats me on the back as we fall into line behind them.

"Yes," I hiss. But it's a lie. Taking a deep breath, I bury my anger and follow them into the house.

The Demachis have suspended their no-shoes policy for the day, and we stand in the hallway, which is frankly crowded now that my mother and *Heath* have joined us, and wait.

Jak squares his shoulders and, with a theatrical flourish, opens the door to the front room, and there in the center stands Alessia Demachi.

She's a vision in lace, satin, and a soft diaphanous material, silhouetted by the light from the window. I stop and stare at the woman who will shortly become my wife and completely lose my train of thought. She's gorgeous. With dark expressive eyes ringed in kohl, she looks a little more sophisticated, a little more... knowing, but demure and sexy as hell.

She takes my breath away.

Her gown is the epitome of elegance: a tight white satin corset covered in lace—lace over her shoulders and arms, and from her waist a skirt that flares softly. There are tiny pearl buttons at the front. Her hair is curled in a delicate updo beneath a fine, gossamer veil.

I realize I'm gawking, saving this moment so I'll remember it for an eternity, and my throat has constricted in a knot of exhilaration, awe, and anticipation.

She looks every inch a goddess... no, a countess. My countess.

Dude, don't get emotional.

Suddenly, I no longer care that what we're doing may not be strictly legitimate. I'm just so glad and thankful that we're doing this today. Here. Now.

"Hello again, beautiful. I could look at you all day."

"And I you," she whispers; her dark eyes, framed with the darkest, longest lashes, are vivid and intense, and I want to drown in her gaze.

I step forward and kiss her cheek. "You look stunning." And I realize this is the first time I've seen her in makeup. She's beautiful.

She strokes my lapel and smiles up at me. "So do you."

"My mother's here."

Her eyes widen in shock.

"Yeah. Brace yourself," I warn, for her ears only, then call, "Mother." And Rowena enters the room. She's removed her sunglasses, so she squints slightly as she observes the exquisite vision in front of her. "May I present Alessia Demachi."

"Darling girl," Rowena says and kisses her cheek, then stands back to scrutinize my fiancée in her usual myopic way.

"Lady Trevethick, how do you do?" Alessia responds.

"You speak English?" Rowena sounds surprised.

"Fluently," Alessia replies, and I could fucking kiss her.

My girl has teeth.

Rowena nods and smiles. I think she's impressed. "It's a plea-sure to meet you on such an auspicious day."

"And you."

It's only then that I become aware of the others in the room. Alessia's cousins, I think. And maybe a couple of her aunts.

"We'll have plenty of time, after this expeditious wedding, to get to know each other. I look forward to it." Rowena's tone is neutral but friendly enough. "We'll go and take our seats." She turns and exits the room. As she does, I notice Alessia blow out a quick breath. Probably from relief. I take her hand and whisper in her ear.

"You were wonderful. Well done!"

"I did not know she was coming," she whispers back.

"Me neither. A bit of a shock, to be honest. We can talk about it later. Shall we go and get married?"

She grins. "Yes."

"Oh, I forgot. The tradition. I'm supposed to give you this." From inside my jacket pocket, I remove a handkerchief. In it is a sugared almond. I hold it up to Alessia's lips.

Maxim is mesmerizing, especially in his sharp, dark suit. She's never seen him dressed this elegantly before, and he looks born to it.

But, of course he is. He's an aristocrat.

His eyes shine a brilliant green as his gaze moves from her eyes to her mouth. His lips are slightly parted as Alessia licks, then presses her lips against the candy he's holding. "Mmm," she mur-murs, and he shuts his eyes for a nanosecond, then pops the sweet in his mouth. The muscles deep in Alessia's belly tighten, and she inhales sharply. He gives her a wicked grin full of sensual promise. It gives her an idea… for later when they're finally alone together.

By then, he'll be hers.

She cannot believe he'll be hers to keep. Her own man.

She wants to strut about the house on his arm, so everyone can see, and shout *he's mine*.

Alessia laughs at herself, feeling a little foolish and giddy.

He loves her—he told her in no uncertain terms this morning—and his declaration has fortified her inner strength.

Since Caroline's shocking revelation, Alessia has realized that his family is challenging her. She squares her shoulders.

Challenge accepted.

Maxim is worth fighting for.

She's just stood up to his mother, and she'll remain vigilant. Maxim has always been circumspect about Rowena, so Alessia will be cautious too. She knows that she must build a bridge with Caroline. After all, she's Maxim's sister-in-law. But still, she's wary. Caroline has her own agenda, and Alessia suspects she's in love with Maxim.

"Alessia, here!" Agnesa calls and hands Alessia her bouquet of white roses.

"Thank you." Alessia smiles as Maxim takes her hand, and she puts her thoughts aside as together they leave the house.

Alessia drops Maxim's hand as she steps out of the house and takes the handkerchief her mother has embroidered for her for this very occasion. As tradition dictates, she pretends to be sad that she's leaving her parents' house and dabs at her eyes, but inside she's dancing.

"Are you okay?" Maxim asks, concerned as he slips his hand over her elbow.

She flashes him a quick grin and winks at him.

His brow creases. He's puzzled but amused.

"It's tradition."

"Oh?"

"There's no prettiness in a bride without tears," she whispers.

Maxim shakes his head, not understanding, but they're soon distracted by the cheers and applause from family and friends as they make their way, flanked by Tom and Joe, toward the spacious tent. Her parents and Maxim's mother follow in their wake as they head into the venue, ready for the wedding ceremony.

We're seated in front of Ferid Tabaku, the registrar, at a small table—with the Demachis, their family and friends, and the scant members of my family sitting at the tables behind us—while he solemnly informs us of our obligations.

Tabaku stands and reads through the code for the family, explaining what is expected of us during our marriage. Thanas quietly translates everything for me.

"Spouses have the same rights and duties toward each other." He peers at both of us, his dark eyes bright with sincerity. "They should love and respect each other, maintain marital fidelity, assist each other in fulfilling all family and social obligations..."

I glance at Alessia, and she squeezes my hand as tears form in her eyes. I look away quickly as a knot forms in my throat.

Deep breaths, mate.

Tabaku goes on and on and on... and I think it takes longer because poor Thanas has to translate everything.

Behind us, the crowd, even though they are seated, begins to fidget. There are coughs and snickers, and a baby starts to cry. A child says something that causes some tittering in the congregation, but I have no idea what he's said. I think it's his mother that removes him from the room, and I suspect he needs the lavatory.

Finally, Tabaku asks if we agree to our obligations and consent to the marriage.

"I agree to all our obligations, and consent," I respond.

The registrar nods, satisfied with my answer, and turns to Alessia, who answers him in Albanian, and I hope she agrees and consents too. She gives me a quick smile.

"I have your consent. I now declare you are married in the name of the law." Tabaku smiles, and the Albanians erupt into applause. "Congratulations," he says. "You may exchange rings."

I wondered when we were going to do the rings.

I fish them from where I've secured them—my inside pocket, next to my heart.

"Lady Trevethick," I say to Alessia, and she gives me her hand. I slide on the platinum ring, feeling a little weird that I don't have to say anything. It fits perfectly. Thank goodness. I raise her hand to my lips, my eyes on hers, and kiss the ring and her knuckle together.

Alessia's answering smile is crotch-tighteningly beautiful. I hand her my ring, and she slips it on my finger. "Lord Trevethick," she whispers, and taking my hand in both of hers, she kisses the ring and my knuckle, then leans forward and kisses me.

The Albanians applaud and cheer, and Tom leans down. "Congratulations, Trevethick," he says, and I stand and hug him. Joe is next.

"Gentlemen, you will need to witness the marriage contract. Maxim, Alessia, you need to sign them too," Thanas tells us.

M axim's family approaches them.

"Congratulations," his mother says to Maxim in her clipped, crisp tone. She places her hand on his arm and offers her cheek.

"Thank you, Mother," Maxim responds, equally clipped and crisp, and his lips barely graze her cheek.

She turns her steely, dry eyes on Alessia. "You make a beautiful bride, Alessia. Welcome to the family." She offers her cheek to Alessia, and taking her cue from Maxim, Alessia gives her a quick peck, mindful that she's wearing lipstick.

Maryanne throws her arms around Maxim, and he hugs her. "Maxie," she says, and she reaches out a hand to Alessia at the same time. "Congratulations, you two. I hope you'll be very happy." She releases Maxim and hugs Alessia. "Reformed rakes make the best husbands," she whispers, but before she can respond, Alessia is distracted by Caroline, who's touching Maxim's lapel, a beseeching look in her big blue eyes.

"Congratulations." Caroline gives him a quick kiss on his cheek.

Stony-faced, he nods. "Thank you."

She flushes a little, and Alessia realizes that Maxim is still mad at her, and Caroline doesn't know how to deal with his anger. She turns to Alessia, her expression cooler, and Alessia's heart starts to pound.

"Congratulations, Alessia. And I'm so sorry. For what I said last night. It was graceless and utterly uncalled for."

Alessia, acting on pure instinct, hugs her before she can say anything else. "Thank you," she says and releases her.

Caroline, embarrassed, nods and moves on, leaving Alessia alone with Maxim.

"How was that?" he asks as he takes her hand.

"Okay," she whispers, and he brings her hand to his lips.

"You coped admirably with my family. Congratulations, Lady Trevethick."

She grins, blossoming under his praise. "We have to sit over there." Alessia points to two gray velvet chairs set up beneath a small arbor, before a table covered in white linen, white roses, and fairy lights. Once they've taken their seats, two children—Alessia's young cousins—present them with plates from the impressive buffet.

The party is in full swing. Alessia is giddy and a little tipsy from the wine. Maxim has removed his jacket and tie, his hair is tousled from all her female relatives ruffling it, and he looks so handsome. The men have started to dance, and her uncles are trying to persuade Maxim to join them.

"Vallja e Kukësit. Come! Chelsea!" her cousin Murkash goads Maxim. "You are Albanian now!"

Maxim rolls his eyes and turns to Alessia. "You didn't mention dancing. With a bunch of men."

"This is the traditional dance from Kukës," Alessia says, grinning at him.

He flashes her a smile as he gets up to join them.

*M*an. *What fresh hell is this?*

"Okay! Okay, I'm coming. Joe, Tom, join me," I call over to them at their adjacent table, where they're sitting with my family.

Murkash puts his hand on my shoulder, then takes my hand, and several of his… no, *our* male relatives join us, linking hands, including Tom and Joe.

"This!" Murkash says, holding a red handkerchief aloft, signaling to Kreshnik, our DJ, and the music kicks in. A traditional ballad with a thumping techno beat, and a slightly off-key melee of strings accompanied by archaic voices, thunders through the room. It's not something I've heard before. But more men get up and join us. It's a real crowd-pleaser.

Murkash slowly shows me the steps, and I follow him step for step—it's not as challenging as it looks. Soon we are circling the room, and a couple of the younger boys have joined us too.

Joe is grinning at me. Tom is concentrating on his steps.

We circle the dance floor once, twice—the men cheering and smiling, enjoying their collective camaraderie and the energetic dance.

By the time the music ends, I'm a little winded.

My bride joins me, looking as radiant as she did when I saw her standing, silhouetted against the window in her front room.

"We dance now." She takes her handkerchief, holds her arms up as the music starts, and begins to sway, her alluring dark eyes on mine. I'm not sure what I am supposed to do. Our wedding party leaves their tables, forming a circle around us, so seizing the initiative, I take her hands, and we dance together, but then I pull away and just watch her because she's entrancing.

My wife slowly twirls her wrists, handkerchief in hand, and turns in time to an ancient-sounding tune with a percussive beat. She's utterly captivating to me and the audience. She beckons me forward again, and I surrender willingly and take another few turns with her before the music ends.

Mr. Demachi takes to the floor with his handkerchief, and the older men of his community join him. The DJ plays a different, traditional track, and Jak leads his fellow men around the venue.

I stand and watch with Joe and Tom. It's… affecting, this expression of male kinship, one that we don't choose to encourage in the UK. Vaguely, I wonder why that's the case. Demachi signals for us to join the throng, and we comply, as do some of the women.

After a couple of hours of exhausting carousing and more dancing, we finally cut the impressive, highly decorated wedding cake and eat it with a glass of champagne. Our guests will continue into the night, but I'm done. I want out. I want to be alone with my bride.

"Our cab should be here shortly," I murmur to Alessia.

"I will go and change."

"Don't take too long." I give her a wolfish grin, and she has the grace to blush. She hurries out of the venue, followed by her mother, and I find Joe and Tom standing by the makeshift bar.

"Trevethick, as weddings go, this has been a good one. Different," Tom says.

"Yeah. It's cool, bro." Joe claps me on the back. "You look happy. Don't let your mother kill your buzz."

"I won't. Thanks for coming. May do this all again in the summer. I'll keep you posted."

"Marrying the same woman twice in the same year? That must be some kind of record," Joe observes dryly.

I nod my agreement and turn my attention to my family. Rowena is in a deep conversation with Heath. He's looking intensely at her, his expression grave as she speaks. He nods as if in agreement and glances at me, a calculating look on his face. He flushes, embarrassed to be caught looking my way, and promptly turns his attention back to my mother. He laughs at something she says and strokes her cheek.

There are certain things a man shouldn't see. His mother canoodling with a man half her age is one of them.

In disgust, I focus on Maryanne, who is talking to one of Alessia's cousins. I think it's Agnesa, who did Alessia's hair and makeup. They're having an animated conversation. Caroline is staring at… me! She gets up.

Shit. I don't want or need any more drama from her.

She sidles up to me, and I know she's had too much to drink.

"Caro, s'up?" I ask, my heart sinking.

"Stop being an arse," she snaps.

"What?"

"You know what!"

I stare at her, trying to convey how monumentally she fucked up disclosing our personal shenanigans to Alessia. Alessia didn't need to hear that from her.

She should have heard it from me.

But I'm tired of being pissed at Caro.

"I'm leaving shortly. What is it?" I ask.

"You're leaving?"

"Yes. Honeymoon. It's traditional."

"Where are you going?"

I make a face. *Like I'm going to tell you.*

She huffs but doesn't press me. "I just wanted to say sorry. Again. Are you going to ignore me forever?"

I sigh. "I'll see. You fucked up, Caro. You need to stop that."

"I know," she says quietly, and she nudges me with her shoulder in a most un-Caroline show of affection that it makes me chuckle. I put my arm around her and kiss her hair.

"Thanks for coming to my wedding."

"Thank you for inviting me." She makes a face... because I didn't. "Am I forgiven?" she asks.

"Just."

"Maxim, might I have a word?" It's my mother.

Hell.

She looks pointedly at Caro, who nods and moves off to give us some privacy.

"Rowena."

"I'll be brief. I wish you every happiness." My mother's smile doesn't reach her eyes. "On the plus side, this young girl will inject new DNA into our gene pool, but she has no idea what she's signed up for. You could at least enroll her in some etiquette lessons, so she doesn't make a complete fool of herself or you when you're in company. Or perhaps send her to finishing school. She might have a hope then."

"Thank you for your concern, Mother. I'm quite sure Alessia will hold her own."

"I'd be happy to pay. My wedding present to the two of you."

I manage, by some miracle, to hold on to my temper.

"It's a tempting offer, thank you, Mother. But we're good."

"The offer stands and I'll see you in London when you're back from your honeymoon. I'll have more to say on this whole... debacle then."

"I can't wait." I smile—a smile so fake I think I'm going to crack wide open.

She raises her cheek to me, which I brush with the briefest of kisses, and she turns to Heath. "Let's go, darling."

Shpresa helps Alessia out of her dress and her veil. "Darling girl, you looked so beautiful today."

"Thank you, Mama. And thank you for all your hard work." She hugs her tightly, trying to convey her gratitude for everything over the last few days.

"You will come and visit, yes?" her mother asks, a desperate tang to her voice.

"Of course, Mama," Alessia says, trying to fight back her tears. "And you know, my offer, our offer, if you want to come with us... and..."

Her mother holds up her hand. "My heart, Jak and I will be delighted to visit you in England once you're settled." She's adamant.

Alessia sighs and hugs her mother again. "The invitation is still there. Whenever."

"Thank you," Shpresa responds. "Now, let me help you into this new dress."

Alessia reappears in our makeshift wedding venue looking radiant. She's changed into a simple emerald dress that clings... everywhere.

Fuck.

My body tightens.

Everywhere.

She's simply stunning. Her hair is in its elegant updo, although some tendrils now frame her beautiful face. She's clutching her bouquet when I reach her side and take her free hand. As I do, all the anger I'd been feeling at my remaining parent fades away. "You look lovely," I whisper. "I can't wait to get you out of this dress." It's then that I notice a slit up one side, and I catch a glimpse of her stockinged thigh and high-heeled shoes.

Oh, man.

"Let's go. Now."

After a half hour of tearful goodbyes, Alessia and Maxim are ready to leave. He drapes her coat over her shoulders as they make their way out of the tent.

There's a chill outside—the ground sparkles with an early

frost—as the waxing moon casts a glimmering path across the lake.

Alessia turns and throws her bouquet at the waiting crowd. It's caught by Agnesa, who jumps up and down in excitement, waving her prize above her head.

The guns begin; Alessia's cousins and uncles fire their pistols in the air, and at the same time, the women shower them with rice.

"Fuck!" shouts Maxim, ducking and clutching Alessia. He looks wildly around at her crazy compatriots.

"It's tradition," Alessia shouts above the noise.

"Hell! Tom!" Maxim says, but Tom is standing calmly next to Joe, watching her relatives with their weapons and shaking his head.

We hurry up the drive, away from the volley of shots.

How the fuck is gunfire at a wedding a good idea?

The Mercedes C class is waiting, and our driver, one of Alessia's cousins, opens the passenger door. Alessia turns and gives the throng one last wave before climbing in. I dash around to the other side and clamber in beside her.

"You don't like the guns," he says.

"No! I don't!"

"Welcome to Albania!" He laughs, then puts his foot down and speeds away from the revelry, the gunfire, and the best wedding a man could have hoped for, given the circumstances and the fact that it was organized within a week.

I take Alessia's hand. "Thank you for becoming my wife, Alessia Demachi-Trevelyan."

Alessia's eyes shine with unshed tears, and her heart, chest… her soul is suddenly too full. "Maxim," she whispers but her voice cracks as she's overcome with emotion. She turns and stares blankly out of the window over the dark waters of the Drin as they cross the bridge that will take them away from Kukës to a new life. A life with the man she loves with her very being. After all that he has given her, and all he's done for her, she only hopes she's enough for him.

"Hey," he whispers.

And she turns to see his eyes shining in the darkness.

"I've got you. You've got me. We've got this. It's going to be great," he says.

And Alessia's tears of joy slide down her cheeks, letting some of her emotion out into the world.

Chapter Eight

A manager shows us into the presidential suite at The Plaza in Tirana, which I've booked for two nights. Alessia eyes the massive vase of white roses that greets us in the small foyer. "Uau!" she whispers. I squeeze her hand, and the porter deposits our bags in what I assume is our bedroom. He returns to the foyer, I hand him some lek as a tip, and he scurries out.

"Can I offer you assistance with the facilities?" the manager asks in accented English.

"I'm sure we'll figure it out." With a practiced smile, I give him several notes, hoping he'll leave. With a nod of gratitude, he exits, leaving Alessia and me alone for the first time in forever.

"Here. Come. Let me show you." I stayed here with Tom when we first arrived in Albania—what feels like a lifetime ago—and I know what I want to show Alessia first. Taking her hand once more, I guide her into the drawing room, which has two seating areas, a dining area, and floor-to-ceiling windows. On one of the coffee tables, I spy a bottle of champagne in an elaborate ice bucket, with chocolate-dipped strawberries artfully arranged on a dish. But that's not what I want to her to see. Over at the window, I draw back the nets, revealing the city illuminated in all its glory at our feet.

"Uau!" she says again.

"Your capital city. It's quite stunning from the twenty-second floor."

A lessia drinks in the view. It's a patchwork of light and shade and darkness—tall buildings and small—and lit-up streets like threads woven through the patchwork flowing toward the distant mountains. She recalls telling Maxim she'd never visited Tirana—and here he is, making her dreams come true.

In so many ways.

"The dark over there." Maxim points with his chin as he stands beside her. "That's Skanderbeg Square. The National History Museum is beside it. We'll go tomorrow if you want." He turns, flashes her a quick smile, and fetches the champagne from the cooler. "Would you like a glass?"

"Yes. Please."

Alessia notes that it has a copper top—it's the Laurent-Perrier rosé, the first champagne she ever drank, not so long ago, in the bathroom at the Hideout. Maxim's smile widens as if reading her thoughts, and his fingers make deft work of removing the cage and cork with a satisfying pop. He fills their flutes with pink, bubbling champagne and hands her a glass.

"To us. Gëzuar, my love." In the soft light, his green eyes glitter with a warmth that stirs her blood.

"To us. Gëzuar, Maxim," she responds, and they clink glasses. She takes a sip, enjoying the taste of a joyous summer and mellow fruits as it slips down her throat. She feels a little shy now that they're finally alone together.

Shy of my husband?

Husband.

She lets the word ring in her head, enjoying the sound of it there.

Maxim turns to the view once more. "'Had I the heavens' embroidered cloths,'" he whispers, almost to himself.

"'Enwrought with golden and silver light,'" Alessia answers.

Maxim turns his head to her in surprise. "'The blue and the dim and the dark cloths.'"

"'Of night and light and the half-light.'"

"'I would spread the cloths under your feet.'" His eyes sear hers, his expression intense.

"'But I... being poor... have only my dreams,'" Alessia whispers, and her throat burns with unshed tears and the truth of the words.

Maxim smiles and traces her cheek with the back of his forefinger. "'I have spread my dreams under your feet. Tread softly,'" he murmurs.

"'Because you tread on my dreams.'" Alessia blinks back a tear, and Maxim leans down and plants a gentle kiss on her lips.

"You never cease to amaze me," he says.

Alessia swallows, searching for her equilibrium. At every turn, she's reminded of what he's done for her—and the difference between them, but she shakes off the idea. It's too complex and too overwhelming to contemplate now. "My English grandmother. She loved her poets. Yeats and Wordsworth. We have books of their poetry. Scandalous in Albania a few decades ago."

Nana.

What would she have made of her granddaughter, married to an English lord, sipping champagne in the presidential suite of a fine hotel in Tirana?

"I wish I'd met her," Maxim says.

She smiles. "You would have liked her. She would have loved you."

"And I her. I know you've been through a great deal over the last couple of weeks. We have two items of business at the embassy tomorrow when we collect your visa. But that's it. We're on our honeymoon now. It's just us. Relax. Enjoy." He slips his arm around her waist, pulls her to his side, and nuzzles her hair.

She rests her head against his shoulder as together they stand in an easy silence and stare out at Tirana and sip their champagne.

"More?" Maxim asks, looking at her glass.

"Please."

He refills their flutes and replaces the bottle in the ice bucket. She watches as he slips off his jacket and drapes it over one of the sofas. At the console table, he connects his phone to a speaker and selects some music. A moment later, the strains of a guitar echo through the room and a man with an American accent starts to sing.

"Who is this?" Alessia asks as Maxim comes to stand beside her once more.

"It's an oldie, but goodie," he murmurs and wraps his arms around her, her back pressed to his front. He rests his chin on her head and starts to sway. "JJ Cale. 'Magnolia.' Hmm… You smell good." He kisses the top of her head.

Alessia relaxes against him, swaying with him, placing a hand on top of his and sipping her champagne.

The song is soft and sensual—more so as Maxim sings a line quietly in her ear.

"Makes me think of my babe…"

She grins.

He can sing! Sweetly too.

"Let's go to bed." His voice is husky and full of promise as he gently tugs her earlobe with his teeth.

Alessia's breath catches, and that sweet, delicious pull tightens deep in her belly. Then she remembers. "Um…"

Maxim takes her glass and sets it on the table.

"Hmm?" he asks and tips her chin up, his eyes burning. He kisses the corner of her mouth. "What did you say?"

"I–I…"

He kisses her again at the pulse point beneath her ear as she presses her hands against his shirt. Her fingers move of their own accord to the buttons.

Just a bit longer.

And she starts to undo them.

He cups her face between his hands and angles her head, bringing his lips to hers.

"Wife," he whispers and gently teases her lips with his, the tip of his tongue seeking hers.

She sighs, and his tongue finds and caresses hers while his hands glide down her body, one pressing her to him while the other skims her backside. Alessia abandons his buttons and tugs at his shirt, freeing it from his pants. Her hands coast up his firm biceps and shoulders, and her fingers fist in his tousled, soft hair as they devour each other.

He groans and pulls back, winded. "I've missed you," he whispers. "So much."

"I've been here…" Her voice is a breathless whisper.

"Not like this." He moves suddenly, scooping her up into his arms.

She smiles, her heart brimming with love, and folds her arms around his neck as he carries her through the suite into the bedroom, leaving behind the velvet timbre of JJ Cale.

The bedroom is decorated in muted creams, minimalist and modern, but Alessia hardly notices as Maxim slides her down his body and sets her on her feet. His fingers move to her hair, and he carefully removes the pins—freeing her hair lock by lock. She closes her eyes, relishing his tender care—and also surprised by it.

But her thoughts nag her.

Tell him.

No. She can't yet. She's enjoying this too much.

"There, that's the last of them, I think," he murmurs, his eyes darkening with desire as he catches a strand and winds it around his fingers. "So soft." He tugs gently, bringing her closer, and kisses the lock before releasing it. "Now, this sensational dress." With a hand at her nape, the other on the zipper, he kisses her once more as he drags the zipper down.

Alessia gasps and crosses her hands over her chest so her dress doesn't fall to her feet.

Tell him.

"Maxim, I… I'm…"

He stops, his brow furrowing. "What's wrong?"

She flushes and clutches her dress to her breasts while staring down at the brilliant diamond nestled next to her wedding ring on her finger. "I'm bleeding."

"Ah," he says and tenderly tilts her chin up, and she's expecting him to be disappointed, or worse, disgusted, but all she sees is his relief, and concern. "Do you feel okay?"

"Yes. I am fine."

"We can wait, if you want…" He kisses the corner of her mouth, then murmurs against her lips, "But just so you know, that doesn't bother me."

"What?"

"I still want you." He trails feather-light kisses along her jaw.

"Oh," Alessia breathes, and she's momentarily stunned.

Can they? Even if…?

Maxim smiles and caresses her cheek with his fingertips. "I've shocked you. Beautiful Alessia. I'm sorr—"

Before he can finish, Alessia lifts her hands, releasing her dress so it slides down to her waist, hitching at her hips, and she encloses his face between her palms and guides his lips to hers.

I catch a tantalizing glimpse of a pretty, lacy bra. But Alessia's lips are on mine, her tongue insistent, and she's pressing her body against me. Closing my eyes, I surrender to her ardour, my fingers in her hair as I hold her to me. Any hesitancy she had about continuing seems a distant memory.

When she pulls away, we're once more breathless, and my dick is straining against my fly.

Fuck.

"What do we do?" Her voice is husky.

It takes me a nanosecond to realize what she's talking about as I step back to behold the vision that is my wife in pretty underwear. "Take your dress off."

She inhales sharply and considers me, her eyes straying from mine to my mouth and then down my body to the hardening bulge at my crotch. With a coy but victorious smile, she shimmies out of her dress so that it skates past her hips and down her thighs to reveal a tiny white lace thong and stockings.

My mouth is suddenly arid, and I'm sure it hangs open in awe as my trousers get tighter by the second.

"Now you," she whispers while draping her dress over the chaise longue.

Quickly, I step out of my shoes and peel off my socks, then undo the remaining buttons of my shirt that Alessia abandoned. I make short work of my cuff links, slide my shirt off, and discard it with the rest of our clothes on the chaise.

"Pants," she prompts, her dark eyes shining and dropping below my waist.

My wife is demanding.

I like it.

With a deliberate leisurely pace, I undo my belt, and she laughs and steps forward to help.

Yes!

She undoes the button, unzips my fly, and drags my trousers down, kneeling at my feet.

Fuck.

A vision of my cock in her mouth while she's on her knees comes unbidden to my mind as we lock eyes. With huge, dark eyes, she reaches up to drag down my underwear... and I watch. Spellbound. And hard. Almost unbearably hard as she tugs down my pants and frees my enthusiastic dick.

Her eyes stray from mine to my cock.

"Alessia," I whisper... and I know it sounds like a plea.

Alessia kneels up, grasps Maxim's erection, and tightens her fingers around him. He's velvet-smooth and rigid in her hand as he gasps and closes his eyes. Alessia knows this is what he wants… It's what she wants too. She's been too shy to do this until now, but she wants to please him, in every way. His lips part, but he seems to have stopped breathing, his body taut with anticipation as he stands over her. She slowly moves her hand up and down like he's shown her before, and gently he places his hand on her head. When he opens his eyes, they're green fire.

His reaction ignites her desire, tightening muscles in the pit of her belly. She loves turning him on. He's used his tongue and his lips on intimate parts of her body often enough, and she's wanted to do this for so long to him. *For him.* She leans in, her eyes still on his, and runs her tongue over her top lip, watching him closely. He's enthralled, his eyes searing hers. He's captivated and entirely at her mercy.

The power she feels. It's heady.

She leans forward and kisses the tip, and her tongue follows, sweeping over him. He tastes salty. Male. Of Maxim.

Mmm…

Maxim groans. And she sheaths him with her mouth, pushing him deeper and deeper.

"Fuck!" he exclaims.

I give myself one nanosecond to enjoy her lips around me—it's fucking heaven, and I want more than anything to push farther into her mouth, but she takes control and does it anyway.

Oh, God.

Instinctively, I flex my arse, gently driving deeper into her mouth, and she clamps down a little harder on me.

Hell. Yes.

She pulls back and then forward again as if she's done this before. And my resolve not to let this continue is a distant memory as I let her take me. Over and over. In her hot, wet, tight, sweet mouth!

My legs begin to tremble as I strain to contain my climax.

Hell.

She's going to unman me.

Now.

O n the bed." He leans down. "As much as I want to do this, I will come very quickly in your mouth if—"

Alessia swats his hands away, silencing him.

She wants him.

All of him.

In her mouth.

"Alessia!" He cradles her head. "I'm going to come!"

She looks up at him from beneath her lashes as he tips his head back and lets go, his warm, salty seed spilling down her throat. She swallows, a little shocked but triumphant that she's done this. She eases back, releasing him, and wipes the back of her hand across her mouth.

As Maxim gasps for breath, he turns blazing eyes on her, reaches down, helps her to her feet, and folds her in his embrace. He kisses her hard and fast, his tongue exploring her mouth, taking all she has to give and surely tasting his seed.

"I love you so much," he breathes.

"I love you," she answers, feeling on top of the world.

She did it!

It!

Finally!

He grins. "How was that?" he asks, and she hears his hesitancy.

"Good." She bites her bottom lip. "For you too?"

"Oh, baby. That was mind-blowing. We can do that anytime. Now you'd better go to the bathroom and… do what you need to do. Bring a towel back with you."

She smiles.

I watch her sashay into the en suite. My cock—game once more—twitches in appreciation as her arse looks like fucking poetry in a thong.

Maybe Yeats or Wordsworth.

My wife is full of surprises.

Who knew she'd be able to quote Yeats?

Who knew she'd be up for giving head on her knees?

Sweet Alessia.

Grinning and giddy with delight, I draw back the duvet and, on a whim, return to the drawing room, gather up our glasses, and place them on the tray with the ice bucket, champagne, and strawberries. On my return to the bedroom, I place the tray on our bedside table as Alessia opens the en suite door and leans against the frame. She's naked except for a towel.

"More champagne?" I offer. She shakes her head, and I watch her gaze travel the length of my body.

My dick responds in greeting, ready and willing for more.

Wow! Quick recovery or what!

"All I want is you," she whispers.

"I'm all yours." I open my arms, and she strolls toward me, opening the towel as she does. I slip my arms around her, and she wraps us both in the soft material.

"Big towel," I murmur.

She giggles. "Big…"

"Room? Head? Dick? What?"

"Dick," she whispers.

And I laugh. "I love it when you talk dirty."

She giggles once more, and my restless cock can wait no longer. Taking her head in my hands, I press my lips to hers, and she opens her mouth, seeking my tongue. I willingly oblige, and as I walk her back toward the bed, we kiss, all tongues and lips and breath, until I'm ready to explode again. I come up for air, and Alessia is breathless too.

"Bed," I whisper, and together we fall onto the mattress.

Alessia tumbles onto the bed, the towel beneath her, and Maxim looms on top of her, but his hands support his weight.

"Now I've got you where I want you," he whispers and nuzzles between her breasts. "Are you sore?"

"No."

"You're sure?"

"Yes!" she says. Emphatic.

I lean up on my arms and look at her. The last time we did this, she had grazes and bruises and God knows what covering her body. But now, she lies beneath me, her hair fanned in a dark mane across the pillow, her eyes shining with love and lust, and there's not a mark on her. She reaches for me, running her fingers through my hair and tugging, bringing me back to half-lie on the softness of her body—my dick cradled between us, against her belly.

But it, like me, is yearning to be inside her.

I kiss the underside of her breast and leave a trail of kisses up to its peak. She tugs on my hair, and I close my lips around her nipple and suck. Hard—feeling it firm and elongate beneath my lips and tongue. I tug gently, and Alessia groans and writhes beneath me, her hips rising and pressing against me. I repeat the action again and again and move to its twin.

"Please," Alessia pleads.

I reach over to the bedside for a condom.

"No," she says. "I started the contraceptive pill."

What?

"It's okay." Her eyes sear mine.

And I can't wait any longer. I kiss her again, grab my dick, and guide it to where it wants to be… "Ah!" I breathe as I ease myself inside her.

Skin against skin.

A delectable first.

She's tight and slick and wet with want, and she curls her

arms around me, her hands moving to my arse, her legs winding around me calves as I start to move and lose myself in the pleasure of her.

In the passion of her.

In the love of her.

My wife.

On and on.

Her fingernails etch her desire on my skin as she gasps and moans close to my ear. She's building, and climbing, as am I, and suddenly she's stiffening beneath me as she cries out, her orgasm pushing me over the edge.

I cry out as I come, and the world around us fades, and it's only me and my wife.

My love.

I lean over her, propped on an elbow, smoothing her hair off her face, as she stares intently at me. We're still intimately connected, and I don't want to move.

"How was that, Lady Trevethick?"

She smiles, lighting up the room and my heart. "That was wonderful, Lord Trevethick. And for you?"

I move then, so she's lying on top of me, and kiss her hair.

"That was muchly."

She giggles, and I kiss her hair again.

"In fact. I'd like to do it again very shortly. But perhaps you'd like some champagne and strawberries first?"

Alessia lies beside me, fast asleep. Her dragon nightlight is with us, a sweet sentinel watching over her, keeping her safe from the dark. I'm delighted that she's brought him with us. I snuggle closer, inhaling her soothing scent, and marvel at how much I enjoy just lying here beside her... just being. Is it because she doesn't make demands on me? Is it because she makes me feel needed? Loved? I don't know. Whatever it is, I've never felt as content as I do now. Content, yet excited. Tomorrow we get to explore her capital city and just be. Together.

Closing my eyes, I kiss her hair.

Until tomorrow, and the rest of our lives, my love.

Chapter Nine

The sun glints off the sparkling Caribbean in Endeavor Bay as my wife paddleboards over the turquoise sea. Her tongue is sticking out as she concentrates on staying atop the board. It's alluring, and I've seen a great deal of that tongue recently—teaching her to paddleboard, play poker, play pool, use chopsticks, give head…

Fuck.

The thought of my wife with her lips wrapped around my rigid dick fellating me has an immediate and significant effect on my body. I shift on the board trying to bring myself under control but lose my balance and fall into the Caribbean with a loud, undignified splash.

When I surface, Alessia is laughing. At me. At *me*.

She's wearing a skimpy, bright green bikini we bought at Pink House, the local store, and her body is beautifully bronzed all over. She looks gorgeous, but she's laughing at me.

Right! This is war.

I grab the paddle, vault back onto the board, and, grinning like a maniac, pursue her.

She screeches and turns her board to the shore and begins to paddle frantically.

The chase is on.

But she's no match for me, and I catch her just before the shallows, leap off my board, and grab her, throwing us both into the sea.

She screams, but the water silences her, and she surfaces coughing, spluttering, and laughing. I reach for her as I'm within my depth and pull her into my arms and kiss her.

Properly.

She tastes of happiness and sunshine and crystal-clear seawater. She tastes of my beloved wife. "That's better," I murmur against her lips.

"Je trap fare!" She pushes at my shoulders but I refuse to let go.

"I take it that wasn't a compliment." I nuzzle her nose, and she giggles.

"I said you are an arsehole."

"Talking dirty again?"

"I am learning from you."

"Hmm… am I a good teacher?" I capture her bottom lip between my teeth and tug gently.

Her dark eyes shine, and her cheeks flush beneath her tan. "You tell me," she whispers.

I grin. "No complaints here."

"My grandmother said the best foreign dictionary is a lover."

Of course, her English grandmother married an Albanian.

"Lover, eh? Does husband count?"

She wraps her limbs around me, cups my face, and kisses me—all tongue and lips and love—weaving her hands into my wet hair. I hold her fast against me. And we're skin on skin, and my body responds, hungry for her again.

Will I ever have my fill of my wife?

I am utterly in her thrall as I surrender myself to her kiss, her tongue… her love.

When we come up for air, I'm aroused and ready for her. "Shall we fuck in the sea?" I whisper breathlessly, half in jest. "There's no one here."

"Maxim!" Alessia is scandalized, but she scans the shoreline where there are a couple of villas, but there's no one in sight on the beach or in the sea. She gives me a coy smile, kisses me again, and grinds against me. Then reaching into my trunks, she grabs my more-than-ready dick.

Fuck… we're doing this!

Our paddleboards hover beside us as they're still attached by their lines to our ankles, providing us with a modicum of cover. Gently, I sweep aside her bikini and ease myself inside her. She pushes down on me, her teeth toying with my lower lip.

Ah!

The surf is gentle, keeping us buoyant as I slowly start to move, holding her to me. She starts tipping her hips toward me, rocking against me at an agile beat. And soon, we're lost in our rhythm. Together. Breath mingling, eyes closed, eyes open, and mouths slack and hungry as we consume each other.

Fuck, she's hot.

She tips her head back and groans as she comes, taking me with her, and I ride out my climax in the clear, blue waters of the Caribbean Sea.

~

It's our last night here, and the candles flicker in the gentle breeze as we sit in the airy gazebo enjoying another of Chef's incredible meals. Alessia sips her rosé and stares out at the sliver of pale sky that straddles the horizon. The sun has long set, but there's a whisper of the day left at the edge of the Earth. She's wearing a green silk dress, again courtesy of Pink House; her hair is tied back, but tendrils have escaped and frame her beautiful face. At her ears are the pearl earrings I bought her in Paris. She looks every bit a countess.

My countess.

I reach across the table and take her hand.

"How is it?"

She turns dark eyes that shimmer in the candlelight toward me.

"Beautiful," she says, but there's an edge to her voice.

"What's wrong?"

"Do we have to go back?"

I laugh. "Sadly, yes. I don't think my uncle's hospitality will extend beyond this week."

My uncle Cameron, my father's brother, was the bête noire of his generation. After a monumental fall-out with my mother and father that happened before Kit was born, he fled to LA and established himself as an artist. During the late '80s, he took the American art world by storm, and these days he's mentioned in the same breath as David Salle and Jean-Michel Basquiat. He now resides in the Hollywood Hills and owns two properties on Mustique.

We are in one of them. An elegant two-bed, Oliver Messel–designed, beachfront villa named Turquoise Waters—it's stunning, and he was delighted when Alessia and I chose to spend our honeymoon here.

Congratulations, Maxim, my dear, dear boy. I'm delighted for you. Of course, you can use the villa. My wedding gift to you.

I haven't been here since my mid-teens when my mother reluctantly let Maryanne and me stay with Uncle Cameron after our father died. There is bad blood between them, so much so that Cameron only made a brief appearance at my father's funeral, and an equally fleeting appearance at Kit's. He didn't stay with us, and he and I only exchanged a few words afterward. I can't decide if he doesn't like us, or if Rowena doesn't like him because he's so much like her—he shares her passion for young male lovers—or because he doesn't tolerate her bullshit.

Either way—they don't talk. Ever.

It had been a pain in the arse to get to Mustique. I couldn't fly Alessia through Miami because she needed an American visa, and we didn't have time to apply for one. I didn't want to fly via London, so we'd come via Paris to Martinique, ferry to Castries, and then we flew to Mustique from there.

And Alessia had never been on a plane before.

Going home will be more straightforward.

"I love that your uncle has a place with a baby grand piano. This place is magical," Alessia whispers.

I kiss her hand. "It is, with you here."

Bastian, our butler, appears. "May I clear for you, my lord?" he asks.

"Thank you."

"A digestif?" he offers.

"Alessia?" I ask.

"I'm happy with the wine; thank you, Bastian."

"My lord?"

"Cognac, please."

He nods and clears away our dessert plates.

"Tell me. Something's troubling you," I ask once more.

"I'm not sure what will be expected of me. When we are home."

I squeeze her hand and sigh. "To be honest, I don't know." I have no idea what Caroline, or my mother for that matter, used to do. I wish I'd taken more notice. "But don't worry, we'll figure it out."

She withdraws her hand and places it in her lap. "I am… um…nervous that I will eat a meal with the wrong knife or I will say the wrong thing to one of your friends, and I will embarrass you."

Shit.

"And there will be staff like here," she says.

"You'll get used to it."

"You are used to this because you have had staff all your life."

"True."

"I have not."

"Hey, stop. You'll be fine. You have been fine here, with

Bastian, with Chef and the housekeeper. Just keep doing what you're doing."

Alessia frowns. "I am out of the depths."

I smile. "Out of your depth. And I don't think you are. You're going to be amazing. I saw how you and your parents pulled together a full-scale wedding in less than a week. All the skills you need are there."

He reaches over and tugs Alessia's hand, and she moves willingly into his lap, where he folds his arms around her and nuzzles her hair. "Besides," he whispers. "Who gives a fuck what other people think?"

Alessia chuckles. "You say that word a lot."

"I do, and your English is improving. I've really noticed on this holiday."

"That's because I spend my time with someone who speaks it so well, apart from the cursing, of course."

Maxim laughs. "I know you love it when I talk dirty."

He's wearing a loose white cotton shirt and linen trousers. His hair is sun-kissed, and his green eyes sparkle in the wavering candlelight.

He's delicious.

"Your cognac, my lord," Bastian says, interrupting them.

"Thank you."

"I've taken the liberty of moving two of the lawn chairs down to the beach and lighting the firepit."

"Thanks, Bastian. We'll enjoy one more paddle in the moonlight."

Alessia climbs off Maxim, and he takes her hand—and his cognac—and leads her down the garden steps onto the beach where Bastian has set up a little bower for them. Torches blaze at the four corners and the firepit flames flicker in the evening breeze.

The lawn chairs, as well as cushions, have blankets draped

over them. Alessia takes a seat in one, and Maxim settles in the other beside her. Taking her hand again, he brings it to his lips. "Thank you for a wonderful honeymoon."

She laughs. "No, Maxim. Thank you. For everything."

He kisses her palm, then her rings—then leans back, and they each gaze out across the dark water that glimmers in the light of the waning moon. They're serenaded by the song of the tree frogs, the crackle, hiss, and spit of the fire in the iron pit, and the gentle wash of the Caribbean lapping at the shore. Alessia takes a deep breath, inhaling the scent of the tropics—the lush earthiness of the rain forest and the salty tang of the sea—and she tries to commit the scene to memory. Above them, there's a spectacular starscape.

"Uau, so many stars," Alessia murmurs.

"Hmm…" Maxim replies, staring up at the sky.

"They look different here."

"Hmm…" The sound of his contentment rumbles in his throat once more.

She gazes at the night sky, feeling that providence has provided the impressive light show above them solely to make amends for all that had befallen Maxim and her before their wedding.

Alessia's heart is full to overflowing.

This is her life now.

She has to pinch herself.

He's shown her the sights of Tirana, whisked her to Paris and then to this magical place.

What has she done to deserve all this good fortune?

She'd fallen in love with him. Her Mister… No, her lord.

"Dance with me?" Maxim says, interrupting her reverie, and he lays his phone on the arm of his chair and hands her an AirPod. He slips one in his ear, and she does the same. He presses Play, and the familiar strains of RY X fills her ear.

Maxim gazes down at her and opens his arms. She walks into his embrace, and together they sway slowly in the sand.

"Our first dance," Maxim whispers.

And Alessia is thrilled that he remembers.

"The first of many," she answers, and he moves his hands to caress her face and turns her lips to his.

They flow together. Taking and giving. Two as one. Alessia clutches the sheets, her body slick with sweat… her sweat… his sweat, and Maxim cries out and stills as he climaxes, triggering her orgasm, so she cries out too and rises and falls through her bliss. She folds her arms around his neck as he collapses on her, then moves them to the side.

"Fuck. Alessia," he whispers and kisses her forehead as she comes back to sanity.

She opens her eyes and strokes his face as they stare at each other. Her finger tracing the outline of his lips. Lips that have been on her.

Everywhere.

"Is it always like this?" Alessia asks.

"No," Maxim says and kisses her forehead again. He eases out of her, and she winces. "Are you sore?" His voice rings with concern.

"No. I'm good." She grins. "More than good."

"I'm more than good too."

Their bedroom is all whitewashed wood, with distressed furniture and discreet art. A four-poster bed, sheathed in nets, dominates the room. Alessia loves the romance of the nets—when in bed, they're cocooned in their own small haven.

As her heart rate slows, a thought that has been nagging her since the wedding strays unfettered into her mind.

"What?" Maxim asks. He's naked and beautiful, his eyes bright in his tanned face, as he hugs his pillow facing her.

She stares at his tattoo of his coat of arms and, reaching over, traces the outline with her finger while she wonders how she should ask this question.

"What?" he presses her and smooths a stray strand of damp hair behind her ear.

"Um… it is something your sister said to me at the wedding."

*O**h shit. What could that be?*
I tense, wondering what Maryanne has blurted to my dear, dear Alessia.

"She said, 'Reformed rakes make the best husbands.'" Alessia's dark eyes glimmer, full of questions in the soft light.

I blow out a breath, trying to think what to say.

"I have read Georgette Heyer. I know what a rake is…" she adds.

"And?"

"Is your sister saying that you are a rake?"

"Alessia, it's the twenty-first century, not the eighteenth."

She stares at me for several seconds, her teeth toying with her upper lip as she assesses me.

Hell. Is she judging me?

Found me wanting?

I have no idea. I hold my breath.

"How many women?" she asks eventually.

Ah. My stomach sinks. This is where her thoughts are going. "Why do you want to know?"

"I am curious."

I reach out and caress her face. "In all honesty, I don't know. I didn't keep count."

"Many?"

"Many."

"Tens. Hundreds. Thousands?"

I make a face. *Thousands! Sheesh.* I don't think so.

"Tens… or so. I don't know." And it's a small white lie.

Hundreds more like, dude.

She stares back at me, and I hope to God she's not seeing through my untruth or seeing me in a sordid new light. It was just sex. "Hey." I shift closer to her. "No one since I met you."

"Not the widow?" she whispers.

And in those three words, I hear her anguish and distrust. I close my eyes as an ember of anger flares in my gut at my loose-lipped sister-in-law.

Bloody Caro!

"No. No one since I saw you clutching the broom in my hallway."

When I open my eyes, she's studying me once more, and I have no idea what she's thinking. But Alessia nods, seemingly satisfied, and I blow out a breath.

Thank fuck for that.

"Here." I draw her to me. "There was before Alessia, and then there's the rest of my life with you. That's all that matters." And I kiss her once more.

As dawn breaks over their little part of heaven, Alessia is curled up in one of the armchairs watching Maxim sleep. He's sprawled facedown and naked on the bed. His legs tangled in the sheets, like the first time she ever saw him… not so long ago.

She was shocked then but fascinated—drawn to the chiseled lines of his athletic body. Now she can appreciate every line and sinew. How sculpted he looks and how young and relaxed he seems in sleep. The tan line between his back and his muscular, curved behind is far more defined, and she'd like to sink her teeth into that butt. Shocked at her wayward thoughts, she sips her unsweetened black coffee, enjoying its bitter, strong taste and the enticing view of her husband.

Should she wake him?

A wake-up call?

He'd like that. The muscles deep in her belly tighten in pleasure at the thought.

Alessia! She can hear her mother's voice.

He's my husband, Mama.

Today, they head back to England.

Her new home.

And she'll have to face his family, his friends, his work colleagues, and she only hopes they won't find her lacking.

And she'll have to find something to do.

What's expected of her, she doesn't even know.

She suspects this is why she can't sleep. It's the excitement and the anxiety.

Maxim stirs and reaches out to her side of the bed, then looks up and around when he finds the bed empty, his green eyes bright in the soft pink light of dawn.

Alessia puts down her cup, lifts the net, and scrambles into bed beside him.

"There you are," he murmurs, pulling her into his arms.

We touch down at Heathrow just after eight in the morning. Once we've disembarked the plane, we arrive at the top of the jetty, where an official from the VIP service greets us. She escorts us airside via a lift to ground level, and we exit the terminal beside the British Airways Boeing 777 that's brought us from St. Lucia. There, a sleek black 7 series BMW awaits us. Our greeter opens the boot and places our hand luggage inside. Then she opens the rear passenger door, and we both climb in and sink into the leather seats.

"This is unexpected," Alessia says, turning wide eyes in my direction.

I shrug. "I'm not dealing with the scrum that is passport control."

Our guide climbs into the car and drives us across the airport to the VIP building.

"You'll need your passport," I tell Alessia as we're ushered out of the car.

The Border Force official gives my passport a cursory glance and a more thorough inspection of Alessia's.

I hold my breath.

He looks up and scrutinizes her face, comparing it to her photograph, and then stamps her passport. "Welcome to the UK, miss," he says.

I blow out a breath.

She's here! Legally! Hurrah!

Alessia rewards him with a dazzling smile, and we follow our escort into one of the stylish and comfortable suites to await our luggage.

"Your butler will be with you shortly to take your breakfast order. We should have an update on your baggage in the next ten minutes. There's an en suite just behind you should you need it. Anything else, just press the call button." She points to a red button on the coffee table.

"Thanks."

With a bright, practiced smile, she leaves us, and I offer Alessia the menu. "Are you hungry?"

She shakes her head.

"Me neither. Did you sleep?"

Alessia nods, taking in our surroundings. "I have never been anywhere like this. Do you always do this at Heathrow?"

"Yes." I kiss her hair. "Get used to it."

She smiles. "I think it will take a while."

I shrug as there's a knock at the door and one of the butlers enters.

"Good morning, Lord Trevethick. May I bring you breakfast and a drink?"

They are back in the expensive black car, and a man in a smart suit is driving them into London. As they sit in traffic on the motorway, Alessia glances over the skyline and notices the towers at Brentford.

Magda! Michal!

She wonders how her friends are doing in Canada. She doesn't have a phone number for Magda, but maybe she can contact

Michal through Facebook. That part of her life seems so long ago, yet it was only weeks. And now here she is in a fancy car with her beloved husband, shooting into London after a holiday in beautiful Mustique.

What has she done to deserve such good fortune?

Maxim threads his fingers through hers. "Seems an age since we were here," he says, and he sounds a little wistful.

"Yes." She returns his squeeze but doesn't know what else to say. She's feeling overwhelmed and a little untethered, as if she's in a dream and she'll wake at any moment to some dreadful reality.

He raises her hand to his lips and plants a sweet kiss. "We'll be home soon. I'm going to need a nap."

"Did you sleep?" They'd traveled first class where their seats converted into comfortable beds.

"Not much. The flight was noisy, but mostly because I'm too excited to get you home."

Alessia smiles, and just like that, her misgivings disappear.

The black car pulls up outside Maxim's building on Chelsea Embankment, and the chauffeur opens Alessia's door. He removes the bags from the trunk and places them in the foyer. Maxim graciously tips him and, grabbing their bags, heads to the waiting elevator. Maxim ushers Alessia inside, and the doors close, leaving just the two of them and their luggage. Maxim presses the button for the top floor, and his emerald gaze moves to hers. Alessia's breath catches at his smoldering look.

He steps toward her and cups her face gently in his hands. "You're safe. We're home," he whispers and leans down to kiss her, a slow, sweet, and grateful kiss, but as his coaxing, teasing tongue finds hers, desire blossoms deep inside Alessia. Her body has become so attuned to his that she wants him. Now. Here. Maxim presses her to the wall, his excitement hard against her belly, and it feeds her lust. She moans, her body molding to his and kissing him back with a fervor that sears her soul.

The elevator stops, the door opens, and Maxim guides them out of the elevator while they are still locked in an embrace, still locked in each other.

Will she ever get enough of him?

"Maxim, how lovely to see you. Have you been away?"

The not-so-dulcet tones of Mrs. Beckstrom interrupt our make-out session, which I'm hoping will lead to some pre-nap hot sex. Briefly, I lean my forehead in frustration against Alessia's, then peek down at her, and she looks as dazed as I feel. Taking a deep breath, I hold Alessia against me to hide my evident excitement.

"Mrs. Beckstrom. And Heracles." I bend and give her annoying lapdog a quick pat. He bares his teeth in disgust. "How lovely to see you. How are you? May I introduce my wife? Alessia."

"Oh, how lovely." Mrs. Beckstrom holds out her hand to Alessia, who's breathless.

"How do you do?" Alessia says as they shake hands.

"You are so pretty, my dear. Wife, did you say, Maxim?"

"Yes, Mrs. B."

"You finally got married. Well, congratulations. That was rather sudden. Are you in the family way, my dear?"

For fuck's sake! I daren't look at Alessia's face as I haul our luggage out of the lift.

"No, Mrs. Beckstrom," Alessia says quickly, and her cheeks are rosy despite her tan.

"But I'll see what I can do about that!" I wink at Mrs. B, and Alessia's blush deepens.

"Well, you young people enjoy yourselves. Heracles and I are going for our morning stroll." And she steps into the lift and presses Ground.

Once the doors close, I turn to Alessia, she bursts out laughing, and I join her. I pull her into my arms. "I'm sorry about that."

"She is, what did you say…oh, yes, eccentric."

"Yes. She certainly is. Now, I have one duty to perform." I lift her into my arms, and she squeals in surprise. Holding her against me, I slide the key into the front door, open it, and step across the threshold with her in my arms.

I set her on the floor and kiss her, hoping to continue what we started in the lift, when I realize the alarm isn't on. We both look up, and there's a "Welcome Home" banner draped over the double doors at the end of the hallway.

Suddenly, Caroline, Tom, Joe, Maryanne, and Henrietta appear at the doors. "Surprise!" they yell.

Fuck a duck!

Chapter Ten

Alessia and I stand in the hall, bewildered and tired from our journey. Mrs. Blake, Caroline's housekeeper, appears at the kitchen door holding a tray of drinks, and I'm struck dumb.

What the ever-fucking-hell is this?

"Welcome home, Maxim, Alessia." With a smile plastered on her face, Caroline steps forward cautiously, holding out her arms in welcome.

Has she been drinking? Already?

This is very un-Caro-like behavior.

"Hi," I say, bemused, as she hugs me and then Alessia.

"Welcome back, Alessia," she says, a little too brightly.

"Hello," Alessia whispers, and I can tell from the waver in her voice that she's rattled too.

My friends surge forward to welcome us while Mrs. Blake serves everyone drinks. Buck's Fizz, champagne, or freshly squeezed orange juice.

"Well, this is a surprise. No, shock, actually. But thank you," I mutter to Caro.

"I thought a celebratory brunch would be in order to welcome you home, and it's a sort of apology." She shrugs impishly and grabs a glass of champagne. I suspect it's not her first.

Mrs. Blake offers the tray to Alessia with what I can only describe as a hostile smile. "My lady," she says, her tone terse. Alessia thanks her and takes a glass of champagne.

Frowning at Mrs. Blake—in the hope that I've misinterpreted her frosty expression—I take a glass of orange juice.

She flushes. "Nice to have you back, my lord."

"Thank you, Mrs. Blake. I hope you and Mr. Blake are well." I give her a pointed look, and she gives me a sweet smile, so maybe I'm imagining her less than warm reception of my wife—though she didn't offer us congratulations.

Maryanne hooks her arms around us both and propels us toward the drawing room, where the table is set for brunch.

Okay. We're doing this.

And all I really want to do is take my wife to bed.

And fuck and then sleep.

But Henrietta, Tom's girlfriend, is there and it's great to see her. She is a beacon of light compared to his pugnacious darkness.

"Maxim, I'm so thrilled for you. Congratulations." She hugs me.

"Henry, how lovely to see you. This is Alessia, my wife."

The grease and grime from the journey stick to Alessia's skin, and here she is, in Maxim's apartment, with… guests. His friends. What she'd like to do is have a quick shower and change. Beneath the black tailored jacket, she's wearing her "It's better at Basil's" T-shirt that Maxim bought for her at a bar on Mustique—and her jeans. She'd prefer to be a little more formal for his friends, but leaving them right now would be rude.

And these women, they all look impeccable.

Especially Caroline.

"Hello, Alessia. It's lovely to meet you," Henry says. Her voice is melodic, measured, and sweet, and she has the face of an angel framed by soft sepia-brown curls. Her tawny eyes are warm and brimming with sincerity.

"How do you do?" Alessia replies, feeling immediately at ease with her.

"There she is!" Tom says and engulfs Alessia in a huge hug. "I do hope he's treating you well, Alessia. I'll horsewhip him if he's not."

Alessia laughs. "It's good to see you, Tom."

"When was the last time you were near a horse?" Caroline scoffs. "Your polo-playing days are long over."

Henry frowns at Caroline, and there's a slight lull in the conversation, and Alessia notices Maxim and Joe are frowning too.

"Alessia," Joe says after a beat and hugs her. "You look so well. Did you have a great time? Where did you guys go? Maxim kept all the deets to himself." He flashes bright white teeth in a broad contagious smile. He looks so smart in his suit—and Alessia realizes he must always dress like this, even on a Saturday.

Maxim slips his arm around her and kisses her hair. "We had a wonderful time. In Tirana and Mustique, if you must know."

"We did," Alessia agrees shyly. "And Paris."

"That sounds heavenly," Caroline exclaims. "I hope you're all hungry. Dear Mrs. Blake has cooked up a storm."

Once I've relaxed into what this is, it's actually rather lovely that Caroline has organized brunch. It's good to reconnect with my friends after our honeymoon and to introduce Alessia to everyone in such a casual setting. And it's a joy to see Henry. Alessia looks relaxed too, or maybe she's just tired. But she's tucking into her smoked salmon, eggs, and avocado toast and happily chatting with Henrietta, who has the rare ability to put everyone at ease.

Even Tom.

Maryanne tells me they all came home from Albania with Rowena on a private jet.

"Private?"

"Yes."

"Hmm… I wonder who paid for that."

"You did, probably," Caro says as she picks at her food.

So, my mother is still charging her shit to the estate.

Well, not for long.

"Your parents did a splendid job at the wedding, Alessia. I have to say it was quite the highlight of this year so far."

"It's only March, Tom," Caro interjects.

He ignores her. "It also inspired me." He stands, looking his usual proud and pompous self. "I'm very honored to say that Henry, mad woman that she is, has consented to be my wife. We are officially engaged." He beams at Henrietta, who smiles back at him and blushes prettily under our collective attention.

"Congratulations, bro," Joe says and raises his glass. "To Tom and Henry!"

A chorus of congratulations echoes around the room, and we take turns to hug and kiss them both.

"Of course, you'll have to time your wedding with Trevethick here for when he marries again," Joe says and takes another sip of champagne.

"Again?" ask Caroline and Maryanne in unison.

Damn.

"Um… yeah."

"Can you do that?" Henry asks with a slight crease on her forehead.

"I hope so. I'll have to find out. We want to get married here too. Don't we, Alessia?" I reach out, and she grasps my hand, a slight frown marring her brow as she digests my panicked expression. Maryanne or Caroline cannot know about the questionable circumstances of our marriage and that we haven't followed the usual protocols.

"Yes. Of course," Alessia responds. "This way all of Maxim's friends can join us," she says sweetly. "We have accom…accommodated…" She glances at me, and I think she's checking her

English. I nod and she continues. "…my friends and family, and now it's Maxim's turn. We want to honor his family and friends too."

Alessia, you fucking goddess.

Caroline narrows her eyes and she takes another slug of champagne. "Another wedding? Well, that will be lovely. In London, Cornwall, or Oxfordshire?"

"We've just got home from the last one, Caro. Give us a break," I retort.

Her lips thin, but she doesn't respond. Instead, she turns to Alessia. "Of course, all the staff at each of the estates are dying to meet you. Do you ride?" she asks.

Alessia gives me a quick, dark look, and an image of her naked, on top of me, breasts bouncing, head back, hair tumbling over her shoulders, mouth open celebrating her passion, comes unbidden to mind.

Fuck.

It's arousing.

My sweet, innocent wife. *She gave me that look deliberately.*

"No," Alessia says, and I hide my smirk. Caro looks from her to me, and back to my wife, and I half expect Alessia to say, "Only my husband," but fortunately, she doesn't.

Mate. Grow up.

"We'll have to see what we can do about that," Caro mutters.

"Caroline is a keen horsewoman, as am I. Maxim, not so much. But, of course, he and Kit used to play polo," Maryanne says.

"You have horses?" Alessia turns her attention to me.

"We do. In Oxfordshire," I respond. "We'll do a tour, don't worry."

A tour. *What does he mean?*

"Of the estates," Maxim answers her unspoken question. "You've been to Cornwall. We have another in Oxfordshire. And one in Northumberland, but that's rented to an American who's made his millions in tech. Why he doesn't buy his own estate, I don't know."

Alessia nods as she absorbs this new information. During their entire honeymoon, he did not mention more estates.

More land. More property!

Just how rich is her husband?

"We should be going. Let you two get some shut-eye," Tom announces. "But I do have one request."

All eyes turn to Tom.

"I missed your epic performance on the piano before the wedding, Alessia, as I was with Thanas at the hotel. Please, will you play for us? I've only heard good things."

"Oh yes, please!" Henrietta claps. "I'd love to hear you. Joe has raved about you."

Oh.

"Are you up for this? You don't have to," Maxim is quick to reassure her.

"No. It's okay. You know I love to play." She smiles, delighted that she can do something for Tom after all his help in Albania. Rising from the table, she makes her way over to the piano. She feels everyone turn to watch her.

Why does she feel so nervous?

Opening the lid that covers the keys, she takes a deep breath and sits down on the stool. She decides what she wants to hear and the colors she wants to see, places her hands on the keys, and closes her eyes. She launches into Rachmaninoff's arrangement of Bach's Partita No. 3. Her fingers find every note as they blaze through her head in soft pinks and lilacs while the prelude echoes delicately through the room—comforting her and consuming her until she's part of the music and the colors.

I've not heard her play this piece before, and as ever, my girl… my wife, is lost in the music, delivering a stellar performance. Our guests are transfixed, as they should be. But what I love about her relationship with her music is that she's submerged in it. It totally absorbs her—no, it possesses her—so much so that I'm sure we've all disappeared, and it's just her and the piano and this delightful piece.

She comes to the final trilling note, and it hangs in the air, holding us all rapt before she lifts her fingers off the keys.

Our guests burst into applause and stand.

"*Alessia, that was amazing.*"

"*My goodness!*"

"*Brava! Brava!*"

Alessia smiles shyly at them as I approach her and place my hands on her shoulders. Her hand clasps mine. "Ladies and gentlemen, my wife." I lean down and kiss her quickly. "And on that note! It's time for you to go home. We're both weary from our travels."

"Yes. We'll be on our way," Tom says.

"Thanks again," Joe adds as he makes his way out of the drawing room.

Mrs. Blake is clearing the kitchen, and I thank her before Alessia and I accompany our guests to the front door. It's then that I notice, much to my delight, that my photographic landscapes are reframed and back on the walls.

Caro hugs me goodbye. "Take Alessia shopping for some clothes, for heaven's sake," she hisses in my ear. "Or let me!"

I release her. "Okay. If you think I should."

"Yes. She's a countess, for God's sake. Not a student. Take her to Harvey Nicks."

Alessia frowns. "What is it?" she asks.

"Let him take you shopping, darling." She hugs Alessia, smiles sweetly, and exits with the rest of my family and friends while Alessia turns to me. But before she can say anything, I'm saved by Mrs. Blake, who comes to the door.

"All the washing is done. The kitchen is clean and stocked with the groceries you requested. The dishwasher will need emptying." She gives Alessia a sly glance. "I know—I mean… I hope that shouldn't be a problem for *you*… my *lady*." Mrs. Blake purses her lips in what I assume is supposed to be a smile but is more of a sneer.

"That's enough, Mrs. Blake," I state in a brusque, rebuking tone, holding the door open for her. "It's time for you to leave."

Alessia places her hand on my arm, to stop me from saying more… I don't know. She draws herself upright and lifts her chin.

"Yes. Of course. Thank you for your help, Mrs. Blake."

"My lord. My lady." She nods, her look uncertain because she's been called out, and she leaves.

Too bloody right.

Maxim's face is carved in stone as he bids the housekeeper good day, but Alessia is delighted that he noticed Mrs. Blake's condescending tone. He turns to face her. "I think Mrs. Blake might need a talking to."

Alessia wraps her arms around Maxim and hugs him.

He noticed and acted.

But Alessia would like to fight her own battles in future. She's sure there will be more. After all, Alessia was his cleaner, and she understands Mrs. Blake's resentment.

She smiles at him. "She is Caroline's servant."

"We would say staff. Servant seems a little… feudal."

"I was your servant," she whispers.

Maxim leans down and runs his nose against hers. "And now I'm yours." His lips are on hers, and he presses her against the wall, kissing her until she wants to curl her toes. "Let's go to bed," he murmurs in a dark tone that speaks directly to her most intimate places.

"Yes," she whispers.

Maxim dozes beside Alessia. His lips gently parted, his eyelashes feathered above his cheeks, his face tanned and relaxed

in sleep—he really is beautiful. Alessia watches him, marveling
at how young he looks. She resists touching him and turns to
survey the room. She has no idea what time it is, though it's
still light outside. When she was last in this room, they'd made
love, and then she left the apartment, and Anatoli was waiting
for her.

Don't think about him!

She distracts herself by studying the room in a new light as
Maxim's wife. It's a masculine space: clean lines, minimal furniture in muted silvers and grays. The only ornate piece of furniture is the substantial gilt mirror on the wall behind and above
the bed's headboard. And on the wall opposite are the two photographs of naked women, their backs turned to the camera, so
they're not too explicit. But still, they're erotic and sensual. And
he said that all the photography in the apartment was his; he must
have taken these pictures.

Darling, he's slept with most of London.

Alessia sighs. This she knows—she saw the evidence every
week in his wastebasket. And there was that young woman in the
pub in Cornwall. Alessia cannot remember her name.

But how many women in this bed?

She shudders.

Don't think about that!

Yet in these quiet moments, she wonders if she measures up to
all who came before her. She snorts at the irony—all who literally
came before her.

The thought is distasteful, and she doesn't want to brood on
it or spend all day in bed. She's not tired, so she slips quietly out
from under the covers and makes her way into his wet room to
shower and clean off the last of their journey and the last of their
fabulous honeymoon.

I wake to the sound of the shower in the wet room.
   Alessia.

Wet and naked.

The thought is immediately arousing, and I bound out of bed to join her.

She's standing beneath the cascade of hot water, her back to me and washing her hair. Her hair hangs down to her waist above her fantastic arse as she lathers the shampoo on her head. I step in behind her and gently place my hands on her head to assist her by massaging the soap into her scalp.

"Hmm… that feels good," she groans.

I stop.

"Oh!" Alessia steps back, pressing her body against mine, but more importantly, my erection is resting in the cleft of her back-side. I grin, and she turns her head, flashes me a bright, playful smile, and wiggles her arse, teasing me.

Oh, man.

"You want me to continue?"

"Yes. Please."

I return to the serious task of washing her hair, spreading soap through her long tresses and gently untangling the strands. She raises her face into the cascade to rinse off the soap, and I reach for the body wash, squirting some onto my hands and rubbing them together to work up a lather. Gently, I slather the soap just over the soft skin of her belly then under her breasts, brushing the peaks with the tips of my thumbs. Alessia gasps with pleasure and arches her back, pressing herself into my palms.

Fuck. She has gorgeous tits.

I skate a hand over her body, feeling the supple lines and planes of her skin while I soap her. My other hand continues to tease her hardening nipples, my hand spanning slightly more than an octave as I tantalize each one. As they lengthen under my fingers, my dick gets heavier and heavier.

"You have beautiful breasts, Alessia," I whisper and tug at her earlobe with my teeth. Reaching down, I move my hand over her sex, my fingers skimming over her clitoris.

She groans, leaning back, and extends her hands around my

neck, her back against my chest. She twists her head and presses her lips on mine.

We kiss. Hot. Heavy. All tongue and desire—my cock still cradled in her arse.

Alessia keeps one hand tangled in my hair, moves the other behind her, and grasps my erection in her palm. She wraps her fingers around me, squeezing hard, and begins to slip them up and down slowly. Oh-so-fucking-slowly. Torturing me. My breath hisses between my teeth, and I walk her forward so her front presses against the dark slate tiles. "Now you're clean. Let's make you dirty."

She frees me, her mouth slack, her eyes dark, and places her hands on the slate tiles.

"Shall we do this? In here, like this?" I ask.

"Hmm…"

"Is that a yes?"

She wiggles her arse against me, and I grin. "I'll take that as a yes."

Carefully, I ease a finger inside her. She's wet. From earlier? From now? I don't care. She's ready. For me. I tug her hips back. "Hold on." And slow as slow, so she doesn't lose her balance, I ease myself into her as she pushes back against me.

Yes!

Holding her hips, I edge back and then slide into her again, relishing every fucking centimeter of my wife. She lets out a loud moan, pushing back against me, and I take that as my cue and pick up steam, building momentum.

Harder. Faster.

Repeatedly. Loving the feel of her around me. As we both climb higher. And higher still.

Suddenly, I feel her contracting inside, and I brace myself, with one hand over hers.

"Ah!" she cries and spirals into orgasm, taking me with her. I cry out her name and hold her as I come…

Then we sink together to the floor beneath the torrent of water.

H ow was that?" Maxim asks as he smooths wet hair off her face, then kisses her temple.

"Good. Very good." Alessia grins.

"Yeah. For me too. I think making love to you is my new favorite pastime."

"It is a...um...worthy... Is that the right word? A worthy pastime."

He laughs. "It works. Very worthy." He folds his arms around her and pulls her close. "I'm so glad you're here, safe with me."

"I'm glad too."

"When I think of what might have happened..." Maxim's voice trails off.

Alessia turns and kisses him. "I'm here. I'm safe. I'm with you."

He kisses her forehead. "Good."

Unbidden, an image of Bleriana, one of the girls trafficked with Alessia, comes to mind. They made friends in the back of the truck that brought them to the UK. They thought they were coming here to work.

O Zot. Bleriana was only seventeen.

Alessia frowns and tries to dampen her anxiety and guilt.

Did Bleriana escape too?

Did Dante and Ylli catch her?

The notion is terrifying.

"Hey, what's up?" Maxim says.

She shakes her head, trying to rid herself of the thought. She'll reflect on it later when she's on her own and not worry Maxim right now.

He's done enough.

"I think I am clean again." She smiles.

He laughs. "Are you hungry?"

She nods.

"Good. Let's go out to eat."

Chapter Eleven

It's early on Sunday morning: the air is cool and crisp, the trees still dormant and leafless as I run through Battersea Park. It's that particular time of day when this place belongs solely to dogwalkers and runners. The sky is gray and threatening rain, but there's an energy in the chilly breeze—the park is waking up from the long winter, spring is on the horizon. As I find my rhythm, placing one foot in front of the other, my mind clears. It's great to be outside with upbeat lo-fi house bouncing off my eardrums while I take deep gulps of London air. I've missed it.

I left Alessia curled up asleep, and we have the whole day stretched before us to enjoy—all we have to do is unpack and settle back into the flat.

As I run, I realize that for the last few weeks, I haven't thought beyond finding Alessia, then the wedding, then our honeymoon. Now, I need to figure out what our married life looks like.

And I have no idea.

I don't think Alessia does either.

Do we stay in London?

We'll need to keep a base here. But we could move to Cornwall or Oxfordshire—though I'm not sure how Alessia will like Angwin, as the estate employs more staff there than at Tresyllian Hall because it's open to the public.

Maybe we should make babies.

An heir and a spare.

A little boy like Alessia?

A little girl like Alessia?

Fuck. Not yet.

We're both still young.

Tomorrow, we'll see the lawyer who will help us with our visa situation. Then we can make some decisions.

Yeah.

Tomorrow will be all about decisions. Let's just enjoy today.

Alessia wakes to find herself alone. There's a note on Maxim's pillow.

> *Gone for a run.*
> *Back soon.*
> *I love you. Mx*

Alessia smiles, remembering how she would have to pick up his sweaty gym clothes from the floor after he'd been running. And then there were the notes she found screwed up on the floor. Usually phone numbers. From women?

O Zot. She frowns and tries to banish the thought.

Don't dwell, Alessia.

She stretches, feeling well rested, then rises from the bed. It's time to unpack and clean the apartment.

Same old, same old.

She grins, her good mood restored.

And she can cook Maxim some breakfast, maybe some bubble bread, provided Mrs. Blake has been as good as her word and stocked up on essentials they requested while on their honeymoon. Happy, she strolls into the wet room for a shower.

Maxim returns as she's unpacking her case in the spare bedroom. Grinning, because he's finally home, she stops to listen as he walks into his bedroom, and then she hears him jog up the hall with some urgency to check the kitchen, then the living room.

"Alessia!" he calls, panic evident in his voice.

O Zot! No!

"Maxim. I'm here!" She steps out of the spare room and stares at him standing at the end of the hallway. His shoulders drop in relief, and he runs a hand through his damp hair.

"Don't do that to me. I thought—I thought you were gone." His voice fades as he strides toward her, a wary expression etched on his face.

"I…" Alessia is lost for words. She did not mean to worry him, and her heart melts that he would be so concerned for her. But why would he think she would leave? She's confused, but he doesn't wait for her explanation; he pulls her into a tight, sweaty hug.

"Don't do that to me again," he repeats, each word a staccato, and he kisses the top of her head. "Last time you weren't here, that fucker had kidnapped you."

Oh!

He blows out a breath as if he's releasing his tension, but his lips are a thin line, so she suspects he's a little annoyed too. "I'm going to shower," he says sulkily, and stalks off in the direction of the bedroom, leaving Alessia wrestling with her guilt in the hallway.

O Zot. O Zot. O Zot.

The last thing she wants to do is upset him—but she didn't think.

"Fuck," she says under her breath and decides to abandon her unpacking and heads into the kitchen.

Using a wine bottle because there's no rolling pin, she rolls out the dough she prepared earlier, then cuts it and forms small balls, placing them on the only baking tray she can find. They will need to shop for more culinary equipment if she's to cook in this kitchen. She frowns, unsure if Maxim will be willing to pay for such things. They haven't discussed money at all—she has her cleaning money, but that's it, and it's dwindling. During their honeymoon, Maxim paid for everything. She knows she'll need to raise the issue with him at some point, but she's unsure how to go about doing it.

Deep in thought, she slips the baking tray into the oven, washes and dries the bowl, and then sets the small round table for the two of them. When she returns to the oven to check on the bread, she's startled to find Maxim watching her. He's leaning against the doorjamb, dressed in a long-sleeved white T-shirt, and his black jeans with the tear at the knee. Her favorite. His hair is tousled and wet, and against his tanned face, his eyes are a vibrant spring green. She inhales sharply, drinking in the sight of him.

He's stunning.

And hers.

He takes her breath away, but his expression is unreadable, and he remains mute as his eyes pin her to a standstill.

She swallows. "Are you mad at me?"

"No. I'm angry at myself."

"Why?"

"Because I overreacted."

She moves forward, standing so close that she feels his heat bathing her skin. "I should have told you I am in the spare room. I'm here. I'm safe."

He tips her chin up as his eyes sear hers. "I was… anxious." He plants a soft kiss on her lips. "It's not a feeling I like."

"I'm sorry. I didn't think." Gingerly she wraps her arms around him, placing her cheek against his chest. He rests his chin on her head, folding her into his embrace and breathing in her scent.

"You smell amazing," he whispers.

"So do you. Clean."

She senses his smile and relaxes as he kisses her hair. He grasps her face between his hands and raises her lips to his. "I need to know you're safe."

"I'm safe. With you."

He kisses her—soft, sweet, wet, and warm, and she surrenders to his skilled tongue. He rests his forehead against hers and blows out a breath. "Is that fresh bread I smell baking?"

She grins. "It is. Bubble bread."

His answering smile is dazzling. "Your father warned me."

"My father?"

"Yes. He said you'd make me fat."

"I will only make this on Sundays."

Maxim laughs, his good mood restored. "Good plan."

Alessia takes a deep breath. "But I will need to go out sometime. Shop for food."

"I know. I know. Of course. I'm being ridiculous." From his back pocket, he produces the key he gave her not so long ago. "Just let me know where you are. Please."

Alessia takes the key. "Thank you." She examines the leather fob. "What is this place… Angwin House?"

"It's our Oxfordshire estate. We'll go later this week if you like. Today even. We could take a quick trip there if you wish."

He takes a seat at the table, and Alessia grabs a tea towel to remove the bread from the oven while she digests this piece of information.

"What were you doing in the spare room anyway?"

"I was unpacking. My clothes. There's no space in your closet."

"Oh. I see." His mouth flattens in a line. "We should get a bigger place for the two of us."

Alessia gapes at him.

"The estate owns a great deal of property," he answers her unspoken question. "I'll talk to Oliver and see what's coming available."

Another home? Just like that? Alessia's brow furrows in consternation.

"What is it?"

"How much land…um…property do you own?"

"Personally, not much. All the Trevethick Estate property, and that includes the three great estates, and all its assets, are held in trust. The trust is the legal owner of the estate, and Kit, Maryanne, and I were trustees. Now, with Kit gone, it's just me and Maryanne—but as the earl, I'm the beneficial owner. Does that make sense?"

A lessia stares blankly at me.

"It's complicated," I concede, knowing it's not easy to understand. "Basically, the estate owns a great deal of property, and its income is made through rents and leases on all the residential, retail, and business premises the estate owns."

"Oh…" Alessia says. "And your job is to…um…run this?"

"Oliver, whom you met through a car window, is the chief operating officer of the Trevethick Estate. He does the day-to-day running. I'm… his boss. It was my brother's job, and Kit had the business acumen for the role. Me, I'm still learning." My mood heads south. This is the crux of the problem I have with assuming the title. I've not been trained to do it, while Kit was skilled at it. Not only that, but he was so economically astute that he increased the fortunes of our individual trusts too.

Hell. I don't want to think about this now.

"Look, it's the last day of our holiday," I add. "Let's enjoy it. We could take a drive up to Angwin. It's about two hours. Have a look around. Then tomorrow, the work will begin." I reach for one of the bread buns Alessia has placed on the table. "We need to find a new home. Organize a visa for you to stay here. Get back to work."

Now, there's four words I never thought I'd utter.

Shaking my head in mock self-disgust, I spread some butter on the roll and watch it melt before I add some blackcurrant jam, then take a bite.

Good God. This stuff is delicious.

Alessia places a cup of coffee in front of me and takes a seat.

"Okay. I would love to see Angwin."

I grin. "I could get used to this, you know." And I raise a piece of bubble bread in salute to my wife.

"You do not have a choice." Alessia smirks.

"But *you* do. You know you don't have to do this. We could go out to eat, or we could hire some help."

"I want to do it. For you. It is my job."

And there it is, her upbringing and our cultural divide. I don't know any women like her. She's waited on the men in her life for years, and her expectations are limited by that. I never thought I'd marry such a domesticated woman. Will she ever get over this?

I mean, I like that she wants to care for me.

Mate.

Okay, I love that she wants to care for me.

But I want Alessia to have options. The sooner we move to somewhere bigger, the better. We can get some help, and she won't have to do this. Besides, there are houses to run, estates to oversee, and people to manage.

Mate. It's a lot.

"I do not know what I would do if I didn't cook and clean for you," she adds as she takes a bite of bubble bread and butter.

"I'm sure you'll be busy once we've established you as countess."

Alessia's eyes widen. "What does that mean?"

"Staff to manage, houses to run, functions to organize and attend."

She gasps, her dark eyes stricken with alarm.

"Sorry." I shrug. "It comes with the territory. Don't look so worried. You'll be fine."

"I think I need lessons!" she exclaims.

"Lessons?" And my mother's contemptuous offer of "finishing school" pops unwelcome into my mind.

"Yes. There must be something I can read, or… a school I can…" Her voice tails off.

"You're serious?"

"Yes," she responds emphatically.

"Well, I'm sure we can find something. If you want. If it would give you confidence."

She smiles. "Yes. That is exactly what I need."

"Are you sure?"

"Yes. I was not born into this… life. I don't want to let you down."

I laugh. "It's me that should be saying that to you. You are perfect the way you are, but we could look into lessons, if that's what you want."

Alessia smiles, her eyes shining.

Etiquette lessons.

How did my mother know?

"I'll unpack." I change the subject, irritated that my mother was right. "Afterward, we could go to Angwin. Go shopping, out for lunch, whatever you want to do."

Alessia nods. "Yes. I'd like that. And I have unpacked your clothes."

"Oh, thank you."

"I would like to go to the store. We need cooking…um… equipment."

"I hadn't thought of that. Yes, I suppose we do. I am not much of a cook."

"You make a good breakfast."

I grin, remembering our time at the Hideout. "I do. Okay. Peter Jones is probably the best place to go. I've never shopped for that stuff. We could look online. We could also get you some new clothes. That reminds me—"

Maxim stands and leaves the room only to return a few moments later with four envelopes addressed to Alessia Trevelyan. Alessia examines them, turning them in her hands.

What could these be?

"I arranged these while we were away. Bank cards. And their PINs. You'll need them. One's a debit card. The other is a credit card."

"Money?" she says, staring at him. "For me?" She's stunned.

"Yes. For you. Magic cards, you called them once. They're not magic; let me stress that. So don't go crazy." He gives her a crooked smile.

And just like that, the issue of money is resolved.

"Thank you," she says.

"You don't have to thank me." Maxim frowns. "You're my wife."

And once more, Alessia tries to quell her rising panic at her good fortune... when she thinks of what might have been. An image of Bleriana crosses her mind again, and her thoughts take a darker turn.

Where is she?

Is she okay?

Could Alessia find her?

"I'll wash up," Maxim says, interrupting her thoughts.

"No. No, you won't. I'll do it."

Maxim laughs. "This isn't up for discussion. I can wash up. And load a dishwasher. Let's do a surprise visit to Angwin when I'm done." He rises, taking his breakfast plate and coffee cup with him.

Angwin is nestled in the Cotswold hills near Chipping Norton. In the Jag, I turn off the road and glide through the main gate and along the majestic beech-lined driveway toward the property.

"Uau," Alessia breathes as she catches sight of the main house in all its Palladian splendor, with its four Corinthian columns and impressive pediment. Between the stark beeches, it dominates the groomed landscape in honeyed stone.

"Yes. That's Angwin."

She grins at me with a suitable look of awe on her face.

I pull into the visitors' parking lot, which I'm pleased to see is busy. Normally, I would park around the back of the house near the stables, but I want to keep our visit low-key. I haven't warned anyone we're coming, and I don't want to overwhelm my new countess. "Ready?" I ask as I switch off the engine. Alessia's smile is answer enough.

Once out of the car, I grab her hand, and we stroll down the driveway toward the main house. "See over there." I gesture to where the driveway forks left to the thriving garden center built where the original, extensive kitchen gardens used to be and explain that beyond that is a children's play gym and our small petting zoo, each hugely popular with the locals and their kids. And a destination for tourists during school holidays. One of our tenant farmers provides the sheep, cows, and pigs for the small zoo, and they join our three resident alpacas and four donkeys— all rescues, and a passion of Maryanne's.

"No goats?" Alessia asks, her eyes sparkling with mirth.

I laugh. "I don't think so. We could go and check. Maybe we could get some just for you."

We stop at the small ticket office, which is occupied by someone I don't recognize. "Good afternoon," the young man offers.

"Two for the house, please." It seems easier to buy the tickets rather than explain that I own the house.

The man hands me two tickets, and I tap my card on the card reader.

Alessia smiles. "You have to pay?"

I laugh. "Not usually. I don't know that young man."

We amble down the drive toward the great house. Through the trees we can see the shoreline of the first of our two lakes, and among the weeds, I spy two coots and some ducks paddling toward the shore.

"Swans," Alessia exclaims with delight, spotting our resident pair of mute swans who are gliding majestically across the still waters, their snowy feathers curled like sails.

"Yeah. This pair have been with us for about ten or so years. I think Kit called them Triumph and Herald, though which is which I don't know."

"Grand names. They're beautiful."

"They are. Kit was obsessed with cars, especially old classics. Hence the names." I laugh at myself. Alessia won't have a clue about old British cars. "They mate for life, you know," I add, turning toward her with a broad grin.

She smiles and lifts her chin, amused but haughty. "I know about swans."

Of course she does.

"These two raise their new cygnets here each year."

And one day maybe we will raise our children here too.

The thought surprises and pleases me.

One day.

She squeezes my hand and I wonder if she's thinking the same thing.

At the front of the house is the impressive lawn, which is about a hectare in size. The nearest half is neatly mowed in stripes. It's surrounded by ancient oaks, elms, beech trees, and the lake. It is a stunning setting, now that I survey it.

"So, anyone can come here?" Alessia asks as she takes in the view from the steps of the main house.

"Yes, as long as they pay. It's not much if you just want to use the grounds. It's very popular in the summer. For picnics. Behind the house are the stables. We provide a livery for the locals with horses, and a friend of Caroline's runs a riding school from there. This is where Maryanne and Caroline keep their horses. Come, I'll show you inside."

Alessia trails after Maxim as he bounces up the stone steps and through the double doors into an impressive reception hall. There are statues in little alcoves and ornate plasterwork over the entire room, even the ceiling. Alessia's chest constricts as she tries to take in the majesty of a room that is merely the entrance to this huge house.

Behind a reception desk, the younger of two women looks up in greeting.

"Hello there. Are you here for the tour?" she asks.

Maxim laughs, and the older woman raises her head. "Oh my goodness! Maxim!" she exclaims. "I mean, my lord."

"Hello, Francine. How are you?"

"I'm doing well, my lord." She bustles around the counter, much to the surprise of her colleague.

"Please, Maxim will do. It's my name. I've said this already when I was last here."

"I know, my lord, but I'm an old-fashioned woman." Her affection for Maxim is obvious as she beams at him.

Maxim wraps his arm around Alessia and pulls her close. "Francine, may I present my wife, Alessia."

"Your wife!" Francine exclaims. "Why, Lady Trevethick, what a pleasure to meet you."

Alessia holds out her hand, and Francine shakes it vigorously.

"Lady Caroline said you'd married. Congratulations to you both, my lord."

Caroline. She was here?

"Thank you."

"I wish you'd told us you were coming—"

Maxim holds up his hand to stop Francine. "We'll come and do a proper introduction later in the month. I just wanted to give my wife a quick and dirty look around the house. Give her an idea of what she's taken on."

Francine laughs, good-natured, her eyes twinkling at Alessia. "I've known his lordship since he was a young lad."

Maxim quickly interrupts her. "You're new," he says, turning to the younger woman behind the desk.

"This is the earl. The owner," Francine hisses at her. "This is Jessica. She's been with us for about three weeks now."

The younger woman stands, flustered. "I'm sorry, sir. Maxim. Um... my lord."

"Welcome to Angwin, Jessica." Maxim extends his hand, and Alessia follows suit, taking Jessica's limp, clammy hand and giving it a reassuring squeeze.

Jessica bows her head in a brief salute, and Alessia's cheeks pink.

"We'll go look around," Maxim says.

"You do that, sir," Francine replies with a huge smile. "I'll let Mrs. Jenkins know you're here."

They walk through a door at the side of the reception hall, into a corridor that's crowded with paintings.

"You didn't tell me he was so good-looking!" they hear Jessica hiss at Francine.

Alessia cocks a brow at Maxim, and he shrugs and laughs.

A lessia is quiet while I drive the Jag through Chipping Norton, heading home to London. Reaching over, I grasp her hand and cradle it in mine. "It's a lot. I know."

Alessia nods. "I didn't realize it would be so... big. Bigger than...um...the Hall, in Cornwall."

"Yes. It's the largest property we own in terms of the actual house and the land. Most of the land's farmed—organically, of course. My father was ahead of his time. An eco-warrior in the late '70s."

My heart swells, and an aching knot forms in my throat. I miss him. *Father.*

And Kit.

I clear my throat. "Angwin mostly takes care of itself because the staff who run it are excellent."

"But you don't live there."

"No. We stay occasionally. As you saw, we have an apartment in the main house. But that's it. I always think of Angwin as a historical document and an amenity for the community. It's open to the public, and they can roam the house and see how the landed gentry used to live. And browse the art collection..."

Alessia nods. "So many rooms..."

"Yeah. I know. The upkeep for that house is astronomical. But we've managed to keep it going and not let it die."

She offers me a slight smile, and my scalp tightens as I wonder what she's thinking.

Is she judging us? My family?

The wealth?

Shit.

"Are you okay?" I ask.

"Yes. Yes. Of course. I am a little…um…overwhelmed. But thank you for showing me your… other home. It is very clear that your staff admire you."

What? Her words are unexpected. "You think?"

Her smile warms. "Yes. Everyone. They are… loyal. It's the right word?"

I snort. "Yes. I suppose so, but I'm not sure I agree with you. I think the jury is out for them."

"I think they want you to succeed."

An unfamiliar warmth spreads through my chest—commendation from the staff, that's new. All praise was usually reserved for Kit.

"I was the family reprobate," I mutter while I muse on Alessia's observation. "Kit was the stable, mature, hard-working brother, but then he didn't have a choice."

"Reprobate?" she asks.

"Definitely." I flash her my most wicked grin in the hope of lightening the mood, and to my relief, it works.

She laughs.

"Put some music on." I point my chin to the sound system, and Alessia scrolls through the tunes.

In the glow of the little dragon, Alessia watches Maxim sleep. He's more boyish when he sleeps. Gently, she smooths his hair off his forehead and plants a tender kiss there. She turns and lies on her back, staring at the dancing, watery reflections on the ceiling, and all she can think about is how one family can own so much property.

And now she's one of them.

She has so much when others… do not.

She closes her eyes to blot out the reflections wavering on the ceiling and to quell her pervading sense of guilt.

Chapter Twelve

Bleriana! Sweet, young Bleriana is outside the locked doors of the ornate reception hall at Angwin House. Trying to get in. She rattles the door.

Banging her fists on the glass of the double doors.

On the glass.

She'll break the glass.

She's screaming. But Alessia cannot hear a word.

Alessia tries and fails to open the doors.

And behind Bleriana... Dante and Ylli emerge from the darkness.

Black plastic bags open and ready.

Alessia is plunged into choking darkness.

Bleriana screams.

"Alessia! Alessia! Wake up!" Maxim's panicked voice penetrates Alessia's horror, dragging her toward the light from the depths of her nightmare. Heart pounding, she opens her eyes—her fear, a tight knot in her chest clawing its way into her throat and choking her.

Maxim.

Her saviour.

Again.

His bright green eyes stare into hers, his face etched in worry. "Are you okay?"

"It was a dream, a bad dream," Alessia mumbles and shudders as Maxim gathers her in his arms.

"I've got you," he whispers, tightening his hold and folding his body protectively around her. He kisses her forehead.

Her thundering heartbeat slows as she clings to her dear, dear husband and inhales his comforting scent—body wash, sleep, and Maxim.

"Hmm," she breathes.

"Hush now," he murmurs in the semi-darkness and lies back with Alessia in his arms. "Go to sleep, sweetheart."

Alessia closes her eyes, and as her fear recedes, she drifts once more.

It's my first day in the office after the tumultuous events of the last few weeks. As the cab pulls up at the front door, I wonder what today will bring. I'm still unsettled by Alessia's plaintive wail in the depths of the night—her cry for help from her nightmare. She seemed fine this morning and couldn't remember her bad dream, but I'm worried her past trauma is catching up with her. She always seems so stoic but perhaps, now that she's safe, the shock of the numerous ordeals she's endured recently is finally taking its toll.

Dude. It's one nightmare.

Taking a deep breath, I push my thoughts aside, pay the driver, and stride up the steps into the office building.

The receptionist greets me with a cheery smile. "Good morning, Lord Trevethick."

"Good morning, Lisa."

"And congratulations, my lord. On your wedding."

"Thank you."

I head through the outer office, knock on Oliver's door, and enter. He grins broadly; if I'm not mistaken, I think he's pleased to see me. "Maxim. Welcome back, and congratulations." He stands and holds out his hand.

"Thanks, Oliver." We shake, and I'm grateful he's been holding the fort. "And thank you for restoring the photography in my flat."

"You noticed! It's a pleasure. You have a good eye. You had a relaxing and enjoyable honeymoon?"

I grin. "I did, thank you."

"We have a long agenda, so I wonder if we should get cracking."

"Yes, of course. I want a moment, though. I've decided that it's time to move into Kit's office."

"Very good, sir," Oliver says gently and gestures toward the door of the hallowed room that was my brother's and my father's domain. "If you need anything," he adds, "I'm here."

"Thanks."

I cross the floor, grab the brass handle, and open the door to the inner sanctum. Taking a deep, steadying breath, I step inside as a wave of nostalgia crashes over me. The smell, the ambience, the décor—it's all Kit.

It's a gut punch of memories.

One wall is lined with books and various curios: a polo ball and trophies, a model Bugatti Veyron, the family crest, and a few of his rallying trophies. The wall behind his desk has pictures, paintings, certificates, and photographs, including a large daguerreotype of Tresyllian House in Cornwall. Beside it is my photographic re-creation in black and white taken with my Leica. I reach out to straighten my print, and I'm reminded that Kit always supported my photography.

The desk is ornate, with intricate carvings and an embossed black leather top. On his desk are more portraits in gilt frames of us, Caroline, Jensen and Healey, his beloved red setters. I glide a finger over the cool, gleaming wood and then test the various drawers. They're all locked.

There's a knock at the door, and Oliver steps in. "You'll need these." He produces a set of keys, setting them down on the desk.

"Thank you."

He looks around the office. "I haven't been in here for a while either." He glances at the photo of Kit shaking hands with some dignitary I don't recognize and then back at me.

"You miss him too." It's a statement that causes a tightening in my chest.

"Yeah," he says and clears his throat. "Those keys should open the desk and the filing cabinet over there."

"Shall we get on with our meeting? We can do it at the rather fine Queen Anne table in here."

Oliver laughs. "I'll fetch my notebook."

I blow out a breath as I remove and hang my coat on the hatstand, thinking about how Kit's death has affected so many of us, even Oliver.

"What's first on the agenda?" I ask when he returns.

"Perhaps you should do a press release about your marriage. The tabloids are pestering our director of communications."

"Really?"

Oliver nods.

I don't want the press delving into the minutiae of my marriage.

"I'll think about it. And can we get me a computer for here?"

"Of course. I'll get that sorted today."

"What's next?"

A lessia is in the apartment sitting at Maxim's desk, using his iMac and trawling the internet. She's trying to find out how to track a trafficked person. It's an impossible task, especially as the intercom keeps buzzing. There are reporters outside, wanting to speak to Maxim. She's feigned ignorance and is now listening to Angela Hewitt's interpretation of Bach's preludes and fugues from the Well-Tempered Clavier through headphones. Alessia was surprised that only a few women artists were featured in the classical albums on Apple Music. The various colors that ring in her head keep her grounded as she reads report after report from victims who have escaped their traffickers and abusers and found safety in England through the work of various charities.

It's sobering reading.

In the back of her mind, she keeps returning to the mantra: *That could have been me.*

She shudders.

If she hadn't escaped from Dante's and Ylli's clutches, she'd have her own harrowing story to tell, and she would, in all probability, become another appalling statistic.

A fractured shard from her nightmare pierces her mind.

Bleriana hammering on the doors at Angwin.

Her face tearstained. Her fear wild and disturbing in her eyes.

O Zot. O Zot. Poor Bleriana.

When Alessia looks up to check the time, she finds tears coursing down her cheeks. She dashes them away, more resolved to try to find her friend. Somehow.

Oliver and I are concluding our meeting. The Mayfair refurbishment is near completion, and it's time to hire an interior designer. I need Caro to decide if she wants the gig.

I've asked Oliver for a full rundown of the expenses my mother has made against the estate for the past year, which means I'll be privy to my parents' divorce settlement. And he'll prepare a list of all the larger houses belonging to the estate, that are or will be coming available for lease shortly.

That's on the agenda for tomorrow.

Throughout our discussions, I've ignored my phone. When I glance at the screen, I'm astonished to find it crowded with a ton of text messages and missed calls.

What the hell! You got married!!!!

When do we get to meet your WIFE?

What's this I hear about you getting married?

You're finally off the market.
My heart is broke!

Maxim. You're hitched!!!

WTF man? You wed!

Who's the lucky girl?

Can I get an interview with
you and your bride?

Shit! The last is from a journalist from one of the glossies. I fucked her back in the day.

How do all these people know?

"You were right about the world knowing about my nuptials," I mutter to Oliver, who is gathering his papers together.

"It's not too late to put out a press release," he says.

I roll my eyes, refusing to contemplate any interaction with the press as I scroll through a flurry of texts Caroline sent a couple of hours ago.

Can we meet today?
You need to see what I've unearthed.
It may affect you.

What fresh hell is this?

Can it wait?

No.

There's a knock on the office door as Oliver rises.

"Come in," I call.

Lisa steps inside. "I'm so sorry to interrupt you, my lord. Lady Trevethick is here."

Alessia! My heart skips a beat, and I rise from the table, a broad smile plastered on my face ready to greet my wife. "Show her in."

Lisa steps aside, and Caroline enters and pockets her phone. *Oh.*

"Expecting someone else?" Caroline snipes. "Your face has fallen several floors, darling."

"Hello, Caro." Ignoring her jibe, I kiss her cheek. "What a lovely surprise."

"Oliver," she acknowledges him, and he gives her a quick nod before exiting. Caroline watches him leave, her face impassive, and then she turns to survey the room. "It's been a while since I was in here." She turns her attention to me, her eyes welling with her sadness.

"Funny, Oliver said that," I whisper.

Her nose pinks charmingly, and she shakes her head, steeling herself. "I was in the area. I wondered if you might want lunch."

"I've just got back and I'm busy, Caro."

She laughs—a sad, sorry sound. "You would never have said that back in the day."

"True. What can I help you with?"

"May I sit? I have something to show you."

"Of course." I gesture toward the Queen Anne table and pull out the chair I've just vacated for her to sit down. While I take a seat beside her, she places her handbag on her lap and ferrets through it, avoiding eye contact.

"You know I've been going through Kit's belongings and his papers."

"Yes." *Where is she going with this?*

"Well, I found all sorts of things. It's amazing what can turn up." She sounds nervous.

"What is it, Caro?"

"Well." She swallows. "This might concern both you and Maryanne." She fishes a couple of letters out of her handbag and places them on the table in front of me.

I glance down at them, then back at her, cocking my head. "What are these?"

"I think you should read them." The haunted look in her eyes sends a frisson down my spine, and I grasp both letters and scan them. Every hair on my body stands to attention.

"Genetic… what?" My mouth dries as I look at her. "Why would Kit be referred for genetic counseling?"

"Exactly," she whispers.

"You don't know?"

She shakes her head, her eyes wide and luminous with doubt. "No. These are a surprise for me too."

What the hell is this?

Carefully, I reread both letters and check the dates. His GP referral was in October last year, and the genetic counseling service wrote back with an appointment in November.

"Have you found any other letters? Results?"

Caroline shakes his head.

"Dates in his diary?"

"No." Caro looks as bemused as I am.

"If Kit's been referred for genetic counseling, it'll be for a reason."

Oh shit.

I feel the blood drain from my face.

If Kit was facing a genetic medical issue, then… I am too, surely. *And Maryanne.*

Hell.

Could there be something wrong with me?

I rack my brain, trying to remember if there are any documented medical conditions in my predecessors. Nothing comes to mind. "Maybe I should get tested too."

"Tested for what? We don't have a clue," Caroline says.

This is true.

"Maybe it was just a precautionary investigation," Caro says. "You know how thorough Dr. Renton can be. He's always overzealous. It racks up the bill."

"Was Kit ill?" I ask.

"Not as far as I know. He had headaches, which you know about."

"He's always had those."

Hell. What could this be? I have no idea. "Did you call Renton's office?"

"Yes. They wouldn't divulge any information." Caro sounds frustrated.

Double hell.

I wonder if my mother knows. "Did you mention this to Rowena?"

"No. She flew back to New York as soon as we touched down from Tirana."

"You knew about this at the wedding?" My voice has risen several octaves.

Caroline's eyes widen, and I have my answer.

And you didn't fucking tell me?

I glare at her, suddenly livid. I might have something wrong with me, and I've just got married!

Fuck. What have I saddled Alessia with?

But before I can get really fucking angry, we're interrupted by a knock at the door, and Lisa enters carrying a tray with coffee. It gives me a moment to rein in my temper.

"I took the liberty of making you some coffee," Lisa says with a bright smile.

"Thanks," I mutter as she places it on the table.

"Thank you, Lisa," Caro says, and Lisa stands awkwardly, surveying us for a moment.

"That will be all. Thanks again." I force a smile, and I'm relieved when she leaves.

"Did you call this place?" I ask, tapping the letter from the genetic counseling clinic.

"Yes. They wouldn't tell me anything either, even though I'm next of kin."

Fucking hell.

"I don't think they'd talk to you either," Caroline says gently.

"Well, maybe I can get some answers out of Renton. After all, he's my GP too. In fact, I need to sign Alessia up. Hell, I may even have to call Rowena."

"Maxim, I'm sure it's nothing," Caroline says.

"How the hell do you know?" I shout, rising from the table, and to my shame, Caro flinches.

Fuck. Fuck. Fuck.

I want to scream.

I'm as angry with her now as I was in Albania when I found out she told Alessia about us. I drag a hand through my hair and pace across the fucking antique Persian rug on the floor.

Dude. Get a grip.

"I'll do some digging before we tell Maryanne," I mutter.

"She might be able to shed some light. After all, she is a doctor."

"Let me find out what we're dealing with here."

She's my sister, and it's my fucking job to protect her.

Caro blows out a breath. "Okay. The other thing we need to discuss is Kit's memorial."

"Not now."

"Well, I've spoken with the Dean of Westminster's office."

"And?"

"They're suggesting a date in April."

"Isn't that a bit soon?"

"Is it?" Caroline says.

"Oh hell, Caro. I don't know. Let me think about it. This is… a lot."

"It is," she admits. "Are you sure I can't take you to lunch?"

"I have to leave shortly. Alessia and I are meeting a lawyer. About her immigration status."

"Oh?"

"Yeah."

Caroline purses her lips, but her expression softens. "I'm sorry," she murmurs. "For not telling you. At the wedding."

I slump into the chair behind what is now my desk. "Perhaps something here might shed some light on these letters." Grabbing the keys, I try the first tiny brass key that looks most likely to fit. The fourth key works and I open the first of the drawers. It contains a rack of suspension files.

Caroline moves to sit in the chair opposite the desk, craning her neck to see if I find anything. I quickly scan through the files, but they seem to be personal—a collection of clippings from car magazines, a file with letters from the LSE, some CVs, and a weighty leather diary from last year. I drag it out, place it on the desk, and quickly leaf through it, checking the dates mentioned on the letters. Alas, the diary holds no clues.

Bugger.

"Anything?" Caroline asks.

I shake my head.

The other drawers don't yield any leads either. Just some cool stationary and some mementos from Kit's trips around the world. My search is fruitless, but a thought occurs to me.

"Where's Kit's laptop? Or his phone for that matter? Or even his journal?"

"I've no idea."

"What do you mean? They're not with his possessions? Perhaps it's here. Or in the safe at Trevelyan House or the Hall?"

Caroline lifts her chin. "I don't know."

"Can you check?"

She shrugs in a noncommittal, un-Caro way.

"Really?"

She shakes her head looking abashed and a little sheepish. "I can try," she mutters.

"I'm going to call Renton, make an appointment, and also try the genetic counseling clinic."

"I hope you have better luck than me." She stands. "I'd better go. I'm sure this is nothing, Maxim."

I rise to my feet, and we gaze at each other, and I'm wondering once more what Kit was doing on his motorcycle racing through the Trevethick lanes in the depths of an icy winter. Is she thinking the same? Was the news so bad that he took his own life?

Fuck.

Neither of us says anything. Caroline's breath catches and her pupils grow darker and larger. I don't like what that telegraphs, but before I can be sure, she breaks eye contact, glancing toward the door. "I'm sorry," she whispers, and she exits the room, leaving me entirely at sea—alone, angry… and scared.

I check my watch and realize I've enough time to walk home and clear my head. Grabbing my coat, I head out of the office.

Oliver looks up and frowns. "You okay, Maxim?"

"Yes. I've got to leave."

"Did you mention interior design to Lady Trevethick?"

Damn!

"No. I will, though. Unless you'd like to?"

Oliver's face falls and he looks a little uncomfortable. "I'd rather you did, Maxim," he responds eventually.

"Okay. I'll do that. I'll see you tomorrow."

Disheartened, I trudge through the backstreets of Chelsea back to the flat. So far, today has been exasperating. I feel like I've been thwarted at every turn. I've made a call to Kit's and my GP, Dr. Renton, and have an appointment to see him tomorrow. Hopefully, I'll get some answers then. The genetic counseling clinic was not forthcoming at all and the clinician dealing with Kit is on holiday, but I have an appointment in a couple of weeks to see her. I've even called my mother and left a message for her to call me… all to no avail.

I cannot believe how bewildering this news has been.

There may be nothing wrong.

But on the other hand, something awful could befall me as I get older.

Hell.

It's the not knowing that's so frustrating.

As I round the corner of Tite Street onto the Embankment, I spy a few people—mainly men—hanging around the entrance to my building.

Wait. These are not people!

Three of the shambolic riffraff are holding cameras.

Paparazzi!

For a nanosecond, I wonder who they're waiting for, and then an older man wearing an Arsenal FC scarf spots me. "There he is!" he shouts.

Fuck. They're after me!

Lord Trevethick! Lord Trevethick! Maxim!

Congratulations.

Care to comment on your marriage? Your bride? When do we meet her?

My mood slides from bad to worse as they swarm around me like cockroaches. I put my head down and walk through them, saying nothing.

This is all I fucking need.

I head into the safety of the building while a couple of the reporters shout questions at me. Leaving them on the doorstep, I vault up the stairs, cursing whoever informed the press about our marriage. Alessia is not going to appreciate the attention; this I know.

I've not been accosted by any journalists since I was with Charlotte, an ex-girlfriend. She loved attention—as an actor… sorry, no, an artist, as she liked to style herself—she lapped it up, especially from the press. I roll my eyes at the memory. She was socially ambitious and hideously pretentious. Thank God she moved on. Apart from my time with her, I've managed to avoid being tabloid fodder, but I'll get the occasional mention in the social diary columns of more discerning publications.

I unlock the front door, step into the hall, and stop.

Alessia is at the piano, and I recognize the melody immediately—*Clair de Lune*, a piece I can play myself but with nothing like her grace. As I listen in wonder, the last few frustrating hours slip away, and I'm transported to a more peaceful, hopeful state. I creep down the hall, peer into the drawing room, and watch her.

Eyes closed, head bent, she's wholly surrendered to the music as it flows effortlessly through and from her. Somehow, she senses my presence and turns and smiles, her face lighting up at the sight of me.

"Don't stop," I say, walking toward her.

She shifts on the piano stool, not missing a note, and I settle beside her, wrapping my arm around her waist while the music caresses and holds the pair of us.

This is sublime.

And I have an idea—I hover my right hand over hers, and she immediately understands what I'm trying to do. She withdraws her hand, and I take over. We stumble over the first few notes, but I watch her left hand, following her lead, and we continue the piece.

Together.

I'm thrilled that I'm able to keep up with her without the composition in front of me. She makes it easy because she's so attuned to the music and its languid rhythm.

Following her lead makes me a better pianist.

It's humbling.

It's exhilarating.

As the final note drifts into the ether and disappears, we grin at each other like fools. "That was amazing," I whisper.

Alessia laughs, threading her arms around my neck and drawing my lips to hers. We kiss. Her mouth is warm, wet, welcoming, and arousing all at once. I tug her onto my lap, deepening our connection, our tongues celebrating each other so that we're breathless when we pull apart.

She rests her forehead against mine. Her eyes closed. "I've missed you," she whispers.

"Oh, baby. I've missed you. And I'd like nothing more than to take you to bed, but we have an appointment with the immigration lawyer."

She pouts but stands, obviously reluctant to leave the safety of my lap. "I am ready." She hands me our passports, our marriage certificate, and the apostille issued by the notary in Tirana confirming our marriage certificate is legitimate. I slip them all into my jacket pocket. Then frown.

"There's a slight problem. We've been besieged by the press outside."

"I know."

"You do?"

"They have been ringing the bell outside. Asking for you. Asking me questions."

"What did you do?"

"I said I was your cleaner and that you weren't here. And then I stopped answering." She bites her bottom lip looking impish.

I laugh out loud. "Brilliant. Apparently, our marriage appears to be in the public interest."

"Are they still outside the building?"

"Afraid so."

"We can escape through the utility room and go that way."

"Of course! Let's go."

Standing outside on the fire escape, Maxim locks the utility room door and grins down at Alessia. "I can't remember the last time I was out here!"

She laughs, then sobers. The last time she used it was to escape Dante and Ylli when they came to Maxim's apartment. And she's used it often to empty Maxim's trash.

"I'll follow you," he says, and gingerly they make their way down the six flights to the side alley.

As they pass the bins, Alessia remembers throwing up beside them. Maxim grabs her hand and threads his fingers with hers. "What is it?" he asks.

She shakes her head, reluctant to tell him and to rid herself of that awful recollection. An image of Bleriana's sweet face imprints on her mind. The poor child. Did she evade their captors? Did the others?

Maxim says nothing, letting her be, and together they make their way to the gate at the side alley. Maxim opens it and peers out. The street is empty.

"This is how you got out and away when those thugs showed up."

"Yes."

"You must have been so scared. Come on. Coast is clear. Let's grab a cab."

Hand in hand, they walk briskly up the street, unhindered by the press, and Maxim hails the first cab he sees.

The offices of Lockhart, Waddell, Mulville, and Cavanagh are on Lincoln's Inn Fields. An office junior shows us into a conference room. "May I fetch you tea or coffee?" he asks, blinking rapidly.

"I'm good. Alessia?"

"No, thank you."

"Very good, Lord, Lady Trevethick. Ticia Cavanagh will be with you shortly." He exits, and I usher Alessia to a seat at the table. Ms. Cavanagh is a partner in the firm, and she comes highly recommended by Rajah—she's an expert in her field.

The door opens before I've sat down, and Ticia Cavanagh enters. She's wearing an expensive black suit and a white silk blouse. In her hand, she clutches a legal paper pad, her scarlet nails vivid against the canary yellow.

Oh, shit.

We stare at each other in instant recognition. The last time I saw her, I'd just untied her from my bed.

Could this day hold any more surprises?

I clear my throat. "Leticia, how nice to see you again."

Chapter Thirteen

"Lord Trevethick," Leticia says in her soft Irish lilt, stressing my title. "How do you do? And your wife"—she emphasizes the word *wife*—"Lady Trevethick." She steps forward, her face etched in disdain as she holds out her hand in greeting, and as she grasps mine a little too tightly, I feel the need to defend myself.

"Recent. Wife. We married. Recently."

Alessia frowns, her eyes darting to me and then back to Ticia Cavanagh as they shake hands. "How do you do?" Alessia murmurs as if her throat is dry, and she casts another glance at me, her eyes wide with insight.

Damn. She knows.

My heart sinks, and I briefly close my eyes, summoning some resolve while realizing I'll have to explain myself later.

Had I known… *hell.*

I'm confused by Leticia's use of a nickname. "Ticia?"

"Here. Yes," she says, her tone terse, and I realize she's not going to offer any other explanation, which is, of course, her prerogative. I wonder if she'll ask us to leave or hand our case to a colleague. "Now, how can I help you and your... recent wife?" Her lips curl into a professional smile that's almost a snarl as she takes a seat at the head of the table, but her eyes remain arctic.

I take a seat beside Alessia. "Alessia and I recently married in Albania, and she needs indefinite leave to stay here."

Leticia taps scarlet nails on the table, and I remember her brandishing them as a weapon.

Mate! I banish that thought. Pronto.

"Tell me. How did the two of you meet? And when?"

I glance at Alessia with what I hope is a reassuring smile, but she doesn't return it. She swallows and stares down at her hands, which are knotted in her lap. With a sigh, I turn my attention back to Leticia.

"Alessia worked for me..."

While Maxim summarizes the last few months' events to the attractive lawyer, Alessia is trying to stay afloat. She feels like a block of cement sinking beneath the weight of Maxim's past liaisons, and she's struggling to breathe.

Darling, he's slept with most of London.

It appears that Caroline was not exaggerating.

Ticia, Leticia—whatever her name is—is older, a mature, elegant woman with intelligent hazel eyes that give nothing away as she makes notes on the lined paper pad. Her voice is soft with an accent Alessia doesn't recognize. She seems to be a woman who does not suffer fools gladly and has something of her nana's spirit—an underlying grit—that's attractive.

Is that what led Maxim to her?

Alessia tries to shake off the thought. She would not want this woman as an adversary, but as an ally—who's slept with her husband, her crimson nails raking his back.

O Zot. Do not think of this.

Maxim tells the lawyer everything.

The trafficking.

The arrest of Dante and Ylli.

Anatoli. The kidnapping.

His trek to Albania.

The speed at which they were wed and the questionable legitimacy of their marriage.

Leticia holds up her hand, interrupting Maxim. "Were you coerced into this marriage?" she asks Alessia directly. Maxim scowls and opens his mouth to speak, but she silences him with a look. "Let your wife speak, Lord Trevethick."

"No!" Alessia says. "Not at all. If anything…it's the…um… other way."

"You were coerced?" Leticia scoffs, looking at Maxim.

"No," he says in a rush. "Her father has an intimidating shotgun, but I went to Albania to marry Alessia. For love."

A lessia raises her head and, much to my relief, offers me the ghost of a smile. Leticia notices and sits back in her chair, looking a tad more relaxed.

"So, you married within a week."

"Yes."

She raises her brows. "I see. Do you have the marriage certificate?"

I fish the documents from my inside breast pocket. "I do. And an apostille."

Leticia gives them a cursory glance. "Good," she mutters. "I'll need a copy of these so we can have them translated. Also, copies of your passports."

I hand them over.

Leticia looks through her notes. "To be clear," she says, regarding Alessia, "you were illegally trafficked into the country?"

"Yes. With other girls."

"Others? Did they escape too?"

"I don't know," Alessia says quietly, her voice laced with guilt.

"Lady Trevethick, this is not your fault," Leticia says, her voice firm. "Now, is there any evidence of the trafficking?"

"The men. They were arrested," Alessia says.

"It's an ongoing case," I add.

"Ah. In the press recently? Part of a ring?"

"Yes," I reply.

"I've read about it."

"They took everything. My passport…" Alessia's voice fades.

Leticia eyes her sympathetically. "Well, that could be a fly in the ointment if your old passport surfaces, but we'll deal with that should it arise."

"What's the worst-case scenario?" I ask.

"Well, I suppose there's a risk that Lady Trevethick could be deported."

"What!" I glance at Alessia who's now ashen.

"Lord Trevethick, it's a slight risk, but I think we'd have a strong case to keep her here, and we're certainly not there yet." She looks from me to Alessia, and she seems more predisposed to both of us. "The validity of your marriage might be an issue if any bad actors discover that official protocols weren't followed."

"That's why we'd like to get married again. Here. So there's no doubt," I respond.

"That's not possible. Under English law, there's only one valid ceremony of marriage that creates the status of marriage, and you have what looks like a legitimate marriage certificate that has been certified with this apostille. If you marry again, your second marriage won't be legally recognized."

"Oh, I didn't realize that."

"You'll have to have the original marriage annulled to get married again. You could have a blessing here if it's that important to you. But"—she examines our marriage certificate and the apostille again—"I think we need to trust the Albanian authorities and the certificate you've been given. This looks very much in order."

"Okay." The skepticism is clear in my tone—this isn't what I expected. "My only issue is the considerable press interest," I continue. "I don't want any zealous reporters digging around and finding out about the speed at which we got married."

"Is that likely?"

"There was a flock of press outside our building today."

"Ah. I see. Okay, let's cross that bridge should we need to." She turns to Alessia and addresses her directly. "First, we need to switch you from your visitor's visa before we can contemplate applying for a family visa for you. Unless you'd consider returning to Albania and applying for the spousal visa from there?"

No," Maxim says immediately.

Ticia's lips press together. "Lord Trevethick, I was addressing your wife."

Maxim scowls but clamps his mouth shut and remains silent.

"How long would I have to go for?" Alessia asks.

"Well, if it's fast-tracked, you can usually get a visa within thirty or so days. You'll have to do an English test, and Lord Trevethick has to meet a minimum income threshold." Ticia glances at Maxim. "I think we can safely assume that you do that and have adequate accommodation in the UK."

"I do," Maxim snaps.

"So, do you want to return to Albania?"

"No. I'd rather stay with Maxim."

"Okay. Then the alternative might be studying in this country. Have you thought about that?"

Alessia is pensive in the cab back to Chelsea. She's not said a word since we left Leticia's offices. The traffic is sluggish at Westminster, and I check the time. It's 5:30—the height of rush hour. I have more missed calls and texts, including one from Caro, that I'm ignoring. Joe has forwarded a short article from one of the London evening tabloids. It's speculation about our marriage and it's illustrated with a photograph of me entering my building from earlier today. Since when did I become so interesting? It's pissing me off.

And I still haven't had a response from my mother.

And I'm getting the silent treatment from Alessia.

Could this day get any worse?

"Do you want to go out to eat?" I ask, in the hope of getting her to talk.

Alessia is gazing up at Big Ben as we round the square. "I'm not hungry," she says.

"Alessia. Look at me."

She turns dark, wounded eyes to me that slice through my soul. "What is it? I don't know what you're thinking. It's driving me crazy."

"You had a relationship with the lawyer?"

"No. She was a one-night stand. Just sex. Once."

Well, more than once that night if we want pinpoint accuracy.

Alessia glances at the cabbie.

"He can't hear us."

"Maxim, I am trying to…ugh…my English." She closes her eyes in frustration.

"Tell me."

She squares her shoulders and turns her dark gaze on me again. "You have a…colorful past, with many lovers. And I don't know why that hurts me so much. I think…um…I am anxious that I am not enough for you. Or you will become bored with me."

There. She said it. Her darkest fear out between them.

Maxim scoots across the cab's back seat and grasps her chin, so she's pinned by his intense green gaze. He leans in. "Never," he says with such conviction that Alessia feels a frisson of alarm. "You own me. Body and soul. Fuck's sake, Alessia!" He releases her and leans forward, placing his head in his hands.

She blows out a breath, startled by his vehemence. "You're angry with me."

"No. I'm angry at myself, but I don't think it's deserved."

"No," she says quietly. "It's not. I'm sorry."

He looks up and gives her a crooked smile. "You don't need to apologize. Like I said, I have a past. Look, let's just go home. It's been a shit day. A really shit day."

Alessia places a hand on his arm. "It's not so bad a day."

"No?" Maxim sits back.

"This morning, I talked to my mother. She's…um…basking— is that the right word?—in the glow…afterglow of the wedding. It is the talk of Kukës. She's happy. My father is happy."

"That's the right word. I'm glad your parents are happy. And it looks like we don't need to get married again, though I wouldn't mind. I would marry you over and over to the end of time if I could."

Alessia blows out a breath in awe at his words and rewards him with a hesitant smile. "I would marry you again too. But it is a relief not to organize another wedding so soon. We have done it once."

Maxim takes her hand. "We have. And it was a beautiful wedding. It's official. We're married. Our lawyer said so."

"And this afternoon, we did a duet together."

Maxim's lips curl into a dazzling smile. "That was exhilarating. You're so talented and easy to follow." He stops. "You've had no formal musical training, yes?" He squeezes her hand and releases it.

"None. I learned at home. You know this."

"Well, not that you need it. But have you ever thought of music school? Here. In London, to formalize everything you've learned?"

Alessia stares at him, nonplussed, as she tries to weigh his words.

"You could study. We could get you a student visa for that."

Study. Music. In London.

Alessia's heart starts to pound with sudden excitement. "That would be expensive."

Maxim snorts. "I think we can afford it," he says drily.

See. Not such a bad day." She beams broadly at me, and her delight is infectious.

"No." I grin back. "Let's do some research when we get home. Etiquette and music. We'll find something."

And just like that, my spirits lift and the atmosphere between us is transformed.

Only two shifty characters, both carrying cameras, are outside our building when we return home. I ask the cabbie to drop us in Tite Street, as I have a Cunning Plan.

Once the cab has left us, Alessia walks around the corner and heads into the building. Of course, the paps have no idea who she is, and they give her a cursory glance, although from my vantage point, I watch one of them ogle her as she walks past him in her tight, figure-hugging jeans.

Dirty bastard.

Once she's inside, I follow, head down, ignoring their questions. I walk briskly into the building and join Alessia inside the lift.

"You have no idea how much of a kick I got out of that." I chuckle. "They didn't have a clue that my mysterious wife walked right by them."

The doors close behind us, and it's just us in the small space. Her eyes meet mine, peering up through her lashes, a smile teasing her lips, and everything tightens in my groin.

"Feeling happier?"

She nods and reaches for my jacket, tugging me toward her. Her hands snake around my head, and her lips meet mine. We kiss. Long. Hard. And I push her up against the wall, pressing my greedy dick against her belly while our tongues slip and slide against each other.

"Maxim," she breathes and shifts, so she runs her fingers over my fly, tracing my erection through denim.

Ah!

The lift stops, the doors open, and I pick her up. "Wrap your legs around me, baby." She complies, her fingers tangled in my hair, our lips locked, as I carry her the short distance from the lift to our front door.

Alessia giggles as Maxim reaches around her thigh into his jeans pocket for the key to the front door. "Not much room in my jeans," he grumbles, retrieving his key and unlocking the door while holding her. The alarm beeps, but he disarms it, carries Alessia into the hallway, and sets her on her feet.

"As much as I want to take you to bed, let's look at music colleges."

"No. Let's go to bed."

He draws back, his expression blank in apparent surprise. "But—"

"No. Bed." Alessia is more insistent.

He frowns and grasps her head, lifting her face to his, his intense green gaze on hers. For a moment, he looks lost and confused, but he closes his eyes.

"What did I do to deserve you?" he breathes, and then his lips are on hers, his tongue taking hers as he walks her backward into the bedroom. As their tongues wrestle, he keeps moving until Alessia feels the bed at her calves. He stops and, with a wicked carnal smile, gently pushes her onto it so she falls back flat on the bed, a strand of her hair settling on her face.

Maxim stands over her, removes his jacket, and tosses it on the floor. With blazing eyes, he yanks his shirt from his jeans and starts to undo the buttons. Slowly. One at a time. His lips are parted, soft and sensual, his breathing measured but increasing.

Alessia licks her lips in anticipation.

Once his shirt is flapping open, revealing the tanned and toned torso beneath, he raises a cuff of his sleeve and undoes that... then the other.

He's stripping for her.

At a wanton and leisurely pace.

Alessia watches. Captivated. Her gaze drinks him in: his broad chest, with its smattering of hair, the toned abs, the trail of hair from his belly that heads down beneath the waistband of his jeans.

His eyes don't leave hers. He's not even touching her and she's seduced, her arousal spreading between her legs and making her squirm. He draws off his shirt, in the way he does, over his head, so it ruffles his hair, messing it up just the way she likes it. Then he discards the garment on the floor without a care in the world.

He undoes the button of his jeans.

And stops.

No!

He leans forward and grabs her ankle—adroitly removing her ankle boot and sock. He then repeats the process with her other boot, running his thumb down her instep when her foot is naked and making her squirm.

He leans over and undoes her jeans. Deftly. He's so quick that he's grabbed the hems of her jeans and yanked them off before she can take a breath. He deposits them with his clothes on the floor.

"You. Your jeans." She waves toward his groin.

Maxim grins and slowly unzips his fly, but he doesn't remove his pants. He steps out of his shoes and removes his socks. Then he sweeps off his jeans and underwear so he's free in all his glory.

Alessia gasps and Maxim moves onto the bed and plants a soft wet kiss at the juncture of her thighs through the soft cotton of her panties. The contact sends a jolt of electricity through her body so that she gasps once more, her fingers tangling in his hair. He strokes his nose up and down along her most precious seam, his stubble prickling her thighs.

"Your panties are wet, sweet Alessia. I like. I like that a lot."

He nips the inside of her thigh, his lips sheathing his teeth, and Alessia tightens her hands in his hair and tugs.

He kneels up between her legs, pulls her into a sitting position, and quickly divests her of her jacket and her long-sleeved T-shirt. They go the way of the rest of their clothes, so Alessia's left in her bra and panties.

She reaches up and strokes his stubbled chin.

"Do you want me to shave?" he asks.

"No. I like. Muchly." She gently rakes her fingernails across his cheek, and he closes his eyes.

"I have an idea," he whispers, and grasping her head once

more, he kisses her. His tongue is insistent, dominating and subduing hers as he lies them both down. His fingers tug down the cup of her bra, freeing her aching breast, and abandoning her mouth, he leaves a trail of wet kisses down her throat, across her chest to the straining peak of her nipple.

Desire courses through her veins, and she turns dark eyes to blazing green as he strokes his chin across the sensitive bud.

Ah!

"Sure you don't want me to shave?" he teases, and he does it again, his eyes never leaving hers.

"No!" she cries out as her nipple hardens and lengthens beneath his assault.

"Feel good?"

"Yes." Her pulse is racing, pumping blood to her breasts, swelling her nipples that ache for his touch, and also to the small powerhouse at the junction of her thighs. "Please!"

He does it again, and she arches her back into his touch.

He grins, tugs down the bra cup shielding her other breast, and begins the same tortuous motion, brushing his stubble over her super-sensitized skin.

She clutches the duvet as his lips and stubble head south, and he nestles between her thighs. He kisses her, *there…*

Then slowly draws down her panties and kisses her *there. Again.*

This time, circling the swollen bud with his tongue.

O Zot!

Alessia closes her eyes and arches her back, and his tongue continues its leisurely assault. Round and round. Licking and sucking.

Ah!

He stops and draws his chin over that sensitive spot, his stubble wreaking havoc with her nerve endings.

"Të lutem!"

"English," he warns. And he does it again.

"Please. Maxim."

He sits up, drags off her panties, and flips her over and undoes her bra.

He lies down on top of her, his erection nestling in the cleft of her behind.

"Shall I take you this way?"

"Yes!"

"You sound like you're in need."

"I am."

She senses his smile at her ear, and gently he tugs her earlobe with his teeth. "God, I love you, Alessia. Wife. Of mine." He pushes her knees apart with his and tugs her backside toward him. He trails a finger down between her cheeks, and her muscles tighten as it trails over and past her arse.

"One day, Alessia," he whispers and then his thumb is inside her, pushing at that sweet spot deep, deep within her. His fingers at her clitoris. Circling. Teasing. Tormenting.

She makes a strangled sound as her body convulses around his thumb. Her orgasm surprising her and spiraling through her limbs.

Maxim withdraws his thumb and flips her back over. With her dazed eyes on his, he slowly enters her, absorbing the last of her shock waves.

He groans his approval and starts to move. Hard. Fast. Taking her higher. So she doesn't have a chance to land. She's flying once more, driven by him. Pushed onward and upward by him. He looms over her. Sweat breaking on his brow. He's relentless. Taking her higher and higher. Her legs stiffen once more, and she cries out as she climaxes a second time. More intense and more draining. Alessia thinks she can see heaven.

"Thank God," Maxim churns out between gritted teeth, and he comes and comes, collapsing on her and holding her close.

Alessia opens her eyes as Maxim eases out of her, leaving a silky, slick trail of his seed across her upper thigh. She doesn't care. She revels in it.

He kisses her brow and smooths damp strands from her forehead. "Okay?" he asks.

"More than okay," she whispers.

He strokes his knuckles down her cheek. "Don't ever think you're not enough. Please. It breaks my heart to hear you say that. I love you. Don't forget it. This feeling is new for me too. I've only felt it since I met you."

She leans up and kisses him. "I know."

"Do you?" He looks lost all of a sudden.

She nods quickly to reassure him.

Nothing's changed, Alessia.

He loves you.

Maxim's smile is cautious. "Good. Look. I can span an Alessia. You're an octave." He stretches his hand out, the tips of his thumb and little finger brushing her nipples. He grins, and she giggles, enjoying his boyishness. "I could lie here and look at you all day, but I need the loo." He gives her a quick peck, rises from the bed, and heads into the bathroom.

Alessia watches him move with his usual athletic grace, his muscular backside pale against his tan.

She sighs as she's still coming back to earth.

He is an exceptional lover.

Not that she has any experience and no one to compare him to… but Caroline's words haunt her. *Promiscuous doesn't cover it. He's proof of the adage: Practice makes perfect.*

Alessia wraps herself in the duvet.

Maxim is *her* lover. *Her* husband. And only *hers.*

He said so…

That should be enough.

But that nagging voice persists. *For how long?*

Chapter Fourteen

The Thames reflections flicker on the ceiling, taunting me as they've done over the years. I can't sleep, though Alessia is comatose beside me. I envy her ability to sleep, but we've made love twice this evening—my desperation driving me to take my wife, so she's exhausted. I want her safe and happy, and I want her to know that I worship the ground she walks on.

Hell, if she knew about Kit, would she leave me?

As much as I've tried to quell the thoughts, my brain continues to chew on the information that Caro sprung on me today, and it won't leave me alone. Carefully, so as not to wake Alessia, I ease myself out of bed, grab my phone and sweatpants from the sofa, and head out to the drawing room. There, I pull them on and stand at the window, staring blankly out at the night.

I've called my mother. Again. And she's not answered.

The woman is fucking useless.

She's the only one who may be able to shed light on this situation. Perhaps Kit talked to her? Confided in her? She thought the sun rose and set with Kit, so they were close.

Sadly, I couldn't find a way to please Rowena when I was young.

Dude. Move on.

I'm tempted to call Maryanne, but I don't want to worry her, and she mentioned she was on nights this week—so she'll be busy right now. The woman works too hard, considering she doesn't have to.

Placing my fist against the cold glass, I lean my forehead against it, stare out at the darkness, and reflect on the day, starting last night with Alessia's meltdown in her sleep. How can I burden her with Caroline's revelation when she's still having nightmares? She doesn't need to know this... not yet, anyway. Especially as she's having doubts about me and my—what did she call it— *colorful* past.

The women.

I hope to God I've reassured her. I don't know what else I can do.

Despite the silent treatment earlier, my sweet wife has been the saving grace of today—joining her while she played *Claire de Lune.* Making love. And her cooking. This evening she made a delicious lamb and aubergine concoction. She's a magician in the kitchen, but I think her father was right; she's going to make me fat—though we burnt off some calories tonight...so, there's that.

A vision of Alessia on top of me, grasping my wrists, tipping her head back and crying out in ecstasy invades my thoughts, arousing my libido, and leaving me hot and heavy with need. I contemplate returning to bed, waking her, and losing myself in her again.

Mate. Let her sleep.

But these fleeting feelings of joy evaporate quickly. As I stare across the glimmering dark river to Battersea Park, I feel numb as my mind gnaws at the news about Kit.

Health-wise I'm fine—in fact, I've never felt better.

But is something awful going to afflict me in later life? Or did this genetic issue, whatever it was, solely affect Kit?

I keep returning to the same depressing theory. Is this why he was riding his motorcycle through the icy lanes? Was the news so devastating that he thought *Fuck it* and let rip on his Ducati, the turbocharged beast that was his pride and joy?

I have no idea.

And if the news was that bad, does that mean I'll suffer horribly? Will Maryanne?

Fuck.

Thank God for contraception.

Until we find out what's happening, I can't contemplate kids. Can I?

Shit. This uncertainty. This ignorance. This powerlessness. It's torture.

Nothing's changed.

My rational self tries to reassure me.

But that's not true. The path I thought I was set on has altered entirely.

Mate, you don't know that yet.

Hell.

I open my texts and notice the one that Caroline sent earlier.

You look good, Maxim.
You always do.
I'm sure this is nothing to worry about.

I ignore her compliment.

Can't sleep.
Keep thinking about Kit.

Me too.

Sorry about today.

You don't need to apologise.
Where's the Albanian?

> Fuck off, Caro.
>
> You make that sound offensive.
>
> My beloved wife Alessia is asleep.

FFS! Chill. She's Albanian!

> Good night.

Maxim, don't be like that.
In spite of the why, it was
good seeing you today.
I miss you.
Cx

What does that mean? In disgust, I toss the phone on the sofa, not wanting to deal with Caro's shit and wondering why I even texted her in the first place. Returning to Alessia, I slip into bed.

As I do, she stirs. "Maxim," she whispers sleepily.

"Hush. Go back to sleep, baby."

She shuffles over, so I'm forced to put my arm around her, and she lays her head on my chest. "I've got you," she murmurs, fighting sleep.

A tangled knot of emotion forms in my throat as I feel her slip away and settle back into her dreams, and I've never felt as grateful for my wife as I do now.

My love. I kiss her hair and close my eyes as a knot of fear and regret forms in my throat. Will we make it through this? Whatever it is?

I breathe in her fragrance, and it's a balm to my misery.

I've got you. Those words, in her accent, float through my brain, soothing me, and I drift.

The following crisp, chilly morning, I walk to my doctor's, which is a few streets away from our flat, for my appointment and hopefully some answers. The brisk, efficient receptionist ushers me into his consulting room as soon as I arrive.

Dr. Renton is wearing his usual sharp suit and red bowtie. In his sixties, with lank, thinning hair, he stands when I enter his office and waves me to a chair in front of his desk. "What can I do for you, Lord Trevethick?" He gives me his familiar avuncular smile as he resumes his seat.

"My brother. Genetic counseling. What do you know?"

"Ah." His bushy gray eyebrows shoot up his forehead—he's taken aback. He leans forward in his chair, and his eyebrows make the return journey as he frowns. Propping his elbows on his desk, he rests his chin on his hands. "I can't help you, my lord."

"What?"

"Your brother, for whatever reason, has decided not to impart information to you, and as his doctor, I cannot breach his privacy. I have a duty of care to him."

My mouth falls open in disbelief. Feeling winded, I watch dumbfounded as he folds his hands in his lap and sits patiently, waiting for me to say something. "Your response is unacceptable. My brother is no longer with us."

"I'm sorry, Maxim. There's nothing I can do. As part of his genetic counseling, prior to being tested, your brother will have discussed the implications and whether or not to tell his immediate relatives."

"But surely—"

"My hands are tied."

"I've just got married."

"Congratulations."

"For fuck's sake, Renton."

His blue eyes narrow, and his voice hardens. "There's no call for that kind of language, my lord."

I huff in frustration, and in my mind, I'm back in my House Master's office at Eton, being admonished for some minor deed.

Renton sighs. "Do you have any health concerns?" He's changing tack.

What? "No."

"That's your answer. I suggest you put all this behind you and respect your brother's decision."

"Did Kit kill himself because of his diagnosis?"

Renton blanches. "Maxim, the late Lord Trevethick died in a dreadful accident."

"Exactly. He won't know that you've told me! And what about your duty of care to me? I'm your patient too."

"But you're not sick," he says gently.

I glare at him, hoping to intimidate him into changing his mind, but as he sits back with his benevolent smile, I realize he's not budging.

Well, how bloody inconvenient is this?

A part of me admires that he's not willing to breach my brother's confidence, so I place a tight lid on my temper and change the subject. "I'll need to register my wife here." I sound petulant.

"I can't wait to meet her," Renton says kindly. "Will that be all, my lord?"

I get up to leave. "I'm disappointed you can't help me."

"I'm sorry to disappoint you, Maxim."

My mood is bleak as the black cab trundles through the traffic on the way to the office. I'm furious at Renton. Perhaps it's time to find someone new—someone a little younger.

Someone less ethical?

Hell.

My phone buzzes with a text. It's my mother. Finally!

Just touched down at LHR.
Need sleep.
I'll call you later.

Fuck! No. I press Dial, and her number goes straight to bloody voicemail. "Rowena. Call me. This is not a fucking request." I hang up and glare out of the cab window. The bright, sunny morning seems to mock my mood.

My mother is driving me insane.

Why won't she talk to me?

As the cab pulls up outside the office, I take a deep breath and bring my irritation under control. I pay the driver and stride up the steps into the building.

Oliver has forwarded details of three properties that are either vacant or soon to be vacant for Alessia and me to consider. I peruse them at my desk, welcoming the distraction as I sip black coffee. One is a mews house that's smaller than my flat—so I disregard that immediately.

The other two have potential as family homes.

Hell.

I want kids—one day. Part of my job is to protect the family's legacy. But if there's something wrong with me, how can I consider having a family?

Yet, Renton asked me how I was feeling.

Maybe that was his coded way of saying I don't have anything to worry about.

Mate. Get a grip.

I push my fears about children aside and decide to stay hopeful.

It's time to move. We need the space. My wild single days are over.

Who knew I'd be content to stay home, eat home-cooked food, and make love to my wife?

It'll be good for Alessia too.

In a new place, we'll be able to forge our own path where there are no memories of my colorful and dissolute past. It's an unsettling idea, mainly because it's accompanied by a pang of lingering guilt.

Why?

I've not done anything wrong.

Have I?

I shake off the thought.

Looking through the details of the properties, the house on Cheyne Walk has a distinct advantage. At the end of the back garden, there's a mews house with a garage that can house two cars. We could use it for staff. I've not raised the issue of having help with Alessia yet, but it will mean that *that* part of her life will be history. I'll always have fond recollections of pink knickers and blue housecoats, but she'll be busy with other things—music school, with any luck. The additional advantage of the Cheyne Walk house is it's between my flat and Trevelyan House, where Caroline lives.

Perhaps I should ask Caro to swap. She could take my flat or another, smaller property. Trevelyan House is mine, after all.

No. It's too soon since Kit's demise to broach that subject.

Picking up the phone, I press Caroline's number.

"Hello, Maxim." She sounds sniffy and aloof. Maybe it's because I scolded her via text yesterday.

I feign ignorance. "Hi, what's wrong?"

"You're all over the press. And they've been calling here. About you. And Alessia."

"Shit. I'm sorry. Just ignore them."

"I am. You should do something. Perhaps host a sort of 'coming-out' party for your wife. Invite everyone, and then you'll be done with all this fevered interest."

The last thing I want or need is the press digging into our hasty marriage.

But I can't let Caro know that!

"That's not a bad idea." I throw her off the scent.

"I could organize it for you!" she says enthusiastically.

Hmm… not sure how Alessia would feel about that.

"Let me think about it. I'm calling because it's crunch time with the Mayfair mansion block refurbishment. Do you want to do the interior design?"

Caroline takes a deep breath. "Yes. I do. It will give me something to focus on and put me back in that world. I've missed it."

"Good. I'm glad."

"Besides, I might need the money," she adds, sounding more like her usual spirited self.

"Caro, you have a huge trust fund and the stipend from the estate."

She snorts, unimpressed, but neither one of us mentions Kit's will, and how he left her out of it.

Dude, don't go there.

"I'll get Oliver to call and deal with the details."

"Oliver!" she says as if she's surprised.

"Of course. He can put you in touch with the developer. Okay?" What is her problem with him?

"Yes. Yes. You're right. Have you told Alessia about the letters?"

"Not yet. Have you spoken to Rowena?"

"No. Why?"

"She's avoiding me. I've left her countless voice messages, and she's not returning my calls."

"Rowena… is Rowena."

"True enough. Any luck with Kit's laptop? I've drawn a complete blank."

"Even with Dr. Renton?"

"He wouldn't tell me."

"The tight-lipped old bastard!"

"Exactly."

"No luck with the laptop. Fact is, Kit never gave me any of the safe combinations. Not for here or for the Hall. Why do you think that is?" Her voice wavers as she finishes her question, and I realize she's upset.

"I don't know. Kit was Kit… a bit like his mother."

"Yes. He was…" Caroline's voice has dropped to a barely audible whisper, and I want to kick myself.

"I'll think about the party idea."

"Do," she responds, brightening. "You know, you should let me take Alessia shopping."

Oh, I'm not sure that's a good idea.

"Maxim, I told you, she dresses like a student."

"Funny you should say that. I'm hoping to get her into college. It will help with her visa. That reminds me. Your stepmother—"

"Stepsow," she corrects me.

"Isn't she a patron of the Royal College?"

"Yes. Ah. Music. For Alessia?"

"Yes. What do you think?"

"I think it's a good idea. Alessia is obviously hugely talented."

"Well, I may need to lean on the Stepsow."

Caroline snorts. "Good luck with that. I've never known her to be helpful or amenable. I don't know what my father sees in her."

Caro is always complaining about her father's wife.

"Did you attend etiquette lessons?" I change the subject.

"Of course I did. Kit insisted. He was a bit of a bore about it, actually."

I gasp, shocked. *Kit? A bore?*

"Yes. Just after we got married."

Kit insisted his wife sign up for etiquette lessons!

What a snob. I had no idea.

"Alessia wants to go."

"It's a good idea. It'll give her some confidence. It did for me. The one I went to was great. In Kensington. I'll send you the details."

"Thanks. And to be clear, this is Alessia's idea, not mine."

"You're so woke, Maxim," Caro grumbles. "My offer stands. I'd be happy to take her to Harvey Nicks. With your credit card." She cackles.

And I find myself smiling reluctantly. "I'll talk to her."

"Good. I need to make amends."

"Yes, you do."

Oliver knocks on the door and enters.

"Gotta go." I hang up and look directly at him. "I've spoken to Caroline. She's up for the interior design."

"I'm glad that's settled. Here are the details of your mother's expenditure against the estate." He hands me a spreadsheet, and the bottom line leaps off the page in all its profligacy.

What the fuck!

I glance at him in shock.

"Yes." His lips are a thin line of disapproval.

"Is this part of her divorce settlement?"

"Here." He hands me another document. "I've highlighted the figures you need."

I scan it quickly.

Wow. A disquieting void lodges in my stomach as I intrude on my parents' private affairs. Their divorce killed my father. He died of a broken heart, and I've never forgiven my mother for his death. "This is more than double her allowance."

"Yes, my lord."

"Okay. I'll deal with this."

"Good luck with that, my lord." He gives me a sympathetic smile and exits.

I call my mother and get her voicemail again. "Rowena. I'm about to cut off your access to estate funds. Call me." I hang up, then call the bank and have a quick word about my mother with my bank manager.

Next, I text Maryanne.

> Please ask your mother to call me.
> I have left numerous messages.
> All to no avail.

I need answers. And I'm stunned that my own mother won't do me the courtesy of returning my call. Life as I knew it hangs in the balance—all my hopes and vague dreams on hold.

Hell.

If this tactic doesn't work, I don't know what will.

Alessia has unpacked, cleaned, and put away all the new cookware she and Maxim ordered online from John Lewis. She's cleaned. Polished. Washed. Everything. The place is spotless. She's prepped dinner. She's practiced several pieces on the piano. She's now sitting at Maxim's desk, poring over the computer comparing music courses, and making notes. As she considers the merits of the Royal Academy versus the Royal College, her eyes stray to Ticia Cavanagh's business card perched on the desk. She recalls the lawyer's shocked statement yesterday.

Others? Did they escape too?

Bleriana's sweet face, laughing at one of Alessia's jokes while they were in the back of that awful, stinking truck, rises in her mind. Perhaps Ticia could help find her. She's a lawyer. She would know. Wouldn't she?

Ignoring her conflicted feelings—this woman has had carnal knowledge of her husband—she fishes out her phone and dials her number.

"Ticia Cavanagh's office," a male voice answers.

"Hello. Um. This is Alessia Trevelyan. I wanted to speak to Ticia Cavanagh."

"I'll see if she's available."

The line goes quiet but a moment later, Ticia answers. "Lady Trevethick, what can I do for you?"

"Please, call me Alessia. Um...I'm, er..."

"Is it about your husband?" Cavanagh asks in a stilted breathy rush.

"No. No. It's not. I think...um...your...acq...acquaintance predates me." Alessia cannot believe that she's discussing Maxim in this way. There's an awkward moment of silence, where Alessia hears Ticia inhale sharply.

"I think so too," she says eventually, and her response is a relief.

To the matter in hand, Alessia.

"I am calling about the other girls who were trafficked with me. I want to find them. Well, one of them at least. If I can find the others, that would be good too."

"I see. I'm not sure I can help, but what can you tell me?"

Alessia sits back in Maxim's chair and stares down at her notes. Ticia has given her the number of a private investigator her firm uses. They're discreet but expensive. She wants to call them; after all, she now has the means. But should she ask Maxim first? By rights, it is his money. Would he approve of the plan? She doesn't know. Perhaps, like Ticia, he would think it's impossible as Bleriana and the other girls could be anywhere in the country.

But Alessia has to try.

Also, it will give her *something* to do.

As much as she enjoys being in the apartment, she's beginning to feel a little claustrophobic. She needs to get out.

But should she tell her husband?

Her phone buzzes, and it's as if she's conjured Maxim to call her just by thinking about him.

"Hi," he says, and the warmth in his voice heats her heart.

"Hi. How is work?" He left early this morning, and he was preoccupied with something. Alessia assumed it was his work.

"It's okay. I have a surprise for you. I'm going to text you an address. It's a short walk from the flat. I'll meet you there in half an hour." She suspects he's grinning. He's excited about something.

"Okay," she says, grinning back.

"Thirty minutes." He hangs up, and a text appears on her screen. It's an address on Cheyne Walk, meaning she has long enough to make a phone call and begin her mission to find Bleriana.

I pace outside the house on Cheyne Walk to keep warm and glance up the street to see if I can spot Alessia. Our potential new home is set back behind the greenery of Chelsea Embankment Gardens, which means—provided Alessia likes this place—I won't have to suffer the watery reflections that occasionally torment me on my bedroom ceiling. I hope she likes it; I think it will serve our needs well.

Through the shrubbery, I catch glimpses of the Thames. Pausing, I breathe in a lungful of air, detecting the muddy tang of the river that's so grounding and familiar.

It's home.

When I look, Alessia is heading toward me down the street. Her face lights up when she sees me, and I jog to meet her.

"Hi." I grab her hand. "Come. I'm excited to show you something."

Her answering smile lifts my spirits, and I usher her toward an iron gate. She gives me a questioning look, her curiosity piqued as I tap the keycode into the electronic lock. The gate swings open with a creaky protest, and we walk across the flagstones to the gleaming black front door topped by a splendid fanlight.

Maxim fishes out some keys from his pocket and unlocks the door. "This could be ours if you like it," he says and waves Alessia inside.

The whole house?

It must be four stories high!

They're met by a wide sweeping hallway that opens onto a stylish dining room and beyond into an extensive modern kitchen that's similar to the glass kitchen in Maxim's apartment. Through the sliding french doors at the end of the room, there's a neat, manicured backyard, and at the other end of the yard, what looks like another house.

"Yes. Two houses. We could make that the staff quarters." Maxim points outside.

Staff!

"Oh," says Alessia.

Upstairs there's a sweeping reception room that spans the whole length of the house, tastefully decorated in muted cream, beige, and taupe.

"We can redecorate," Maxim says, his brow furrowed with what Alessia thinks is concern.

"It's lovely," she says automatically.

Alessia's intimidated by the sheer scale of the house. There are five bedrooms, all with their own en suites. The principal suite comprises a large bedroom, a bathroom with two sinks—in marble—an egg-shaped tub, a shower big enough for four people, and two walk-in closets that would more than serve her and Maxim's needs.

"What do you think?" Maxim eyes her anxiously.

"You want to move here?"

"Yes. We need the space."

"Five bedrooms?"

"You'd prefer something smaller?" He frowns.

"I had not thought somewhere so big… I suppose one day, we'll have children." She flushes at the thought, though she doesn't know why.

"Yes. One day," he says quietly and closes his eyes as if this is a painful idea.

"One day," Alessia responds, wondering why this should be a painful thought for him. "You do want children. Yes?"

He nods, but his eyes say something else. He's fearful.

Why?

"Could we put a piano in here?" Alessia asks brightly to distract him.

He laughs. "Of course. I'm not leaving the baby grand behind. Let me show you the basement."

H and in hand, we walk back to the flat.

"Have you lived there before?" Alessia asks.

"No. I've never even been inside until today."

"Do you like it?"

"Yes." I squeeze her hand. "Do you? We can make our own memories there."

Alessia regards me with—awe, relief—I don't know, but she offers me a beautiful smile. "Yes. It will be just us."

We round the corner, and I'm relieved to see no paparazzi lingering outside the front of the building. We're yesterday's news.

As we head into the flat, my phone buzzes.

It's my mother. *Finally.*

Chapter Fifteen

"It's Rowena. I need to take this," I mutter, and leaving Alessia to close the front door, I head into the privacy of our bedroom and answer the phone. "Rowena. Thank you *so much* for returning my call." My sarcasm is heavily laced through every word.

"Maxim. Your messages are insufferably rude. Why would I want to talk to you? And what the fuck do you mean, you've cut me off?"

Swearing now! My mother is in a snit.

"Exactly what I said. I rang you days ago, and you've not replied. *That's* insufferably rude."

"Once you've learned to be a little more gracious when leaving messages, you'll receive a quicker response. You'll catch more flies with honey than vinegar, Maxim. Surely a man of your appetites understands that."

What!

"Lord help the estate with you barking down the phone at everyone," she continues.

"That makes you the fly in this analogy," I snap. "And it's only you that elicits that response, Mother. And I don't think you're one to preach about appetites!"

She inhales sharply. "So you've cut me off to bring me to heel?"

"No. I've cut you off because you're overspending the allowance you're entitled to under your divorce settlement." She's silent on the other end of the phone, and I know she's seething. "Did you think I wouldn't notice? Perhaps Kit let you get away with it." Again I don't get a response—and this isn't helping my cause. I take a deep calming breath in an attempt to bring my temper under control. "But this isn't why I called. Did you know that Kit was seeing a genetic counselor?"

There's an audible gasp on the other end of the phone. "What?" she whispers, and I know by her quiet tone that she's been shocked into next week.

"Yes. I was hoping you could enlighten me as to why."

"No." She chokes back a gut-wrenching exclamation that makes my scalp tingle and my entire attitude shift.

"What do you mean no? What do you know?" I sound breathless.

"This is nothing to do with you, Maxim. Nothing. Just forget it." She's curt and panicked.

"What do you mean?"

"Forget about it!" she shouts, and the line goes dead.

She's hung up on me!

She's never done that before, and she was *shouting*, which is completely out of character—she's normally so cool and detached. I press Redial, and the call goes straight to voicemail. I do it again, with the same result.

Something's wrong. Seriously wrong. I stare at my phone in a chasm of confusion.

What the fuck?

I phone Maryanne and get her voicemail. "M.A., call me. The Mothership is behaving more irrationally than usual."

As I slip my phone into my pocket, it buzzes.

I glance at the screen and answer. "M.A."

"Maxie. What the hell did you say to your mother? She's just slammed the front door as she went out."

Bugger. I have to come clean with my sister.

"My mother! She's your mother too. And I didn't want to bother you with this, Maryanne." I give her a brief explanation about the letters that Caro found from Kit's GP and the genetic counseling place, Dr. Renton's refusal to shed any light, and now our mother's refusal too.

"And you didn't think to tell the only medically qualified person in this family?" Maryanne spits.

"I didn't want to worry you. I know you're busy."

"Maxim! You are such an arse sometimes. What exactly did your mother say?"

"Basically, your mother said it's none of my business."

"That's weird."

"Exactly."

"Oh," Maryanne whispers as if she's just had a rather unappealing thought.

"What?"

"I'll call you back."

"Maryanne—"

She's hung up.

What the hell?

The female members of my family are driving me crazy.

Alessia tries to quell her anxiety but it expands in her chest, causing her heart to race. What's happened? Why is Maxim taking a call from his mother in private? He's not a secretive man generally. Is he? But what does he not want her to hear? What does he have to hide?

She heads into the kitchen so she's not tempted to press her ear to the door and listen. To divert her thoughts, she busies herself with final preparations for dinner. But her mind turns to how preoccupied Maxim has been over the last couple of days.

Except in bed.

She frowns at the thought. She figured his absentmindedness was due to the surprise meeting with Ticia Cavanagh and Alessia's subsequent reaction. But maybe not. While they explored music colleges last night on the internet, he'd been distracted by something, so much so that she'd asked him if he wanted to continue. He'd reassured her that he did, but something was bugging him. It still is. She can feel it.

Maxim is leaning against the doorjamb, watching her, when she looks up from grating parmesan. He looks anxious. Bewildered even.

Oh no.

"What is it?" Alessia asks.

Maxim moves into the room and rakes a hand through his hair, leaving it tousled and unkempt, just the way Alessia likes it. But his eyes are wide with disbelief and confusion as if he's wrestling with some inner turmoil.

"What did your mother say?" Alessia prompts.

"She hung up on me." He raises his hands in dismay. "And I need answers from her…" His voice tails off, but he steps forward and brushes his knuckles over her cheek, the contact reverberating enticingly through her body. "It's nothing for you to worry about."

"But you're worried," she murmurs.

His stance changes, his jaw tensing, and he rakes a hand through his hair again, his frustration apparent.

"Do you want to go and see her?"

"It's tempting. Rowena lives with Maryanne when she's in London. They share a townhouse in Mayfair. She bounces between there and an apartment in Manhattan. She's here at the moment." He glances at his watch. "Perhaps I could go and confront her." But his mouth turns down and he shakes his head.

"What answers do you need?"

He blows out a breath. "Honestly, don't worry about it. It's something Caroline showed me on Monday—"

"Caroline?" Alessia's immediately on high alert.

Maxim frowns, and his eyes widen—as if caught in headlights. "Yes. She came to the office with some letters concerning Kit."

"Oh."

Caroline.

Why is she going to see Maxim at his office when Alessia's never been to his office? And Alessia knows it isn't jealousy that's bothering her—she doesn't want her husband alone with his sister-in-law.

His ex-lover.

Because, deep down, she doesn't trust Caroline.

Does she trust her husband? Well, she's only hearing about this visit that took place yesterday.

Alessia ignores the nagging voice in her head while Maxim's lips press together in an angry line and he closes his eyes. When he opens them again, he looks irritated.

"Alessia," he says. "This is nothing for you to worry about. Let's go out. I need a change of scenery. We'll eat out." He sounds exasperated.

"Okay," Alessia capitulates immediately. She can cook the lasagna tomorrow. Or freeze it.

Maxim narrows his eyes. "We can stay in if you want to. You need to tell me what you want to do. This is a partnership." He waves a hand between them, his tone terse.

Is he angry with her?

Alessia suddenly feels they're on the edge of some precipice, and she doesn't know what to say or do.

Why is he so agitated? He didn't tell her about Caroline. Or letters concerning Kit.

How is she supposed to feel about that?

But she can tell he's distraught about something, and she doesn't think it has to do with Caroline, and Alessia doesn't want to add to his worries.

"We can discuss the house," he adds in a gentler tone.

She nods and instinctively reaches out and grabs his hand. "Whatever's going on, you'll figure it out. You always do." She steps into his arms and holds him close.

I'm touched by Alessia's faith in me, though I think it's misplaced. Yet her caress and her words are soothing—the warmth of them spreading through my chest as I gradually relax in her embrace. Holding her close, I kiss her hair, grateful she's with me. "Both my mother and my sister are behaving strangely."

"That sounds…um…frustrating," Alessia says. "We can go out. I'll go and change my clothes."

"You look fine in jeans." I stop, grab her hands, and raise them in midair as if we're about to begin a folk dance. I let my gaze sweep over her body, ignoring the familiar tightening below my gut.

Caro's right.

Alessia needs clothes fit for a countess. Not a student. "Let's go shopping. You need clothes. Proper clothes."

Alessia gapes at him.

"Yeah. Let's do that." I check the time. "Harvey Nicks should be open for another couple of hours."

"But… but… I don't know where we would start."

"There's a personal shopping service. We'll start there."

And it will be a wonderful distraction from all this genetic bollocks.

Alessia's head is spinning. In less than ninety minutes, she's become the proud owner of a "capsule wardrobe" with "key pieces" that will see her through the next few months. The cost is staggering, but Maxim seems delighted, and deep down, so is Alessia. She'll no longer feel like a cleaner when standing beside Caroline.

Maxim scrawls the delivery address on headed notepaper for the personal shopper.

"These will be with you tomorrow morning, Mr. Trevelyan."

The young woman bats her lashes at Maxim, but he ignores her—and doesn't correct her about his title.

"Shall we go eat?" Maxim takes Alessia's hand.

"Yes. And thank you. For all this." Alessia eyes the bags containing her new clothes and shoes.

"You don't have to thank me." He frowns as if a monumental thought has just occurred to him. "I want to provide for you." He leans in and kisses her quickly. "We'll go across the road to the Mandarin Oriental and have dinner there."

Alessia grabs her new Saint Laurent tote, and hand in hand they head out of the store, with Maxim's words ringing through her head.

I want to provide for you.

Alessia is not sure how she feels about this. She wants to be more than a chattel handed from her father to her husband. Her brief bid for freedom when she first came to the UK was an attempt to work for herself. Alas, that failed. But she found Maxim. Except now, she's a little at a loss.

He wants a partnership.

What can she do to contribute to a partnership?

Maxim tightens his hold on her hand, distracting her from her thoughts, and weaves them through the traffic as they cross the road to the magnificent building that is the Mandarin Oriental Hyde Park. "This way," he says, and they walk toward The Aubrey restaurant.

Alessia's tongue pokes out between her lips in studied determination as she grips her chopsticks, and I remember the first time she used them, in Mustique. Chef had prepared a sushi and sashimi extravaganza, and with her on my lap, I'd wrapped my hand around hers as I demonstrated how to use them. As ever, she was a quick learner.

"You've remembered how to use the chopsticks."

She flashes me a quick hopeful smile as she reaches for some hamachi.

"So you like the house?"

"How could I not like the house, Maxim? It's beautiful."

"Good. Then I'll make arrangements to have us move in. But if you want it redecorated, we should do that before we move."

"I like it how it is now. Perhaps we should live there before we decide if it needs decorating."

"That sounds sensible."

My phone buzzes. It's a text from Maryanne.

Mama is at the airport.
She's heading back to New York.

I give Alessia an apologetic glance and text back.

What? Why?

She didn't say.
She texted from the gate.

That's it. No explanation?

None!

What the hell?

She's only just left New York, and now she's on her way back.

"Excuse me," I murmur to Alessia. I leave the table and press my mother's number as I walk into the vestibule. As I feared, her phone goes to voicemail.

"Mama, please. What's going on? What do you know? Is this serious? I just got married. I–I... *we* want children. Call me. Please."

I'm tempted to head out to Heathrow and follow her to Manhattan, but I know I've missed the last flight out tonight. Maybe my plea will ignite a modicum of maternal feeling if she has any left.

Mate.

My mother is not renowned for her sentiment or her maternal feelings.

Fuck.

Perhaps Alessia and I should fly out to see her together?

Bugger. Alessia will need a visa.

I head back to the table, and she looks up. "Okay?"

"Yeah. I called Rowena again and left a voicemail. She's returned to New York, so I won't hear from her this evening. Let's enjoy ourselves." I take a swig of sake, and Alessia raises her small porcelain cup.

"Gëzuar, Maxim," she says.

"Your good health, my dear wife."

"In Japan, there is sake; in Albania, raki. What do the English have?"

"Gin, I suppose. There are many new distilleries popping up to quench the nation's thirst for English gin."

She smiles. "I would like to try this."

I don't have any meetings in the morning. "Okay. We can do that."

It's midnight, and my wife has had too much to drink. I've seen her tipsy before when we were in Cornwall, and she took a tumble into the sea, but she's never been like this.

And it's my fault.

Alessia is new to drinking, and I should have kept a better eye on her. I bet she'll have a hangover tomorrow.

"Come on, princess. I've got you." I hold her tightly to my side as we stagger out of Loulou's to a hail of flash photography and clamber into the cab. In the back seat, I direct the cabbie to take us home and keep an arm wrapped around my wife.

Alessia gives me a crooked smile. "Maxshim."

"I think you've had too much sake and gin, baby."

"Yesh. I like the gin. But it is fun. Was fun," she corrects herself. "S'good to meet your friends."

"I think you dazzled them."

"You have many friends. Women too. How many have you had sexual…intercourse with?"

Whoa! "What?"

"How many?" She gazes at me, dark eyes hazy and unfocused. She closes one and squints, trying to look serious.

Two. I think.

"Let's talk about this when we get home."

When we started our evening, I didn't know we would end up at Hertford Street. But after these last few shitty days, it seems we both wanted to let off steam.

This much steam?

I pull Alessia closer and kiss her forehead. She raises her face to mine and puckers her lips, looking adorable.

How can I resist?

I offer her a quick peck on the lips.

"Why so many lovers, Maxshim? I don't understand," Alessia says.

"Can we talk about this when you're sober?"

She considers my response. "Yesh. I will not forget."

Oh, I hope you do.

I'm worried about her line of questioning. I thought we had settled this the other day. She seems obsessed with my sex life prior to meeting her, and I don't know why. I didn't behave inappropriately with any of the women we met tonight. Did I? I was friendly enough. But just that—friendly, even with Natasha and Sophie, two one-night hook-ups. I sigh and nuzzle Alessia's hair, wondering how to reassure my wife.

Maxim sits Alessia on the edge of the bed. "Let's get you undressed." He sinks to his knees and removes her boots.

Alessia reaches out, running her fingers through his hair. "So soft," she whispers.

Maxim removes her socks, then stands up and wrestles her out of her jacket.

"The photographs in here," Alessia says and sways as she turns toward the nudes. "You know these women?"

"Yes." He tosses her jacket on the sofa.

"In the…um…biblical sense."

Fuck.

Maxim grasps her chin, forcing her gaze on him. She squints so that he's in focus. "Alessia, you've got to let this go. For your sanity and mine. I'll take these photos down. It was thoughtless of me to leave them here. I'll do it tomorrow." He leans down and kisses her, his tongue warm and wet, and Alessia wraps her arms around his neck, tugging him onto the bed. He falls to her side, still in her arms.

In the light from the bedside lamp, she studies him.

Her husband.

Her lover.

Her lothario.

His eyes gleam, a brilliant emerald, the pupils dilating. She runs her fingers over his stubble and traces the soft cushion of his lips, which part as he inhales.

"I love you," she whispers. "But I don't want to be a chattel."

"Chattel?" His eyes cool. The fire in them doused with doubt.

"You want a partnership. What do I bring to our partnership?"

He gasps. "Everything." The word is a prayer.

Alessia cups his cheek—her throat suddenly raw.

"Hey. What's this about?" Maxim peers into her eyes, and his beloved, concerned face blurs through her tears. "Alessia, what's wrong?"

She shakes her head as the question spirals through the drunken haze in her mind.

So many women.

"Tell me," he pleads, and when she doesn't answer, he continues. "Oh, my love, we'll figure this out. It's going to be okay. Have faith." He kisses her forehead. "I love you." He tugs her into his arms and holds her.

The knot in her throat gradually dissolves, and her anxiety recedes as she falls into a drunken sleep.

Alessia's breathing settles, and I know she's fallen asleep, but I don't move. I don't want to disturb her. Instead, I stare at the ceiling, mystified. What's brought about her emotional outburst? Is it the drink talking? I thought she was happy. But have I been deluding myself? I've been so hung up on my own shit that I haven't thought about how she's been settling into her new life in London. She's been present and giving, consoling me while I deal with my mother and Kit's mystery genetic issue—even though she knows nothing about it. And I'm loath to tell her because it'll add to her anxiety.

And she might have second thoughts about us.

Dude. Don't go there.

Being cooped up in the flat may be affecting her. It's spotless— that hasn't gone unnoticed—but she needs more. She needs friends. She's here on her own, isolated, and only has me.

Fuck. Mate.

Tomorrow we'll start applying to the music conservatoires in London and find a finishing school for etiquette lessons. She'll be less isolated and have more to do. If that's what's bothering her, that should help.

It's you, dude. You're bothering her.

Your fucking fucking.

I sigh. Caroline spilling the beans didn't help. I understand why Alessia is sensitive about her. By revealing our sexual past, Caro sowed doubt in Alessia's mind about my fidelity, and then we met Leticia, which only worsened matters. I rub my face, trying to forget that awkward moment. Alessia has been confronted with my sexual antics since she's known me.

I blow out a breath, and a thought occurs to me. Maybe it's our cultural differences that she's finding difficult. One aspect I observed of life in Kukës was the casual segregation of men and women.

Maybe that's it. She doesn't understand that here people can fuck *and* be friends.

Why so many lovers?

It's a good question, and I think this is the answer. Sex, here, is a recreational activity for many, including me. It still is, but it's so much more satisfying with my wife.

Why is that?

Love?

Yes. Love.

Avoiding intimacy has been a way of life for me, and it was never an issue until I found Alessia and fell in love.

There. That's it. And she doesn't understand. I grin. Relieved. I think I've cracked the code to her anxiety.

Gently I untangle myself from my girl, stand, and strip.

Before I head into the bathroom, I remove the two photographs from my wall and place them in the walk-in wardrobe.

Shame. I like these photographs.

Some of my best work.

And yes, I knew them both in the biblical sense, or should I say recreational sense?

When I emerge from the bathroom, I feel much calmer. Carefully I undo Alessia's jeans and gently peel them off. I drape the duvet over her, clamber into bed, and snuggle up to her sleeping frame. "What are you thinking about, baby?" I kiss her hair, and she mumbles my name.

Me?

The thought pleases me far more than it should.

Maybe she's overwhelmed by being here. A new life with an ex-player—a rake.

Maybe that's what this is about.

She needs to understand that all that is behind me.

Yeah. That's it.

I close my eyes, and with Alessia's scent invading my senses, I drift off to dream about my love.

Chapter Sixteen

The smell of fresh coffee rouses me from my beguiling dream.

Alessia.

Blue nylon housecoat.

SpongeBob pajama bottoms.

Pink knickers.

Opening my eyes, I find her standing beside the bed dressed in cream silk, looking her usual beautiful self—except for her uncertain smile. "Good morning," she says as she sets a cup on the bedside table.

"Morning, my love. Thank you for the coffee."

"It is after 9:30."

"Oh dear, I've slept in." I rub my face and haul myself to a sitting position, and she sits on the bed beside me. "How are you feeling?"

"Okay. I had a headache."

"Better now?"

She nods. "I'm sorry. I did not mean to get so drunk. I hope I didn't embarrass you."

"Sweetheart, you do not need to apologize. You were fine." I'm horrified that she feels the need to express remorse. "My friends adored you. How could they not?"

"It was good to meet them."

"I hope you liked them. I have to confess that used to be me most nights—drunk in a club, somewhere. Meeting you has probably saved my liver."

Her eyes soften. "I liked your friends. They were entertaining. And I liked the gin. Maybe too muchly." She looks down at her hands in her lap.

"You did? Good. Maybe friends and gin in moderation next time." I run my fingers beneath her chin, turning her face to mine. "You said some things last night. I've been consumed with my own problems, and I haven't asked you if everything's okay or if there's anything I can do to make settling into this new life easier for you."

"We have only been back from our honeymoon for a few days."

"I know. But still."

She swallows and steels herself as if garnering some inner strength, and I don't know what she's going to say. From nowhere, my apprehension beats fast, furious wings in my gut.

"Maxim, I want to see if I can find one of the girls who was trafficked with me."

My relief is instant. "Oh. Okay," I respond cautiously. "But how the hell would you start to search for someone who could be anywhere?"

"I spoke to Ticia Cavanagh."

Shit. The apprehension returns full force.

"And?"

She smiles, and I think she's reading me like the open book I am. "We did not talk about you. Though maybe we should…um, compare notes?"

She's teasing me! "Alessia!" I don't know if I'm warning her to back the fuck off or congratulating her on her gumption.

"She gave me a number of a private investigator," Alessia says hurriedly, "who might be able to help. I need to find her."

I stare blankly back at her as my anxiety returns.

This seems an impossible task.

"Bleriana's only seventeen," she says, her voice low.

"Oh, God. That's awful." I close my eyes, not wanting to wrap my head around the horror that Alessia and her young friend have endured. "Did she run when you did?"

"I think so. I ran for my life. I didn't have time to check…" The words trail off as if this is a failing.

No!

I haul her into my lap and wrap my arms around her. "I didn't mean to imply—God, Alessia. I'm so glad you escaped. Heaven knows what would have…" My words die as horrific scenarios scroll through my head. "Look, I don't think it's a good idea that you get involved in that gruesome world again. Even from a distance. I'd never forgive myself if something happened to you because of your search."

She stiffens in my arms.

"I'm not going to lose you again." I tighten my grip on her and bury my nose in her hair. "Please."

"But—"

"No. Alessia." I breathe in her scent. "The answer's no. It's too big a risk. I'll talk to Tom. His company does PI work too. I'm not sure if they locate missing persons, but perhaps he can help."

She pulls away, her dark, dark eyes luminous, and I don't know if she'll fight me on this. "Thank you," she says and wraps her arms around my neck. "If Tom can find her—" Her breath is warm against my throat, but her voice catches. "I… I was lucky. And I feel guilty. I managed to escape."

My blood curdles in my veins. "Oh God. No. Never feel like that. Jesus, Alessia." If those thugs had caught her. I close my eyes again, imagining all the circles of hell—and Alessia in the infernal heart of the worst of them. "Don't ever feel like that, sweetheart. Ever. I'm not asking. I'm telling you. Those men were monsters." I cradle her head in my hands, and she turns her eyes to mine.

"Okay," she whispers, and after a beat, her fingers twist in my hair, and she draws my lips to hers.

"My coffee is cold." I sweep my nose down Alessia's as I lie beside her, spent.

She giggles. "I can make you some more. And some breakfast."

"No. Don't go. I'll make it. And some for you." I kiss her cheek.

"No!" Her fingers tighten in my hair, scraping my scalp. "Don't go." She presses her fantastic breasts into my chest and winds her leg around my hip.

Oh boy… again!

I stand beneath the shower and wash away my hangover, feeling more settled.

It's the sex.

Twice in one morning—I can get on board with that.

Alessia is voracious. *Who knew?* I grin into the water cascading over me.

She seems much happier today, and my mind turns to her emotional state last night. I think she's suffering from being cooped up, a lack of friends, and her survivor's guilt. Maybe it's reminders of my old life too.

Alessia and I are still getting to know each other. But she's usually so self-contained and stoic, so her outburst was a surprise.

I'm glad we talked, and I'll call Tom today and get the ball rolling on what's probably a futile search—but for Alessia's sake, and her friend's sake, we can try.

I turn off the shower, stagger out, and inspect my chin, ready to shave.

No. Not today.

I leave the stubble—my wife likes it—and head back into the bedroom with a towel wrapped around my waist. The bed is already made.

You can take the girl out of Albania… I smile.

I'm glad she's out of Albania.

With me.

But I'm not sure what to think of her mission. Is it wise? I imagine it'll be fruitless. How can you find a trafficked, undocumented immigrant?

We can try from a safe distance because there's no way I'm letting anyone pull her back into that hideous underworld.

I need to keep her safe.

Oliver is running through the monthly profit-and-loss accounts for each of the individual estates. We're in surprisingly good shape, and I know my instinct to leave everything well alone until I understood how it all works was a good one.

"So we're not making massive profits on any of the houses, but it's enough," Oliver says.

"I've been thinking of a way to plow these profits back into each of the estates."

Oliver raises a brow, surprised by my rare display of entrepreneurial spirit, so much so that I want to laugh. "I'm thinking gin, Oliver. Trevethick gin."

"Now, that is an interesting idea."

"I'll talk to Abigail Chenoweth at Rosperran about her potato crop. And Michael at the Hall about the north pasture barn."

Oliver nods. "That could be a good place for a still."

Alessia presses the intercom on the anonymous-looking door in a backstreet in Covent Garden that bears the discreet sign: MPPI. Maddox Peacock Private Investigators. "Hello," answers a gruff, disembodied voice.

"Hello. My name is Alessia Dem…Trevelyan. I have an appointment." She didn't have the courage to tell Maxim she'd already made the appointment to see the private investigator.

What harm could it do?

Two companies searching for Bleriana might yield better results.

She knows she's acting in defiance of her husband, and she feels guilty, but as Maxim himself once told her—it's better to ask for forgiveness than permission.

She did ask for permission.

He said no.

An emphatic no.

O Zot. The door buzzes and Alessia steps into a grubby hallway and heads up the flight of stairs. At the top is a waiting area with cushion armchairs and a coffee table. The door to one of the offices opens, and a tall, well-built man with a shock of blond hair comes out to greet her. "Alessia Trevelyan, I'm Paul Maddox." He has bright blue eyes that coolly assess her as his large hand engulfs hers in a firm handshake.

Alessia swallows, trying not to feel intimidated.

"Please, come this way." He ushers her into a small, cluttered office that his broad shoulders seem to fill and directs her toward a chair in front of a wooden desk piled with papers. Alessia takes the seat and waits for him to sit down. "What can I do for you, Mrs. Trevelyan?" he asks as he glances at her wedding ring, and she knows he's appraising her. She's glad she's worn her new tailored trousers, cream silk blouse, black jacket, and Gucci loafers.

"I'm looking for a missing person and want to trace a family."

"Are these related?"

"No. I'm trying to find a girl who was trafficked to England from Albania, and I'd like to trace the family of an English woman. Her name was Virginia Strickland." From her purse, she pulls a small faded black-and-white picture of her grandmother as a young woman—in pearls, a dark sweater with short sleeves, her head cocked to one side, her smile lighting up the frame. She hands it to Maddox.

"I see, Mrs. Trevelyan. Two cases. Let me take some notes."

After my meeting with Oliver, I call Tom and ask him if Alessia's mission to track down her friend is a fool's errand or if it's possible to find someone after they've been trafficked into the country.

"Well, this is a challenge," Tom says after I've explained the situation, and I can almost hear the cogs in his brain whirring. "How many women?" he asks.

"I believe there were six, including Alessia."

"Dreadful business."

"Yes. Alessia tried to get the others to run when she did."

"Where was this?"

"All I know is that it was a motorway service station."

"It's possible we could track the girls down—tall order, mind. I need more information. I can make inquiries with the police. I have a contact. You know him. Remember Spaffer from school?"

"How could I forget him?" Charlie Spafford had been a fearsome bully. No wonder he joined the plod.

"He's a highflier at the Met. I'll call him. I think he's with the organized crime division. He may know something about the traffickers you apprehended in Cornwall. I'll see if there are any leads that may direct us to find the girls."

"Sounds like a plan, but I don't want your inquiry to lead back to Alessia." We don't need Sergeant Nancarrow breathing down our necks.

"I hear you, old boy. I had no idea that poor Alessia's experience was so traumatic."

"She needs to be kept out of this. She was here illegally."

"Understood. I want to talk to her, though. If she has any recollection of where she was, we could work out which service station and some of the girls may still be in that area."

"I'll talk to her."

"Roger that."

I roll my eyes. You can take the man out of the army. "Thanks, Tom." I end the call and check my phone for the millionth time for any messages. There's still nothing from my mother.

What the hell is wrong with her?

And I know deep in my bones it's because she despises me. She always has. It was always Kit. Kit. Kit with her.

I used not to care, but now it cuts deep, and I wonder what I did when I was young to inspire such contempt.

Fuck it. To hell with her.

There are, however, texts from Caroline.

You went to Loulou's without me!

How do you know?

You're all over the Daily Fail.

WTF!!!

Yes. Staggering into the night.
Drunken Earl with Mystery Wife?

Hell.

Just ignore them.

They're still calling here.
Blake is deflecting.

Good.

I miss going out.
How long do I have to stay in purdah?

That's up to you.

I've had an invitation to
Dimitri Egonov's party.

It's on Saturday.
Are you going?

> I've always thought he's a bit dubious.
> His father is anyway.
> Are you ready to face the world again?

My phone rings. It's Caro.

"What?" I ask.

"I think I'm ready. It's sweet of you to care."

Shit. In a fraternal way, Caro! I don't want her to get the wrong idea.

"I'm not sure I could bear another night in," she continues. "And Dimitri knows how to throw a party. Everyone will be there."

"I'll think about it."

"In fact," she says with the enthusiasm of a new idea, "this might be the perfect place to launch Alessia."

"She's not a boat!"

Caroline laughs. "Listen, Maxim. Everyone will be there. It's perfect. And she'll need a new frock. Something ultra-glamorous. Please let me take her shopping!"

"Caro, I'm not about to unleash society on Alessia."

"She'll be fine. Sink or swim, to keep your boat analogy."

"Boats don't swim. They float."

"She'll float. She'll fly! She is lovely. I'll give you that."

That she is. It's not a bad idea. And Alessia needs friends—it's a perfect place to make connections. "I'll talk to her."

"You can't keep her hidden away forever. You're not ashamed of her, are you?"

"Fuck off, Caro. Of course not."

"It will be fun. And I need some fun. And mention the shopping!"

"Well, I think she's lonely. So I'll think about it. I've got to go."

⌒

"Are you okay?" Alessia asks when Maxim leans oh-so-casually against the doorjamb of the kitchen. This is a habit of his that Alessia enjoys—he likes leaning there and watching her, and she can admire him; his hair is rumpled, his chin stubbled—he's a welcome sight. This evening, he's just returned from work, and his face is tense, his jaw strained.

"I'm fine. Just another day at the office." He smiles, and Alessia snakes her arms around him and tilts her face up for a kiss. Maxim obliges willingly, his mouth firm and demanding against hers.

"That's better," he whispers.

She grins. "Dinner is in the oven."

"How was your day?"

"It started very well. Very well indeed."

"Why, Lady Trevethick, whatever do you mean?"

The heat rises in Alessia's cheeks, and she bats her eyelashes. "I think you know."

"I do." Maxim kisses her again—longer this time, so they're both breathless when he pulls away. He rubs her nose with his. "Seriously. How was your day?"

Tell him.

Alessia debates whether to tell him about Paul Maddox, but because he's brooding about something, and she's not sure how he'll react if he finds out she went against his wishes, she distracts him with a question. "It was good. Did you hear from your mother?"

His face shutters immediately, and Alessia knows this is what's vexing him. "No," he says. He blows out a breath. "But I did speak to Tom. He wants to talk to you. About your friend."

"Bleriana?"

"Yes. Call him after dinner."

"I can call him now."

"I'll text you his number."

It's just after 9:00 p.m., and Alessia and I are sitting at my desk, staring at the computer. I feel like I've taken my school entrance exams again, but it's been a welcome distraction. We've signed Alessia up for an intensive weeklong social etiquette course at the academy that Caroline recommended.

"Caroline did this course too?"

Alessia was incredulous.

"Yeah. Kit insisted." I'd shrugged, still shocked that Kit would insist on such a thing.

And we've completed four applications to music conservatoires in London. Her favorite is the Royal College of Music because it's within walking distance.

"I don't know if my English will be good enough," Alessia says.

"You'll be fine. And let's hope you can start in the summer term, after Easter. You said your mother was going to send your exam certificates."

She chuckles. "Yes. My Matura Shtetërore. I should have packed them. I didn't know I'd need them."

"You got top marks in English, which will help." I blow out a breath, a rosy sense of achievement glowing in my chest. "Now that this is done, what would you like to do?"

"It's late."

"Not that late. I know what I want to do."

He grins, boyish and breezy, and taking her hand as he rises from his desk, he moves toward the coffee table in front of the sofa and grabs one of the remotes. He's not been this upbeat since their honeymoon.

"Sit," he says, and Alessia settles on the couch beside him.

We're going to watch TV?

Alessia is surprised. They've never watched television together, even in Kukës. The large flatscreen pops to life with an electronic hiss of static, but instead of a TV program, there's a strange white logo on a black background.

"Here." Maxim hands her a game console controller.

She frowns up at him.

"*Call of Duty?*" he prompts.

She smirks. "I thought that's what we always do?"

Maxim laughs. "Duty?" he scoffs in mock horror, then pounces on her so she's suddenly prone on the sofa, his weight pressing her into the soft cushions. He grins. "Duty, Lady Trevethick?"

She giggles. "Well, duty and pleasure."

He kisses her quickly and sits up. "Your English is getting so much better. No. I fancy playing a game that I know I can win. It's what my ego needs right now."

Alessia laughs and sits up beside him. "How do you know you can beat me?"

"I didn't see a PS4 in Kukës. And you're holding the console upside down. Here, I'll teach you."

Games! He plays video games! This is a side of Maxim she's not seen before.

"Okay?" he asks, green eyes bright but less sure.

"Yes!" Alessia declares enthusiastically because she's never played computer games before.

"Right. Bring it!" Maxim means business.

S o, how's doing your duty going so far?" I whisper against the soft skin of her inner thigh.

"Maxim. Please." She tugs my hair, trying to shift me from between her thighs.

I grab her hands and hold them fast against her. "Oh, no." I blow gently on her clitoris and follow with my tongue, provoking the greedy, swollen little bud between her thighs. She garbles my name in a cry, and it's a gratifying, cock-hardening sound. It's such a heady thrill to tease and tantalize my passionate wife. I stop because I think she's close and trail wet kisses over her plucked labia along the edge of her soft, warm belly.

"Please. Maxim." It's a desperate cry.

I nip her hip bone, kiss the sweet well of her navel, and then skim my lips up her body, to her peaked breasts, where her nipples are hard and ready, begging for me.

"Oh, Alessia," I whisper in awe as I take each in turn, sucking and tugging until they're straining for the ceiling, and she's squirming beneath me, her hips moving in a reckless counterpoint. I rear up over her, and her dazed eyes meet mine, full of longing and love. I release one of her hands and slowly sink two fingers inside her.

Ah! She's so wet and ready for me.

"Baby," I murmur as she hungrily tilts her pelvis to meet my fingers. She's so close. I jerk my fingers free and quickly flip her over onto her stomach. Grabbing her hips, in one swift move, I tug her onto my straining cock.

"Ah!" she cries and pushes back against me, wanting and taking all of me.

Oh, my thirsty girl.

Doing her duty.

I lose myself, over and over in my wife, and time and space are suspended. It's just us. Now. In this moment of love. She lets free another garbled cry and stiffens beneath me as she peaks. Her body pulsing around me as she rides out her orgasm. I don't stop. I want it all. Onward. Rocking into her. Pulling her back against me. Driving onward and onward until I can't hold on anymore.

I come. Loudly. Calling out her name and collapsing on top of her.

Engulfing her with my body.

Holding her fast as we both return to the present.

Duty done.

I'm slippery and sticky from our combined sweat. *Yes.* I'm also bone tired.

Fuck, that was good.

I kiss her cheek as she pants beneath me.

"Wow…" I whisper in her ear.

Her lips lift in a tired grin. "Yes. Wow."

"Duty done, baby." I ease out of her, enjoying the slip and slide of it all. Her back. Her arse. Her sex.

Yeah.

Wow.

Alessia blows out a breath and gives me a sleepy smile. "You have also fulfilled your duty."

I nuzzle her ear. "I'm glad to hear it. And I got to beat you at *Call of Duty.* I'd call that a good day."

"Tomorrow, I will practice. Then we shall see."

I laugh. "God, I love you." And in the light of the little dragon, she closes her eyes with a most satisfied smile on her face, and it makes me feel that I have some worth, after all.

Chapter Seventeen

Alessia's fingers rest on the keys, the last of Bach's fugue ringing through the room—the bold blues dissipating as the notes fade. If—and it's a big if—she gets an interview at one of the music colleges in London, she'll have to audition. She's been playing through her repertoire for the last two days and trying to decide what would be appropriate. Maxim thinks the Beethoven *Moonlight Sonata* third movement would *crush it*. She smiles, recalling how bright-eyed and sincere he looked as he uttered those words.

Alessia wants to crush it.

Completely.

The thought of studying in London is one she'd never contemplated before. She's excited, and her parents are thrilled, but she doesn't want to fail; she wants Maxim to be proud of her. Next week she'll start the etiquette course that Caroline recommended. It confounds Alessia that Caroline, who's so poised and elegant, had to attend such a course. She always imagined that her gentility was innate. Alessia hopes she'll learn such propriety too, enabling her to move seamlessly in the circles that Maxim inhabits.

Her smile fades.

She wishes she knew what she could do to help her husband. Maxim is still distracted and frustrated by his mother not returning his calls. He's reassured her that it's nothing for her to worry about, but she does. Alessia loves him and wants to help. She finds his relationship with his mother unfathomable. She's sure Maxim loves his mother, but does he like her? She thinks not. And her instinct is that Rowena feels the same antipathy toward Maxim.

Why?

Perhaps his mother will speak to him today and put him out of his misery.

Alessia checks her phone to see if Maxim has texted her—there's nothing, but an email from Paul Maddox appears in her inbox. Her scalp tingles, and butterflies flutter in her stomach.

He has information about her grandmother's family.

Already?

With trembling fingers, she dials his number.

axim. Max!"

"Sorry. What?" I look up from my desk to find Oliver standing in the doorway.

"May I come in?"

"Of course."

Fuck. Dude. Pay attention.

"I have some brochures here for distilling equipment as requested. I have a favorite. Let me know what you think. There are many, many rules and regs to overcome, but nothing insurmountable. My second question relates to the Cheyne Walk property, and if you wanted it decorated before you move in?"

"It looked like it had been newly decorated."

"It was. Ready for the next tenants."

"Alessia's happy with it, though I think in time she might want something less… beige."

Oliver laughs. "True. Do you have a move-in date?"

"Not yet. Soon, I suppose."

"Anytime is good, Maxim."

"I'll talk to Alessia. I should bring her here to meet you all."

"You should." He nods. "We'd all be delighted to meet the new Lady Trevethick. Incidentally, the press are still calling."

"They'll get bored."

"They've been at it every day."

I shrug. "I want to keep Alessia out of the limelight. I'm sure she'll be uncomfortable with any press scrutiny."

"Hmm, perhaps. Or you could show her off to the world, and then the press might leave you alone."

"Maybe," I mutter, knowing that Caro is of the same opinion.

"Maxim, are you okay?" he asks as he places the brochures on my desk.

"Yes. Fine. Thanks, Oliver."

He nods, but his brow creases with concern as he exits.

I glance at my phone. Still nothing from my mother. How can she be so callous?

I text her once more, switching to super-groveling mode.

> Mama, please.
>
> Call me.
>
> I'm begging you.

I'm not seeing the genetic counselor who advised Kit for another week, and I need to know. *Am I a walking time bomb or not?*

Virginia Strickland's remaining relative was easy to trace. She has a brother. He's still alive. I'll email you everything we have," Paul Maddox says.

"Thank you," Alessia replies, feeling a little light-headed. She hadn't expected this to be so fast. "Do you have any information about Bleriana?"

"No, Mrs. Trevelyan. Not yet. Finding her is far more tricky. But, as her traffickers are in custody and there's an ongoing criminal investigation, we're hopeful that we might get a lead from our contacts in the police."

Alessia remembers Tom mentioning he also had a contact in the police. She shudders.

Dante and Ylli.

Still in custody.

Thank God.

She blows out a breath. "Okay."

"I'm going to close off the Virginia Strickland case. But we'll continue with the hunt for your friend. I'll send you an itemized invoice, but we have enough funds in the retainer you gave us to last for a week or two—depending on how our inquiries go."

"Thank you."

"I'll be in touch when I have further news." He hangs up, and Alessia checks her email. Sure enough, there's one from Maddox with a PDF attachment. She clicks it open and reads. There's information about her Nana's parents but, most importantly, her grandmother's older brother.

TOBIAS ANDREW STRICKLAND

Date of Birth:	4th September 1952
Age:	66
Address:	The Furze House, Kew Green,
	Kew, Surrey, TW9 3ZJ
Marital Status:	Single
Employment:	Emeritus Professor of Music.
	Worcester College. Oxford.

Alessia has a great-uncle who was a professor of music! Musical ability must run in her family. Virginia had taught Shpresa the piano, and they both taught her. Alessia quickly checks Google Maps and finds that Kew is only a few miles from Chelsea. As she studies the map, a frisson of recognition travels up her spine.

Kew is over the river from Brentford.

Where she had lived for a couple of months.

He was so close!

She's stunned.

All that time when she was worried about where she could live, and he was just across the river.

She should visit. Introduce herself. Tell him about his niece in Albania. Her mother will be delighted. Surely. She hugs her phone.

Should she tell Maxim?

Perhaps she should meet Tobias first.

Alessia skips over to the piano, sits down on the stool, and starts on her favorite prelude in celebration.

Caroline texts me when I'm in a cab on the way home.

I'm taking Alessia shopping tomorrow.
No ifs or buts.
Warn her.

She might not want to go shopping!

Maxim, she's female.
She'll want to go shopping.
And I'm not giving her a choice.
You are coming to Dimitri's.

Hell. Caro is not going to let this go. But on the other hand, Alessia needs to get out more and meet people, and frankly, after the past week, so do I. It would be a welcome distraction to see everyone. No doubt Tom and Joe will be there. Oliver suggested I show her off to the world. This would be one way of doing it.

Okay!
We'll come.

Great!
I'll be there in the morning.
Tell Alessia.

Caro is so bossy, and I don't know if Alessia will be up for this. After Caroline's behavior before the wedding in Kukës, it could go either way. But Caro is a force of nature, so maybe she'll prevail. I need to warn my wife.

My phone buzzes again with a number I don't recognize. "Trevethick," I answer.

"Lord Trevethick. My name is Donovan Green. I'm a journalist for the *Weekend News*."

"How did you get this number?"

"Lord Trevethick, is it true that you married your cleaner, Alessia Demachi?"

His question winds me as if his fist has slammed into my solar plexus. I hang up without making a comment. How the hell did the slimy bastard get my number? And how did he get Alessia's name?

My phone rings again, but I block the number.

Fuck a duck.

What am I to make of this? I'd better warn Alessia's parents that some stringer may turn up on their doorstep looking for a story. I know Shpresa will stay quiet, but my father-in-law, who, let's face it, likes a little drama and attention, might not be so taciturn.

Maybe I should throw these vultures a bone.

Tomorrow night, Alessia and I will be guests at Dimitri Egonov's annual spring bash, which will be attended by the great and the good and the not so good, so there'll be no doubt. The world will know that we're married, and the Grimy Slimy *Weekend News* can fuck off.

The cab stops outside my building, and it's a relief that there are no reporters or paparazzi outside. I pay the driver and hurry inside, anxious to see my wife.

～

Alessia wraps languid limbs around me as we both return to earth. I nuzzle the special pulse point beneath her ear and move over onto my side, taking her in my arms. "You are the world to me," I murmur as I hold her close. It's early Saturday morning, and I want to spend the whole morning getting lost in my wife.

The buzzer from the building intercom sounds.

"What the hell?" I grumble.

Is it the press?

"Can we ignore them?" Alessia whispers against my neck, her breath tickling the fine hairs there. The buzzer sounds again, and this time a garbled, disembodied voice echoes through the hallway from the intercom.

"Bugger." I sit up.

Who the hell is that?

"Do you think it's that reporter?" Alessia is wide-eyed with alarm.

"I don't think so."

The buzzer sounds again, and I clamber out of bed and wander naked into the hall to answer the intercom. "Hello," I grunt into the speaker.

"Hi. It's me."

"Caro. What gives?" *Shit!* I forgot to mention Caroline's plan to Alessia last night. I'd been too distracted by the journalist.

"I'm here to take Alessia shopping. I told you. Let me in."

Shit. I haven't broached this with Alessia. I press the door release and pad back into the bedroom, where Alessia is up and draped in the quilt.

"Caroline is on the way up," I mutter as I hunt for my jeans. "She wants to take you shopping. Do you want to go?"

"Shopping for what?"

"Clothes."

"I have clothes."

"For the party tonight?"

"Party?"

Hell. I'd forgotten this too! "We're going to a party. An acquaintance. That's if you want to."

"Okay," she says, but her eyes are wide with uncertainty.

"It should be fun. Go shower. I'll entertain Caroline." I zip up my jeans.

The front doorbell buzzes, and Alessia gives me a hesitant, unreadable look as she hurries into the bathroom. I pad out to the front door holding a T-shirt.

"Good morning, Maxim," Caro says brightly, offering her cheek for a quick peck. I oblige, then drag on my T-shirt to stop her from checking out my torso. "You're only just getting dressed? Did I interrupt you shagging?"

"Fuck off, Caro."

"Yes. I'd love a coffee. I'll make it." She breezes into the kitchen, leaving me standing barefoot in the hallway.

I follow her in.

"Where's Alessia?" she asks.

"Showering. And black. No sugar, please."

"I know how you take your coffee," she chides.

Alessia showers in record time. She doesn't trust Caroline, and doesn't want to leave her sister-in-law alone with Maxim, who happens to be Caroline's ex-lover. Caroline is still in love with him, or so Alessia thinks.

Draped in a towel, Alessia dashes into the spare room where all her clothes are kept, to dry herself and dress.

Maxim and Caroline are in the kitchen. She hears him laugh at something she says. And Alessia is spurred on to be quicker. Three minutes later, she's dressed in black trousers and a white long-sleeve T-shirt, with Gucci loafers.

"Good morning, Alessia," Caroline says brightly when Alessia walks into the kitchen. "You look nice."

"Thank you," Alessia responds, surprised at the compliment. "So do you." Caroline is dressed in dark jeans, knee-high boots, and a fitted tweed jacket. She gives Alessia a quick hug and peck on the cheek.

"Sorry to interrupt your morning shag," Caroline says with a wink.

Alessia blushes and turns her attention to Maxim. He hands her a coffee. "Here you go. Just ignore her."

Alessia smiles and takes the coffee.

Why is this woman so brazen? Are all English women like this?

Or is this awkward because Caroline knows Maxim intimately, and they used to "shag"?

"Do you want to go shopping?" Caroline asks, utterly unabashed by what she's just said. "We can find you something gorgeous for this party. And for me too!"

"Sure," Alessia responds.

"Great." Caroline beams.

Caroline intimidates Alessia. On every level. But this friendly, happy Caroline is something new.

Alessia gulps down her coffee. "I'll get my things." She escapes into the spare bedroom to collect her jacket and handbag.

Spare room? Don't tell me you have separate beds already!" Caro scoffs. "Because you being half-dressed is not what that looks like."

I give her an exaggerated sigh, irritated by her teasing. "No. Separate wardrobes."

"Ah. Look, I get it. She's a tempting little morsel, isn't she?" She sounds wistful, and I cock my head in warning. "Oh, relax, Maxim. You're newlyweds. You must be at it like rabbits."

I rake a hand through my hair. "This is none of your fucking business. Where are you taking her?"

"Knightsbridge or Bond Street. I'm not sure yet. But I was thinking about what you said."

"Oh?"

"About her being lonely." Caroline glances down, avoiding eye contact. "I know how that feels. I have friends, but they were Kit's friends too, and it's extraordinary how grief has spirited them away." Her face falls, and for a moment, she looks devastated.

"Oh, Caro. I'm sorry." Without thinking, I reach out and hug her.

She gives me a watery, grateful smile. "Maybe I can forge a friendship with your wife."

"I'd like that. I hope you do."

A lessia watches their exchange from the hall. He does love his brother's wife. His words are kind and sweet.

But not like he loves Alessia.

You are the world to me.

And he wants them to be friends. She sighs. For Maxim, she'll try.

Alessia shoulders her bag and steps into the kitchen doorway, and they break apart. Not guiltily, because right now, they don't have anything to feel guilty about, Alessia can see that, but still—she wishes that Caroline would keep her hands off her husband. "Shall we go?" she asks.

"Yes!" Caroline exclaims with an overexuberant enthusiasm.

"Don't go crazy," Maxim warns, and he leans down and kisses Alessia hard and fast on her lips.

"Of course we're going to go crazy. It's Dimitri's party." Caroline winks at Alessia once more, grabs her hand, and together they set out the door.

A lessia with Caroline. I'm not sure how I feel about this. I don't want Caro upsetting Alessia again. Though she seemed genuinely remorseful after the last time, Caro is like the proverbial bull in a china shop regarding other people's feelings. I hadn't noticed before… before Alessia.

Hell.

Alessia can look after herself.

Can't she?

The apprehension that's become familiar since I lost Alessia reverberates in my chest, and I'm suddenly a little overwhelmed, standing in the echoing silence of my hallway. This is the first time I've been alone in the flat since Alessia went missing.

Shit. Mate.

Pull yourself together.

I drag out my phone and text Joe.

> Bout?

Bro! The missus letting you out?

> Mate!!!
> My missus is shopping with Caro.

Sounds expensive!
I'll grab my blade.
See you at the club.

Alessia closes her eyes as Jimmy, one of the young men at the beauty salon, massages conditioner into her hair. She's shocked that most of the staff at the salon are men, and it's the first time a man has washed her hair. She smirks. Technically, Maxim was the first man to wash her hair. But they were naked together in the shower. This experience is entirely different, and the strong-fingered young man gives a good massage. The sensation is blissful, and after a hectic morning, it's a welcome respite from shopping with her full-on sister-in-law.

Caroline's been more than friendly, chattering nonstop and

offering her opinion on *everything*. She's encouraged Alessia to buy two dresses—no, gowns—that were outrageously expensive.

Darling, you'll have to get used to spending money. It's all about quality, not quantity. These pieces are classic and will last you for years, and you look fabulous in both.

Alessia loves them, and she hopes Maxim does too.

Darling. He'll love them!

She's also bought matching high-heeled shoes and a little black Chanel evening bag.

These are perfect accessories for those frocks.

Afterward, they had a quick lunch at a champagne bar, where Caroline quizzed Alessia about her life in Albania.

Caroline was fascinated and continued her friendly interrogation at the salon while their finger and toenails were trimmed, shaped, and polished a bright scarlet.

But the truth is, Alessia feels indolent; this is not a life she ever aspired to—spending outrageous amounts on high-end fashion and grooming. But her apartment is spotless, Maxim's and Alessia's clothes clean and ironed… and now and again, a woman needs to spoil herself, or so says Caroline.

"Mmm." She smiles, drifting off as Jimmy continues his massage and grateful for a few minutes' peace.

M ate, you are easy meat. Your game is way off. You okay?" Joe says as he tugs off his fencing mask, having scored the winning point.

I gape at him through the mesh of my mask. My mother is AWOL. My brother may have killed himself because of a genetic disorder that I may or may not have, and some scummy hack is digging into my nuptials. "Just a lot of shit going on," I mutter, breathless, as I pull off my mask. "Besides, you're performing way too well for my liking."

"Practice. That's all it is. What with you married, and Tom all loved up with Henry, I'm on my own."

"My heart bleeds, bro."

He laughs and claps my back. "You going to Dimitri's tonight?"

"Yeah."

"Let's have a swift drink, and then I'll let you go."

"Okay. But it needs to be a swift one. I need to pick up some jewelry from the vault."

"For your countess?"

"Yep."

Joe grins. "Need a hand selecting something?"

"Mate!"

"Just asking."

Alessia and Caroline are in the back of a taxi cruising back to Chelsea from Knightsbridge. Alessia's phone buzzes. She has a text from Maxim.

What color is your dress?
Mx

> One is black.
> The other is red.
> Why?

You'll see!
Mx

"Is that Maxim?"

Alessia nods.

Caroline smiles. "I think he'll be pleased with today's endeavors."

"I hope so."

"It's been fun."

"It has," Alessia acknowledges, surprised.

"Of course, this is my last hurrah for a while," Caroline says.

"Last hurrah?"

"Yes. I start work on a project for Maxim next week."

"Oh?" Alessia glances at Caroline, who seems oblivious to the alarm writ all over Alessia's face.

"In my old life," she continues, "I was an interior designer, and one of the Trevethick properties in Mayfair is being refurbished. He wants me to add my special sparkle to it."

Special sparkle. What does that mean?

Caroline works for Maxim. This is news.

How closely do they work together? A chill grips Alessia's heart as she recalls them hugging this morning. "And you enjoy it. Working?" she asks, trying to keep her voice level.

"Yes and no. Depends on the client. Maxim will be fine, but some can be a complete nightmare." Caroline makes a face, and Alessia can't help but laugh because it's so unexpected. "Yes. I've had some dreadful, demanding, delusional clients in the past. But I've missed being in the fray. And now, well, I need to get back out there since, since Kit…"

Caroline exudes a confidence that Alessia envies, but one mention of her deceased husband and her confidence crumbles— her shoulders droop, and her face clouds. Instinctively, Alessia reaches out and clutches her hand. Caroline turns raw blue eyes to her that shimmer with unshed tears and returns her squeeze. "Thank you," she whispers.

Alessia's compassion shines in her kind smile, and they continue their journey in silence for a few moments.

Alessia glances out of the cab window, wondering what it would be like to have a proper job. "I'd like to work, but I can't because I don't have a visa," she says, almost to herself.

"Oh?" Caroline is surprised.

"It's frustrating. I'd like to…um…contribute."

"I see." Caroline looks thoughtful. "I'm sure you contribute in other ways." She gives Alessia a quick smile, and Alessia wonders if she's referring to sex as she usually does, but there doesn't seem to be any malice or vulgarity in her expression.

"Yes. I may go a little crazy in the apartment."

"Oh, you'll have enough to do once you've established yourself. There are two estates to oversee as countess. Incidentally, Maxim asked me about finishing school. I recommended the one I attended. It was just what I needed. It's a good idea that you go."

"I was surprised you needed to go."

Caroline scoffs. "Kit wanted me to go. Darling, I'm not aristocracy. He was very particular in how things were done."

"Oh." Alessia is surprised.

"Yes. He was a bit of a snob, to be honest. Everything had to be just so. Maxim isn't like that."

"No." And Alessia is waiting for her to say—*he married you*—as an example of how he's not a snob.

But she doesn't.

"Once you're done, you'll have the confidence to assume your place, and then you should have a proper introduction to both the estates as Maxim's countess."

"That's the reason for doing the course. My confidence."

"You'll be fine."

Astonished by Caroline's sincerity and kindness, Alessia fixes a smile on her face, which her sister-in-law returns.

Caroline cocks her head to one side as she scrutinizes her. "Your hair looks so pretty blow-dried in these soft waves, Alessia." She sighs. "I envy your thick hair. It looks so healthy. You should go twice a week and have Luis style your hair each time. They'll cover grooming during etiquette lessons. It's fun. Nails. Hair. Everything. Tonight you will stun, darling. You'll meet everyone, and they're all dying to meet you. Once tonight's over, the press should stop bothering you."

Alessia is bewildered by Caroline's candor and that she envies Alessia, when it's the other way around—Alessia hopes to emulate Caroline's elegance, poise, and confidence. She's her only role model as to how Alessia should look and behave. The fact that Alessia will be attending the same finishing school gives her hope that she will.

"I know very little about the party we are attending."

"Has Maxim not told you about Dimitri?"

Alessia shakes her head. "Who is Dimitri?"

"He's some Russian oligarch's son. Bit of a player. Likes to throw lavish parties. Spends oodles of money. You'll see. Kit knew him well, Maxim less so. Dimitri likes to surround himself with the influential and the glamorous, beautiful people."

Uau. Of course Maxim would be invited to such a party.

And Caroline.

Alessia can only hope that she won't let Maxim down.

"He's ingratiating himself into society. Everyone can see that, and rumor has it that his father is ex-KGB. Exciting stuff. And he knows how to party. It will be fun." She smiles at Alessia, unaware that her nerves are now on edge.

The party sounds totally intimidating to Alessia.

"You really are very pretty." Caroline changes the subject and pauses for a moment while Alessia flounders for what to say in response to such a statement. "He's different with you. Protective. You know." Caroline's tone softens, her fondness for Maxim apparent. "He's head over heels. Must be nice."

It's such a gear change from what they were discussing. "It is," Alessia replies quickly and firmly. She knows she's staking a claim on her own husband.

"It's admirable what you've done. He's avoided intimacy all his life—you've achieved the impossible."

Alessia squirms in her seat, uncomfortable with the direction of their conversation. "Thank you," she mutters, because she doesn't know what else to say—but inside, she wants to shout from the rooftops.

He's mine. Keep your hands off him.

"Do you want to stop for anything else?" Caroline asks.

"I should get home. Though I've enjoyed today, thank you."

Alessia is surprised that she means what she says, in spite of all of Caroline's intimate observations and personal questions. It has been fun to get out of the apartment and spend time with her sister-in-law.

Perhaps she's not a rival.

Perhaps.

"I have to prepare dinner," Alessia adds.

"What? You cook? For him?"

"Yes."

"Wow." Caroline is stunned. "I suppose it's not surprising. I saw you cooking up a storm with your mother in Albania. That was nice. Intimate. You have a good relationship with her."

"I do. Do you have a good relationship with your mother?"

Caroline scoffs. "My mother lives in the South of France. I don't see her very often." She tucks her hair behind her ear as if she's distracting herself from an unpleasant thought and continues, "And the food at your wedding was delicious. I don't cook. But then I have Mrs. Blake." She lowers her voice as if her sadness has returned, and Alessia remembers overhearing her conversation with Maxim.

Caroline is lonely too.

"You are welcome to join us for an evening meal. I'll cook something light."

Caroline laughs. "Normally, I would love to, but I must get ready for this evening. And so do you. And can I ask, may I come with you and Maxim to the party? I don't want to go on my own."

"Of course," Alessia says automatically, knowing Maxim won't mind.

"Thank you," Caroline gushes. "I'm looking forward to it. I haven't been out since your wedding. And I need some excitement. In fact, why don't you two come over for a pre-party cocktail?"

"Sure." Alessia smiles, but her nerves flare again. She's excited about this party, though she's terrified too. Supposing she puts a foot wrong...or says the wrong thing...or...or... She swallows her rising panic and clasps her hands together.

Alessia, calm down. It will be fun.

What could possibly go wrong?

Chapter Eighteen

My mouth dries. Beneath the hall chandelier, the light burnishing her dark hair, Alessia is a screen siren. She's wearing an ankle-length soft silk dress fitted at the waist and fastened at her neck, exposing shapely shoulders. The skirt sculpts her hips, tapers to her knees, and then falls in swathes of ruby red to her feet. Her dark eyes are framed in kohl, her lips are as scarlet as her dress, and her hair falls in soft, gentle waves around her. She is a goddess. Aphrodite. And she's mine. I clear my throat. "You look stunning." My voice is hoarse.

She smiles, knowing and shy and sweet at once, and I feel it in my dick.

Fuck.

"You look edible," she says.

I laugh. "This old thing; it's my lucky suit."

"You could get lucky," Alessia purrs, teasing me.

I reach up and take a strand of her hair between my fingers. "I hope so, but only with you. Your hair looks lovely."

"We went to a salon at the store where a man washed it, and another man gave me a blowout."

A momentary pang of what I can only assume is jealousy slices through me. "Did they now?" I pull her into my arms. "I'm not sure how I feel about that."

Alessia giggles. "It was a first for me too."

Tenderly, I clasp her face between my palms and press my lips lightly against hers. "Then I don't approve."

"Of my hair?"

"No. The men. But whoever it was, they did a great job. Come, let me show you something."

On the dining table, I've laid out three velvet boxes. I open them all, revealing their sparkling secrets. Alessia inhales in wonder.

"Yes. Trevethick booty. Part of a substantial collection."

A lessia is awestruck. On the table, nestled in velvet, is some of the most exquisite jewelry she's ever seen.

Diamonds.

Diamonds winking in the soft light of the chandelier.

"I think these," Maxim breathes eventually, and he reaches for a pair of starburst cluster diamond earrings. "Let's see what they look like." Gently he tucks her hair behind her ears and inserts first one, then the other earring. "You're beautiful. You don't need any embellishments, but these earrings are fit for a goddess. And in that dress, that's what you are. Do you like?"

Alessia stares in the gilt mirror on the wall at the unrecognizable woman gazing back at her. She looks and feels… different. Confident. Potent. "I love them," she whispers, her eyes shifting to her husband's in the mirror and she drinks in his beauty. His emerald eyes glint, and his sculptured lips part as he inhales. He's in a fitted black suit, with a white shirt.

He looks virile. Elegant. Gorgeous.

He gives her a dazzling smile. "Good. Let me put these back in the safe."

"You have a safe?"

"*We* have a safe. It's in my wardrobe."

Hand in hand, Alessia and Maxim walk up Cheyne Walk toward Trevelyan House. Alessia tries to stifle her nerves, remembering Mrs. Blake's less than enthusiastic welcome last weekend.

What kind of reception will she receive today?

"This house has been in my family for generations. In fact, since it was new," Maxim says as he opens an iron gate that leads down a short stone path in a neat garden. They stop outside an impressive old building with a gleaming black front door that looks remarkably like the door at the house on Cheyne Walk. "I grew up here."

Alessia smiles. "Are there photographs of you as a boy here?"

Maxim laughs. "Yes. Many." He reaches up and pushes the bell, which rings shrilly somewhere inside the house. "You've met Mrs. Blake." Maxim's mouth flattens into a bleak line. "She's been with the family for years, since my father was earl. Mr. Blake, her husband, is the family butler."

"Okay." Alessia inwardly girds herself.

A stout, balding man in a pristine black suit answers the door. He turns his shrewd brown eyes on Alessia, then Maxim. "Lord Trevethick," he says and, bowing his head, holds open the door.

"Blake." Maxim is tight-lipped as he takes Alessia's hand and guides her into the hall. "This is my wife, Lady Trevethick."

"Congratulations to you both," he says kindly. "Lady Trevethick, welcome to Trevelyan House. May I take your coats?"

"Caroline is expecting us," Maxim informs him as he hands over his coat. Following his lead, Alessia removes hers too.

"Lady Trevethick," he murmurs as he takes it, his eyes bright with admiration. Alessia returns his smile. "Lady Trevethick is in the drawing room, my lord. Brace yourselves. I believe cosmopolitans are on the menu."

Maxim chuckles. "Thanks."

Blake gives them both a nod, turns on his shiny black shoes, and paces down the long black-and-white tiled hall. Alessia's gaze follows him. The walls are adorned with photographs and paintings. Two large chandeliers are hanging from the ceiling, much like those in Maxim's apartment, but these are bigger. An ornate gilt mirror sits above an old wooden console table where two elaborate lamps with golden lampshades cast a gilded light over the hall.

"The drawing room is upstairs," Maxim says, smiling at her.

Their footsteps clatter up a broad staircase made of rich, russet-brown wood. Above them, on the walls, are more paintings and photographs. Alessia catches sight of one with Maxim. He looks younger, and he's posing with a blond, curly-haired man who seems a little older than him. They're in a uniform: white britches, long leather boots, and darker T-shirts with LAURENT PERRIER emblazoned on the front. A long mallet is casually propped on Maxim's shoulder, while the other man, who has an arrogant, imposing air, is resting his hand on a similar mallet.

"That's Kit and me in our polo gear. It's from about five years ago."

"You both look very handsome."

Maxim grins, looking boyish and pleased at once. "Thank you." He leads her through a door on the landing into a large drawing room where Caroline is waiting. She's impeccably dressed in a floor-length black gown with a plunging neckline, single pearls at her ears, and a long, knotted pearl necklace that falls between her breasts. She steps forward and grasps both Maxim's and Alessia's hands.

"Welcome, Alessia, you look stunning. Maxim." She kisses Alessia's cheek and offers her own to Maxim.

"Caro. You look lovely." Maxim gives her a brief peck.

"I do so hope you're both in need of a cosmo." She squeezes their hands, then turns and presses a button on the wall. "Do take a seat."

Alessia glances around the room, taking in its opulence and antiquity. It's comfortable yet imposing. A marble fireplace with impressive columns dominates the room, and there are several overstuffed red-patterned couches. There are paintings of landscapes and still-lifes but also photographs of Caroline and her husband, several of an older man who Alessia recognizes from the portrait in Cornwall as Maxim's father, and a few of Maxim, Kit, and Maryanne as children.

"May I look at the photographs?"

"Of course, Alessia," Caroline responds. "Please, be my guest."

There's a brisk knock at the door, and Blake enters, making his way over to a silver bar cart that's laden with bottles of alcohol, sparkling crystal glasses, and a cocktail shaker.

"That dress does suit you," Caroline says. "Do you approve, Maxim?"

"I do. Very much." Maxim's expression heats as he stares at Alessia.

Alessia smiles. "Thank you," she whispers, warmed by his gaze. She turns, flushing a little, to examine one of the family photographs. Maxim must be nine or ten, handsome even as a child, his father's hand cupping his shoulder. Maryanne stands between Maxim and his brother—who's taller with a mass of blond curls—while Rowena stands behind Kit, her arm draped around her eldest son. There's a steely glaze in her eyes as if she's daring the photographer to reveal the truth.

What truth?

"I have those items of Kit's," Caroline says to Maxim and gestures to an elegant wooden box on the coffee table.

"Oh." Maxim eyes the box, eyes suddenly wide with doubt. "Um…"

"Now might not be the right time," she adds quietly.

The atmosphere in the room cools, only to be revived by the loud rattle of a cocktail shaker. All eyes turn to Blake, who holds the silver shaker aloft with a flourish. He smirks, enjoying himself. Maxim grins while Caroline laughs and joins Blake at the drinks tray. "Let me help."

Deftly Blake pours alcohol into three cocktail glasses, and

Caroline adds a slice of fresh orange zest to each. "There we go," she says, handing a glass to Alessia then Maxim. "This is a cosmopolitan. Or, as we say, a cosmo."

"Cosmo," Alessia repeats.

"Cheers," Caroline says, smiling at Maxim.

"Gëzuar," Alessia and Maxim say in unison, and Caroline laughs in response. Alessia takes a sip. The tangy, sharp taste is delicious. "Mmm… what is in this?"

"Vodka, a dash of Cointreau, lime juice, cranberry," Maxim responds, his voice husky as his eyes meet Alessia's.

"Oh, for God's sake, get a room, you two!" Caroline says. Maxim winks at Alessia, and Caroline continues, "I thought a vodka-based cocktail might set us up for Dimitri's."

Maxim nods. "Yes. The vodka will be flowing this evening. Let's drink up and make a move."

D imitri lives in a newly renovated pile in Mayfair. The house is redbrick, squat, and furnished by the interior designer du jour. I've been a couple of times. The décor, the furnishings, and the art are on point and utterly soulless. I've never felt fully comfortable in his company—not that I've met him often—but his is the place to be seen, and if I'm going to out Alessia as my wife, there's no better way to go public. We'll be plastered over all the tabloids in the morning.

"Are you ready for this?" I ask Alessia as our cab stops close to his house. She nods, her eyes dark and shimmering from the streetlight. "Caro?"

"Yes. Time to get back on the horse," Caroline says.

"Okay. Let's go. Don't answer any questions."

As we climb out of the taxi, I see there's a steady stream of the well-heeled already entering the property. The paparazzi step forward with shouts and cameras poised.

Lord Trevethick!

Maxim!

Look this way!

I wrap my arm around Alessia and grab Caroline's hand, and we walk through a sea of flashing cameras and shouted questions. It feels like forever, but it's probably seconds later that we're through the shining black door and into the relative safety of the courtyard.

Though it's still early, the place is already heaving.

An attractive young woman with slicked-back hair, dressed entirely in black, takes our coats, and we head into the courtyard proper. As we do, we're given a shot of vodka each from a waitress who looks the spit of the cloakroom attendant.

"Thank you." Alessia looks dubiously at the concoction.

"Welcome to Dimitri's," I mutter in as reassuring a voice as I can manage and down the shot. I'll say one thing for him—he does good vodka. Alessia downs hers as does Caroline.

"Uau! Ah! That's strong!" Alessia splutters.

"Yeah… maybe not too much, eh? Let's find Joe and Tom. They should be here."

"Trevethick!" The booming voice of Dimitri Egonov interrupts us. "I am so glad you could make it. And who is this beautiful young lady?" His accent is faint, but it's there. Could he sound any more oily? And he's wearing a white dinner jacket like he's Gatsby or Bogart.

"This is my wife, Alessia Trevethick. Alessia, our host, Dimitri Egonov."

He takes her hand and brings it to his lips, his dark eyes searing hers. "The rumors are true," he murmurs. "My dear Lady Trevethick, you are exquisite."

"Mr. Egonov." Alessia smiles, but even I notice that her smile doesn't reach her eyes.

"You'll need to be careful of this one," Egonov warns me. "She's a rare diamond."

"She is," I agree, wanting him to drop her hand.

Get your hands off my wife.

I've never felt as territorial as I do now.

"Please enjoy my hospitality. There's all manner of entertainments to delight here. Maybe next time you'll DJ for me."

Never.

"I think my DJ days are over, Dimitri." My smile is polite, but I want him to release my wife. Finally, he does and turns to Caroline.

"Lady Trevethick, how lovely you look this evening."

"Dimitri, darling." She air kisses him on each cheek, but he pulls her into a tight hug.

"I am so sorry for your loss," he says, holding her close.

Caro turns a panicked look toward me, but it's Alessia who takes her hand.

"Caro, please show me around," Alessia asks sweetly.

"Thank you, Dimitri," Caro purrs, and with a dazzling, knowing smile, he releases her and moves on.

Fuck.

"Are you okay?" I ask Caro, whose hand is still clasped in Alessia's.

"Yes. He is… extra."

"He is. Let's go grab a drink."

Alessia is dazzled by the spectacle of the event laid out before her. The courtyard is covered by a black silk canopy festooned with tiny, twinkling fairy lights. In the center, on a black plinth, there's an ice sculpture of tall carved flames that branch in all directions. It's lit with red and orange flickering lights, so the flames look real. Three bartenders stand before it, serving shots from the vodka that's pouring through its icy flames.

How does that work?

"Vodka luge," mutters Maxim. "Let's avoid that and find some champagne."

"I'll have another shot," says Caro, and leaving them, she saunters up to the bar and greets a tall young woman standing there. Maxim turns abruptly away from them as if he's avoiding the other woman, grabs two glasses of champagne from a passing waiter, and passes a flute to Alessia.

"Let's move over there, and we can hold court and people-watch," he says.

The area is crowded with men and women all dressed in their finery. Alessia recognizes a few movie actors, celebrities, and a couple of British politicians that she remembers from the free newspaper she read on the train to and from Brentford. On the fringes of the throng, several conspicuous, burly men in dark suits, wearing earpieces, watch over everyone.

Security? For what? Alessia doesn't know.

Various people accost Maxim to offer their condolences at his brother's passing and to meet Alessia. She shakes hand after hand, aware that a few beautiful women she meets are eyeing her with ill-concealed envy. She wonders if they know Maxim intimately.

Alessia, don't go there.

She tightens her grip on her husband's arm.

A photographer asks for a picture, and Maxim pulls her closer. "Smile," he whispers. "This will be all over the tabloids tomorrow, and I want the world to see that you're mine."

Alessia beams at him, her doubts erased, and the photographer snaps a few shots, thanks them, and moves on.

"Trevelyan!" There's a shout, and Tom, in black tie, strides toward them, dragging Henrietta behind him through the crowd. "Dear Alessia, you look stunning. Maxim, my goodness, what an extraordinary turnout. Of course, everyone here wants to meet your new bride!"

Henrietta lights up when she sees Alessia. "You look lovely," she gushes.

Alessia beams back. "Thank you, so do you!"

Maxim and Tom begin an intense discussion. Alessia picks up the words *prying journalists*, *security*, and *kompromat*—whatever that might be.

"I've never been here before. Shall we go and explore?" Henry's brown eyes sparkle with curious delight and a little mischief.

"Okay," Alessia replies, inspired by Henry's infectious enthu-siasm and of course, Alessia is curious too. She's never been to a mansion owned by a Russian oligarch.

"Where are you going?" Maxim asks as soon as they move away.

"Exploring." Henry smiles, and Maxim casts bright eyes that widen with concern at Alessia.

"Be careful," he murmurs, and Alessia knows he disapproves, but he's not going to stop her.

"We will," she says with a sweet smile. He nods in response, and Henrietta takes two glasses of champagne from another pass-ing waiter, and they walk through the affluent crowd and into the house.

The residence is impressive, decorated in beige and browns and creams with touches of gold everywhere. It's opulent; the fur-nishings are in satin and silk. Abstract and figurative art hangs on every wall. It's stylish but a little sterile for Alessia's taste. Guests mingle, talking, laughing, and drinking in each room. In the first—a sitting room—a couple of close-up magicians entertain the milling folk. One produces a gold coin from behind Henry's ear. What's more, to her utter delight, he lets her keep it.

They move on through a dining room set with a lavish banquet. Alessia recognizes the caviar and pink salmon roe, but there are dumplings and little pasties. *Pirozhok*, Henry informs her. The table, which must seat twenty people, is laden with food. Tall, attractive male servers with slicked-down hair dressed in their uniform black stand at points ready to serve. Henry and Alessia choose caviar with blinis, the little dumplings, and pasties.

"This will fortify us," Henry declares, and they move with their plates into the next room, another sterile space crammed with beautiful people. Henrietta introduces Alessia to all who approach. A thin young woman in black accosts them—her flow-ing dress appears a little big for her. "So you're the woman who snared Maxim Trevelyan," she drawls as her brown eyes sweep over Alessia.

"Maxim is my husband," Alessia responds stiffly, aware that she's been the subject of speculation and the occasional side-eye as she and Henry have wandered through the gathering. No one's been as overt at this woman.

"Pretty little thing, aren't you?" she says, and Alessia suspects she's had too much to drink.

"And you are?"

"Arabella Watts. Maxim and I used to date. Many moons ago. I must congratulate you on snaring one of the UK's most eligible—"

"Thanks, Arabella," Henry interrupts. "We have to find Maxim." She grabs Alessia's hand, and they move through to another room. She whispers, "Maxim's ex. A complete addict and a nasty piece of work too. Though I'm not sure if the two things are related."

"Oh. Ex-girlfriend?"

"Yes. Has he not told you?"

"Briefly. But not…um…with…details."

"Probably wise," Henry adds. "I mean, we don't want to hear about our partner's ex-lovers, do we?"

Alessia shakes her head and doesn't want to dwell on Maxim's exes at all.

There are too many.

Henry stops by a window so they can finish their food. When they're not being interrupted for introductions, Henry chats about her day. She's a nurse who met Tom while working at the veterans' hospital in London. Alessia listens attentively, feeling more relaxed and oh-so-comfortable in Henrietta's presence. She wonders vaguely where Maxim might be.

Once they've eaten, and with more champagne in hand, they wander through the hallway. The atmosphere among the revelers has heated up. The chatter louder and freer. They pass a magnificent wooden staircase that leads to the floor above and down to the basement, from where colored lights flicker up the walls and thumping music can be heard.

Henry makes a face. "We don't want to go down there," she warns, and they move on into the main sitting room.

It's another opulent room, furnished as the others, though this has a modern gas fireplace where flames flicker, adding a little color and life to the space. There's an excited buzz from the well-off crowd that hangs over the spacious room, accompanied by the chink of champagne and shot glasses.

Above them is a mezzanine floor. "Look," Henry says when she spots the grand piano on display above them. She grins. "Let's go up there." Henry downs her champagne, grabs another two glasses from a waiter, and leads the way to the spiral staircase. Alessia is keenly aware that their journey is followed by the curious eyes of the partygoers mingling in the room. Alessia downs one of her glasses of champagne and follows Henry up the staircase to the mezzanine. It houses an impressive library, the hardbacks sorted by color and size, and the gleaming black piano. Alessia inhales sharply. It's a Bechstein.

"Well, hello there. Do you play?" A young man with black hair, tousled a little like Maxim's, steps out from behind one of the library shelves. His accent echoes Dimitri's.

"Not me," Henry responds. "But Alessia here does."

He steps forward; his clear blue eyes scan Alessia's face, then skim down her body, so that she raises her chin to meet his challenge.

He smirks at her attempt to intimidate him and holds out his hand. "Grisha Egonov, and you are?"

Alessia shakes his hand, alarm bells ringing in her head. His grip is too tight, his smile too warm. She withdraws her hand and resists the urge to wipe it against her dress. "Egonov. Dimitri's...?" Alessia asks.

"Brother. Well, half-brother. Same father."

"Alessia Trevethick."

"Ah! The new countess." He bows quite formally, takes her hand once more, and kisses her knuckles. "My lady."

A shiver runs up her spine.

"This is my friend Henrietta Gordon." Alessia removes her hand and introduces Henry, who is watching Grisha with the same wariness as Alessia.

He gives a nod to Henrietta and turns his attention back to Alessia. "Your accent. Like me, you are not from around here."

"I am Albanian."

"Ah. Interesting. Please." He gestures toward the piano. "Be my guest."

"I wouldn't want to…um…disrupt the party."

His eyes glow with an unwelcome intensity. "Maybe it's exactly what this party needs. Or perhaps your friend's claim that you can play is… overstated?"

Henry laughs—at him, not with him—and Alessia glances at her friend. "Show him," Henry mouths. Grisha's gaze slides between the two of them, arrogant and amused.

"Please." He gestures once more to the piano, and because Alessia doesn't know if she'll ever have the opportunity to play a Bechstein again, she concedes with a graceful nod. She sits on the stool, rests her fingers on her lap, and stares at the beauty before her. The piano gleams beneath the inset lights, and the golden words C. BECHSTEIN glint irresistibly on the fallboard, enticing her to play. Alessia presses middle C, and the note rings out, the tone deep, rich, and more golden than their surroundings.

Perfect.

Alessia glances up at Grisha, who's holding his phone and eyeing her speculatively.

She'll show him, arrogant arsehole.

Alessia smiles and winks at Henry. Turning to the keyboard, she places her hands on the keys and launches into Bach's prelude number 2 in C minor… her angry music.

The music rings through the room in oranges and reds, warmer and hotter than the colors of the ice-fire in the vodka luge outside, and Alessia loves it. And because she's had a little to drink, she's free and fast, letting the music overtake her and blotting out the arrogant fool beside her.

I've left Tom and Joe deep in conversation about the merits of rugby over soccer, to try to find Alessia. Ignoring the rising panic in my chest, I move through each room as Dimitri's guests offer me condolences or congratulate me on my marriage to my beautiful wife whom they've just met!

Where the hell is she?

Then I hear it. The sounds of Bach wafting over the hum of conversation.

Alessia.

She's in the main drawing room. I follow the sound, and with the crowd gathered in the room, I look up and spy her with Henry and Dimitri's arsehole younger brother Grisha on the mezzanine.

Now that I have her in my sight, I relax and listen. I know this is her angry music and I wonder what Grisha's said to piss her off.

"Maxim!" I turn and find Charlotte staggering toward me.

My ex.

Shit.

They're both here, though I've managed to avoid Arabella. Caroline was talking with Charlotte earlier, and I wonder what about.

"Hello, Charlotte." I place my index finger on my lips to silence her because I want to listen to my wife's exquisite take on Bach. Charlotte glances up at Alessia in full flow.

"I've missed you." She grasps my hand. "Do you want to come and join me downstairs?" Charlotte's invitation is clear, but her eyes are unfocused as she weaves on her high heels at my eyeline.

She's drunk or high, or both, and I'm a little stunned.

Does she not know I'm married?

Alessia finishes the prelude, and as the final notes fade in the room, the gathered crowd erupts into applause. I extract my hand from Charlotte to applaud with them, but Charlotte grabs my lapels, surprising me, and plants her lips firmly on mine, pressing her wet tongue into my mouth. I'm vaguely aware of a flash of light.

What. The. Fuck.

I twist my head and grab her hands, pushing her gently back, escaping from her clutches. "Charlotte! What the hell are you doing?"

Alessia hears the applause coming at her from what feels like the far end of the room.

"Brava, Lady Trevethick," Grisha says. "I was doubtful, but that was impressive."

"Thank you," Alessia says and grins at a smiling Henry before glancing down at the audience in the living room, her eyes straying to her husband.

He's kissing another woman.

And Alessia's world crashes to a halt.

What?

Chapter Nineteen

Alessia looks away, the sight too painful to endure as her head spins and bile rises in her throat. She swallows down the bitter taste, feeling light-headed. The room is suddenly too warm and too small for her to remain. The notion that she's intruding on her husband crystalizes in her mind.

Perhaps he always behaves this way.

Alessia wouldn't know, as they've not been in a large social setting like this before.

This is him. This is what he does. Caroline warned her.

Alessia stands, swaying slightly from the shock of what she's witnessed, and refusing to glance in *his* direction again. She turns to Grisha. "I need to get out of here."

"Are you okay?" Henry asks.

Alessia shakes her head.

Grisha's brows knit together, his concern almost tangible. "Do you feel faint?"

Alessia nods. She just wants to get away. *Now.* "I need air."

Frowning, Henry turns to view the now-disinterested congregation below. "I'll get help," she says, stepping to the balcony rail to scan the crowd.

"Here." Grisha grabs Alessia's hand and leads her to the bookshelves, where he presses an unseen button, and one of the bookcases swings open, revealing a hidden passageway. "Follow me."

Alessia stumbles after him and hears the click of the bookshelf closing behind her.

Sit down, Charlotte. You're drunk. And haven't you heard, I'm married." Shocked at Charlotte's behavior, I guide her to sit in a vacant armchair, so she'll have less chance of falling flat on her face. She peers up at me, her expression scornful.

"I hear you married your daily."

"I married the woman I love."

She snorts. "Is she up the duff? How very eighteenth century of you, Maxim."

"Fuck off, Charlotte," I mutter and turn to go.

She grabs my hand. "I can't believe you're finally married," she says.

"Believe it." I raise my left hand, fingers spread so she can see my wedding ring. She's never behaved like this. I wonder if she's here alone or with her boyfriend. I look around but can't see anyone paying attention to her. "Are you here on your own?"

"With a friend."

"Where are they?"

She waves toward the crowd in the courtyard. "Caroline said…"

"What?" My scalp crawls. "What did Caroline say?"

Charlotte shakes her head. "That you'll fuck any woman with a pulse."

Fucking Caro.

"Even me. He's dumped me," she wails.

"Charlotte, show some bloody dignity. Plenty more fish and

all that bollocks. Now, if you'll excuse me, I'm going to find my wife." I leave her, feeling a little tarnished after our encounter. Glancing up at the mezzanine, I can see Henry looking at one of the bookcases. Alarm skitters down my spine.

Where's Alessia?

And where's Grisha?

I work my way through the crowd, ignoring the curious looks and the odd offer of condolences and congratulations, and vault up the spiral staircase.

"Henry! Where's Alessia?" I snap.

"Maxim. Hi. She disappeared with Grisha through this bookcase."

What? Why?

I start feeling around the bookcase and find the hidden button. I press it, and the bookcase swings open.

"I was looking for that!" Henry exclaims.

"Come on. Let's find her."

The passageway is lit by a couple of inset LEDs, and it ends in a door that opens onto a spacious open-air terrace above the drawing room. A couple in a dark corner among the lush pot plants are having sex against the wall. I catch a glimpse of blond hair, and I'm relieved it's not my wife. But I'm distracted by a shift in the light. A curtain closes in a room across from the terrace.

Has Grisha taken my wife in there?

Suddenly furious, I bolt through the terrace door, turn right, and burst through the bedroom door. Three men in various states of undress and arousal turn to face me in all their glory. A fourth is snorting a line of coke.

Shit.

"I'm so sorry." I back up immediately, almost knocking over Henry, who's hot on my heels. "Don't go in there. It's Ganymede central."

There's a muffled cry from inside the room. "I thought you'd locked the bloody door!"

"Dimitri's parties never disappoint," Henry says breathlessly.

"I think one of them was a cabinet minister. Come on. Alessia must have gone downstairs."

Grisha leads Alessia into the kitchen, where he barks at one of the staff in what Alessia assumes is Russian. The young woman scurries off to fetch a glass of water and returns to Grisha moments later. "Here you go." He hands Alessia the cut crystal tumbler, and she gratefully takes a long draft.

Perhaps Grisha is not so bad.

"Do you want to come down to the basement and let off some steam?" he asks, a gleam in his eye.

"No. I'd like to go home now," Alessia responds, still wary.

"I'll summon my driver." He takes out his mobile and makes a call. "Where to?"

Alessia gives him the address on Chelsea Embankment, and he snaps the orders in the same foreign language into his phone, then hangs up. "My driver will be outside in a moment. You can leave out the back, the way we do, and avoid the cameras out front." From his pocket, he fishes out a card. "Call me. When you're home."

"Why are you being so kind?" Alessia responds.

Grisha cracks a smile. "It would be very ungallant of me not to help such a talented and beautiful woman."

"Thank you," she whispers, but she can't believe her luck… in fact, she *can't* believe her luck, and a frisson of fear sends shivers up her spine.

Perhaps she's been too hasty.

Maxim will be furious.

She lifts her chin.

Well, *she* is furious. How dare he bring her to this opulent event to "announce" their marriage and then kiss someone else?

"The car's here. Let me see you out," Grisha says and offers her his arm.

I cannot find my wife. I've been in the basement, where the fun is heating up. Several people are naked in the swimming pool, and writhing bodies cover the floor of the softly lit studio. A woman flings herself at me, throwing her arms around my neck, cocaine dust on her upper lip. And I gently set her aside. "I'm looking for my wife," I growl. A quick scan of the bacchanalian horde in the studio tells me that Alessia's not a participant.

Not that I'd expect her to be here—not my sweet, innocent wife.

But these people. *It's like they're teenagers again.*

And they're probably being recorded.

Fuck. Where is she?

I head back upstairs, pull out my phone, and call Alessia once more. "Where are you?" I snap when I get her voicemail again, and I try to think what would make her run.

Someone from her recent past?

Maybe the traffickers.

Perhaps they have her. Again.

This is my darkest fear.

Hell. I find Tom and Joe. "Joe, please find Caroline and make sure she gets home in one piece. Tom, I can't find Alessia."

"Henry told me. She's gone off to look for her in the other rooms. We'll mount a search." He grabs my upper arm and gives it a brief squeeze. "We'll find her. Don't fret, Trevethick."

Fret! I'm going out of my fucking mind.

I nod in gratitude, unable to speak because there's a slight risk I might lose it. Last time she disappeared—she'd been fucking kidnapped.

My phone rings and hope swells in my chest.

Fuck, it's Oliver. I ignore the call.

A lessia sinks into the sumptuous leather of the Bentley SUV. The rear passenger door is super heavy, and she suspects the car is bulletproof. The driver gives her a cursory glance in

the rearview mirror and, without saying a word, sets off into the
night.

Only now, in the privacy of the vehicle, does Alessia allow
herself to replay what she witnessed.

Maxim kissing another woman.

Kissing. Another. Woman.

Tears well in her eyes.

Caroline had warned her.

Darling, he's slept with most of London.

Maryanne had tried to reassure her.

Reformed rakes make the best husbands.

Do they, though? Maybe they'll always be rakes. But does this
mean he loves her less?

I want the world to see that you're mine.

Does it not work both ways?

*Spouses have the same rights and duties toward each other. They
should love and respect each other, maintain marital fidelity.*

Their vows haunt her. Did they mean nothing to him?

O Zot. Was this inevitable? Her husband is just too promiscuous. Too handsome. Too charming.

A lump swells in her throat.

Her Mister. Her man.

She knew deep in her bones it would come to this.

She was never enough.

Alessia, you have been deluding yourself.

What will she do? Accept this? Leave? Alessia stares unseeing out of the window at the darkness between the lights of
London.

Was it always going to come to this? A decision to stay or go?
And for a moment, Alessia thinks of her mother and how her
mother decided to stay… and her father is far worse than Maxim.
Perhaps this is the lot of women as it has been for all time. The
Albanian saying from the *Kanun of Lekë Dukagjini* springs to her
mind: "Gruaja është një thes, e bërë për të duruar."

A woman is a sack, made to endure.

I spot Grisha coming out of one of the sitting rooms and make my way toward him. "My wife? Where is she?"

"She's gone home, Trevethick. You should take better care of her."

What the hell? And I want to ask him why she left, but it's none of his fucking business, though he seems to have made it so.

"What do you mean home?"

"She wanted to go home. I sent my car for her." His simpering swagger makes me want to punch his stupid, arrogant face. "She was feeling unwell. You really need to—"

I walk away before I deck him and find Tom. "She's gone home. Tell Joe to watch Caro. Last time I saw her, she was three sheets to the wind."

"Will do, old boy. Glad you tracked down Alessia. I'll check out that journalist you mentioned."

"Thanks."

In the cloakroom, I hand in my ticket and collect not just my coat but Alessia's too. She's left without her fucking coat. And she couldn't be bothered to tell me.

What the hell?

What did I do?

Maybe she's having second thoughts. I brought her to this den of iniquity and depravity, and she's disgusted. Let's face it, Alessia has not seen how the over-affluent can behave.

Fuck. I didn't think of this.

I storm outside, past a blaze of flashlights from the paparazzi, and make my way down the road to grab a cab.

Much to Alessia's relief, the Bentley draws up outside Maxim's building. The driver climbs out and opens her door, holding his hand out for her.

"Thank you," Alessia says as she takes it.

He nods and walks with her to the building. From her evening bag, she extracts the keys and unlocks the front door.

Once she's inside, the driver turns and clambers back into his vehicle.

It's only as she calls for the elevator that she realizes that there are no paparazzi outside. They're probably all still at Dimitri and Grisha's.

Thank goodness.

In the elevator, she finds her phone and texts Grisha her thanks and to tell him that she's arrived safely. There are a couple of missed calls from Maxim. She listens to his message as the elevator travels to the sixth floor.

Where are you? He sounds angry. Hurt. Confused.

The man doesn't even know he's behaved badly!

Maybe he doesn't think he has!

Alessia storms out of the elevator and, using her key, opens the apartment door, slamming the door behind her.

The alarm is off.

Did they not set it when they left?

The familiar cloying scent of expensive perfume hangs in the air, and the hairs on Alessia's neck stand to attention. The click, click of high heels alerts her to the end of the hallway, and standing in the doorway of the living room is Maxim's mother.

Rowena.

I n the back of the cab, my anger mounts. What the hell was she thinking? Abandoning me at a party? But why? I don't understand what's happened. Did Grisha say something? Did Caroline?

I check my phone. There's the missed call from Oliver, but still nothing from Alessia.

Did she meet Arabella or Charlotte?

My scalp tingles.

Fucking Charlotte. That kiss.

Alessia must have seen us. That's the only reason I can think of that could explain why she left without so much as a goodbye.

My relief is monumental.

That's it. I lean back in the cab, feeling I finally have a handle on what's going on.

But wait. Charlotte kissed *me*. Not the other way around. I have zero designs on my ex. I have zero designs on any other women. Surely Alessia should know that… Why would she doubt me? And the fact that she does doubt me grinds my gears. She's punishing me for something that's not my fault—and punishing me with the worst of my fears.

It's aggravating.

Actually. I'm fucking furious.

Why the hell would she think I'd be interested in anyone else?

And from nowhere, loud and clear, the thought rings like a klaxon through my head.

Because of your past.

Your reputation.

Fuck.

My mood plummets even further. I'm going to have to convince my wife—*again*—that my past is in the past.

Alessia's reeling and stands immobilized in the hallway while Rowena gawks at her.

Why is she here? How is she here?

Her mother-in-law purses her lips. "On your own, in Trevethick diamonds, I see. You've not wasted any time getting your little hands on our trinkets. Those earrings were one of my favorites back in the day. They're a little de trop, now, don't you think?"

Alessia finds her voice. "Hello, Rowena. May I help you? If you're looking for Maxim, he's out."

Maxim's mother folds her arms, remaining in the doorway, unmoving, unwavering, unwelcoming.

Hostile.

O Zot.

"You look very… nice, dear. But you'll never make a countess.

There's a saying that we have in this country—you can't make a silk purse from a sow's ear. How much money do you want to walk out of my son's life?"

Alessia feels like she's been gut-punched. "What?"

"You heard." Rowena slowly advances on Alessia. "My friend Heath has been doing a little investigation. Turns out you haven't followed the correct procedure in this farce of a marriage to my son. It can easily be annulled."

Not for the first time this evening, Alessia feels a little light-headed.

Heath? Her mother-in-law's lover?

Rowena smiles. A smile so chilling that a shiver runs down Alessia's back. "I'll write you a check, and you can go. Lead the life you were meant to lead. Not this one—it's not for you. And it's not for Maxim either. He'll need someone with a gentility and refinement that you couldn't possibly achieve. Someone with breeding who won't bring scorn and embarrassment to the Trevethick legacy. He needs someone worthy. Someone who can offer him more. And that's not you, my dear. What could you possibly give him?

"He's only married you to spite me. He's a man who likes a good time; I'm sure you're aware of what I mean by that. It won't be long until he strays. He doesn't want the job of the earldom, and he's set himself up to fail by marrying you. You can see that, can't you?

"So, how much?"

"I want nothing from you," Alessia whispers, her heart beating a frantic tattoo. "And maybe, if you'd been a better mother, your son might have a better respect for women, and chosen some-one with all the qualities you wish for in a daughter-in-law. But maybe, because *you* are his mother, he didn't. He chose me. And I am glad to say I am nothing like you."

Rowena gasps, shocked.

Alessia walks to the door. "I think it's time you left."

The key rattles in the lock, and Maxim appears on the threshold.

When I open my front door, I'm met by my mother and my wife facing off in the hall, in an atmosphere so frigid, it might freeze my nuts off. My relief that Alessia's home and safe is tempered by my anxiety.

What in the name of hell is going on here?

Chapter Twenty

Rowena and Alessia stare at me—my mother cold and brittle in black Chanel, my wife magnificent in red Alaïa—and I know in my soul they've exchanged heated words. Alessia's eyes shine with unshed tears, and I suspect my mother has been a complete and utter bitch.

But, magnificent or not, I'm also really fucking angry with Alessia right now. Angrier than I've ever been. "We'll talk later," I mutter to her, holding up a finger in warning. "Though, I'm glad you're home. Safe."

And what I really want to do is grab her and kiss her and fuck her until she forgets everything but me, but now is not the time. I turn to Rowena. "Mother, to what do we owe the pleasure?"

She purses her scarlet lips and squints at me in her myopic way, radiating tension and irritation. The doorbell rings, startling us all, and because I'm right beside it, I open the door, wondering who in the hell is calling at midnight. Maryanne stands on the threshold, wilting and wrung out in her scrubs. She casts a tired, wary, I-may-know-what's-going-on-but-I'm-not-sure look at me and shuffles in as I step aside.

"A family reunion. Past midnight. How quaint." My sarcasm hides the fact that I'm completely blindsided by them both being here. It's after fucking midnight, I'm about to have a massive row with my wife, and I thought my mother was in New York avoiding me.

Maryanne follows in our mother's expensive-perfumed wake, and they head down the hallway to the drawing room.

"Please. Come in. Make yourself at home," I offer to their backs, altogether bemused that they're both here. The Mothership has come all the way from Manhattan. I just wanted her to return my call. Not turn up on my bloody doorstep.

I hang up the coats and turn to find Alessia eyeing me warily. She's said nothing. I reach for her hand, and she snatches hers away.

Okay. She's pissed off. "We'll talk about whatever's bugging you and why you fled without telling me once I've dealt with the Mothership."

Alessia raises her head, her eyes flashing.

Okay, she's really fucking pissed.

"She was here when I arrived home," she says.

"In the flat?"

"Yes."

How the hell did she get in?

"Let's see what she wants." Icily formal, I motion for my wife to proceed me and walk toward the drawing room. "After you." I'm relieved when she does as she's asked. I'm anxious to hear what my mother has to say because she's felt the need to make a personal appearance.

This is very out of character.

Rowena stands in the center of the room, and from the disdain on her face, I suspect she's appraising it and finding it lacking. She scans me from head to toe and reaches the same conclusion. "Hello, Maxim." Her tone is clipped and, if I'm not mistaken, weary.

No niceties.

No cheek for me to grace with a kiss.

Not even her usual nasty sarcasm.

"You had a fine evening out, with or without your... wife?" The word *wife* is a sneer.

Ah. There she is. The Rowena I know. What the hell has she said to Alessia?

I glance at Alessia, who's frozen beside me, her dark eyes obsidian as she stares at my mother with thinly veiled hostility.

"What I've been doing with my wife is none of your concern. And how did you get into my flat?"

"I bullied Oliver into giving me a key and the code for your alarm. He said he'd send you an email."

Ah. I remember his missed call. I'll have words with him on Monday, but I can only imagine the altercation they had for him to surrender my keys. Maryanne, who's said nothing, shrugs, her face a picture of tired bemusement, and she flops onto the sofa.

"You and your dubious marriage are all over the press." Rowena purses her lips in disgust.

"Mother, you are the fucking press!" I retort.

Is this why she's here? My marriage? Or is it Kit?

She peers down her nose in that annoying, haughty way she has. "I'm the editor and proprietor of one of the UK's leading women's lifestyle magazines. Not the gutter press."

Alessia moves, recovering some of her composure. "May I take your jacket? And would you like some coffee?" she interjects quickly.

"Please," Maryanne half sighs, half gasps from the sofa. She's obviously exhausted. "Then we can get this masquerade over, and I can get some sleep."

"Really, Maryanne," Rowena scolds, her lips pinched. "I'll keep my jacket. And yes. I'd like some coffee. Real coffee." Her tone is that of a woman in charge, but it's only now that I notice she's clutching a dainty handkerchief like her life depends on it.

Alessia squares her shoulders and lifts her chin. "It's all we have." And she gives her mother-in-law a slight smile she doesn't mean, turns on her Jimmy Choo heels, and struts out of the room in her sensational dress.

"So, to what do we owe this honor, Rowena?"

She turns bright blue eyes to me, and in them, I see… raw pain and uncertainty. It's completely confounding. All the animosity I usually feel in her presence evaporates, leaving me defenseless.

A torn white flag in a storm.

Fuck. Mate.

"Please. Sit," I whisper, gesturing feebly toward the sofa.

She takes a deep breath. "No. You sit. You'll need to."

Like an automaton, I do exactly as she asks and perch on the sofa, waiting for whatever devastating news she has to give Maryanne and me.

Because something's wrong.

Seriously wrong.

She gathers herself, in that way she does—as editor, former countess, former It-girl—and raises her chin, just like my wife. "I felt your last text message regarding Kit and his condition needed a personal reply." She starts to pace while clutching her monogrammed handkerchief—and Maryanne and I watch wide-eyed, not chancing a glance at each other as our mother continues to act entirely out of character. "In answer to your message, you have nothing to worry about, Maxim. Neither of you have anything to worry about. Nothing."

Maryanne nods as if she's confirming a diagnosis.

What the hell does she know that I don't?

"Mama, please. I just got married. We want children."

Her lips thin. "You figure it out. I repeat. It's nothing to do with you or Maryanne."

I frown as I fail to make any connection with what she's saying and what could possibly have been wrong with Kit, and why that has nothing to do with me or my sister.

"Oh, for fuck's sake, you're so obtuse, Maxie!" Maryanne explodes.

What?

"Daddy was not Kit's father." Each word is a staccato expletive from Maryanne's mouth.

There are times when the world tips on its axis and starts to spin at a different and untried trajectory. When the world that you knew stops being and begins anew.

Like when my mother left my father.

Like when my father died.

Like when Kit died.

And, more hopefully, when I met Alessia.

And now, all that I knew and took for granted from my childhood has disappeared in five devastating words.

"So, you see. You have nothing to worry about," Rowena says, her quiet tone tinged with the grief of a mother who's lost her favorite child.

Not a child of the family.

Her own boy.

Her own blue-eyed boy.

Alessia appears in the doorway, bearing a tray with delicate espresso cups and saucers and an elegant cafetiere that I didn't know we had. She places it on the coffee table in front of the sofa and looks warily at me before sitting at my side.

No one moves.

"Did Daddy know?" Maryanne's question echoes with righteous indignation through the oppressive atmosphere within the drawing room.

"Yes." My mother fists her hands.

"And he took your shame to his grave," Maryanne continues in the same vein.

Rowena closes her eyes. "Yes."

She turns to me, a tear sliding down her cheek.

Fuck. I have never seen my mother cry, and my emotions crowd into my throat and stay there. Expanding and smothering me.

"Say something," she hisses.

But I'm hollow. Lost for words at her treachery and betrayal—a mere casual observer to a family tragedy.

My poor father.

My champion.

It all makes sense now.

"So, to be clear," Maryanne says as she stands, "it was Kit's biological father who had an issue."

"Yes. He died last year from his condition."

Fuck.

What I should feel… is relief. But there's nothing.

Except perhaps a bottomless rage on behalf of my father.

On behalf of Kit.

"Did Kit know?" The words are out of my mouth.

Rowena makes a strange, strangled noise.

"Did he find out over New Year?" Maryanne's voice is quiet with recrimination as tears pool in her eyes. My faithless mother closes her eyes once more, grasps her handkerchief, and emits an unearthly, spine-tingling cry as if she's being disemboweled.

Fuck. He knew.

That's why he was out on his motorcycle, haring through Trevethick's wintry lanes.

Maryanne lets out a similar sounding sob, her green eyes blazing with the ugliness of this tragic news; she stands and storms out of the room, down the hallway, and leaves, slamming the front door.

"Does Caroline know?" I ask.

My mother shakes her head.

"Good. We should leave it that way. Thank you for clearing that up. I think perhaps you should leave now." I'm back—the detached persona I've cultivated over the years to deal with my mother restored.

She nods, unable to speak.

"May I get you anything?" Alessia asks.

Rowena seems to recover and peers down her nose at my beautiful, compassionate wife. "No. I don't need anything from the likes of you."

My detachment evaporates, and behind it is a seething caul-dron of rage. "Rowena, don't you dare speak to my wife like that," I warn between gritted teeth.

"Maxim. Now you know. You are your father's son. A knight in shining armor—a sucker for a damsel in distress. Well, this damsel"—she points an elegant scarlet fingernail at herself—"was up to the task of the Trevethick legacy. I doubt your... *daily* will be. You need someone of your own class, someone English who understands the pressures of the title and your position in society. Someone who can help you fulfill the role you were born to and help protect our legacy. Besides, it's not as if your marriage was legal. Heath has done some research."

Alessia flinches as if she's been physically assaulted.

What the hell! Heath? Heath!

Get out. Get out now." Maxim is on his feet, and Alessia stands too.

They're a show of force. Together.

His mother casts a superior, scornful eye over them both, but Alessia sees through her veil of detachment as Rowena swallows, her jaw strained; she's wounded and hurt—rejected by both of her children—and she's lashing out, especially at Alessia who's an easy target. She's already been at the bitter end of Rowena's vicious tongue this evening.

"And you finally addressed me as mama," Rowena whispers as she regards her son. "It was too much to hope that you might find some compassion for me." She turns and waltzes out of the room, her heels clicking on the hardwood floor, echoing down the hallway until she exits quietly through the front door.

Compassion? For her?

And she knows! About our marriage because of Heath! Her fuckboy! *Shit!*

Alessia turns her elfin face to me, her eyes impossibly large, and I blow out a breath I didn't know I was holding. "You okay?" I ask, my heart beating at a furious pace, pumping adrenaline through my body, so I'm ready to fight or flee.

I'm ready to fight. But Rowena's gone. Is Alessia going to fight?

She nods. "You?"

"I don't know how I'm supposed to feel after that… bombshell. I'm so sorry that you had to witness that and bear the brunt of her meltdown." I drag a hand through my hair, trying to assimilate what's just happened.

Kit was my half-brother.

Hell.

"I heard what she said. Did you know?"

"No. I'm stunned. My mother, a pillar of the establishment." I take Alessia's hand and pull her into my arms.

We stand dazed and confused in each other's clutches for seconds… minutes—I don't know—as I try to recalibrate my life from within this new prism. All I have is questions that I was too stunned to ask before she left.

Did my father know when they married?

Who was Kit's father?

Shit.

Alessia pulls away, and I remember that she and I have yet to clear the air.

I s this why you have been distracted?" Alessia asks as she tries to find some equilibrium.

"Yes. Caroline came to the office with the letters from Kit's GP and a genetic counseling service."

Alessia's hackles rise, equilibrium lost, and she stiffens. For the life of her, Alessia does not trust Caroline. Even after the pleasant time they spent together today. She knows Caroline is in love with Maxim. Maybe she was always in love with him but married his brother for the title, wealth, and social standing.

Maxim regards her warily. "She needed to show me the letters. I told you."

"She said she's working with you. You didn't tell me that."

Maxim frowns. "No, not with me. For me, I suppose. Well, for the estate. Honestly, Alessia," he huffs in frustration, "Caroline isn't important. She's the least of our issues right now. What is important was I thought that I might have a debilitating condition. I texted my mother to see if she knew anything about Kit. She wouldn't talk to me. Until now."

"And you didn't tell me that either."

Maxim closes his eyes and rubs his forehead. "No. I thought you'd leave me."

It's the third time this evening that Alessia's felt winded.

Uau. How could he think that? "I would never leave you—"

Y ou did fucking leave!" I almost shout. "At the party, tonight. Without even a goodbye. Why?"

Her eyes cloud, and her face falls, her heartache writ large in the tension at her jaw. "But you…you…" she whispers, unable or unwilling to say it out loud.

My chest constricts. "The kiss?" Deep down, I know that's what she's trying to say. Alessia meets my gaze and gives me the same haughty look my mother gave us before she left. She's hiding behind that look, protecting herself. I see that now, and it cuts me to the quick. "Charlotte was drunk," I state. "She's an ex-girlfriend, and for some bizarre reason, she threw herself at me. I was taken by surprise. *She* kissed *me*—not the other way round. I peeled her off me, sat her down, and came to find you. And you'd disappeared with fucking Grisha! Grisha!" Anger infuses my veins once more with heat. I step further away from her and run a hand through my hair, trying to hold on to my temper.

Fucking Grisha Egonov. Renowned arsehole. Possible underworld criminal.

"I saw the kiss," Alessia says quietly. "I had to leave. Grisha helped me. He sent me home. He was kind."

"He is not kind! You cannot trust him," I snap and reaching out, I grab her and pull her into my arms. I want to shake her, but I don't. "You put yourself in what could have been a dangerous situation. Why do you do this? Why do you run? You have to learn to confront me. I didn't do anything wrong. And we could have sorted this out there and then."

"I thought… I thought perhaps this was how you always behave," she says quickly.

What? No.

"There are so many," Alessia whispers, and in those four words, there's a world of hurt that I don't really understand, and can't do anything about.

"Alessia. We're married. I have a past. You know this. But I only want you. No one else. I don't care what my mother says. I don't care what the world says. The press… fuck them. I just want you. And you fucking left me when you know how anxious I am about your safety." I rest my forehead against hers and close my eyes.

Fuck. This night.

"Look, it's really late. We've had enough drama tonight. Let's just go to bed." I kiss her forehead.

Alessia feels like a scolded child. She wishes she hadn't looked away when she was on the mezzanine, just to verify Maxim's story. It sounds so plausible that it's probably true. She wants to believe that it's true. Then she finds out he's been wrestling with all these issues, which he hadn't shared with her.

Does he think she's incapable of handling this news?

Does he think she's a child?

She's young and inexperienced. But she's no child.

"What?" he asks, bright green eyes burning into hers.

"You should have told me about your brother." She sounds sulky even to her own ears.

"I didn't want to worry you until I knew for certain what I was dealing with. Please. I'm tired. It's been a shitty few hours. Let's go to bed." He releases her, steps back once more, and they stare at each other.

They're raw. And sad. And on either side of a huge divide that Alessia doesn't really understand.

Was it always there, or did the divide suddenly appear?

Maxim closes his eyes, and when he opens them, they're dim with defeat. "You look beautiful. Every inch a countess, no matter what my mother may have said to you. And I know she said something else and for that I'm sorry. I'm here. I love you, but if that's not enough, I don't know what more I can do. I'm tired, and I'm going to bed." He turns and walks from the room, his footsteps echoing down the hall toward his bedroom, leaving Alessia reeling and utterly alone.

Chapter Twenty-One

In our bedroom, I strip off my jacket and toss it on the sofa. So much for my lucky suit. I think I'll burn it. Like an idiot, I turn toward the closed door and *will* Alessia to join me. If she doesn't, I don't know where we go from here, and if she does, she can remove my cuff links and undress me, and we'll go to bed and fuck and spoon and hold each other. The little dragon catches my eye, unlit and spiritless. He looks how I feel—dim and glum. But wherever Alessia sleeps, she'll need him, so perhaps she'll come and fetch him.

Hopefully.

I don't know how long I stand there dazed and confused, staring at a small piece of molded plastic, but there's no sign of my wife. She's abandoned both my dragon friend and me.

I remove each cuff link and start on the buttons, fatigue wrapping around me like a shroud. Sinking onto the bed, I sit with my head in my hands and try to process the last couple of hours.

This evening has been… *intense.*

I've dealt with a drunken ex, my missing wife, my faithless mother and her revelations, and her meddling fuck toy. I wonder if Heath was the one who tipped off the press. He has the connections.

Fucker.

And then there's Kit. *My half-brother.*

Did he know? Rowena didn't answer the question. I cast my mind back to the New Year when we were at the Hall. "*Not now, Maxim!*" he'd snapped as he stormed out of the kitchen back door into the dark, icy night. And I'd turned and watched my mother stalk down the corridor, her heels tapping their brisk percussive beat, as she walked stiffly away from Kit's office.

Had they been talking? Fighting? I don't remember hearing any raised voices.

But maybe I was my usual oblivious self.

If she *had* told him—he'd have known he was an impostor, and he might lose everything. He would have been shocked and dumbfounded and furious, and that's probably what spurred him onto his Ducati.

Anger. At Rowena.

And now she has to carry that guilt.

His death is on her.

He'd lost everything. Except he hadn't. Not really—only he and Rowena knew.

Fuck a duck.

That's it. She feels responsible for his death. Her favorite child. The eerie sound she made this evening—the half-sob, half-cry—was proof enough. I'd not seen her shed a tear for him until tonight when the truth was finally aired.

Perhaps, before then, she grieved in private.

I'll never know.

Unless she and I talk.

And that's not going to happen anytime soon.

How the hell do we come back from this?

Alessia slumps onto the couch, tears welling in her eyes.

What has she done?

Somehow, during their fight, she's been made to feel like the villain.

How? She'd watched her husband kiss another woman, and she left because she didn't want to witness his betrayal. Is that so unreasonable? Then she arrived back at his apartment, and she'd been berated and found thoroughly wanting by her mother-in-law.

And insulted too!

As if Alessia is motivated by money!

It had taken all her resolve not to rip the earrings from her ears and toss them at Rowena.

All Alessia wants is Maxim's love.

You have that! The still, small voice of her conscience reminds her. He's told her often enough. And again! Just now.

What has he done to make her think he doesn't love her?

He's explained the kiss. He can't help how women react to him. He's probably had to contend with that kind of attention since he was in his teens. And what hot-blooded male wouldn't take advantage?

He only changed when he met Alessia.

She saw the proof… or lack, in the wastebasket in his bedroom.

No one since I saw you clutching the broom in my hallway.

I've only felt it since I met you.

Her ire dissipates, leaving a burning hole in her chest.

He didn't have to marry her. He could have left. He stood up to his mother on her behalf, and that's not something an Albanian man would generally do.

Maxim's given her the world.

Is that not enough?

Why is she so insecure?

The other women.

All of them. Including the ones she's met. Caroline. Ticia. Arabella.

Alessia. Alessia. Alessia.

Enough!

She must stop comparing herself to all the women he's bedded.

She has to learn to trust him. And now he's explained about that kiss—he's given her no reason not to. And if she does doubt him, she has his permission to question him. He's asked for that… *Confront me. Talk to me.*

It's not the first time he's said that… *You need to tell me what you want to do. This is a partnership.*

The hole in her chest deepens and darkens. He'd received such troubling news, and he didn't think he could share it with her because he thought she might leave.

Does he think she's so faithless and lacking in compassion? *Where's the sense of partnership in her reaction?*

Guilt slices like a scythe through her heart. She's been so absorbed in her own misgivings that she missed all these clues to Maxim's state of mind.

Maxim's in a new, demanding role that he wasn't expecting; he's fallen in love, he's rescued her from kidnappers, he's newly married, and he's been harboring the news that he might have a potentially life-altering illness.

He's protected her from this.

And Alessia's just consumed by the number of women he's slept with and his ex-girlfriends. Remorse follows the scythe through her heart, filling the gaping hole and almost choking her.

O Zot. Fool! Go to him!

And I have my wife's insecurities to deal with. My beautiful, stoic, talented wife who thinks she's less than the women who came before. Rowena can be a complete bitch sometimes. Did she say something that's making Alessia reassess our relationship?

I hope not.

But I'm not giving up. I just need a moment to get my head together.

My sweet, sad wife.

Emotion gathers in my throat. Maybe she'll never get beyond my past. It preoccupies her in ways I don't understand. Perhaps it *is* our cultural divide, and in my defense, I can categorically say I've never looked at another woman since I met her and I'm as obsessed with her now as I was then.

But I didn't expect to feel this… vulnerable.

Or this… miserable.

What if she leaves?

Fuck! It's unthinkable.

I'll be crushed.

I remember when the Arsehole spirited her away and how devastating that was. I rub my face, trying to scrub the feeling away, and catch a whisper of her scent and hear the rustle of silk. An ember of hope lights up the cavern that is my heart, and I open my eyes. On the floor beneath my gaze are her bare feet, her toes painted scarlet. I look up, and she's standing in front of me, and the sight of her tearstained face rips through my soul.

"Oh, love," I murmur and stand in one swift movement.

"I'm sorry." Her voice is barely audible.

"Oh, baby, so am I." I pull her into my arms, breathing in her scent and holding her fast and hard against my body. As she nestles against me, her tears dampen my neck. "Hey, love, please don't cry."

She tightens her arms around me and starts weeping.

Hell. This is my fault. I've done this, and I remember her sobbing in the room next to mine at the Hideout. She was overwhelmed then and maybe now.

Frankly, so am I. I tighten my hold on her and let her cry. Perhaps that's what she needs. Sitting back on the bed, I cradle her in my lap, rocking gently, and it's soothing. Perhaps this is what we both need—an outward expression of the frustrations of the last few hours.

It's cathartic.

I calm just holding her close. My beautiful, stoic wife needing me. *Me.*

My mother was right.

I am a sucker for a damsel in distress, or maybe—it's just Alessia.

Eventually, she quiets, and I reach over to the bedside and grab a tissue. "Here. Better?" I ask.

She nods and wipes her nose and eyes, which are all smudged kohl and running mascara and even like this… she's gorgeous.

More so.

"Good. Me too." I kiss her forehead. "Let me get you out of this dress, and we can go to bed." Lifting her off my lap and onto the floor, I stand behind her, brush her hair over her shoulder, and unfasten her dress at the neck. Leaning down, I press my lips to her nape, inhaling her scent, and then turn to undress myself.

She wanders into the bathroom while I strip and clamber into bed. When she emerges a few minutes later, she's fresh-faced and wearing one of my T-shirts. She switches on the little dragon nightlight while I flip back the quilt, and she climbs in beside me and snuggles up, her head on my chest, her arm across my body.

"I love you," she whispers, and her words unfurl inside my heart, filling the void left by my treacherous mother.

"I know. I love you too."

I kiss the top of her head, close my eyes, and fall into an exhausted sleep.

My footsteps echo an urgent beat on the hard reflective floor, and I squint beneath the unremitting light of the fluorescents.

I've been here before.

"This way." The A&E consultant stops and opens the door to a cool, stark room that is the hospital mortuary.

I don't want to go in. I don't want to see.

The A&E consultant stares. Scarlet lips pursed.

Rowena?

"In you go," she says in a clipped tone that's not to be contradicted.

Inside, on a table, beneath a sheet, is my brother.

Kit.

No! That's not him.

It's *me*—lying bruised and broken… cold… dead.

What?

From my prone position on the table, I watch Kit lean over and kiss my forehead. "Goodbye, you fucker," he rasps, the strain of unshed tears heavy in his throat. "You've got this. This is what you were born to do." He smiles, his crooked, sincere smile that's reserved for those rare moments when he's fucked up.

Kit! No! You've got this wrong.

Wait!

"You've got this, Spare," he says again, then disappears. And I'm looking down at him once more, leaning over him while he sleeps. Except his battered body belies that… he's not asleep—he's dead.

No! Kit! No! The words stay stuck in my throat. I can't speak. This is all wrong.

And I'm outside the room watching my mother walk stiffly away, her heels beating a terse tattoo on the tiled floor as she moves farther and farther away.

Rowena! Mother! Mama!

I wake drenched in sweat, my heart thumping a furious rhythm, my blood pumping frantically through my veins, and I'm sure I'm shaking the bed. I take a deep, cleansing breath and my heartbeat gradually slows.

It's quiet and dark. Even the shimmers on the ceiling are absent.

Alessia mumbles something unintelligible but settles back to sleep.

Thank God she's here.

I turn over to face her, resting my head on my arm and watching her slumber, her features delicate and lovely in the soft glow of the little dragon.

It's just a dream.

No. A nightmare. A prophetic nightmare.

I rub my face and lie on my back, trying to drive out the images of Kit and me on the cold slab.

Was my mother's revelation such a shock to me? Did I know? Maryanne and I share similar coloring—a straightforward blend of our parents. Kit did not. He was blond and blue-eyed, driven and imperious. He was harder, more arrogant, and meaner, maybe, than both Maryanne and me. It's been a revelation that he made Caro attend etiquette classes. He was always a bit of a snob, and I wonder if he knew deep down.

Hell. This changes nothing. No one need ever know.

I should contact Maryanne and find out how she's doing.

We can keep this within the family—provided my mother hasn't blurted all to *Heath.*

When I turn back to Alessia, she's watching me, her dark eyes gleaming in the soft light from the little dragon.

"Did I wake you?"

"No," she whispers, placing her palm on my cheek and steadying me in the storm. I close my eyes, cherishing her touch and grateful that it distracts me from my fevered thoughts. "Are you okay?" she asks. "Is there anything I can do?"

With my eyes intent on hers, I try to articulate how I feel, but I'm lost in my own turmoil.

Alessia nods as if she understands and brushes her lips against mine. "You will figure this out. And until then, I've got you. I'm sorry I wasn't here for you early...um...earlier." She snuggles closer, resting her head on my chest, and I wrap an arm around her, holding on tight.

"It's okay, baby," I murmur. "I should have told you."

When she's not angry with me, she's my guiding light, and with her so close, her scent fills my senses, soothing me.

As Alessia's breathing settles into the rhythm of sleep, I close my eyes and join her.

Chapter Twenty-Two

I wake with a start. It's a bright spring morning, and a glance to my side tells me I'm on my own.

Hell! Is she here?

I leap out of bed, grab my jeans, slip them on, and stalk out of the bedroom. Alessia is in the kitchen making bread, her face etched in furious concentration. She's bent over the counter kneading the dough like it's deeply offended her, or her life depends on it—I'm not sure which. She's barefoot but not pregnant, I think idly and watch as a tendril from her ponytail escapes and curls down her cheek and under her chin. She shakes it loose, peers up, and freezes when she sees me.

"Good morning." My voice is a whisper.

"Hi," she says and stands upright. She's in tight jeans and a tighter T-shirt, and it's stirring as hell, but her dark eyes are wary.

Is this a hangover from yesterday's debacle? "You okay?"

She presses her lips together, quickly rinses her hands, and grabs her phone from the countertop. "My mother. She sent me this. She has the Google alert."

My heart sinks as she hands me her phone, and sure enough, she reveals a tabloid article titled "The Earl, the Ex and the Wife." A series of photographs from last night accompany it—Alessia, Caroline, and me arriving at the party, together at the party, and there's a photograph of Charlotte kissing me. In it, I'm obviously taken aback and not a willing participant. I'm vindicated, though I'm sure that's not what the picture editor who chose the photo intended. I slide my gaze to Alessia's. "I love the one of you and me." I hand her phone back. "Your mother sent that?"

Alessia nods and sets her phone on the counter. "She worries."

"Did you reassure her?"

"I did."

"Good. Are you reassured?"

She bites her lip, her eyes shining with unshed tears—and I have my answer. Reaching up, I run my thumb over her trembling bottom lip. "You didn't sign up for any of this, did you?"

She inhales sharply, and I dread what she's going to say. But she runs her tongue across my thumb, then purses her lips and kisses the tip. The jolt travels like lightning to my groin, heating everything in its path, and I suppress a groan, taken completely by surprise.

Alessia's eyes, intent on me, widen a fraction.

Not from fear or anger.

From the same jolt of desire.

Her sharply exhaled breath dries the spot on my thumb moistened by her kiss, sending my blood racing.

South.

Her eyes follow, and my dick rejoices as I drop my hand.

"Alessia," I whisper, and I don't know if it's a plea or a warning. Her darkening eyes lift, pinning mine. Gone are the unshed tears; there's just her burning gaze full of carnal promise. I step closer so I'm bathed in her scent and the warmth of her body. I want nothing more than to grab her, strip off her jeans, and fuck her on the kitchen counter. But I want her to make the first move. "What do you want, my love?"

Tentatively, she raises her hand and traces my bottom lip with her thumb. "No, I didn't sign up for this. But I did sign up for you."

The words are softly spoken.

And in them. There's hope. For us.

My senses heightened, I feel the air thicken between us, full of lush anticipation.

And heat.

And expectation.

It's heady and addictive.

I've never felt like this with anyone else. My sweet, siren wife. She has no idea about the potency of the magic she weaves and the spell she casts over me.

Or maybe she does.

"What do you want, Alessia?"

"You," she whispers, and using one hand, she runs the tips of her fingers down my sternum, firing synapses throughout my body. Then across my chest, so my nipples pucker at her touch, and down my stomach, my belly, and my happy trail to the button on the waistband of my jeans. Keeping her eyes on mine, she undoes the button in one nimble move. And her fingers skirt lower, cradling my heavy erection through the denim.

"You have me." I tilt my pelvis, finding some friction against her palm, and close my eyes, fisting my hands to stop myself from wrapping her in my arms.

Alessia regards her husband through heavy-lidded eyes.

You'll have to fight for him. Her mother's words from their call this morning ring through her head. And fight, she will. Using every available weapon she has.

She loves him.

She knows this.

She wants him.

And she wants him to want her. She skirts her fingers over his unyielding erection once more. The rigid proof at her fingertips means she's succeeded.

It's an intoxicating feeling. Seducing her husband.

Or maybe he's seducing her...

She doesn't care.

She didn't sign up for all the other women.

But they are out of his life. He said so, and she's chosen to believe him. Even though there's questionable evidence splashed all over the papers. She can see he's the reluctant party in the photograph.

And now she wants him. But he hasn't touched her since his thumb skirted her lip.

It's frustrating.

Confront me. Talk to me.

Those were his words. "Take me," she says, because that's what she wants. Here. Right now.

Maxim groans and steps forward, bringing his body flush against hers and clasping her face between his palms and bringing her lips to his. His tongue unleashed, he searches and finds and provokes her own. Her hands fist in his hair as she revels in his kiss—wanting and giving more. When they're both breathless, he pulls sharply away and drops to his knees. Deftly, he makes fast work of her jeans, unfastening them and sliding them and her panties down her legs and off. He grabs her thighs and tugs her against his waiting nose and mouth.

"Ah!" she groans and grabs the countertop for balance. Maxim's tongue is on her.

Big time.

Teasing.

Circling.

Coaxing her higher.

Making her wetter and wetter.

Alessia tilts her head back, one hand tugging his hair, the other gripping the counter, and she moans, surrendering to his masterful ministrations.

I think I'm going to burst. Standing ready to bury myself in my wife, I grab her glorious behind and lift her onto the counter. "I've never done it here," I mutter as I unzip my jeans, freeing my straining dick. Alessia approves and wraps her legs around me, hauling me closer, digging her heels in my arse. She rests her arms on my shoulders, and we both pause, our breath mingling, eyes on each other. She kisses me. And pulls away.

"I taste me," she whispers.

"Best flavor in the world."

She grins, her whole face lighting up like a blissful spring day, and she cups my face, bringing my mouth to hers and we kiss, our lips covered in a heady combination of her arousal and my saliva.

It's slippery and wet.

And wonderful.

And oh-so-slowly, I sink into my wife.

"Ah," she cries, tipping back her head and hitting it on the cupboard behind. "Ow!"

She laughs, and I cup her head, knowing she's not hurt—and thrust harder and deeper inside her. She clings to me as I set a punishing, forget-everything-else pace. She bites my earlobe, her breathing hot and harsh in my ear as I lose myself in her.

And I feel her. Climbing. Higher and higher.

I keep going, banishing all thoughts from last night, so it's only her and me in the now.

Alessia.

She's rising and soaring, taking me with her.

"Maxim," she cries as she comes, and the power of her orgasm pushes me over the edge, and I climax hard and fast, buried in my beautiful wife.

I have flour on my backside," Alessia mumbles.

Maxim raises his face from the crook of her neck and grins. "There's a sentence I never thought I'd hear." He runs his nose down hers and kisses her sweetly. They're still intimately joined, and neither of them seem to want to move.

"I love you, Lady Trevethick."

"I love you, Lord Trevethick," she responds.

"Good."

She tightens her hold on him, keeping him anchored inside her. "If you kiss anyone else, I will remove this organ," she says, digging her heels into his naked butt.

Maxim laughs and eases out of her. "Understood, my lady."

Alessia smiles. "I will fight for you," she says as he tugs up his jeans.

He caresses her face with both his hands, his thumbs tracing the outline of her lips and his green eyes blazing. "Oh my love, you don't have to fight for me. I'm yours. Always. I'll be yours for as long as you'll have me."

Alessia is winded by his quiet but passionate entreaty.

He studies her as he stands between her legs. "What can I do to convince you?"

She frowns. Where is he going with this?

"I know," he says, his face lighting up with sudden inspiration. "Let's have a baby."

Chapter Twenty-Three

Alessia gasps and stares back into bright green eyes, totally blind-sided. "A baby?" she squeaks.

He plants a soft kiss at the corner of her mouth. "Yes. A boy." He kisses her again. "Then a girl." Kiss. "Then another boy." Kiss. "And another girl." He kisses the other side of her mouth.

Alessia giggles. "Four children! I'm not sure it works like that."

"I know how it works," he growls, amused.

"*Call of Duty?*"

Maxim laughs. "Oh, my love. Funny and talented. Never change." He nuzzles her nose with his.

"My backside is covered in flour, and you want babies."

He nods.

"Can I shower first?"

He grins and looks at the counter beside her, where the dough lies neglected but rising. "I was rather hoping for breakfast." He kisses her again, and she swats him away.

"Help me down, and I will make you breakfast."

"Only if you promise not to put your jeans or knickers back on." He gently lifts her from the counter and slides her down his body until her feet touch the floor. He cradles her head in his hands. "I want babies—lots of them. I thought—" He swallows. "I thought that maybe with Kit… and his…condition. That…"

"Oh, Maxim," Alessia whispers, realizing that this is another reason he's been so preoccupied. She leans in, bringing her lips to his, and kisses him, a sweet, remorseful kiss.

All the worry, and she never knew.

"Let's have breakfast and talk about it."

"We could go out," Maxim offers.

"I like making breakfast for you, Maxim. I want to take care of you, like you want to provide for me. That's a partnership."

Alessia's fingers make patterns in my hair as we lie in bed. Spent. Replete. Together. My head on her stomach, I turn and kiss the soft skin of her belly and allow myself a little fantasy that it's swollen with our child.

Alessia doesn't have the same sense of urgency as I do. She doesn't realize that I'm trying to bind her to me in any way I can, but we've talked, and she's right. She's young and wants to see a little of the world before we embark on babies.

Mate. What were you thinking?

I wonder what my mother would make of being a grandmother.

I sigh. I have no idea how I'll repair that relationship.

Do I want to?

"What is it?" Alessia asks.

"I'm just thinking about my mother."

Alessia stiffens beneath me.

Shit. "Did she say something horribly dreadful to you?"

Alessia is quiet, and her fingers have stopped fiddling with my hair, so I look up.

Eyes gleaming, she swallows. "She wanted to know how much money I wanted to leave you."

What. The. Fuck?

Sitting up, I lean against the pillows and gather my wife in my arms. "I'm so sorry."

"I was hurt and angry, but she was only acting in what she thinks is your…um…best…um…"

"Interests?"

"Yes. That."

"It's not in my best interests at all. The woman wouldn't know my best interests if she tripped over them and they smacked her bloody arse. You don't deserve to be spoken to like that. If anything—" I stop because what I'm about to say about my own mother is… *un-fucking-becoming.* "Who the hell does she think she is?" I shake my head in disbelief and kiss the top of Alessia's head.

"She did come here and had the courage to tell you and your sister face to the face about your brother."

"Well, that's putting a positive slant on what happened. But I suppose you're right." I offer her a smile. "And it's 'face-to-face.'"

Alessia grins. "There he is—my English teacher."

"For as long as you need me."

"I will always need you." Alessia's burning sincerity and love is in every syllable of her soft-spoken statement, and it feeds my soul. Curling my fingers around hers, I bring them to my lips. And to think we were at loggerheads last night—and I wonder what would have happened if my mother hadn't put in her untimely appearance. "I wonder why she came all the way from Manhattan to tell us in such a hostile way."

"Perhaps she is punishing herself?" Alessia offers.

Wow. "That's insightful. Do you think so?"

She shakes her head, and it's plain that this is just Alessia's hypothesis, but it's credible. Perhaps my mother is filled with shame.

Who knows? Is she capable of shame?

"Shall we go out for lunch?" I ask, and Alessia grins. "We'll probably have to dodge the press after that sordid article," I add.

Alessia shrugs. "We say nothing."

I grin. "Exactly."

On Monday morning, Alessia and Maxim leave via the fire escape to avoid the cluster of reporters outside the building. Maxim hails a cab, and together, feeling pleased with themselves, they settle into the back seat and head to the London Academy of Social Etiquette and Graces.

"What's that place?" Alessia asks, pointing with her chin at an enormous, ornate, gothic building.

"That's the Natural History Museum. We should go. Beside it is the Science Museum. Many a Saturday afternoon was spent there. Our nanny at the time had a passion for science. But it has a great place for kids to play and explore."

Alessia grins. "One day, we will take our children."

Maxim glances at her. "Or the nanny will." He finds and fondles her knee.

"Nanny?" Alessia had not thought that they might have help with childcare.

"Just a thought. I had one. Well, several, actually. And look how I turned out."

Alessia laughs. And Maxim scowls, pretending to be offended. "What are you implying? Am I not the epitome of well-bred manhood?"

"Of course you are." She giggles. "You have the best manners. And after this week, so shall I." She pats his knee, suppressing her laughter.

The cab pulls up outside an impressive white building in Queen's Gate, South Kensington. "We're here." Maxim opens the taxi door and steps out while the cab idles. Alessia follows him, staring up at yet more imposing architecture. "Do you want me to come in with you?" Maxim asks.

Alessia tries to suppress her smile. He's been fussing like a mother hen all morning, and it's a side of him she's not seen before. "I'll be okay."

"Text me if you need anything." He kisses her quickly and

climbs back in the cab, and Alessia strides up the stone steps to the glossy black door.

So many shiny black doors in London.

She rings the brass bell, ignoring the fluttering of nerves in her stomach, and the door buzzes open. Alessia steps inside a wide hallway painted a brilliant white, and from behind a reception desk, a young woman in a gray suit looks up, an open, expectant expression on her face.

"London Academy—" Alessia asks.

"Up to the first floor. Registration is through the door on the left."

"Thank you," Alessia says, surprised to be interrupted. She heads up the wide staircase that creaks beneath each footfall to the first floor and turns left toward a door with a discreet sign that reads: L A S E G. Inside the white, high-ceilinged room, she's greeted by an older, smartly dressed woman with pearls at her ears and her neck, carrying a clipboard.

"Good morning," the woman says pleasantly, her smile reaching her bright brown eyes.

"Hello," Alessia replies.

"My name is Belinda Donaldson, I'm the administrator, and I'll be checking you in. We use first or given names for our delegates here at the Academy to protect everyone's identity."

"Alessia," Alessia replies.

"Excellent. Welcome, Alessia. You're the first to arrive. Punctuality is the politeness of kings… and queens. Please help yourself to tea or coffee, and do take a seat."

Alessia pours coffee into one of the delicate cups and takes a seat. She watches as women arrive and are greeted in a similar fashion by Belinda. They're all elegant, some in dresses, some in pants like her, and most are young, like Alessia, but there's one older lady who must be in her fifties. Alessia is grateful to be wearing her new black pants, white shirt, and tailored jacket; knowing she's well-dressed has boosted her confidence. For the first time, she feels like she belongs with these women.

A breathless young woman with flowing red hair stumbles

into the room. "Hello," she says, gasping for air. "I thought I was going to be late."

Belinda regards her coolly. "Good morning. Take a moment. You have time."

"Great. Thanks. My name's Tabitha, Lady—"

"I'll stop you right there, Tabitha. We operate on a first-name basis only. Please. Come and sit down and help yourself to tea or coffee. We will begin shortly."

After a delicious pub lunch yesterday afternoon, Alessia and Maxim had attended an exhibition of pre-Raphaelite art at Tate Britain, a gallery not far from their apartment. With her long red hair and flowing chiffon dress, Tabitha reminds Alessia of one of the subjects in the paintings.

The assembled women resume their quiet chatter among themselves as Tabitha sits down beside Alessia. "Hi, I'm Tabitha," she introduces herself. "I thought I'd be late!" She makes a face, and Alessia smiles, feeling a little more relaxed as she introduces herself. She's drawn to Tabitha's bright grin.

"I was too early," Alessia confesses. "I am nervous."

Tabitha beams as if she's met a long-lost friend. "You'll be fine," she says and Alessia feels lighter, buoyed by Tabitha's warmth.

On Sunday, my phone had blown up with texts about Dimitri's party and the photos of Alessia and bloody Charlotte. I'd ignored the messages, choosing to spend quality time with my wife. And what a wonderful day we had—we seem to have turned a corner. We've survived our first major argument, my mother's interference and her revelations, and some extremely unwelcome press attention.

And Alessia *finally* seems to be standing up for herself.

If you kiss anyone else, I will remove this organ.

I shake my head, smiling at my possessive, jealous wife.

But as I sit at my desk and try to read up on the rules for

distilling alcohol in the UK, I'm finding it impossible to concen-
trate. My brain continues to pick over my mother's disclosure
like it's carrion. I've called and left messages for Maryanne so we
can compare notes on the drama, but she's not returned either.

Is she angry with me?

I suppose I prompted the fallout and didn't tell Maryanne
about Kit's genetic counseling.

Hell.

And I'm not sure how I'm supposed to feel after Rowena's
shocking news.

Numb?

Distracted?

Angry?

Yeah, all those feelings.

Dude, get a grip.

My second meeting of the day is at the Mayfair mansion block
refurbishment with Oliver and Caroline. We're going through
design and décor plans for the foyers, the common areas, and the
show apartment. Caroline and Oliver are already in the foyer,
making what sounds like awkward small talk. Oliver, for some
reason, looks a little flustered while Caroline observes him with
cool detachment.

"Maxim!" Caro brightens, greeting me with a quick peck on
my cheek.

"So, what do you think?" I ask.

"This is a light, airy space, and we can do a great deal with it.
What, is up to you. What do you want this space to say? What do
you want to achieve?"

I'm not sure if she's mocking me or not—we've never had
a professional conversation before. "What I want is something
classic that doesn't date and doesn't need redecorating every
year."

Oliver smiles in approval. "Yes. Pragmatic," he pipes up.

"You sound just like Kit," Caroline huffs, and a tangle of conflicted emotions fill my throat. Kit. My half-brother.

And Caro doesn't know. "Thank you," I mutter. "I'm going to take that as a compliment."

She smiles. "It was meant as such."

"Let's see the common areas so you can have an idea of the extent of the work required," Oliver says, his gaze intent on Caroline.

She offers him a polite, cool smile. "I can sketch some plans and take a few photos as we walk through."

A lessia is paying attention to Jennifer Knight, their social etiquette instructor and the owner of the school. "And our mission is to empower all of you to present your best selves. You'll have the confidence to walk into any room and know exactly how to behave. From the boardroom to the banqueting hall, you'll be equipped to handle any work and social situation. We'll start with the basics: introductions—both formal and informal—what forms of address you should use, and while mainly focusing on British etiquette, we'll touch on cultural differences that you should be aware of to make those you meet and greet feel respected and comfortable in your presence." Jennifer gives the class a broad smile. "If you'll turn to the first page in your workbook, we can begin."

Alessia does exactly that, while Tabitha is trying and failing not to look bored.

I think I have all I need," Caroline says.

"Excellent." Oliver gives us a rare, relieved smile.

"Do you have a budget in mind?" Caro looks to me.

"Do the designs and give us options," I state, and Oliver nods with approval again—I think—which is heartening.

"Okay. That shouldn't be too difficult. If we're done, can we grab a coffee, Maxim?"

"Sure. There's a café across the road. Oliver, I'll see you back at the office."

"Of course. I'll wait to hear from you, Caroline," he says stiffly. *What is it with these two?*

"Something troubling you?" I ask, watching Caroline slide into the banquette.

"Yes. Rowena. Have you managed to track her down and ask her?"

I take the chair opposite Caro as I struggle to find something to say. "Ask her what?"

"About Kit! The genetic stuff."

I clear my throat. "Yes. Of course. I did. And she said there was nothing to worry about."

Caro narrows her eyes, pinning me with her most intrusive gaze. Inside, I'm flailing. This is not a conversation I expected to have just yet. I'm still coming to terms with my mother's bombshell.

"What are you not telling me?" Caro's tone is terse. She's irritated.

"Nothing."

"Maxim, you're lying. I can always tell. Your whole face becomes completely immobile while your brain frantically works out what to say."

"It does not! And I told you. She said there's nothing to worry about."

"It was all a false alarm?"

I make a noise in my throat that I hope passes for agreement. I don't want to lie to her.

"I'm trying to organize Kit's memorial service, and you won't confirm the date, and Rowena is not taking my calls."

"Oh." *Hell.* Kit's memorial had slipped my mind.

"It's not like her," Caro continues. "I don't know if I've offended her. But it must be something. Can you talk to her?"

"She's not talking to me either."

"Really? Why? Do you think she's okay?"

"I don't know."

"When did you talk to her?"

"Over the weekend."

Caroline huffs. "Maryanne's disappeared too. Perhaps they've found some late winter sun together."

"Maybe. Do you have a guest list for the memorial service?"

"Yes. I'll send it over, and you can add people. I'm waiting for your mother's additions."

"I told Rowena I'd write the eulogy."

"Can we discuss readings?"

"Of course. Whenever. We're around. Alessia is on that etiquette course this week."

"Good. She'll feel a lot more confident afterwards. And she should make some friends."

"Yeah."

"Are you worried?" Caroline scoffs. "For heaven's sake, Maxim. She's a grown woman."

"I know. I know. But the kidnapping. I… I…" I shrug. *What can I say?* Alessia's safety is my priority.

"Of course. But she's here now. With you. She'll be fine."

"Incidentally, what did you say to Charlotte Hampshire at Dimitri's party?"

"Nothing!" she says far too quickly and holds my gaze, but I'm not sure I believe her.

"Caro?" I arch a brow in warning.

What did you say?

"Is this about the photograph? It's everywhere. Are you in trouble?"

"Was that your intention? To cause trouble between Alessia and me?" I glare at her, and the temperature between us drops to below zero.

Caroline's eyes widen. "No! Why would I do that?" she says in a gush of faux indignation. "Is that what you think?"

"Caro, I don't know what to think. But Alessia and I are fine. Stop inter-fucking-fering, or there will be consequences."

She bristles but stays silent, and I know she said something to Charlotte.

"And what's with you and Oliver?" I ask to change the subject.

"What do you mean?" she snaps.

"I don't know, but there's some weird energy between you."

"Oh, for goodness' sake. You're coming across all woo-woo. I'd better go and get on with this work." She stands. "Let me know if you hear from Rowena."

A nd that's a wrap for today, ladies," Jennifer says. "Tomorrow, we'll be covering communication. Everything from texting to writing letters. Thank you for your time and attention today." She smiles, and Alessia almost sags with relief but stops herself as she's endured a whole afternoon of deportment lessons and learned about correct posture.

"I am desperate for a drink," Tabitha hisses beside her. "Please say you'll come."

"Um…" Alessia is hesitant. This is a first for her—a stranger asking her to come for a drink. But she likes Tabitha. A woman her own age. Maxim won't mind.

Will he?

"Don't tell me you have to get back to your husband, Alessia."

"How did…?"

"Your ring. I assumed you were married. But you seem awfully young to be wed."

Alessia smiles. "In my country, it is normal to marry young."

"Tell me all over a drink! Please."

M y phone buzzes. It's a text from Maryanne. *Finally.*

I'm in Seattle.
Will text when home.

Are you okay?

No. Still reeling from dear
Mama's revelations.
Here for some R&R.

How did you get the time off?

Skillz!

What! Her response makes me laugh. It's a most un-Maryanne text. But I'm glad that she's still speaking to me and that she's getting some rest. Has she gone to see that guy she met when she went skiing? I daren't ask.

Enjoy yourself.

Oh. I am.
Are you okay?

Of course.

Maxie, it was you all along.
Not Kit.

What?

The earldom.
It was yours.

My scalp prickles.
It was me all along.
I was the viscount. Then the earl.
Not Kit.

That's hard to hear.

I know ❤
But it was you, Maxie.
It was always you.
Remember that.
Poor Kit. Finding out like that.
He must have been furious.

Yes. I can't stop thinking about that.

I wonder what he had.

What he had?

His genetic condition.

Something awful, I suspect.
I don't want to know.
Poor man.

Yes. Maybe you're right.
We loved him.

We did.

I'll be back later this week.
We can talk then.
I've got to get up.
We're going sailing on a super-
duper catamaran.

Be safe.
Mx

I blow out a breath. Maryanne is still speaking to me, unlike my mother. And she's focused on something that I've not thought about. My family has been obsessed with bloodlines since the earldom was created in the 1600s. My mother was driven by legacy too. It was drummed into all of us.

Kit most of all.

How ironic.

And with his death, my mother's secret has died. And no one need ever know.

She didn't have to tell us.

She could have claimed that Kit's genetic issues were all a false alarm. Perhaps Alessia's right. She's atoning for her sins.

Her lies.

Hell. I need to talk to her. But after what she said to my dear wife, I'm not sure I want her in our lives.

My phone buzzes again, and I think it might be Maryanne with more pearls of wisdom. But it's Alessia.

I am going to a bar with a woman

I met on my course.

I will try not to be late.

Alarm tightens my chest. I'm not sure how I feel about Alessia on the loose in London with a stranger. Caroline's words from earlier come back to me.

For heaven's sake, Maxim. She's a grown woman.

Yes. But she's led a sheltered, claustrophobic life. I've seen it. I lived it for a week.

Sounds great. I'm finished here.

May I join you?

Yes!! 😃

We are at the Gore.

xxxx

Alessia is fascinated by Tabitha. As they sip gin and tonics, Tabitha divulges that she lives in a castle in Scotland, though Alessia can't discern a Scottish accent. Tabitha finished her History of Art degree last year at Bristol University and has been on a gap year trekking through Kenya and Tanzania with a friend. It sounds exciting and beyond anything that Alessia's experienced. Apart from her harrowing journey to England—but Alessia decides to keep that story to herself.

"Oh look, Maxim Trevelyan just arrived, or should I say Maxim Trevethick, now."

"Oh." Alessia turns to see Maxim scanning the room.

"I've not met him. But my sisters *know* him. You know. In the biblical sense."

Alessia's spirits sink.

"They're twins."

Twins!

"I heard he's married, though I know nothing about the lucky woman who bagged him."

Maxim spies Alessia, and his face lights up with what she suspects is relief.

"Oh my God, he's coming over here!"

Alessia turns to Tabitha. "Maxim Trevethick is my husband."

Tabitha chokes on her gin. "Oh my God."

"I'm the lucky woman who…um…bagged him."

"Oh no. I'm so sorry. About what I said."

Alessia gives her a reassuring smile. "His reputation is… extra."

"Yes. It is!" Tabitha says quickly, her face flushed.

Alessia stands as Maxim approaches them, and he gives her a sweet, chaste kiss, suitable for public consumption. "Hello, darling. How are you? How was the first day?" Maxim's husky tone suggests he's asking her something indecent.

"Good. Thank you." Alessia is a little breathless. "May I introduce Lady Tabitha."

"How do you do," Maxim says.

"Lord Trevethick." Tabitha offers her hand, and Maxim takes it. "I'm so sorry to hear about your brother."

"He's sorely missed. May I join you?"

"Of course." Tabitha summons the waiter, and Maxim orders an old-fashioned.

"So, what did you learn today?" Maxim turns his intense gaze on Alessia, his expression glowing with curiosity.

"How to sit. Walk. And how to say hello." Alessia grins.

"Ah. The basics." He grins back, and he's breathtaking, a licentious gleam in his eyes.

"I really should be going," Tabitha says.

"Please don't leave on my account," Maxim says.

"I should be getting back to the flat."

Maxim stands when Tabitha does, and Alessia knows he doesn't need any lessons; his manners are innate. "I'll pick up the tab," he says.

"Thank you. Alessia, I'll see you tomorrow." Tabitha gives her an embarrassed wave.

"I look forward to it," Alessia says.

He sits back down.

"Twins?" Alessia asks.

He frowns, then glances at Tabitha's retreating figure. "Ah. That Tabitha." He looks back at Alessia. "Do you really want to know?"

Alessia feels her cheeks warm but rolls her eyes. "No."

He laughs. "Now, that is an appropriate reaction. A good eye roll."

Alessia smiles, despite her misgivings, and leans forward and kisses him once more.

She's learning. This is growth. His past is his past.

"Shall we go out to eat?" he asks. "We could eat here if you'd like?"

In the back of the cab, Alessia studies me. "How are you?"

I blow out a breath. "Honestly? A little numb. Dinner this

evening was a welcome distraction. And Maryanne has finally texted me back. She's in Seattle but says we'll compare notes when she's back."

"And have you heard from your mother?"

I snort. "I think that's unlikely for a while."

Alessia reaches out and takes my hand. "She is your mother…"

"I know." I swallow. "It will take time."

She nods sympathetically. "Do you want to talk about it?"

"What's there to talk about that we haven't already said? My mother has proved to be as duplicitous as I thought she was, and mean. And a terrible snob."

"She is… human."

I laugh, and it's a hollow sound. "That may be the first time anyone has accused Rowena of being human."

Alessia smiles. "What do you want to do?"

"Well, I should read up on stills."

"Stills? More landscape photography?"

I chuckle. "No. Still. For distilling gin."

Alessia's expression brightens.

"Yeah. I want to make gin. My wife likes it."

The cab pulls up outside our building and it's besieged by photographers.

"Fuck," I growl under my breath. "Ready?"

Alessia nods.

"Say nothing. Let me clamber out first, and I'll open your door."

"Okay."

I do exactly that and tuck Alessia under my arm as we make our way into the building.

Trevethick! Trevethick!

What about your relationship with Miss Charlotte Hampshire?

What does your wife have to say?

We ignore them, but Alessia stops us at the front door of the building. "What?" I ask.

She grabs my lapels, then slides her hands around the nape

of my neck, dragging my lips to hers. To a blaze of flash photography, she presses her body to mine and kisses me properly, her tongue insistent and possessive.

It's… hot.

And takes me by surprise.

When we move apart, we're both winded. She pushes open the door, and without a glance at the cheered crowd, she ushers me into the building.

Wow.

In the lift, I pounce, hungry for her, and we kiss all the way to the sixth floor.

"You know, we could play *Call of Duty* again," I murmur against the corner of her mouth.

She tips her head back and laughs.

Alessia toys with Maxim's hair as they lie in bed, fresh from their lovemaking. Her limbs are boneless as her heart rate settles into a satiated, steady rhythm. Maxim rests his head on her stomach, his favorite post-lovemaking position, and draws a faint circle around her navel. It almost tickles, and she knows he's preoccupied.

"My father was always my champion," Maxim interrupts their easy silence. "Now it makes sense."

Alessia stills her fingers, and he turns gleaming green eyes to her. "I'm wondering if my mother overcompensated with Kit because of my father's… indifference to him. No, indifference is too strong a word. I didn't notice it then. I was too caught up in my own world, but now, looking back, perhaps he favored me more."

"No one suspected?"

"No. I don't think so…" He trails off. "No. Wait. My mother and father had a huge falling-out with my uncle Cameron. Perhaps he knew."

"He's never said anything?"

"No. Never." Maxim rests his head on her belly once more.

"He escaped to LA in the late '80s. But now I think of it, Kit never felt comfortable with Cameron. We didn't visit him when we were in the Caribbean last Christmas. Now, I know why."

They're quiet as they each digest this tidbit of information. Alessia realizes that the only person who can shed any light is Rowena.

"Are you going to talk to your mother?" Alessia asks.

Maxim snorts. "We had a fractured relationship already. I don't see us coming back from this."

Alessia says nothing but teases his hair once more. She wants to tell him that, in spite of how he and Alessia feel about Rowena, maybe he should listen to his mother's side of the story. They don't know all the details, but she doesn't think Maxim is ready to hear that yet.

One day.

Soon.

After all, Rowena is still his mother.

Chapter Twenty-Four

Tabitha makes a beeline for Alessia as soon as she walks into their classroom. "Good morning, Alessia. I'm so sorry about yesterday."

Alessia shakes her head. "Don't worry."

"Did you know you've gone viral?" Tabitha gushes.

"No. What? Where?"

"Here. I Googled you last night after my dreadful faux pas. And look. This is what I found." She holds up her phone, and there's a video of Alessia playing the piano at Dimitri's party. It's an Instagram reel in the name of GrishaEgonov.

"You're very good," Tabitha says.

"Thank you," Alessia says automatically. She's staggered. She doesn't remember him filming her—she was too caught up in the music. The post has over eighty thousand likes and thousands of comments. The caption reads *Lady Alessia, Countess of Trevethick. Beautiful and talented.*

She gapes at Tabitha, who grins. "Grisha's not wrong."

"Good morning, everyone." Jennifer Knight brings the room

to attention, ending their conversation. "Today, we'll be discussing written communication and the correct forms of address, whether by email or snail mail."

Abigail Chenoweth, our tenant farmer from Rosperran farm, and Michael Harris, Tresyllian Hall's estate manager, are beyond excited at the prospect of making gin. I conclude my conference call with them, pleased that, if we get this project right, we might bring some welcome revenue to the estate and provide employment for the locals from the surrounding villages. There's a great deal of work to be done to obtain the necessary licenses, planning, and all that bollocks, but I've got to say, I'm stoked: my first project for the estate—and all inspired by my wife.

My phone buzzes. It's Caroline. "Caro."

"Hi, have you seen that video of Alessia?"

What now?

"Video? No?"

"She's on Grisha's Instagram."

"Well, I'd look at it, but I'm talking to you. What's she doing?"

"What do you think she's doing? She's playing his grand piano—and don't worry, darling, that's not a euphemism." Caro cackles at her tasteless joke.

"And?" I know about the piano playing. I was there!

"The Stepsow has seen it. She wants to know if Alessia has applied to the Royal College of Music."

Whoa!

"Yes. She has applied."

"What name did she use?"

"Alessia Trevelyan."

"Good. I'll let her know."

"You two are on speaking terms?"

"She called. I thought Daddy might be ill or worse, so I took the call. But no, she wanted to know about Alessia, and she was sounding me out about you DJing?"

"Why?"

"The Demon Spawn is eighteen this year, and she wants a rave in the grounds at Horston."

"Your little sister is eighteen! How the hell did that happen?"

"Stepsister!" she snaps. "And yes. Cordelia's of age to spread her demon spawn-ness. The world should tremble."

"Caro, my DJ days are over, unless your stepmother gets Alessia into the school. In which case, I might reconsider. It's the only way I can get her a visa without her returning to Albania."

"Ah. I see. No more spinning the decks for you?" Caro sounds surprised.

"I don't have the time. Besides, the arseholes who trafficked Alessia stole my decks, and I haven't found a minute to replace them."

"Oh." Caro is momentarily silenced, but before I can say anything, she continues. "I'll let her know. Although the Demon Spawn will be terribly disappointed. You know she has a huge crush on you."

"Does she now?" *What the hell am I supposed to say to that?*

Caroline sighs, and I'm not sure why.

"Anyway," she says. "I should have some ideas sketched out for you by the middle of next week."

"Great. Thanks, Caro." I hang up, relieved that she changed the subject from Cordelia's crush, and open my Instagram app.

Alessia! Viral.

Does she know?

I search for Grisha and find his profile. There are several photos from the party—he's posing, of course, with many of the famous actors, TV personalities, and models who were present at the party, but on his reels, there's my wife playing Bach as if that's what she was born to do.

Wow. The video has a hundred thousand likes.

Grisha's right, though it pains me to say—Alessia is gorgeous and talented.

And mine.

I take a moment out of my day and watch the video again. Then again. The fourth time, a movement in the background catches my eye.

I grin. Something to show my wife.

Their lessons finish early, and Tabitha invites Alessia to take tea. But Alessia politely declines and asks for a rain check; she has plans. She eyes her watch: 3:30 p.m. She has time—she's researched the journey a few times on the internet. Out on the street, she bids goodbye to Tabitha and hails a passing cab, just like Maxim, and clambers inside.

"Where to, love?" the cabbie asks.

"Kew Green, please." Alessia sits back in her seat and takes out her phone. She texts Maxim.

> Hello My Lord
> We finished today early.
> I am going out.
> Axx

Alessia wants to see where her great-uncle lives. Maybe even meet him. During her lessons today, she'd written him a letter, and she hopes to post it through his door. Once they've made contact, she'll tell her husband that she's tracked him down, and only then. After all, Maxim didn't want her to contact the private detective.

And she did.

Her phone chimes.

It's a text from her husband.

> Good afternoon, My Lady.
> I love when you text me.
> Out where? Curious minds need to know.
> I'll come and join you if you wish.
> Mx

Oh no.

> I am going to Kew.
> I will not be long.
> See you later.
> xxxx

What the hell is Alessia doing in Kew? The last time I was near that part of the world was when I drove out to Brentford after those arseholes showed up at my flat, and Alessia fled. *You are your father's son. A knight in shining armor—a sucker for a damsel in distress.*

The memory of my mother's words sours my mood and my concern for Alessia mushrooms.

> What are you doing in Kew?

Alessia huffs. Her husband worries too much—she can tell by the brusque tone of his text. She thought she would reassure him by letting him know she was going out, but it appears to have added to his anxiety. She texts back.

> It is a surprise.
> Do not worry!!! :D
> xxxx

Alessia's text is moderately reassuring.
For heaven's sake, Maxim. She's a grown woman.

> Okay.
> Stay safe.
> Text when you're coming home.

Mx

PS: Not sure I like surprises! ☺

Alessia sighs with relief. This is more like it. He seems to have recovered his sense of humor. Feeling reassured, Alessia stares out the cab window and spots a mother pushing a stroller. She wonders what Maxim would be like if she was with child. He'd probably be a great deal worse.

Maxim's child.

She loves the idea.

Just not yet. She was shocked when he mentioned it at the weekend, and she's glad he's eager for children. But the temptation to study at one of the best music schools in the country is too great a lure.

Parenthood can wait.

But if he insisted, she would capitulate. She wants children too.

Yes. She could see herself doing this.

Her parents would be thrilled, and so would Maxim.

But he agreed to wait. He wants to show her some of the world too.

My phone rings, and it's a number I don't recognize. "Trevethick."

"Lord Trevethick, it's Ticia Cavanagh."

"Hello, Ticia. Please call me Maxim." *Jesus, we've bumped uglies, for heaven's sake.* "What gives?"

"I'm calling to let you know that, as we thought, all your marriage documents are completely bona fide. We've done the research. You are legally married."

I laugh, more from relief than anything else. "That is good news."

After all that, Demachi and Tabaku's plan worked.

"I wondered if you'd made any movement on finding a place for Lady Trevethick—"

"Alessia, please."

"For Alessia to study. I'm concerned about the rabid press interest you're attracting."

"Oh. You've seen it?"

"Yes. 'Oh' is right. You realize that if the Home Office finds out Alessia was here illegally earlier this year, they could refuse her a family visa. And *you* may also be in trouble, as you breached immigration rules, given that she was working for you and didn't have the correct visa in place."

"Oh, shit."

"Exactly. I'll follow up with a colleague to find out how the police investigation into her traffickers is progressing and if they have anything that might connect your wife to the crime. This will all be done anonymously, but the cost will come out of your retainer. So, I'm asking if—"

"Go ahead. By all means. And if the retainer doesn't cover it, let me know."

"Okay. Good."

"I'm hoping we'll secure a place for Alessia at one of the music conservatoires in London."

"I've seen the video. She's very talented."

I smile but shake my head. My wife has gone viral! "She is, and she wants to study at the Royal College."

"Good luck with that. In the meantime, it might be helpful if you could be a little more under the radar."

"Point taken. We may go to Cornwall. We'll be off the grid there. Thanks for the warning."

"You're welcome… Maxim." She hangs up, and my brain feverishly starts processing this information. Perhaps going to Dimitri's was a mistake.

Of all the times to go viral!

Alessia fingers her grandmother's cross at her neck. Butterflies are forming in her stomach the closer she gets to Kew. The cab stops at a red light, and Alessia can see Kew Bridge before her and the road to Brentford off to her right. She remembers how happy she was living with Magda and her son for those few precious weeks. Michal has told her via Facebook that he and Magda are doing well in Canada. He has a bunch of new friends and is learning to skate. He has ambitions to play ice hockey like his new stepfather, Logan. From his posts, he looks happy, as does Magda.

Idly she wonders about grumpy Mrs. Kingsbury, and Mrs. Goode too. Her old clients. Do they have new cleaners?

Alessia shakes her head. She's come a long way since then.

The lights turn green, and the cab moves on, crossing Kew Bridge before stopping and turning into a side road. It draws up outside a large old house that would not look out of place on Cheyne Walk. It's one of several surrounding a pretty green pasture, flanked by enormous sycamore trees. Alessia pays the exorbitant fare with her credit card and climbs out of the cab.

It moves off, leaving her facing her great-uncle's house. The house is immaculate. There's a neatly trimmed tree at the front, and through the bay window, Alessia can see a baby grand piano.

A piano!

He plays too?

Her heart starts pumping with excitement, anticipation, and also, a little fear, but in that moment, she decides to call on him.

He might tell her to go away.

She grips the little gold cross that had belonged to her Nana, *his* sister, and with her mind made up, she walks the short driveway to the gleaming black door and pushes the doorbell. It rings faintly inside, and seconds later, an older woman, her hair in a tidy bun, answers the door.

"Hello. Can I help you?" she asks.

"I am here to see Tobias Strickland."

"Do you have an appointment?" she asks sternly.

"No. I was hoping he'd see me. I am his sister's granddaughter. Um…his great-niece."

Given that Leticia Cavanagh is concerned, I call Tom Alexander to see if he's made any headway with finding Alessia's young friend and if he has an update on the police investigation.

"Trevethick. How goes it? I take it you found your wife."

"I did. Grisha offered her his driver, and he took her home."

"What? Why?"

"Don't you read the press, Tom?"

"Are you joking? Of course not. I told you. Never bother with that nonsense, unless I have a client who makes headlines. Suggest you do the same. Ignore the arseholes."

"You're right. But if you happen across a lurid headline, Charlotte, my ex—"

"The actress? Not very good? Always plays herself?"

I chuckle despite myself at Tom's bluntness. "Yes. That's the one. She jumped me." There's an awkward pause in the conversation, so I continue, "Alessia witnessed that and got the wrong idea. Anyway, I'm not here to dredge up recent history. I want to know if you've made any headway with the police investigation and finding Alessia's young friend."

"Certainly nothing on the girl. But the details that Alessia gave us were so vague, I'd be surprised if we tracked her down. I spoke to Spaffer—he's actually working the case. They're still gathering evidence. He says he's getting inquiries from a private detective about the same case."

A frisson of alarm runs down my back.

"Journalists?" I ask.

"He doesn't know. But there was a recent raid on a place in South London; they found four young women there."

"Shit. Really?"

"Yes. They're now in the care of the Salvation Army."

"Any of them Albanian? Any of them Bleriana?"

"I don't think so. But without speaking to them directly, we can't be sure."

"What will happen to them?"

"To be honest. I don't know."

"It's fucking grim."

"It is, old boy. It is. We'll keep working. See if we can trace
these women."

"Good luck with that."

"Oh, and while I remember, you don't need to worry about
that journalist who called you."

"Really?"

"No. He's got nothing." Tom sounds definitive.

Okay then.

"Thanks for the update."

The lady with the tidy bun must be in her fifties. She peers
behind Alessia to see if she's shielding anyone and then
casts a critical eye over her, and Alessia is relieved when the
woman steps aside; she seems to have passed inspection. "I'm
not aware that Professor Strickland has a niece. Let alone a
great-niece. You'd better come in." She allows Alessia into the
hallway.

The hall is much like Trevelyan House, where Caroline lives,
and Alessia concludes they must have been built around the
same time. "Follow me," the woman says, and she leads Alessia
down the hall into an airy room with a prominent fireplace, an
impressive mantelpiece, and french windows that look out onto
a lush back garden. Seated at a desk, in front of a laptop, is a man
with a full mane of blondish gray hair, an outrageously curled
mustache, and a beard. He looks up with polite interest. His
eyes are the same baby blue as her beloved Nana's, his mouth
the same shape and creased from his readiness to smile—it's
her grandmother in male form. Alessia is blindsided; a well of
emotion rises from her chest into her throat, and she's unable
to speak.

"Well, my dear," he says. "What can I do for you?" When she
doesn't reply, he frowns in confusion, looking from Alessia to

the woman who, Alessia suspects, is a servant of some kind. No. Staff. Not servant.

"She says she's your great-niece, Professor."

He pales and turns luminous wide eyes back to her. "Alessia?" he whispers.

What! He knows her!

Tears well in her eyes, and she nods, still unable to speak.

"Oh, my dear!" he exclaims, rising from his chair. He steps around the desk and takes both of her hands in his. "I never thought…" His voice trails off as he chokes up, and they stare at each other, holding each other's hands. She takes in the smile lines around his eyes and his ridiculous mustache that peaks at each end. His neat beard. His impressive mane of hair just like her grandmother.

"Virginia?" he whispers.

He doesn't know.

Alessia shakes her head.

"Oh no," he says and tears pool in his eyes. He squeezes her hands while they face each other for several seconds, and myriad emotions flit across his face as he absorbs the sad news. Finally, Alessia's tears fall, streaming down her face as she remembers her dear, dear Nana. Tobias pulls a cotton handkerchief from his pants pocket and wipes his eyes.

"My dear, you have quite undone me. My dear, dear sister. I wondered. I hadn't heard from her for a long while. I hoped…" He takes a breath. "Mrs. Smith. Tea. Please. You'll take tea, won't you, my dear?"

Alessia nods, and she reaches for a tissue from her handbag. Mrs. Smith, whose gentle smile reveals her demeanor has transformed from suspicious to solicitous, hurries out of the room.

"That gold cross. It looks familiar. Was it hers?"

"Yes!" Alessia says. "It was." Automatically, Alessia's fingers fly to her throat, and she fiddles with the cross. "It's very precious. I loved her dearly."

He smiles. A sad smile. "I remember it. My parents were

terribly religious. Ginny too. That's why she went to Albania, to spread the Word during the Communist era." He shakes his head as if to rid himself of some unpleasant memory. "Let's move to the drawing room." He ushers Alessia toward the door.

"So, I never had an address for Ginny, but she would write to me very occasionally. That's how I know about you. I think she was concerned that my parents would go and 'rescue' her from the depths of Albania. They did not approve of her marriage at all." Toby sighs. "Dreadful business. They lost a daughter."

"She married well. She was very much in love with her husband. He was a fine man. Her daughter, my mother, was less lucky, though that seems to have changed."

"Your mother. Shpresa?"

"Yes."

"So, Alessia, tell me about yourself. How do you happen to be in England? Tell me all."

Honey, I'm home," I call as I close the front door. It's deathly quiet, and the unsettled anxiety I've felt since Alessia announced she was going *out* rears its ugly head. "Alessia!" I shout, just in case she's deep in a wardrobe or one of the bathrooms. But the flat has a ringing emptiness that I never noticed until Alessia moved in.

Hell. We forgot to set the alarm.

And she said she'd text. Scowling, I take out my phone and call. But it rings through to voicemail. "Where are you?" I ask and hang up, blowing out a breath in frustration.

Alessia can look after herself.

Can't she?

She handled my mother. She handled Grisha.

The apprehension that's become familiar since Alessia was kidnapped flutters in my chest. I text her, keeping it light.

> Where are you?
> The flat is cold and lonely without you.
>   Mx

Also, I'm hungry. That isn't helping my mood. Feeling miserable, I drift into the kitchen, where the fridge is stacked with goodies.

No. I change my mind, head into the bedroom, and put on my running gear. A run will clear my head, and she'll be back when I'm done.

I cannot believe that you were living across the river. That's extraordinary," Toby says.

"Yes. I was happy there," Alessia replies.

"West is best, I think the saying goes." He smiles kindly.

Alessia glances at the time. It's after six! "The time. I must go. My husband will be anxious."

"I'm sure he will. Maxim, you say?"

"Yes. That's his name." Alessia hasn't told Toby about Maxim's heritage. She's going to save that for their next meeting. "I can't wait for you to meet him. He's a good man." She stands and glances at the piano.

"Do you play?"

"Yes. I do. Nana taught my mother. Nana and my mother taught me. Do you?"

He chuckles. "Musicality runs in the family. Sadly, I don't play as much as I used to." He holds up his hands and waggles his fingers. "These aren't what they were, but I've studied music all my life. It's more a science to me now than an art, yet it started in a blaze of color for me."

"You have synesthesia?"

"I do, my dear. I do." He's stunned. "But I call it chromesthesia."

Alessia grins. "Chromesthesia. I have not heard this."

"It's specific. Sound to color synesthesia."

"I have this!"

"Ha!" he hoots, and he takes her hands. "I have never met another synesthete! And when I do, we're related! How do you see the colors?"

"They match a key. You?"

"Mine are less defined, but listen, we can discuss this at another time. I know you need to go. I'll order you an Uber, and while we wait for it to arrive, will you play something for me?"

Alessia is giddy with joy as she climbs into the vehicle. Toby waves her off from the doorstep, and she waves frantically back until she can no longer see him. She hugs herself as the car turns and slowly eases into the traffic on the bridge. Toby is thoughtful, kind, musical, and super-smart, but most of all, he's interested in her and her life in a way that her male relatives at home were not, and he cannot wait to meet her husband. She digs her phone out of her handbag to call Maxim and apologize for not texting. But it's dead.

O Zot!

Well, there's nothing she can do until she gets home. So she sits back and replays her entire conversation with Toby. Her great-uncle. Synesthete.

Honey, I'm home!" I announce to an empty flat when I'm back from my exercise. The endorphins conjured by my run disappear as I head into the shower.

Where the hell is she?

By 7:00 p.m., I'm climbing the walls. I've left more messages but received no word from my wife. There's no one I can call, nothing I can do. I'm powerless.

I hate not knowing where or how she is.

I pace the drawing room, and every time I pass the double doors that open onto the hallway, I glance at the front door, willing Alessia to appear.

I. Am. Going. Crazy.

Hell.

I step into the echoing silence of my hallway. And I'm suddenly overwhelmed. I don't know where my wife is, and for some unknown reason, the memory of my mother's Louboutins clicking across the hardwood as she left springs to mind—reminding me that I've already lost another family member this week.

Was that the last I'll ever see of her?

And as much as Rowena annoys the hell out of me, that thought is depressing.

She's my mother.

Mama.

Fuck.

How do we come back from this?

I shake off the bleak feeling and text her.

> We need to discuss Kit's memorial service.
> When you're over your snit,
> perhaps you can give me a call.

And I want to add *you faithless whore*, but I don't. She's my mother. Next, I text my absent wife. Again.

> I am going crazy here!
> Call me.
> Please.
> M

Suddenly the key sounds in the door, and it opens to reveal Alessia. She looks fine. When we lock eyes, her warm smile lights up the darkened hallway and my heart. My relief and anger seize the day in equal measure.

Thank fuck she's safe.

But as she steps into the hall, the anger triumphs, and my cry echoes off the walls. "Where the fuck have you been?"

Chapter Twenty-Five

Alessia freezes as I stride toward her, wanting to vent my spleen. I'm overwhelmed with fury, but as I step up to her, she raises her face to mine, all innocence and beauty and beguiling dark eyes. "I'm sorry. My phone died," she whispers.

"Oh." This is not what I thought she'd say. I'm expecting a spirited argument that will help me offload some of my frustration and fear. Her simple apology and admission steal the wind from my sails, and in a nanosecond my temper softens.

"I was worried," I grumble.

Tentatively, as if she's about to beard a lion, she reaches up and strokes my cheek. "I know. I'm sorry."

Sighing, I rest my forehead against hers and close my eyes, taking a moment to calm the fuck down. Slowly, I circle my arms around her, drawing her close so she molds herself against my body, bathing me in her reassuring warmth. She kisses my cheek. "I am sorry. I lost track of the time."

"Where were you?"

She grins. "If you promise not to be mad, I'll tell you."

"No. No, I don't promise. Not at all. I'm mad already. You have a disturbing tendency to put yourself in perilous situations. Tell me."

"I met my grandmother's brother, my great-uncle."

Maxim steps back, releasing Alessia. "Uncle? You have family here?"

She nods, still radiating from the joy of finding her relative.

"Why would I be upset about that? Does he live in Kew? How did you find him?"

Alessia takes Maxim's hand and leads him into the kitchen. "Sit," she says and points to the kitchen chair.

He frowns, confused, but obliges and looks expectantly up at her, his hair tousled and green eyes no longer flashing with anger but bright with curiosity.

"Remember when I asked you about finding Bleriana?"

Maxim stills, and Alessia doesn't know how he'll react.

"I went to see the detective."

"I see. And?"

"I asked him to find my grandmother's family."

"Ah."

"And Bleriana," she whispers as if she's confessing a great evil.

"Even though I asked you not to." Maxim's mouth flattens, his eyes frost, and she knows he's irritated. She nods, trying and failing to feel guilty. He shakes his head and, taking her hand, hauls her into his lap. "What the hell, Alessia? I don't want you involved in that world, even from a distance. Tom's on it. Admittedly he hasn't got very far. Call the private investigator and ask him to stop. Let Tom deal with it. Someone I trust. Please."

"Okay," she says quickly. "I'm sorry. I'm just anxious to find her."

Maxim sighs. "I understand. But why didn't you tell me you were going to meet your great-uncle? I would have come with you."

"I didn't plan to meet him. I was going to deliver a letter. We learned about correspondence and letter writing today in class. But I saw the baby grand in his living room through the window, and once I saw that… It was…um…fate." She shrugs, trying to convey that she felt compelled to knock on the door after seeing the piano.

Maxim sighs again. "I see. Well, if you have any other hidden relatives, I'd be happy to take you to meet them. Let me. Please?"

"Okay."

"Tell me about him."

Alessia kisses his cheek. "Thank you for not being too mad at me."

"I am still a little mad at you. And we say 'angry.' 'Mad' is American. And I was fucking incandescent earlier. With worry more than anything."

"I know. I'm sorry. Shall I cook? Are you hungry?"

Maxim sits back, a reluctant smile tugging at the corners of his mouth. "Yes. I'm famished."

She smiles and caresses his face. Her husband is *hangry*. "I'll cook and tell you all about him."

So he was just across the river when you lived in Brentford?" I ask as I watch Alessia stir a tomato sauce. "So near, and yet so far."

"Yes. It is a grand house. He is a musician too, but he was a teacher. At Oxford. A professor in music. He has synesthesia like me, but calls it, um…chrom…chromesthesia."

"Wow." *What are the odds?* "Is it genetic?"

"I think so!" She beams as she stirs in some capers. Whatever she's concocting, it smells delicious. It smells so good—it deserves a glass of full-bodied red.

"Wine?" I ask Alessia.

"Please. He wants to meet you. And my mother!"

"Has he not met your mother?" I grab a bottle from the rack.

"No. He's never been to Albania. And my mother doesn't know he exists. My grandmother was shun…shunned by her family for marrying an Albanian." Alessia's voice fades, and she stirs the sauce.

Shit.

My family haven't shunned her.

Have they? My mother— "That's awful," I mutter, immediately shutting that thought down.

"But he knew about me. She would write occasional letters to him."

"He should go and meet your family. I can recommend it, in spite of your scary father. Have you told Shpresa?" I uncork the wine and, giving it zero time to breathe, pour two glasses.

"No. But I will after dinner." She drains the spaghetti and adds it to the sauce, stirring it in. "This is ready."

Alessia places the last of their plates in the dishwasher, wipes down the countertop, and retrieves her phone from her purse. Setting it down, she plugs in the charger. Maxim is in the living room at the piano. She hasn't heard him play since he duetted with her. She leans against the doorjamb, unseen by him, and listens for a moment. He's improvising a melody in A minor. The notes sparkle across the room and through her head in a vibrant blue, sounding upbeat and full of warmth and hope, unusual for a minor key.

He sounds… happy.

Alessia smiles. The theme is a complete contrast to his melancholy composition that she played for him not so long ago in the Hideout in Cornwall. He turns, noticing her, and she sidles over and sits beside him at the piano.

"This is a happier tune."

"I wonder why that is?" Maxim smirks, and she smiles. "It's from *Interstellar.*"

Alessia frowns.

"The film?" he asks.

"I don't know it."

"Oh. We'll have to watch it. Amazing movie. Great soundtrack by Hans Zimmer." He stops and puts his arm around her. "That reminds me. I spoke to Leticia today."

Alessia tenses—despite the fact that she likes Ticia, she doesn't like him talking to women he's bedded.

Alessia! Stop.

Maxim continues either because he doesn't notice her tension or chooses not to. "She says we should keep a low profile and avoid the press. So when you've finished your course, I think we should go to Cornwall. I have work to do at the Hall anyway. I know we were going to pack the flat up this weekend so we can move. But maybe we can get someone to do that for us. Or we can wait."

Alessia's heart skips a beat. "I love Cornwall," she says breathlessly. "Especially the sea."

"Me too." Maxim kisses her hair. "That's settled then. We can go on Friday evening. And between then and now we can stay at home and watch films. You know, Netflix and chill."

"I thought that was another way of saying sex on the couch."

Maxim laughs. "We can do that too." He kisses her quickly.

"Play some more *Interstellar*."

"I feel a little self-conscious playing for you."

She laughs. "Why? Don't, please. I love your compositions."

"Well, this isn't mine. But if you listen, you'll probably be able to play it better than me."

"Maxim. Play."

He grins. "Yes. My lady."

With the music from Maxim's performance still ringing in her head, Alessia fetches her phone to FaceTime her mother. There are several messages from Maxim; he sounds more frantic and annoyed with each one, and she swallows down her guilt. She didn't mean to worry him.

There are emails from four of the colleges she sent applications to—the one she reads first is from the Royal College of Music.

She has an audition!

They are keen to see her.

Uau! She runs back into the living room. Maxim looks up. "I have an audition at the Royal College of Music!"

He grins and applauds, rising slowly to his feet. "My talented wife. That's fantastic news!"

Alessia opens the other emails and finds they all want to see her.

She gapes at Maxim. "All of them want me to audition!"

"Of course they do! They'd be fools not to." He cups her head in his hands. "You're beautiful. Talented. And I'm so glad you're my wife." He brushes his lips against her. "Go. Tell your mother."

Alessia beams and heads back into the kitchen to FaceTime Shpresa with the good news.

M aybe I worry too much. Alessia's fine. She came back in one piece. She's a functioning adult, for heaven's sake.

Who has been abducted.

Twice.

Fuck.

I thought… What did I think? She'd left? She'd been abducted again?

Mate. Let it go.

She's fine. She's here.

I take a sip of the extremely satisfying Bordeaux, which has had a chance to breathe now, and I briefly wonder if I should raid the cellar at Trevelyan House before Caroline drinks it all.

The doorbell rings. From outside the front door rather than the outside of the building.

Who the hell is that?

Rowena?

A dark shadow looms outside the front door. It's a man, not a woman. I open the door.

Fuck. It's him.

All slicked-back hair and expensive camel coat and brogues.

Ana-fucking-toli. Arsehole.

"Hello, Englishman," Anatoli says, with an arrogance and swagger that makes me want to deck him.

"What the hell are you doing here?"

"I've come to see you."

Me! "Why?"

"Aren't you going to invite me in?"

"No. I'm going to tell you to fuck off."

"And they say the English are so polite." He steps in, and contrary to how I feel, I let him.

What the hell?

In the hallway, he stops and turns to address me. "Where's your wife—the woman who should be my wife? Has she had enough of the upper-class snobbery and left you yet?"

"Do you mean the woman you abused and kidnapped and dragged across Europe?"

Alessia appears in the hallway and pales when she sees the Arsehole.

"I got her out of the country in one piece. She's back here legally. I did you both a favor," Anatoli scoffs, eyes like flint.

A natoli," Alessia whispers. "What are you doing here?"

His expression changes, his pale blue eyes warming as he studies her. "I'm here on business," he answers in her own language. "It's good to see you, carissima. You look well. Your father says a journalist called at their home. He sent them away. The press don't approve of you here, like I told you. The English are such snobs. They say your marriage is not legal."

"But we know that's not true!" Alessia exclaims.

Anatoli makes a face. "Jak also told me that you're not with child. You lie well."

Alessia flushes.

"Is the Englishman taking good care of you?" he murmurs.

"Enough!" Maxim snaps. "You two speak in English, or I will throw him out." Maxim glares at Alessia as if it's her fault that Anatoli is standing in his hallway.

Alessia frowns and moves to Maxim's side. He slides his arm around her and pulls her close.

"Don't get your panties in a wad, Englishman. It is you I came to see."

"Me. What the fuck do you want with me? And why would I want to see you?"

"Such language. From an aristocrat too."

Maxim tenses, and Alessia worries he might explode and hit Anatoli like he did before. She grips his shirt.

"Why are you here?" she pipes up.

"Your father sent me."

"Baba? Why?"

"I told you. I have a message for the Englishman."

"And my esteemed father-in-law can't send a message through his daughter?" Maxim scoffs.

"Jak is not proficient in English. Unlike my good self." Anatoli's smug grin is annoying, his mockery unmistakable. "And this is private. For you. Not for his beloved daughter."

Maxim scowls. "You turn up. Barge into my home. Chat up my wife at some unseemly hour. What is it you want?"

"I need to talk to you. It's a matter for men. And only men." Anatoli looks pointedly at Alessia.

"I am not going anywhere," Alessia exclaims. "If you have something to say to my husband, you can say it to me. I'm not in Kukës anymore."

"No, carissima. This is for your husband's ears only."

Alessia turns her bewildered gaze to me. It's obvious she has no idea why the Arsehole has appeared on our doorstep. I blow out a breath. "Her name is Alessia. Or Lady Trevethick, to you. Now, say what you have to say, and then you can leave." I give him a frosty, fuck-off smile, and Anatoli narrows his eyes.

"Is there somewhere private we could go?"

Fuck's sake.

"Not really. Unless we step outside. This is Alessia's home too."

"Maxim, why don't you go into the living room, and I'll bring you another glass of wine."

"There she is!" Anatoli grins. "Alessia, you are an Albanian woman to your soul." His face lights up. He's still smitten with my wife.

It's sickening.

"No. Arsehole, you're not welcome in this house. You took Alessia from here against her will. You threatened and abused her. And you have the fucking nerve to turn up here and expect us to invite you into our home—"

"I am an associate of Lady Trevethick's father. And he has a message for you, asshole."

A lessia is tempted to step between them as they glower at each other.

"Let's take this outside," Maxim says through gritted teeth.

Alessia looks up at him, eyes wide and her face etched in panic. He gives her a reassuring smile and turns his attention to Anatoli.

T he Arsehole's icy glare doesn't intimidate me.

"Are you armed?" Alessia asks him suddenly, the words coming from her mouth in a distraught, breathless rush.

What the fuck?

He shakes his head. "Not this time." And he smirks. "I came by air. Okay, Englishman, have it your way."

I don't even want to think about the implications of Alessia's question. No wonder it was easy for him to take her—the monster was fucking armed. I scowl at him, trying to keep a rein on my temper. He brought a fucking gun into my home and threatened my wife.

Or me.

That's how he was able to whisk her away.

Fucking monster.

"Well, Englishman?" he says.

My blood boils, but I grab my jacket and head out, not bothering to wait for him. I don't take the lift—I bolt down the stairs, buoyed by my anger, and quickly reach the small foyer on the ground floor.

We'll do this. And then he's gone.

For good. Hopefully.

He follows me down the stairs, and I know he didn't expect me to move so fast because he's breathless when we reach the bottom.

It's hugely satisfying.

Fucking bastard brought a gun into my home.

"Here," he shouts when he reaches the foyer before I can leave the building. "There's light."

I stop, and he pulls out a newspaper clipping from the inside of his coat and hands it to me. It's from an Albanian newspaper, so I don't understand the headlines, but there are grimy photographs of two men.

The hairs on the back of my neck rise in recognition.

Those fuckers!

The traffickers.

I shoot my gaze to him.

"This them?" he asks.

I nod. "Why?"

He says nothing and then produces another newspaper cutting. It's the photograph of Charlotte kissing me.

Oh shit. "This reached Albania?"

"It did. It made the papers. Jak thinks you should be more discreet with your affairs."

"Whoa!" I hold up my hand. "This is not what it looks like."

"No?"

"No. For the record, I'm not having an affair. Also, it's none of Jak's or your fucking business."

"Alessia has seen this?"

"Of course she's seen it. She was there."

"Oh." He looks crestfallen—so much so that I feel a nanoparticle of pity for him. He still holds a torch that shines brightly for my wife. He loves her. In his own way.

What an idiot.

"You know," he growls. "You fuck this up between you and her—I'm here. Waiting. It's obvious your gutter press, they don't approve. The snobbery and disdain is in every word they write about her. I'll be in her home country where we love her. I love her."

"No, you don't. And keep away from my wife. If you hadn't mistreated her, she might be with you now. But you did. *You* fucked up. And she's mine now. In every way. And I don't give a flying fuck about the press. Leave Alessia alone. Now, you can see yourself out."

Without looking back at him, I vault up the stairs, and when I reach the top floor, I've expended enough energy to calm down.

Alessia is still in the hallway. "Where is he? What did he want?" she asks.

"Nothing important."

She puts her hands on her hips. "Maxim. Tell me."

And suddenly, I want to laugh. She runs off to meet her uncle without saying a word. And here she is, demanding answers. "You really want to know?"

"Yes. And why are you smiling?"

"Because you're making me smile."

"Tell me!"

"Your father wants me to handle my mistresses more discreetly."

Alessia pales, gaping at me as if I'd just slapped her.

Shit. I was joking!

"Hey. It's nonsense. Anatoli had a clipping from an Albanian newspaper with Charlotte." And I'm suddenly inspired. Reaching out, I take Alessia's hand. "Let me show you something."

I guide her into the drawing room, sit at my desk, and seat Alessia on my lap. Grasping my iMac's mouse, I wake the computer. On Instagram, I find Grisha Egonov's reel of Alessia at the piano. "Watch," I say, and switching on the sound, I listen to my wife's exquisite performance of Bach. She squirms on my lap, unused to watching herself. "It's good, don't worry," I murmur.

A lessia watches the recording, noting her finger work and the sound from the piano. It's good. The tone is mellow yet bright. As she finishes the piece, there's a burst of applause from the audience. Maxim pauses the video. "See?" he says, and with the cursor, he circles some blurred figures in the background, then presses Play. Alessia's scalp tightens. There's Maxim, leaning back from Charlotte as she kisses him. He twists his head, grabs her hands, and eases her gently away from him.

He stopped her.

Alessia slides her gaze to him. "She kissed you."

"I told you. *She* kissed *me*."

"I believed you."

"Did you, though?" he says, with a sideways look, his lips curved into a teasing smile.

Alessia laughs and throws her arms around his neck. "Yes. A thousand times, yes. Of course I believed you."

"So you should. Shall we Netflix and chill?" He kisses her, his hands in her hair, his tongue invading her mouth, stealing away her breath and making her heart sing.

Chapter Twenty-Six

"That was a good meeting. You're getting a handle on all of it, Maxim." Oliver's smile is benevolent as he gathers his papers, so I don't think he's being sarcastic—just sincere. It's humbling and heartwarming at the same time. We've just concluded a discussion with the managing agents for the residential and commercial property divisions, and I'm pleased that all is well, though they're keeping a watchful eye on the retail sector—online shopping has much to answer for—and the churn on our retail property is up.

"I felt it went well. In fact, so much so, I might bunk off and walk home right now."

"Good plan. You're off to Cornwall, yes?"

"Hoping to throw off the press."

"Good luck with that."

"Have a good weekend. And thanks, Oliver. For everything."

"I'm just doing my job, my lord. Have a great weekend."

He exits my office, and I remember when I thought he might

not have my best interests at heart. Well, I was wrong. He's an asset to me and the estate.

I bounce down the steps into a brisk March afternoon. I've decided to walk home, as I have plenty of time and I want to stretch my legs. I've only managed two runs this week, and I resolve to do better in Cornwall.

Alessia will conclude her course today and mentioned going for drinks afterward with her classmates. I'm tempted to join her, but I haven't been invited, and I have to drive this evening.

Mate. Let her be.

As I walk through Berkeley Square, a nagging, skittering itch travels up my spine, and I find myself glancing behind me.

Am I being followed?

Reporters? Paparazzi?

I can't see anyone acting suspiciously, but I quicken my pace.

Mate. Get a grip.

I hurry on, tempted to grab a cab—but I need the exercise.

The uneasy feeling follows me to Chelsea Embankment, and I'm relieved that my building is press-free when I arrive home. I stride through the doorway and jog up the stairs, grateful to be home.

Alessia is seated beside Tabitha and two of her course colleagues at the bar in The Gore, enjoying a glass of champagne. The atmosphere among them is fizzing with celebration.

"I think my father will find my manners vastly improved. He'll be pleased. I hope," Tabitha purrs. "He wants me married off as soon as possible, like my sisters. You wouldn't think we're in the twenty-first century. Did your husband send you on this course?"

Alessia smiles. "No. It was my decision. I'm thankful. I've learned so much. And the first banquet that we host, you must come."

"Complete with minstrels? I'll be there!"

Alessia giggles. "I am not sure about minstrels, but Maxim

has guitars, though I've never heard him play. We are moving to a new place soon. I hope we entertain there."

"Oh! A housewarming party. That would be splendid. When and where are you moving? Tell me all."

I'm about to head into the shower when the external buzzer sounds.

What now?

It better not be a reporter.

In the hall, I answer the intercom. "Hello?"

"Hello. Alessia. Please," a soft, hesitant feminine voice rasps.

"Who is this?"

"Friend. Alessia friend. Please." A quiet desperation in her tone raises the hairs on my neck. English is not her first language. "Sixth floor. Use the lift." I buzz her in.

We'll see who this is.

Tabitha hugs Alessia. "It's been such a pleasure to get to know you these last few days," she gushes. "Please, please stay in touch."

Alessia returns her hug. "I will. And yes, it's been lovely. I feel I have made a friend."

"And we both know how to sit correctly. Deportment is important," Tabitha mimics their tutor and Alessia laughs.

"And I know the difference between a salad and dinner fork. My life is now, um…complete."

Tabitha grins.

"I have to go. Maxim will be waiting."

"Don't stay in Cornwall forever. Please keep in touch."

"I will. Goodbye."

Alessia gives quick farewells and handshakes to her other classmates, and she's out the door and onto the street. There she waves down a cab and gives the cabbie her address.

I open the front door and wait for the lift to arrive. When it does, a young, slight woman steps out onto the landing. She has long, dark hair and dark eyes that regard me warily, and I suspect they've seen too much of the world.

"Hello," I offer cautiously. "Can I help you?"

"Alessia?" She's a little breathless. From nerves? I don't know. She's pretty in an understated way, but stands awkwardly in mismatched clothes at a distance from where I am, and I recognize the same reticence that Alessia used to have with me... with men.

Christ, where did that thought come from?

"She's not here, but she's on her way home."

She frowns, and I step aside and gesture toward the inside and the hallway. "You can wait in here. What is your name?"

"Me?" she asks.

"Yes. Your name. I am Maxim." I place my hand on my chest.

"Bleriana," she says.

"Bleriana!" I exclaim, beaming. "Alessia has been looking for you. Come in."

She tightens her fists as if she's steeling herself and regards me with dark eyes that hint at harrowing secrets beneath their sheen.

Fuck.

I offer her a reassuring smile because I don't know what else I can do while she takes a moment to decide whether or not to come in, and whether or not to trust me. Nervously, she licks her lips, and it's either curiosity or desperation that wins, and she steps past me and into the flat. I stand well back, not wanting to freak her out in any way, and close the door. In the hallway, I fish out my phone and call Alessia. Her phone rings and rings, then goes to voicemail.

Damn.

I text her under Bleriana's watchful gaze.

> I have a surprise for you.
>
> Come home.
>
> Mx
>
> PS—A good surprise.

"I think Alessia is on her way home. She shouldn't be too long."

Bleriana stares with dark, haunted eyes, a little like my wife used to.

What has this young woman been through?

"Do you speak English?"

She nods, then shakes her head in response.

"Okay. Do you want a drink?" With my hand, I motion a cup at my lips.

"No. Thank you." Her voice is hesitant and soft, and her arms are crossed in front of her—I suspect to try to make her already slight frame look smaller. She's trying to be invisible.

Oh, sweetheart. I see you.

"Come. You can wait in here." I head down the hall, hoping that she'll follow, which she does, and I motion her into the drawing room. "Sit."

Bleriana perches on the edge of the sofa, stiff and scared, radiating a tension that I can't even imagine. She clutches her hands in her lap while her wide eyes dart everywhere, taking in her environs. I wonder if she's looking for an escape route.

I stand in the doorway, wondering what the hell to do or say.

"Um. Are you hungry?" With my hands, I motion eating.

She frowns, then nods, and then shakes her head.

Of course—she's Albanian.

"Yes. No?"

"No."

I check my watch. "Alessia. Here soon."

The cab pulls up outside the building, and Alessia steps out and pays the cabbie. In the foyer, she has to wait for the elevator, and Alessia suspects that Mrs. Beckstrom has returned from walking Heracles, judging by the time it takes to come from the top floor. While she waits, she fishes her phone from her bag. There's a missed call and text from Maxim.

A surprise?

Alessia smiles to herself, intrigued, as she finally steps into the elevator. She's excited to get to the Hall. Perhaps the surprise is something to do with Cornwall.

She opens the front door, and Maxim is standing at the end of the hallway, dressed in suit pants and a white shirt. His hair is tousled, his eyes bright green, and he smiles, relieved to see her.

"There you are. You have a friend here!" he says.

"Alessia!" Her name echoes with such hope down the hall, and a young woman comes to stand in the living room doorway. They gape at each other, neither quite believing what they are seeing.

Bleriana!

"O Zot! O Zot! O Zot!" A well of emotion bubbles from Alessia's chest into her throat, and she dashes down the hall, scooping Bleriana into her arms. "You're here. How are you here? Are you okay? Did you escape?"

Bleriana starts to cry, and Alessia's tears push past the hope and joy and incredulity that's knotted in her throat, as they hug and sob, together.

*H*ell. *Weeping women.* Weeping women chattering fast and furious in Albanian.

Their emotional reunion chokes me for a moment.

Alessia turns a teary face to mine. "How?"

I shake my head. "I don't know. She found me. I think she might have followed me from my office. Ask her."

Alessia poses the question to Bleriana, who turns a now teary but more hopeful face to me and answers her.

"Yes. She did," Alessia says.

"I thought I was being followed. Look, I'm going to have a shower. I'll be a few minutes. I'll let you two reconnect."

Alessia reaches out and takes my hand. "Thank you," she mouths.

"As much as I'd like to take the credit, this is not me. She found us."

Alessia turns back to Bleriana. "Tell me. How did you find us? We have been looking for you. Did you escape?" She takes Bleriana's hand, and they sit on the sofa, hands clasped tightly together.

"They caught me." Bleriana whispers the words like she's confessing a terrible sin and with a fear and horror so deep that Alessia's revulsion rises with the bile in her throat.

She wraps her arms around Bleriana and holds her like she'll never let go. "You're here now. You're safe."

Bleriana sobs—a dam bursting within her—and holds on to Alessia like she's her life raft in a sea of awfulness, horror, and terrible abuse. Alessia rocks her gently, as Maxim has done for her, and they both shed tears and more tears. And more. And yet more.

"You're safe. I've got you," Alessia repeatedly murmurs, comforting herself and Bleriana at the same time.

This could have been her.

Eventually, Bleriana quiets and wipes her nose and eyes on the tissue Alessia hands her.

"If you want to tell me, I am here. I will listen."

Bleriana's bottom lip trembles, and she tells her story in a slow, halting voice while Alessia listens and dies a little inside.

From the safety of the doorway, I watch them talk quietly but intensely. I don't understand what they're saying, but Alessia's calm compassion for this stricken young woman resonates through her entire body. The way she gently holds her hands, strokes her back, her eyes warm with concern. Her concentration is utterly centered on Bleriana and nothing else.

It's... affecting.

Whatever Bleriana's telling her, it's distressing for both of them. I turn away, it's too painful to watch, and my morbid imagination kicks into overdrive.

Fuck. Fuck. Fuck.

ow did you find us? We had men looking for you," Alessia asks.

"We were… rescued. By the English police. I am staying with an English family in a safe house. It's part of a charitable organization. They are kind. And I must wait to find out if I can stay in England. Anyway, I saw the newspapers. And I recognized you."

"Ah!" And for a brief moment, Alessia forgives the British press for hounding her and her husband.

"The daughter of the family who is hosting me. Her name is Monifa—she is very kind. She went online. And we found your husband and where he worked. And today, I came to London to find you."

"And you succeeded." Alessia beams and Bleriana's answering smile is radiant, even on her tearstained face.

"So tell me. Alessia, Lady Trevethick. How did this happen to you?" Bleriana's eyes are alight with her curiosity, the dark shadows momentarily hidden behind her joy in her friend's good fortune.

"It is a long story."

I return to the doorway when I hear laughter. Under Alessia's tender, calm care, Bleriana has relaxed and no longer looks like the harrowed young woman I met on the doorstep. Her face has softened, and there's a trace of the young, pretty girl she is, despite the unimaginable horrors she's endured.

My only hope is that she doesn't trigger Alessia's trauma— her nightmares. I didn't want her back in that awful world. Yet here we are.

Hell. I'm standing in the shadows as a bystander, feeling utterly useless.

What can I do?

And it dawns on me that this used to be my norm.

This was how I felt all the time. *Useless.*

It's only since I met Alessia that I've felt worthy and purposeful.

Fuck. I shake off the notion as it's a little disturbing.

There's no way we're going to the Hall this evening, so I head into the kitchen and call Danny to let her know.

"Oh, my lord. That is a shame. We are so looking forward to seeing you and our new countess."

"We'll be down tomorrow. Something's cropped up here. I'll let you know."

"Very good, Maxim."

Next, I call Tom and tell him to call off the search for Bleriana.

"She's turned up here."

"I say, Trevethick. What are the odds!"

"I know."

When I'm off the phone, I wander back into the drawing room.

"Ladies. Shall we eat?"

Alessia jumps to her feet. "Maxim! I'm sorry. The time has flown away."

"It's okay. Talk to your friend. I'll order us a take-out."

"No. No. I'll cook. We are not going to Cornwall this evening?"

"We'll go tomorrow."

Alessia turns to Bleriana. "Can you stay? Are you hungry?"

Bleriana's slight smile signals her agreement.

A lessia makes quick work of preparing some lamb chops with olive oil, garlic, and rosemary for grilling. Then she starts making a salad with feta cheese, onions, tomatoes, and various types of lettuce from a bag. Bleriana helps chop the onions and tomatoes with Alessia. Maxim opens a bottle of red wine for them all to share.

"Alessia, ask Bleriana where she's staying," Maxim says, pouring the wine.

"Reading," Bleriana replies to Alessia's question.

"Can she stay here tonight?" Alessia asks.

"Darling, you don't need my permission. This is your home, too, and she's your friend."

"I wanted to check you do not object."

"Why would I?" His forehead creases with a frown. "What I would say—is it okay with Bleriana? Does she need to get back to Reading this evening? Does she need to let anyone know where she is?"

"Good points." Alessia beams at her husband.

He's so capable.

And asks the right questions.

Alessia quizzes Bleriana, who tells her that she can stay the night but must call the family she lives with to tell them. "I have a phone. They will be anxious if I don't call them. I'll do it now."

She steps into the hallway to make her call, leaving Alessia and Maxim alone for the first time since she arrived. Maxim folds his arms around Alessia and nuzzles beneath her ear. "Can I tell you how much I love you," he whispers.

His lips against her skin, the soft words in the shell of her ear send tingles down her spine. "I am very lucky to have you." He kisses, then nips her earlobe, taking Alessia by surprise and making her yelp. She turns in his arms.

"I am lucky to have you. Thank you for being so understand-ing about Bleriana." She leans up and kisses him.

"Why wouldn't I be? She's been through hell. If she lives in Reading, we can take her back tomorrow on our way to Cornwall."

"Okay." Alessia wants to ask if Bleriana can come to Cornwall with them, but she'll bide her time and wait for the right moment.

How is Bleriana settling down in the spare bedroom?" I ask when Alessia eventually glides into bed beneath the covers.

"She is okay now that she has the little dragon." Alessia snug-gles up to me and slips her hand over my torso and belly, bringing it to rest just beneath the waistband of my PJs. "You are dressed," she murmurs, as her fingers skim the edges of my pubic hair, waking my dick.

"I am. We have a guest. I don't want to frighten her during the night."

She removes her hand, much to my disappointment, and trails it over my body up to my chin, where she cups my face. Leaning over me, she whispers, "Thank you." And she offers me a quick, sweet kiss.

"Oh, no. I want so much more than that." Pulling her into my arms, I turn us both, so she's lying beneath me, her dark hair splayed out over the pillow, her dark eyes gazing up at me, her body cradling mine.

I pause, drinking her in.

But something's off.

"Thank you," she says once more, but this time it's with a breathy, quiet plea that's sobering. She cups my face with her hands, and tears pool in her eyes.

My breath catches in my throat.

Oh, God.

No.

Her soft entreaty almost undoes me and kills my desire. I gather her in my arms and roll back, holding her hard and fast on top of me.

It could have been her.

That's where she's gone.

It could have been her.

But she got away.

My girl. My wife. My sweet, sweet wife.

She lets out a gulping sob and starts to cry, and I hold her while she grieves for her dear, young friend and maybe for herself and all she's endured too.

I kiss her hair and murmur, "I've got you. Let it all out. You're here. You're safe." While my own tears stay lodged like a cinder block in my throat.

Chapter Twenty-Seven

When I stir, Alessia is pressed against me, her arse against my groin as we spoon. My arms are wrapped around her, and my nostrils fill with her delicious, arousing scent.

My dick, thwarted last night for compassionate reasons, is raring to go. Without opening my eyes, I kiss her hair. "Good morning, my love," I murmur and hear a gasp that doesn't emanate from my wife.

What the hell!

Opening my eyes, I raise my head, and Bleriana is staring at me all wide-eyed and pink-cheeked while she's lying next to my wife from the other side of our super-king.

I'm momentarily stunned.

I mean, it wouldn't be the first time I've woken up with more than one woman in bed, but never in this situation.

"Good morning," I say because I can't think of anything else, and I'm conscious of the slow flush that heats my cheeks while my boner dies.

Alessia squirms as she rouses beside me, brushing my dick and bringing it instantly back to life. She reaches out and places a hand on Bleriana's cheek.

Wait a minute! What about me?

G ood morning. Did you sleep okay?" Alessia asks, her voice soft and welcoming.

Bleriana blinks a couple of times. "Yes. Very well. Your husband is awake. Is he mad?"

Alessia smiles. "No, why would he be?" and with a smirk, she continues, "I think he's woken up to more than one woman in his bed before."

Bleriana gasps once more, scandalized but amused by her friend's candor, then lets out a bubble of laughter and Alessia giggles too.

"I shouldn't tell you that. It's a good thing he doesn't understand Albanian." Alessia turns over to face her husband.

M y wife is tousled and sleepy and giggly and utterly beautiful. "Good morning, Lady Trevethick. Something you want to tell me? We seem to have acquired a stowaway during the night."

Alessia's gaze is alight with mischief and love, and to my relief, the anguish from last night seems a distant memory. Her dark eyes are focused on me, and all I see in them is her adoration— and I yearn for her. In every way, even with our audience present.

But I can't fuck her right now—though I'd like to—because… Bleriana.

"I hope you don't mind. Bleriana was afraid in the night. She came in here. I moved over, and we didn't wake you. There is more room in this bed than in the spare room; more important than that, *you* are here, keeping us safe from our bad dreams."

"I thought the little dragon did that."

"He does. But you do too. You always do." She strokes my cheek, her fingers brushing my stubble, and the contact of her skin on mine and her sweet words lead directly to my dick.

"Oh, Alessia," I murmur and kiss her lightly on the lips, though I want to do so much more.

Damn cockblocker!

To indicate my need, I tilt my hips forward, prodding her with my erection. "I'd get out of bed, but this gives the game away."

"Maxim!"

I grin. And plant a swift kiss on her forehead. "This will take a moment."

"We'll make coffee." Alessia grins, turns, and ushers Bleriana out of bed.

D oes he make you get up every day and make coffee?" Bleriana asks when they're in the kitchen, her disapproval apparent in her frown.

Alessia laughs. "No. He makes coffee, even breakfast some-times, but I like to do these things for him. He's a good man. I love him so much."

"I can see that. You are lucky."

"I am." Alessia beams.

After her shower, Alessia quickly pulls on jeans and a sweater while Bleriana showers in the spare room en suite.

Maxim is already freshly washed, dressed, and sitting at his computer in the living room when Alessia interrupts him. "My lord, I have a request."

He turns his attention from the screen to her. "Why are you standing so far away?" He reaches for her and tugs her onto his lap. "What is it, my lady?" He nuzzles her ear. "And if it's about Bleriana joining us in Cornwall, I would rather she didn't."

"Oh." Alessia slumps against him, disappointed.

"Love, it's not what you think," he says quickly. "When Leticia rang earlier this week, she said that the Home Office might refuse you a family visa if they find out you've been in the country illegally. You were trafficked with Bleriana, and she's known to the police." A crease forms between his brows. "I'm worried that someone will make the connection between you two, and if the press get hold of that…"

"Oh." Alessia pales.

"Exactly. But I suggest we ask Leticia to expedite whatever's happening with Bleriana's case for asylum. It's Leticia's area of expertise, and Bleriana might get a visa before you do."

"Okay," Alessia says, but she's still ambivalent about Maxim dealing with Ticia.

Alessia! Ticia is an expert.

"That is a good plan. You will ask Ticia?"

He smiles. "I'll email her now. And when this is all sorted, Bleriana can come to Cornwall anytime. Though I would prefer it if she slept in her own bed."

"She's… um…trauma…traumatized," Alessia says quietly.

"I know." He brushes her hair behind her ear. "But it's not appropriate." Maxim shrugs, his smile rueful.

Alessia nods in understanding. *If the staff find out, they will assume the worst.*

"She's very young," he says. "Does she want to go back to Albania?"

"No. She will be shunned. The stigma…" Alessia's voice trails off.

"Wow. That's awful. Her parents?"

Alessia shakes her head in answer to his unspoken question.

"Okay. Let's take her back to Reading and put her in touch with Leticia."

Bleriana is quiet. She's seated with Alessia in the rear of Maxim's bigger car, the Discovery. They hold hands and make occasional small talk, but Alessia can sense her friend's growing anxiety as they get closer to their destination. Maxim, following the route guidance, comes off the motorway, and they head toward Reading town center.

"I wish I could come with you," Bleriana says quietly.

"I know." Alessia squeezes her hand and glances at Maxim. Their eyes meet in the rearview mirror, and she wonders if she should press Maxim to change his mind.

"I have to be here because of meetings," Bleriana says.

"You do?" This news slightly consoles Alessia. "Meetings?" she asks.

"Yes. A counselor. And a social worker."

Bleriana can't come to Cornwall. "I see. I am glad you are seeing a counselor."

"When will I see you again?"

"Soon. I promise. You have my mobile number. Call me. Whenever."

We pull up outside a modest terraced house in the back-streets near Reading station. I climb out and join Bleriana and Alessia on the small driveway. The front door opens, and a middle-aged woman steps out. She has a friendly, open face, and her teeth are dazzling against the darkness of her skin when she smiles. "Bleriana, welcome back."

A pale, portly, balding man, who must be in his early fifties, appears behind her, wearing a Reading FC shirt and jeans. His smile is as warm and friendly as his wife's. Well, I assume they're married, and these are Bleriana's foster parents. Alessia introduces herself as Alessia Trevelyan and me as her husband. I like that she doesn't flaunt her title. Sometimes, it's just not the done thing.

And she gets it.

Mr. and Mrs. Evans seem like lovely people, but when they ask us to join them for tea, I politely refuse. I'd like to get on our way.

Bleriana turns, hugs Alessia, and murmurs a teary goodbye

in Albanian, then offers me a goodbye, with a nod, from a safe distance.

"Come." I hold out my hand to my wife, and we head back to the car.

From the passenger seat, Alessia gives them a wave, her eyes shining, and I know she's tearful. I put the Discovery in drive, head down the street, and reach over to grab her hand.

"She's going to be okay. They seem like good people."

"They are. Bleriana is overwhelmed by their kindness."

"You'll see her soon."

Alessia nods and turns to stare out of the window.

"Do you mind if I put some music on?" I ask.

"No."

"Any requests?"

She turns dark, sad eyes to me and shakes her head.

"Oh, baby. Do you want me to turn around and pick her up?"

"No. No. We can't do that. She has to see her social worker and her counselor."

I blow out a breath. Relieved. "I'm glad she has support. She's going to be okay. She's like you. Self-sufficient. She came to find you through me. That was courageous on her part."

Alessia gives me a slight smile. And I'm tempted to remind her she was crying the last time we headed to Cornwall but decide against it. Instead, I switch BBC Radio 6 on the sound system and let the music wash over me from an old timer, Roy Harper, his song "North Country" from 1974.

Hmm. I'd like to learn to play this on guitar.

D o you want to stop for lunch?" Maxim asks.

"I'm not hungry." Alessia's heart is heavy.

"I can't tempt you with a panini?"

She smiles, albeit reluctantly. "That seems so long ago."

Maxim laughs. "It was. A world away. I'm hungry. Please, can we stop?"

Alessia's smile broadens. "Of course. I don't want you to be hungry."

A lessia stays glued to my side, her hand in mine, as we make our way through the motorway services building at Sedgemoor. We buy ham-and-cheese toasties and coffee at Costa Coffee but decide to eat and drink on the road.

"One day, you won't think twice about being in a service station," I try to reassure Alessia when I open her car door.

"I hope so," she replies, but her eyes follow me as I walk around to my side of the Discovery, and I know she doesn't feel safe. The thought is depressing. I knew this might happen if she was exposed to her recent past and that awful underworld again.

It will take time, mate.

Time.

Once inside, I place the coffee cup in a holder, remove my sandwich from its wrapping, and take a big bite. I start the car and pull out of our space. "You didn't get to tell me about your last day on the course. How was it?" I ask, with my mouth full and some butter dribbling down my chin.

She laughs at the state of me before passing me a napkin, and the sound warms my heart. "The course was very…um…informative. We shall see. And I made some friends. Especially Tabitha."

"That's great." Out of the corner of my eye, I watch her take a delicate bite of her toastie as she deliberates over something. Her napkin is neatly laid on her lap, pointing the correct way, and it makes me smile. She's every inch a lady.

"I think they will help."

"The lessons?"

"Yes. I want to prove to your mother and people like her that I am worthy of you and your…your legacy."

Her softly spoken statement is a gut punch, sending shock waves to my soul.

Fuck a duck.

Rowena must have said something truly nasty and scathing last week, and my poor wife has taken my mother's poison to heart. I remember what she said when we were both with her in our drawing room, which was bad enough.

You need someone of your own class, someone English who understands the pressures of the title and your position in society. Someone who can help you fulfill the role you were born to and help protect our legacy.

The antagonism that I've come to associate with Rowena—that's been a part of my life since she walked out on us so long ago—simmers in my chest, and I grip the steering wheel harder. The resentment is my familiar—never really far away.

"You are more than worthy of me. If anything…" I mutter, trying to keep a handle on my temper. "You are worthy of everything. Never think anything less than that, please." I offer her an apologetic smile. "You were on the receiving end of some dreadful diatribe from Rowena. I can only apologize."

Alessia sighs. "She was upset, Maxim. She thinks you married beneath you…a foreigner, a woman with nothing, and she was there to confess her…um…"

"Sins?" I sneer.

"She was there to put your mind…um…at ease. You should hear her side of Kit's story. Sometimes women find themselves in"—she swallows—"difficult situations."

I inhale sharply. My sweet, compassionate wife reminding me of the brutal truth of the world. *And she would know. Her awful travails brought her to me.*

It blows my mind.

My sweet girl. Defending my mother.

I clear my crowded throat. "How's your toastie?" I ask because we're in difficult territory. I don't want to feel any compassion for my mother.

She left us.

She was cruel to my wife.

"Delicious," she whispers, and another glance at her tells me she knows exactly what I'm doing.

Deflecting. Away from the sore spot that is my Mama.
Mate.

"You are too kind to my mother. But I'll think about it," I mutter, and because I don't want to discuss the Mothership, I turn on the sound system.

At just after five in the evening, the sun low in the sky, I turn right at the North Gatehouse and drive over the cattle grid and onto the northern driveway of the estate. Alessia leans forward to take in the rolling north pasture on our right. We've not been this way before.

"You have cows!"

"Cattle. Yes. Organic."

"They are so pretty!"

I laugh. "They're Devons."

Alessia casts a look at me, her brow furrowed.

"The breed. Of cattle."

"Oh."

"You can meet them later."

Alessia grins. "Still no goats."

I laugh. "No goats."

She looks ahead, and gasps as Tresyllian Hall comes into view. The magnificence of this house never fails to impress. It's always a moment for me as well. There's a sudden tightness in my chest. I'm bringing my wife to what will be a home for her, for our children, and hopefully for their children.

Fuck.

Dude. Steady.

That's a weighty thought.

Accompanied by weighty emotions.

Enough.

I shake it off. This place has been my haven, and I hope that Alessia will be happy here too.

I round the drive, run over the second cattle grid that rattles our teeth, and steer us around the old stables to the kitchen door where I park the Discovery.

I switch off the ignition and turn to Alessia.

"Welcome home, wife."

Her smile lights up her face. "Welcome home, my lord."

The kitchen door opens, and Danny stands on the threshold, clasping her hands in excitement, her joy writ large in her sparkling blue eyes and beaming smile. Behind her, Jensen and Healey, Kit's beloved red setters, come barreling out onto the gravel, curious to see who's arrived.

I clamber out of the car, and the dogs jump up, delighted to see me, insisting on some attention. "Hello, boys. Hello!" I ruffle them both behind the ears. And they turn their enthusiastic attention and demands on Alessia when she comes to stand beside me. She pats them both, a little more reticent than me.

"Welcome home, my lord and my lady!" Danny gushes.

Danny gushing. It doesn't happen often.

She grabs Alessia's hand. "I am so pleased to see you again, my lady."

"Thank you, Danny," Alessia says. "Please, call me Alessia."

"Alessia is fine, Danny. For heaven's sake." And I give her a quick kiss in welcome. "It's good to see you."

"And you too, my lord." She pats my face, and if I'm not mistaken, she's a little teary.

Oh, this will never do. "Maxim. Please," I instruct her. "But wait, I have an important duty to perform." I take Alessia's hand and lift her into my arms, making her squeal in surprise. The dogs jump up in encouragement and start barking. And rather than go in through the kitchen door, I hold Alessia to my chest and trudge over the gravel toward the front of the house.

"What are you doing?" Alessia laughs as she puts her arms around my neck.

"I'm taking you through the front door, which we rarely use. We should go through the boot room, but everyone uses the kitchen door, as it's the most welcoming part of the house.

However, as the new countess, I think you should go through the front door."

The dogs are with us when I glance behind me, but Danny has disappeared. I know she's heading to the front door through the house. I round the corner and follow the path, lined with ancient yews, toward the old front door inset in the spacious stone porch. It's a quicker journey for Danny, who opens the old oak door. Beside her, Jessie, our cook, and Brody, one of the estate hands, stand ready to welcome us.

I carry Alessia inside and set her down in the hallway in front of my family coat of arms and our staff. "Welcome, Countess Trevethick." I cup her face, bring her lips to mine, and give her a sweet kiss that stirs my soul.

My wife.

Here. At last.

"Aww." There's a collective sound of approval from the team, and I must remember we're not alone.

"Welcome home, both of you. And congratulations," Jessie offers.

"Thank you. Danny, Jessie, Brody, may I present Alessia, Countess of Trevethick."

A lessia is overwhelmed by the unexpected and warm welcome. The staff—even the dogs—are delighted to see her. Danny and Jessie have left to make a "wee spot of tea," and Brody has gone to replace some light bulbs somewhere. The dogs, sensing food might be forthcoming, have followed in Danny's and Jessie's footsteps.

Maxim and Alessia are alone in the front hall as they gaze at each other. From nearby, a rhythmic tick from an old clock beats a sensual, relentless pulse.

"How is it?" Maxim asks, his eyes searing hers, and he tucks a wayward lock of hair behind her ear.

His gentle touch echoes through her body, waking her up.

"It's good. Very good," she whispers, unable to avert her gaze from his striking green eyes that darken as he stares at her.

"It's not so long that we were here."

"No. But it was another lifetime."

"It was," he whispers and brushes his thumb along her bottom lip, sending a bolt of delicious electricity south through her muscle, sinew, and bone and all the soft tissue in between. It's arousing.

"I know that look," he breathes, his words barely audible.

"I know your look." She can feel it. Their desire. Coursing between them. Electrical. Magical. Their own special alchemy.

"Let's go to bed," Maxim whispers, eyes dark with carnal appreciation and bold promises.

How could she resist? Why would she want to?

"I'd like that very much."

He grins, grabs her hand, and leads her toward the considerable staircase with its two-headed eagle newel posts.

"Race you?" he challenges with a wicked grin and bolts up the stairs taking two at a time. Alessia follows, trying not to laugh at his boyishness.

He waits at the top of the stairs, all tousled hair and licentious smile.

"Eager?" Alessia teases, a little breathless, and he laughs and dips suddenly, grabbing her around her thighs and hauling her over his shoulder so that she squeals and giggles in equal measure.

"You bet!" he exclaims and smacks her backside before striding down the corridor toward his bedroom with Alessia bouncing on his shoulder.

Fortunately, it's not far. In his bedroom, he sets her on her feet, and they regard each other, drinking each other in—all eyes and smiles and desire.

"I love you," he breathes and leans forward, catching her lips with his, slowly snaking his arms around her and pulling her against his body. They kiss. And kiss. Tasting and teasing one another. Losing each other in their tongues and lips and teeth.

Her hands fist in his burnished chestnut hair while his are at her nape, cradling her head, and skimming her body to her behind, and squeezing hard, so she's flush against his growing erection.

"You taste so good," Alessia breathes when they come up for air.

"So do you, baby. So do you. I want you so much. But for a moment, I just want to hold you. Here. Now." He tightens his arms around her and rests his forehead against hers.

She smiles to herself and for him as she catches her breath, and they stand in each other's arms, at peace in the eye of their passionate storm.

Together, they hold each other.

Own each other.

"Oh, Maxim. I love you," she whispers. "More than you'll ever know."

"I *do* know."

But her love, her gratitude, her desire can't wait for long. "I want you," she whispers, reaching for Maxim's sweater and tugging it over his head. She jerks his shirt out of his jeans and starts to undo the buttons.

I stand as placidly as I can, given I want to jump my wife.
    Now.

And I let her undress me. She's as driven by her longing as I am. My fingers are itching to undress her, but I'm happy to stoke the heat in my blood just watching her.

She slips her hand into the waistband of my jeans and undoes the button.

"Your turn," I say, halting her, and I sweep off her sweater. Then I kneel at her feet, slipping her boots off one by one and peeling off her socks. I stand, and under her unremitting gaze, I remove my shoes and socks.

There. Ready.

So ready.

"Take your jeans off. Now," I whisper.

Alessia gasps, and with her darkening eyes on mine, she steps back, slowly undoes her jeans, and lowers the fly at a glacial speed.

Tease!

Then she shimmies, swinging her fine arse to and fro, tugging her jeans down and stepping out of them.

My beautiful wife stands before me in a pretty lacy bra and panties.

And I take a moment to admire the fucking view.

She is gorgeous.

She reaches behind her back, undoes her bra, tosses it at me, and laughs when I catch it. Then she shimmies out of her panties.

"You are so beautiful, Alessia."

"Now you," she says with an imperious look that's hot as hell.

"Yes. My lady." I make quick work of my jeans and underwear, so my ready, ready dick springs free, enthusiastic for her.

Alessia smirks and steps forward, taking me in hand.

It's my turn to gasp.

Her fingers are cold!

"Ah!"

Alessia laughs, and I join her. "Enough!" I grab her around the waist and lift her. "Wrap your legs around me, baby." She obliges, and holding her, I walk to our bed and lower us onto it, so I'm lying cradled between her thighs.

"First time. As man and wife. Here," I whisper, suddenly beset by a sense of history or legacy or something that's more than the two of us. She gazes at me and gently pushes my hair off my forehead.

"Husband," she whispers, and the word echoes in my groin.

Fuck.

I want to be inside her. I run a hand down her body, skimming her nipple, so it stands to sweet attention, and continue, my hand celebrating the dips and shallows of her skin down to her belly and over her sex. Slowly, I insert a finger into her warm, welcoming wetness, and her hips rise, meeting my finger, and pushing against my hand, wanting relief.

Oh, baby.

I withdraw my finger and slowly ease myself into her and take her mouth with mine, my tongue mirroring my cock. Her body rises to meet mine, and she wraps her arms and legs around me. Holding me fast. It's intoxicating.

And I can resist no more.

And start to move.

Hard.

Swift.

Claiming the woman who is my wife.

Taking her higher as her nails etch my back.

Vaguely, as I lose myself in her, I hope she leaves marks on me.

I'm hers.

She's mine.

For all time.

"Maxim," she cries as she comes, and I let go, finding release inside the only woman I've ever truly loved.

My wife.

Chapter Twenty-Eight

Alessia takes a break from practising her audition pieces and watches Maxim from the mullioned windows of the great music room. He's trudging up the driveway with Michael, the estate manager. Maxim is dressed in his long coat and wellingtons, holding what looks like a walking staff as he paces the ground. They are deep in discussion, probably about the still, Maxim's passion project. He's excited to get it up and running.

Behind him, Healey and Jensen are bouncing along the lane, stopping to sniff and mark their territory like dogs do. Even from here, Alessia can tell that the dogs are delighted to be with her husband. They adore him.

Like she adores him.

Maxim and Michael laugh at something Michael says, and it warms Alessia's heart to see him so happy. This is where Maxim belongs. He looks every centimeter the lord of the manor and so much more relaxed here in Cornwall than in London. And who could blame him? The pace of life is easier, and it reminds her more and more of her homeland.

In the pasture beside them, the deer congregate around the water trough. Maxim stops to admire the herd with Michael.

Alessia is distracted by the sound of footsteps. "Ah, what a pleasure it is to listen to you play, my lady," Danny says. "I've brought you some refreshment." She places a tray with a small coffeepot, cup, and saucer on the console table beside her.

"Thank you."

"His lordship has always had a fondness for the herd," she murmurs as she glances out of the window.

Alessia nods. "When I was here last time, we saw one on the road. A great stag. It stopped in front of us."

"You did! Well, I never." Danny looks shocked.

"Why is that a surprise?"

"Did Maxim not tell you?"

"No."

"About the legend?"

Alessia shakes her head.

"Och, that boy," Danny scoffs. "Legend has it that the first countess, Isabel, encountered a stag out in the forest shortly after her wedding to the first earl. The stag spoke to her and told her that if her family cared for the wild herd, then she would be blessed with a long life and many children. And that's exactly what happened. The Trevethick estate has long been a haven for the deer. They're seen as a sign of good luck. That's why the two stags are the support in the family coat of arms. They symbolize protection for the earldom, the estate, and the family, my lady."

"I did not know this. They are not…um…hunted?"

Danny shakes her head. "No. Not for centuries. They're humanely culled every other year to keep their numbers sustainable. And the venison is much coveted around here. Keeps the herd strong, and while the herd stands strong, so will the Trevelyans and the Earls of Trevethick."

Alessia doesn't know what to say, but a frisson of hope for the future—a future for her and her husband skitters over her skin.

After all, the stag they saw when Maxim took them shooting seemed to be welcoming her. She grins at Danny.

"It's a good omen, my lady. The Trevelyan family is responsible for the well-being of the estate, the village, forests, fields, and pastures surrounding it. Their land extends many thousand acres. And they and their kin have kept it together and thriving since the 1600s. Long may they continue." Danny's smile reflects her own. "Now, once you've had your coffee, I was wondering if you wanted to see the private apartments and the attic—though that floor is mainly for staff and storage."

"Yes. I'd love that. Thank you, Danny." Alessia has cherished the housekeeper's thorough tours of the house. She's given Alessia a detailed history of each room that's open—not all are—and its place within the great house. She's introduced Alessia to most of the staff, who, so far, have been kind and accommodating. Alessia is increasingly in awe of the woman that keeps the entire house running smoothly. And she feels safe in her hands—after all, it was Danny who cared for her after Dante and Ylli's kidnap attempt.

And it's obvious she dotes on Maxim, and he on her. She seems more maternal than his own mother…

Alessia!

She tries not to think uncharitably about Rowena, but sometimes it's impossible. Perhaps, to make up for her unkind thoughts, she can do something to help repair the fissure between her mother-in-law and her husband.

But what?

"And then there's the all-important decision of moving his lordship into the earl's bedroom and you into the countess's room." Danny distracts Alessia from her thoughts.

"Countess's room?"

"Yes. You each have your own apartments here."

Separate bedrooms! Separate apartments!

"Sometimes it's good to have a bolt hole, my lady," Danny says as if reading her thoughts.

Bolt hole? Alessia doesn't understand what that means and does not like the sound of it or the idea of sleeping elsewhere.

Is this what Maxim wants? To sleep without her?

Like the ancient Gheg custom! The thought depresses her immediately.

"Ach, my lady. It'll not be like that," Danny says. "I'll show you once you've had your coffee."

Michael and I survey the motors in the old stables—these vintage and classic cars were Kit's pride and joy. I can almost see him, walking toward me in his filthy overalls, his hands covered in grease and smelling of oil and Swarfega. He'd have his cloth cap on, an oily rag protruding from his pocket, and he'd be so fucking happy.

Well, Spare, fancy a spin in this Ferrari?

He loved it here.

He loved his cars.

Me, not so much. However, I didn't mind the odd spin around the grounds in one of these beasts.

And now I have to decide what to do with them.

"You're right, Michael. This building would be a much better place for a still. It's more secure, closer to the house, there's room for expansion, and these old stables are in better condition than the north pasture barn."

"Only problem is the cars."

"I'm going to have to sell them. I have no need for all of these." Michael gives me a rueful smile. I know selling them would have broken Kit's heart, but he's not here. "I'll keep the Morgan, and everything else can go. I'll ask Caroline if she wants any of them, but I doubt it. Cars were Kit's passion, not hers."

"Yes, my lord."

I head back into the house via the boot room while Michael returns to his office. We've had a good morning, and I'm ready for lunch. Michael was extolling the virtues of regenerative farming.

Apparently, it's the next step in green agriculture. I've vowed to read up on it, to see what the fuss is about.

I find Alessia in the small sitting room, seated at a table set for lunch. She looks up from the Daphne Du Maurier that she's reading, anxiety etched on her face.

"What is it?" I ask as I take a seat opposite her.

"Do you want me to sleep somewhere else?"

"What? No. What's this about?"

"Danny was talking to me about moving rooms."

"Ah." The penny drops. "I'm not sure I want to move rooms. Do you?"

"No. I want to stay with you."

I laugh. "I'm glad to hear it. We can sleep where we like. The earl's room has been my father's and my brother's." I shrug. I'm in no mood to move in there. "And as for the countess's rooms, that's up to you. They're not far from my bedroom, and there's a dressing room there that might come in handy. You don't have to sleep there. I'd rather you slept with me. Unless I snore."

She exhales and laughs. "Good. That's what I thought. And you do not snore."

"I have an idea of what we can do this afternoon." I change the subject.

"Oh?" Alessia tilts her head to one side with a coquettish look, and I know she's thinking about sex.

I laugh. "No. I'm going to teach you to drive."

"Drive! Me?"

"Yes. You don't need a license on private land. We can take the Defender, or maybe another, smaller vehicle, and I'll teach you."

Danny enters, holding two plates. "Lunch, my lord."

I roll my eyes. "Maxim. That's my name."

"Maxim, my lord," Danny concedes, and she places two plates on the table. "Salad Niçoise with a Cornish twist."

"Cornish twist?" I ask, intrigued, examining the plate in front of me.

"Pilchards, sir, instead of anchovies."

I laugh. "Okay then."

"Steady, a little more gas, and slowly ease the clutch up," I direct Alessia. We're in the Defender that Danny normally drives around the estate. It's battered but quite serviceable.

Alessia is grasping the steering wheel like her life depends on it, and her tongue peeks out between her lips because she's concentrating so hard. The car suddenly jerks forward and stalls, and Alessia stamps on the brakes.

I'm thrown forward, my seat belt cutting into my chest. "Whoa!"

Alessia lets out a string of invective in her mother tongue, which I've never heard her do before.

She's not happy.

"It's okay," I reassure her. "It's about finding the biting point on the clutch when the engine engages. You just need a little more gas. Take it steady. We have all afternoon. And it's okay—driving can take a while to learn."

She gives me a quick, determined scowl and starts the car again.

My girl is not going to give up.

"Take it slow. Put it into gear," I murmur.

She fights the gearshift to put it back into first, and I wonder if we should have chosen an easier car.

Hell, if she can drive this, she can drive anything.

"Okay. Deep breaths. You can do this."

The gears grind as she thrusts it into first and revs the engine once more.

"Easy does it. Not too much gas."

She scowls at me again, and I shut up because if I don't, I suspect she'll be tempted to remove one of my limbs. I've never taught anyone to drive, and I learned here on the estate when I was fifteen. It was one of the last duties my father fulfilled before he died. He was calm and reassuring, his best self…and I hold that memory dear. He was a great teacher.

I want to be the same for Alessia.

At a snail's pace, we roll forward.

Yes! I let out a silent, internal cheer so as not to distract Alessia, and we inch across the gravel behind the stables.

"Okay, now into second. Clutch. Second gear. Ease up on the clutch."

Her tongue appears again, and she shifts smoothly into second gear, letting the Defender pick up a little speed.

"Well done! Okay. Take it steady. Head straight toward the gates. Yes. Good!"

Alessia gingerly drives toward the gateposts where the cattle grid lies.

"We're going into the lane. Keep it going."

She steers—successfully—between the gateposts and heads down the lane. A wild grin erupts on her face, and it's infectious.

"You're doing it. Keep your eyes on the road."

She continues to drive slowly but solidly down the lane, concentrating hard; her tongue makes the occasional foray, peeking from her mouth.

It's sexy as hell.

But now is not the time to tell her. Or to think about that—it's distracting.

"You're doing so well. But beware, there might be deer in the lane. They should get out of the way when they hear this crate coming. You don't want to hit one. Kit did. Once…"

Shit.

And look what happened to him.

Hell.

I clear my throat, pushing my grief away, though I'm reminded that there's a mythical story about the deer that ties them to the estate, which I've forgotten. I must try to remember to tell Alessia. "At the end of the lane by the north gatehouse, let's take the left fork. Take that, and we'll do a crisscross tour of the estate."

Alessia is giddy with delight. She cannot believe she's managed to move the tank she is driving. But most of all, she's
thrilled because she doesn't want to let Maxim down. He seems
to think that she should be able to do this.

And so she has.

His faith in her is touching.

As they round a bend in the lane, she spots the gatehouse and
the cattle grid and the road forks in three directions.

She panics for a moment.

Which is left?

O Zot!

Rather than turn at all, she slams on the brakes, throwing them
both forward and stalling the car.

"Sorry!" she says quickly.

"It's okay. You don't need to apologize. You remembered the
brakes and stopped the car. That's the most important thing. Not
sure of your left?"

Alessia laughs, and she suspects it's more in catharsis than
amusement. "No. I was confused."

"It's okay. You could have gone either way. This is all estate
land. Turn the ignition off. Car into neutral. Brake on."

Alessia follows Maxim's instructions and takes a deep breath.

She can do this!

"Do you want to try again?"

She nods.

Maxim sweeps his hand forward. "Go ahead."

She turns on the ignition, and the engine grumbles into life.
She stamps on the clutch, wanting to show it who's in charge,
and she slides, then pushes the stick into first. The gears make
an awful grinding noise. Alessia chances a glance at Maxim,
who's wincing, so she quickly looks back at the road and revs the
engine, easing her foot on the clutch, releasing the handbrake…
and they're off once more.

No stalling!

Alessia wants to cheer from the rooftops.

She turns the heavy steering wheel, and the car moves slowly to the left and continues along the lane.

"Second gear?" Maxim says gently.

She nods and changes gear, keeping the car going. They pass one of the fields, and Alessia catches a glimpse of Jenkins on a tractor pulling a trailer. He gives them a wave, which Maxim returns, but Alessia keeps her hands firmly gripped on the steering wheel. As they head down the lane, Maxim continues to offer his support with sweet words.

He's pleased.

Alessia catches sight of another gatehouse and slows down as she approaches it. From beyond the gate, a small motorbike shoots in and across their path, the driver wearing black trousers and boots, and fastened to the rear, there's a carrier holding what looks like a small furry passenger. Alessia slams on the brakes as the motorbike continues at a pace up the driveway and doesn't stall the car!

Go, Alessia!

"Shit. It's Father Trewin," Maxim exclaims. "Driving much too fast. It must be God's will that he's still in one piece. Better follow him."

Alessia does and speeds up to see if she can catch him.

"Steady," warns Maxim, and she slows down again. "We'll see him at the house. He's probably here to congratulate us. Or he's going to berate me for not coming to church yesterday. Probably both."

Alessia stops beside Father Trewin while he's unfastening his Norfolk terrier, Boris, from his carrier on the back of his moped. Jensen and Healey are eagerly waiting to play, their tails frenetic flags.

I clamber out of the car, walk around to open Alessia's door, and turn to greet Father Trewin.

"Maxim, my lord. Congratulations on your marriage. How are you?" He offers his hand and gives me a firm handshake.

"Good. Thank you, Father. May I present my wife, Alessia, the Countess of Trevethick?"

"Lady Trevethick, what a pleasure to meet you again."

"Father Trewin, how do you do?" Alessia shakes hands with him. "Would you like to join us for tea?"

"I'd be delighted." He gives us both a broad, benevolent, reserved-for-parishioners smile.

We make our way through the boot room and out into the west corridor, where we're met by Danny. "Good afternoon, everyone," Danny greets us. "How was the car, my lady?"

"It was a tank!" Alessia beams. "But I got it going."

"I'm glad to hear it."

"May we have some tea?" Alessia asks.

Danny smiles. "Yes, my lady. The west drawing room?"

Alessia glances at me. I nod.

"Please."

"We didn't see you at our service this Sunday," Father Trewin says once we've sat down.

Bugger. I knew it. I'm going to get a lecture. "Yes. I had to catch up here," I mutter, desperate to change the subject. I lean down and scratch Boris behind his ears, wondering where Jensen and Healey are. "And I was showing my wife around the estate."

"Well, my lord, as I've said before, we lead by example. Perhaps next Sunday, you could do a reading."

What?

I clear my throat. "Sure. I'd be delighted."

Liar.

"Your brother was a keen supporter of the church."

Trust Kit. The nerd! I smile, my heart sinking.

That was Kit—the perfect earl. It's not me.

Mate. The irony.

"Will you choose a reading?" I ask.

"Of course. And might we expect to see Lady Trevethick there?" He casts his beady eyes at my wife.

Alessia smiles, but her eyes dart to mine in a silent plea for help.

"Alessia is Albanian, where religion was outlawed for many years. But her people are Catholic. As high Anglicans, I'm sure that won't be an issue."

"We are a broad church, my lord, and welcoming of all faiths."

"Of course, I'll be there," Alessia says.

Danny enters and places a tray with cups and saucers on the table in front of Alessia. She gives her a nod and then leaves.

"Tea, Father Trewin?" Alessia asks.

"Yes, please, Countess."

If the use of her title disconcerts Alessia, she gives nothing away. She takes the teapot and pours a cup, using the tea strainer that Danny has provided, and hands the cup and saucer with a small teaspoon to Father Trewin. She offers him milk and sugar, pours some for me, and gives me the cup and saucer.

Hiding my smile, I accept it. She's learned how to serve tea. Properly. "Thank you, my love." She gives me an impish smile before serving herself, and I know, that she knows, that I know that she's putting her social etiquette training into full force.

She's not put a foot wrong.

Would I expect anything less?

She's amazing. And adorable.

Even more so because I know she's done this for me.

And maybe for herself.

I turn my attention to our guest, who is fully conscious of Alessia and me grinning inanely at each other. His cheeks become rosier as he looks from me to my wife.

Yeah. We're in love.

Deal with it.

Which reminds me… "Father Trewin, I had hoped that Alessia and I could marry again in the UK as we're now back home, but I've been reliably informed that it's not possible. Therefore, I was hoping we could have a blessing at the church. Give us a chance to celebrate here. Preferably in the summer?"

"That's a splendid idea. Of course we can do that. I'd be delighted."

Alessia escorts Father Trewin back to his moped. He is positively blossoming under her attention, and I think she has a new fan. I head to the study to make some notes on the gin project, to find someone to sell Kit's car collection, and to read up on Michael's new passion—regenerative farming.

It's dusk when I look up from the computer. My head is buzzing from what I've learned about sustainable agriculture. Leaning back in my chair, I take in my surroundings to ease the strain on my eyes.

I've not really sat here since Kit died. There was that time when Oliver talked me through the burglary at Chelsea Embankment, and before then, when I visited the Hall for the first time in my capacity as earl, I sat here and mostly talked to the estate workers in turn.

A faint melody drifts through the hallways from the music room; Alessia is at the piano, no doubt practising her audition pieces. As I try to make out what she's playing, my gaze wanders over the desk that was once my brother's and once my father's. There are mementos that belonged to both of them: my father's Georgian tea caddy where he kept paper clips and such nonsense, two vintage Matchbox Bugattis from the 1960s—they were my father's, but I remember he used to let Kit play with them. He and Kit shared a passion for cars.

They *were* close.

And here I am, selling his prized collection.

Kit. I'm sorry, mate.

I open the tea caddy, more out of nostalgia than curiosity, trying to capture some essence of my beloved father.

There is a small set of keys sitting on top of a slightly larger key, which I know is for the safe.

The safe!

Maybe this is where Kit's missing laptop, phone, and journal might be.

Grabbing the key, I stand and open the large wooden built-in cupboard that once served as the serving platter closet, where the old Cartwright & Sons safe is situated. The larger key fits the lock, and I open it, revealing Kit's laptop.

But no phone or journal.

There are also various papers that I don't have the energy to explore right now. I take out his laptop and place it on the desk.

Perhaps his journal is in a drawer.

I try one of the drawers, but it's locked.

A key from the small bunch opens it, and as I slowly tug the drawer open—there, in all its glory, is Kit's battered, brown leather journal and his dead iPhone.

I ignore the phone and laptop because they're probably password protected, so I'll need expert help to hack them.

It's the journal that will answer my questions.

My scalp tenses as I take it out—clasped with reverence between both hands—and place it on top of his laptop. I stare at it for a full minute before I decide to invade his privacy. Slowly, with a slight tremor in my hand, I unwind the leather tie ragged from overuse and pull the covers apart. It opens on the last entry.

2nd January 2019

Fuck! Fuck! Fuck!
A thousand times fuck!
I'm fucked!
Fucking Rowena!!!
First my wife, now my mother!!!

Chapter Twenty-Nine

Every hair on my body rises in shock as I pore over the entry time and time again.

First my wife, now my mother.

The words ring through my brain, a loud klaxon of wrongdoing.

My wife? Caroline?

And guilt surges like a tsunami through my chest.

But. But…we…we—Kit was dead when Caro and I fucked that first time. I never touched her while they were together.

Not once.

Before they were together. Yes. But… not while *they* were a couple.

First my wife!

Was she having an affair? And he found out?

Is this why he left her nothing in his will?

That makes sense. It always seemed such a shockingly cold-blooded move. And Caroline was angry… but she accepted the exclusion readily.

Was she aware that he knew?

Did he confront her?

He must have—his will was changed in September last year.

But an affair with whom? One person? Two people? More?

Fuck. Poor Kit.

I think back to Christmas in the Caribbean. There was no hint of marital un-bliss between them. Or maybe I didn't notice because I was too busy fucking my way through the American tourists.

Oh hell.

The answer is probably chronicled within these pages.

Dare I look?

Do I even want to know?

There's a knock on the door that startles me. I close the book and instinctively lean over the journal to hide it from view. Danny enters, and I must look as guilty as sin because she doesn't tell me why she's there. "Are you okay, my lord?"

"Yeah. Yeah. What is it, Danny?"

"The countess has gone out with Jenkins to the sheep. She didn't want to disturb you. But she wanted to help. We have twenty-seven ewes lambing right now."

"That many!"

"Yes, my lord."

"But it's just the beginning of the season!" I frown—that's a lot at once. "I'd better go and help too." I rise from the desk, taking Kit's journal with me. I don't want any prying eyes seeing this, and on a whim, I grab the Leica M6 I brought from London and automatically check that it has film in it.

"I'll hold dinner, my lord."

"Okay, thank you. I have no idea what time we'll be back."

Alessia rides with Jenkins in the Defender as it bumps down one of the lanes in the dark. The high verges, covered with brambles and grass, seem to loom out of the night, so Alessia's grateful she's not driving. Jenkins glances at her, his brow etched in concern.

"My lady," Jenkins almost shouts above the noise of the engine.

"Alessia."

"Yes. I have to ask…" His words trail off as if he's reluctant to say more.

"What is it, Jenkins?"

He clears his throat. "Are you… are you in the family way?"

Alessia frowns. *Family way? What does that mean?*

Jenkins tugs his ear. "Might you be… might you be pregnant, my lady?"

Alessia's blush warms her cheeks, and she hopes it's not visible in the darkness of the car. "No!" she exclaims. "Why… why would you ask me such a thing?"

His shoulders fall as Jenkins visibly relaxes. "No. 'Tis a good thing, my lady. We don't want pregnant women around lambing."

"Oh. Oh yes. I understand. I am sorry."

"No need to apologize, ma'am. I forgot to ask earlier."

Alessia flashes him a smile. "I know pregnant women should not be around lambs and goats."

"Goats?"

Alessia laughs. "Yes. Where I am from, we have goats."

He turns by a large structure that Alessia realizes is a substantial barn. He parks next to a steel door, where three other cars are stationed.

"We're here," he says. "You'll be glad you wrapped up warm."

The barn is cavernous and chilly, and there must be a hundred or more ewes inside. Several are bleating loudly, in the throes of labor—these have been separated into smaller pens away from the pregnant flock. Among the pens, a few newborn lambs are already being nuzzled and licked by their mothers as they root for milk from swollen udders. A couple of the estate workers are busy with lambing among the pens.

They're just in time to watch one of the farmhands, whom Alessia has not yet met, help deliver a lamb. Wearing surgical gloves, he cleans the lamb's nose to help it breathe and places it in front of its mother to be licked clean. He grabs a bottle and dabs a little of the ointment, which Alessia notices is iodine, on the lamb's navel.

"Good evening." He nods a greeting to Alessia. "Oh, there's another," the young man says, and he sits back while the ewe delivers that lamb on her own. "Good girl. Easy there," he says in a soothing voice to the ewe and repeats the same cleanup process with her lamb.

"Where are the gloves?" Alessia asks Jenkins.

"The workstation over there." Jenkins points with his chin. His eyes are on the ewes and who's going to pop next. "We try to let them do this themselves. New Zealand Suffolk rams tup the sheep. Means they should have narrow shoulders and finer heads. Makes them easier to deliver. But some of them need help, my lady. It's good we keep an eye. We don't usually have them all lamb at once."

Alessia smiles at the young farmhand, who is now trying to get both lambs to feed. "Colostrum. Very good for new lambs." He grins.

Alessia heads to the workstation, spreads the disinfectant over her palms—paying particular attention to between her fingers—then slips on some disposable gloves. Jenkins joins her. "It's all hands on deck. It's just observing. Checking they're not in distress."

Alessia nods. "I have done this. But with goats. And not with this many."

Jenkins gives her a broad smile. "You're going to fit right in, m'lady."

I pull up at the Home Farm barn and, grabbing my camera, leap out of the car. I've stowed Kit's journal in the glove box and locked it. It should be safe there. Inside the barn, I scan the interior for my wife, but I can't see her. There are about thirty ewes in the birthing pens. I spot Jenkins, who's in the nearest pen attending a ewe. I squat down to talk to him.

"My lord."

"All at once? What did we do to deserve this?"

"Maybe it's the moon," he says as he pulls a lamb into the world. Its mother is very keen to get it cleaned up. Jenkins sits back.

I laugh. "What can I do? And where's my wife?"

"She's in the thick of it, somewhere in here. She wants to help."

I frown. *Does she know what she's doing?* But I keep that thought to myself.

"Okay, I'll get ready." I head to the workstation, disinfect my hands, and pull on some blue gloves. From there, I spot Alessia, her hair snaking down her back in a long braid. She's in a pen, clearing the nose of a newborn lamb and placing it in front of its mother. As I approach her, I hear her cooing in her own language. "Hej, mama. Hej, mami, ja ku është qengji yt. Hej, mami, ja qengji yt." Gently, she strokes the ewe's nose and repeats whatever she's just said in her soothing tone, then sits back to see if the ewe will produce another.

I'm suddenly overwhelmed with a swell of emotion that mushrooms in my chest and stops me in my tracks. My heart is full. Full to bursting—just watching my sweet wife interact with a sheep. A Trevethick sheep.

One of ours.

I have never seen Caro, or my mother, help like this on the estate.

And in that moment, I know Alessia is the best thing that's ever happened to me.

To us.

All of us. Here. Now.

I clear my crowded throat as I kneel beside the pen. "Hi," I whisper, my voice hoarse.

"Hello." She grins, and it's obvious she's pleased to see me, and she's in her element. She's thoroughly filthy, with blood, mucus, and heaven knows what all over her gloves, jeans, and sweater, but she's radiant.

"You okay?"

She nods. "And so is this little one." She rubs the lamb's head. "The mama did good. She may have another."

"This is not your first rodeo?" I ask.

She frowns.

"Not the first time," I clarify.

"No. Our neighbours. They came to our wedding. They have goats. I have helped when they are in kid. Often."

"Alessia, you never fail to amaze me. We're lucky to have you."

She waves off the compliment with a dismissive flutter of her hand. "You do this too?"

I laugh. "It's not my first rodeo either. I'll go see where I'm needed. But first…" I raise my camera and peer at my beautiful, disheveled wife through the lens as she smiles back at me, and I press the shutter. "I'm going to take more if I can. I don't have enough of you. And right now, you're absolutely fucking beautiful. I'd better go."

She grins, a dazzling smile just for me, and I'm reluctant to leave her, but needs must.

It's three o'clock in the morning when I guide Alessia into the shower to clean her up from the evening's exertions. We're exhausted and squalid from a full shift in the sheep shed. But we have seventy-two new lambs. I don't think I've ever, ever worked as hard in my life, but I'm thrilled. Only one stillborn, no rejections, and all the ewes are in good condition. That's an epic start to lambing. And I am so glad that we were here to help.

Now, I need to get my wife clean and into bed.

Alessia leans against me under the welcome warm water, her eyes closed.

My love.

She's nothing short of amazing.

She's scooped her braid into a gravity-defying knot and manages to keep it out of the cascade of water. I grab a cloth and soap and gently start to wash her hands, her arms, and her face. Then hold her up, while I wash myself.

Maxim towel-dries Alessia. She can barely keep her eyes open and thinks even her hair is exhausted. But she's exhilarated too. Finally, she feels that she's helped and given back to Maxim, and to the estate workers who have welcomed her so warmly.

"Can we just go to bed?" she mumbles.

Maxim gently clasps her chin and tips her head back so Alessia opens her eyes. "Your wish is my command, Lady Trevethick. Thank you for this evening and tonight. You were spectacular. You must be starving too." He brushes her lips with his.

"No. Just tired. So tired." She gives him a sleepy smile, and he drops the towel, scoops her up off the floor, then places her on the bed.

Alessia is asleep before I step back and cover her in the duvet. I move a stray strand of hair off her face, and she doesn't move. "My brave, strong girl. Thank you," I whisper and kiss her forehead.

I finish drying myself, drag on my PJs, and crawl into bed beside my wife, where I snuggle up to her and inhale her scent…

It's the rattle of cups that wakes me. Danny has entered our room with a very welcome tray of coffee and breakfast. The smell is tantalizing, and my mouth pools with saliva.

I am fucking famished.

"Good morning, your lordship. I hear you had quite the night."

"Good morning," I mumble, not wanting to wake up. I open my eyes, and Alessia's eyes flutter open but close again.

Danny places a tray at the end of our bed. "It's after eleven, my lord. I thought you might need some breakfast," she says, and I cannot remember the last time she brought me breakfast in bed.

I must be in her good books.

Or maybe it's Alessia.

It's probably Alessia.

"Thank you, Danny." I sit up, and Alessia is still fast asleep beside me.

Danny looks down at my sleeping wife, her face soft and sweet with a fondness I don't think I've seen before. "Oh my lord, you chose well," she says, and with that, she seems to come to her senses. She straightens, clears her throat, gathers our filthy clothes from the floor, and leaves.

Breakfast smells enticing.

Bacon, eggs, mushrooms, toast.

I pull the tray toward me, and Alessia rouses.

"I smell food," she says sleepily.

"Hungry?" I ask.

She offers me a sleepy grin. "Starving."

Alessia is becoming familiar with the rhythm of the house. In the morning, after they've washed and dressed and maybe made love, she and Maxim have breakfast with the staff in the large kitchen—usually, it's the second sitting. Afterward, she and Danny meet to discuss the day's menu, bookings, and requirements for the holiday houses, which includes the Hideout, and any household issues or tasks that need to be completed. When that's all done, Alessia has been going to the great barn to help with the lambing and moving ewes with their progeny to the bonding pens.

She's even driven herself.

Without Maxim.

He was anxious, but he let her go.

And she succeeded.

She needs to apply for a driver's license. And take a test.

All in good time, Alessia!

During the week, the Home Farm has welcomed 197 lambs and counting.

Alessia has done two more night shifts to help. And she loves it.

She loves it here.

She loves that she feels… useful.

She now knows all the estate workers by name, who lives-in, who lives nearby in Trevethick village, and who lives farther afield. They are all delighted that she's there to share the workload.

And she is m'lady.

To everyone.

In the early evenings, she enjoys a walk with Jensen, Healey, and her husband. The dogs adore her husband almost as much as she does… though he assures her the dogs were Kit's. The four of them have roamed the estate, and Maxim has regaled her with stories of his youth and his many, many misdemeanors, and she's built a mental picture of an idyllic life led by Maxim and his siblings here on the estate.

No wonder he loves it so much.

They've taken a couple of walks along Trevethick beach, and she's breathed in the fresh, salty air by the sea.

He has given her the sea… again.

And she loves it.

But tomorrow will be different. Tomorrow, after church, they're returning to London for Alessia's audition that will take place on Monday. She's been studying for that in the afternoons. Losing herself in the colors of her music in the great music room.

Maxim, too, has been busy. As well as the new still idea, he's been preoccupied with the concept of regenerative farming. He's holding a meeting of all the tenant farmers at the Hall this evening, with a farmer who's come from a place called Worcestershire— which she finds impossible to pronounce—to share ideas. Snacks and drinks are being provided—Danny, Jessie, and Melanie, one of the part-time staff who helps Danny, are serving, but Alessia will also be on hand. She's looking forward to it, as it's the first time they've entertained at the Hall, and she, too, wants to learn about these new farming practices.

Alessia's only concern is Maxim. He seems a little distracted sometimes. And she's not sure if it's the estrangement with his mother or something else. She's asked him about it, but he says he's fine. In fact, he says he's never been happier.

It's all good.

We're here together.

And I'm loving life right now.

Thanks to you. I love you.

Alessia feels the same, but she wishes he'd reconcile with Rowena because, deep down, she suspects he's hurting.

Sitting at my desk, I read through my notes for the meeting this evening. I'm excited. Michael, our estate manager who's in charge of the Home Farm, has lit a fire under me. My father was ahead of his time when he went organic. Michael's father, Philip, who ran the Home Farm back then, helped persuade all our tenants to go the organic route too. Today, with Michael's help, I hope to convince our local tenant farmers that regenerative farming is the next step in our ecological journey. Sustainable, regenerative farming is the way forward—it helps the estate, our producers, our land, the locale, and the planet. It feeds and repairs the soil, sequesters carbon and increases biodiversity. Through all my research, I've become a passionate fan. We have an advocate in a farmer from Worcestershire, Jem Gladwell, who will join us this evening. His substantial farm uses the latest regenerative techniques, and he's enough of a convert that he wants to spread the word and talk to fellow farmers using language that they understand.

I'm looking forward to meeting him, and he'll stay the night.

Our first guest!

And if tonight is a success, I hope we can repeat this process at Angwin and Tyok.

Once I finish my notes, I check my email, and my thoughts turn to Caroline, and from her to Kit's journal. I have squirreled it into the safe and pocketed the key. I haven't read any more pages, but I'm torn. I don't know if I want to find out more or if I should leave Kit to his secrets. After all, he's no longer with us.

I should let him rest.

But it gnaws at me… Caroline, faithless.

Is it any wonder we fucked when he died? I thought it was some grieving alchemy that got us together. It probably was, but as I look back, there was no restraint from either of us.

Hell.

Was she faithless throughout their marriage?

She said she loved him.

She was devastated when he died.

Devastated enough to sleep with me?

Fuck.

I hate that these thoughts plague me. Neither one of us behaved well.

Caro's sent me her interior design ideas for the mansion blocks. There are three options, all of them good. But I haven't picked up the phone to discuss them with her. Oliver wants the cheapest option, but that's no surprise. We'll be back in London for a few days from tomorrow evening—I'll arrange to speak to her then.

There's a soft tap on the door, and Melanie, one of Danny's protégés from the village, peeks around the door.

"Good afternoon, your lordship. Sergeant Nancarrow is here to see you."

What! Shit!

Anxiety rises like the tide in my chest. What does he want? To interview Alessia? On a Saturday? I thought we'd avoided all that.

"Offer him some refreshment and show him into the main drawing room. I'll be with him shortly."

"Yes, milord."

I blow out a breath. What could he possibly want?

When I enter the room, Nancarrow is sipping a cup of tea and examining the family photographs displayed on one of the Queen Anne tables. Notes drift from the music room, where Alessia is at the piano.

Keep it together, dude.

"Sergeant Nancarrow. Good afternoon."

He turns, and I extend my hand.

"My lord. It's good to see you." We shake, and I usher him over to where Melanie's set up tea, and we both take a seat.

"Congratulations on your recent marriage," he says and offers me a kind smile.

So far, so good.

"Thank you. What can I do for you?"

He blows out a quick breath and sets down his teacup, his expression now grim. "I've brought news, my lord. Unfortunate news. Earlier this week, the two men we apprehended at your rental property were murdered while on remand."

My scalp tightens, and I'm suddenly a little dizzy; I'm sure all the blood is draining from my head.

What the fuck? "How?"

"Details haven't yet been released," he mutters, watching my expression intently.

I sit back, utterly stunned… and a memory of the Arsehole showing me the newspaper clipping looms large and ugly in my head.

"I thought I should come and inform you. The case against them will lie on file but neither you nor Lady Trevethick will need to testify in court."

"Yes," I breathe as my mind goes into overdrive.

Did Anatoli *murder* them?

Does he have that kind of capability?

Was it someone else at his behest?

Fucking hell. Should I tell Nancarrow?

"So I wanted to return this." His voice has softened, and he hands me a large Tesco's shopping bag. In it are my laptop and sound mixers.

"How did you come by these?"

"The gear was in the back of their car. The BMW. We were holding the car and these as evidence—but now the case is defunct." He shrugs. "The serial numbers match those of your missing items. I thought I'd return them."

"Thank you."

His eyes darken, and I don't know what that heralds. "And there was this too." He reaches into a pocket, pulls out a brown envelope, and hands it to me. "We were waiting for the Met to ask for all the evidence, but they hadn't got around to it. And now, well, there's not much point."

Intrigued, I open the envelope. Inside is a passport—Alessia's old one.

Shit.

My eyes meet his, and I have no idea what he's going to say or what my response should be.

"I thought Lady Trevethick might want this back, my lord."

I'm stunned into complete silence.

He smiles at my expression. "And let that be the end of it."

I gape at him, not sure if I quite believe what he's implying. "Thank you," I blurt.

"I hear she's made quite the impression here, my lord."

"Maxim. Please."

He grins. "Maxim."

"She has. On all of us. That's her, playing now."

"The piano?"

"Yes."

"I do love a bit of Beethoven."

"Come and meet her. She doesn't mind an audience."

"I wouldn't want to intrude."

"It's fine. Come."

"Goodbye, Sargent Nancarrow," Alessia says as they shake hands.

"My lady, such a pleasure." His face flushes, and I know my wife has captured yet another heart.

"My lord. Maxim," he corrects himself, and with a nod, he heads out toward his squad car.

I blow out a breath. He didn't mention the death of the traffickers to my wife, and I decide to keep that information to myself for now—I know how unsettling it is for her to hear about that part of her life.

"He seems very nice," she says but sounds uncertain. "Why did he come here?"

"He was returning some of the gear that the arseholes who were arrested at the Hideout stole from my flat and also to return this." I retrieve Alessia's old passport from my pocket.

"O Zot! He knows!" She bites down on her bottom lip, her eyes wide with worry.

"He does, but he's chosen to give us both the benefit of the doubt. He's not going to pursue it."

Alessia frowns. "But when Dante and Ylli go to trial…" Her voice fades, and I shift my focus to Nancarrow's car as it disappears down the lane. "Maxim. What is it?"

Fuck.

"Tell me!"

I turn to face her, and her jaw is set in grim determination.

Hell.

"They died in custody."

"What? Dante and Ylli? Both of them?" Her voice is barely audible.

I nod. "That's the main reason Nancarrow came to see me… us."

"They're dead," she whispers again as if she can't quite believe it.

"It would appear so."

"Murdered?"

"Yes."

Her gaze scans my face, and I watch as a dozen emotions cloud her eyes, until they harden. Frigid. Callous. Unlike my girl. "Good," Alessia says, with such passion that I'm a little shocked. "I hope they rot in hell."

Whoa. But yeah. I hope so too.

"It also means there'll be no trial. We're free from all that," I whisper.

Tears well in her dark eyes.

Shit. No. "Please don't cry. Not for them." I circle her in my arms, pulling her close and kissing her hair.

"No. Not for them," she responds. "For their victims. But I am relieved. We are free."

"We are."

She exhales, and her body relaxes in my arms as if a great weight's been lifted. "It is a relief." She tilts her head up, offering her lips, and I kiss her, falling under her spell as her fingers twist and tug my hair.

She pulls back, rewarding me with her sweet smile. "Now. We just need you to talk to your mother."

I scoff and shake my head. "What? That's a change of subject. And it's my mother who needs to talk to me. I have texted her."

"You have? Good. She will. She loves you. She wasn't ready to tell her story. Only the shocking…um…headlines. And you weren't ready to listen."

I stiffen. "I don't know if I'll ever be ready to listen, and I don't know if she ever loved me. She loved Kit."

Alessia caresses my face. "Of course she loves you." She draws my lips to hers. "How could she not? You're her son… and I love you," she whispers.

There's a cough in the corridor behind us, and we straighten up and release each other.

"Danny?"

"My lord. Jem Gladwell is here to see you."

"Great. Show him into the main drawing room."

～

We're stretched out on our bed when we should be sleeping. "Can we come back here?" Alessia asks, her head resting on her pillow, and I face her as she traces the outline of my tattoo with her finger. It tickles… but I love the attention.

"Of course we'll come back here. It's our home."

"But soon." Her hand cups my face.

"Once you've done your auditions. Sure."

"Good. I love it here."

"Me too. I feel hopeful in this place. And now more hopeful for the future of it and for the estate as a whole. I thought Gladwell was inspiring."

"Yes. And funny too. He is good…um…company?"

"Yes. That works. He is good company. I look forward to seeing him again when he comes to Angwin." I haul her into my arms. "I think he liked you." I nuzzle that pulse point beneath her ear.

Alessia squirms and giggles in my arms. "That tickles."

I stop torturing her and gaze at her beautiful face. "We should sleep. I have to do my reading in church tomorrow morning, and then there's the long drive back to London."

"Are you nervous about your reading?"

I lean against the pillows while considering my response, and Alessia snuggles against me. "No. I'm not nervous at all. I feel a little hypocritical, to be honest. I'm not religious. Never have been. But Trewin is right. He's here for the community, and I need to step up and be here for the community, too, whether I like it or not.

"Tonight, listening and watching all our tenants and estate workers, I realized that all of us bind together to make a cohesive whole. We all work for the good of the community. And you and me, we're a part of that. I never thought about it before… when Kit was in charge here.

"Now, I want to be part of it more than ever. It's important to keep this place together and thriving for us and everyone who lives in and around Trevethick. We are its beating heart."

Alessia's dark eyes are luminous. In them, I see her hope and… dare I say it, admiration. "I want to be part of it too," she whispers.

"Oh, baby, you are. More than you know already."

"I have loved our time here. I can't believe that this is my life now. It is like a dream. Thank you."

I skim my fingers over her cheek. "No, my love. It's I who should thank you. This place has come alive with you here."

Alessia shakes her head as if she doesn't believe what I'm saying and kisses me. Properly, her hand skimming down my body… waking everything.

Again? Oh boy!

Chapter Thirty

"Do you want me to wait?" Maxim asks. They're standing on an ornate mosaic floor in the impressive foyer of the Royal College of Music, and Alessia's audition is in forty minutes.

"I don't know how long this will take. But I'll be okay." Alessia ignores her racing heart to reassure him. "You have work to do. I'll come to your office afterwards."

He frowns, unsure, and she places her hand on his chest, feeling the heat from his body through his shirt.

Comforted by his warmth, her heart rate slows to something approximating its usual rhythm. "I'll be okay," she repeats and tilts her head back for a kiss.

"Okay. I'll see you at the office. Good luck," he says and brushes his lips against hers. "As we say here, break a leg."

Alessia's brow creases and she looks down at her feet.

Break a leg?

Maxim cups her chin with his thumb and forefinger, and lifts her gaze to bright green eyes that sparkle with humor. "It's just an expression of good luck."

"Oh." Alessia returns his smile.

"Go. Warm up. You've got this."

Alessia takes her bag, and with a final glance at her handsome husband, she follows the young student who's been patiently waiting for her.

They head up two flights of stairs and along a corridor. The student introduces himself as Paolo and welcomes her to the college. He's casually dressed in jeans and a sweater, and Alessia hopes she's not too smart in her black trouser suit. He stops and opens one of the doors to a small rehearsal room. "You can warm up here. I'll be back to take you to the audition in about twenty minutes."

"Thank you," Alessia says, looking around the intimate space but, more importantly, at the upright Steinway and stool. They're the only pieces of furniture in the room. Paolo closes the door, and Alessia places her bag on the floor and sits on the stool.

This is it. She's here. She's practiced and practiced and practiced some more. She knows her pieces backward. She's watched YouTube video after YouTube video on audition techniques and what to expect. She's ready.

Taking a deep breath, she places her hands on the keys and launches into her warm-up... loving that the piano's tone is warm and immediate in this soundproofed cocoon.

In the cab on the way to the office, my phone buzzes, and I think it might be Alessia. No. It's another text from Caroline. She's sent me a few over the last few days begging for feedback on her designs.

For heaven's sake, we're meeting later this morning. I didn't know she was professionally so needy! Now she's trying a different tack.

How was Cornwall?

A303 or M5/M4?

In spite of myself, her text makes me laugh.

You know I hate the A303

It's for pensioners!

See you later

My eyes stray to the battered briefcase beside me on the seat. Within it are my notes from our meeting with Jem Gladwell, which I want to share with Oliver, and also Kit's journal—its mere existence searing a hole in my conscience and nagging me.

Should I read it?

Fuck.

Maybe I should burn it?

Alessia dampens down her nerves and steps into the audition room to meet a flank of the faculty, two men and a woman, sitting behind a long table. This room is airier than the last—big enough to house the Steinway grand piano in the center of the room—and there's a large sash window that looks out over the Royal Albert Hall.

The older man rises from behind the table. "Alessia Trevelyan. Welcome. I'm Professor Laithwaite, and I'm joined by Professors Carusi and Stells."

Alessia takes his offered hand. "Good morning, Professor. Good morning," she says to the other staff, who offer her smiles in greeting.

"Do you have your music?"

"Yes." From her bag, she retrieves all the scores and places them on the table in front of the tutors.

"Please take a seat at the piano."

"Thank you."

"Oh. What's this?" Professor Carusi asks as she looks at one of the scores. "Valle e Vogël?"

"Yes. By an Albanian composer. Feim Ibrahimi."

"Please. It's short. Let's hear it. And then move onto the Liszt."

Alessia nods, pleased that they want to hear from one of her country's leading composers. She takes a deep breath and places her fingers on the keys, the familiarity of the ivories calming her, and starts to play. The music is bright and expressive, an homage to an Albanian folk song darting through the room in shades of purples and blues, morphing into paler blue colors. Once the final notes fade, Alessia places her hands on her lap, takes another deep breath, and begins the Liszt… the notes taking her back to the apartment in Chelsea, with the snow swirling through the window as she played for Maxim that first time.

"That's enough, thank you," Professor Laithwaite interrupts at the beginning of the penultimate crescendo.

"Oh."

"The Beethoven. I'd like to hear that from the thirty-seventh bar," Stells says.

"Okay," Alessia says, feeling a little shaken. *Did they hate it? Is she bad?*

She blows out a breath while her mind zips through the hues of the score to the thirty-seventh bar. She settles her hands on the keys once more, then starts pouring her heart and soul into the rest of the piece while the colors flare in angry reds and oranges around her.

O liver's beaming smile and hearty handshake imply that he's delighted to see me. "What did you think of Gladwell?" he asks.

"I thought he was fantastic. What's more, so did our tenants."

Oliver claps his hands together in an unusual and spontaneous act of delight. "Michael has been trying to get this regenerative farming idea off the ground for over a year."

"He didn't tell me that."

"Yes. Kit just wasn't interested." Oliver shakes his head and looks away as if he's embarrassed or he's said too much, and I realize he doesn't want to be disloyal to his friend, my brother.

"Well, I think Kit missed a trick. I'm excited about it. Our next move is to galvanize the tenants at Angwin and Tyok. Gladwell's up for it. And we should talk in more depth about purchasing or leasing some capital equipment. It's going to be pricey."

"We can budget for it. I'll talk to each of the estate managers and get a date in."

"Great. Anything pressing?"

"Just the interior design for the mansion block."

"Caro?"

"Yes." And I don't think I've ever heard him say that word with such weariness.

"Is there a problem?"

"No. Of course not." Oliver clears his throat, and I make my way into my office.

That was weird.

My first task is to call Leticia and tell her about Sergeant Nancarrow's news.

"And why do you want to study at the Royal College of Music?" Professor Carusi asks, her shrewd eyes assessing Alessia.

"I need a backbone to my music. My musical education so far has been…um…quite local. No, parochial, and I know I can take it further with the right tuition."

"Where do you think you need help?"

"With my technique. I want to develop my voice, my playing. And my musical vocabulary."

"To what end?" asks Professor Stells.

"I would love to perform. All over the world."

Alessia cannot believe she's said that out loud.

They nod as if this might be a possibility, and Alessia is thrilled at the thought. She doesn't want to tell them that the other reason she needs to be there is because she needs a student visa.

"Well, thank you for coming to see us. Are you auditioning for other conservatoires?"

"I am."

Professor Laithwaite nods. "You'll be hearing from us."

Alessia has no idea if it went well, but she's relieved it's over. She knows she played well... but was it good enough? In the cab, on a whim, she calls her great-uncle on FaceTime.

"Alessia, my darling. How are you?"

She fills him in on the past week in Cornwall and tells him about her audition.

"Who did you see?"

"What do you mean?"

"Who auditioned you?"

Alessia tells him.

"Hmm... All good people. You'll do fine. I know it. Have you told your mother? She'll be thrilled. We've spoken often, though her English is not as good as yours."

Alessia grins, thrilled that they have been in touch with each other. "No. I will call her now."

"Well, good luck, my dear. Let me know how you get on and when I can see you again."

Next, she calls her mother to share her news.

At my conference table, Caroline talks Oliver and me through her moodboards and designs, and it's clear she's put a great deal of thought into her process. The first option is opulent but elegant; the second, upscale, warm but airy; the third, bold but minimalist. I have to admit, they're all quite different but clever. Caro has excellent taste.

"I think I prefer the second option." It's not the most expensive, but not the cheapest either. I glance at Oliver to see if he's on the same page.

"I concur," Oliver says, nodding.

"Good. Let's do it. I'll crack on." Caroline preens.

"Great. If you'll excuse me." Oliver rises from the table and leaves.

Caroline watches him go with a frown. She turns back to me. "So, how was Cornwall? How did Alessia fit in?"

"Great. Thanks. It was cool to be back. Alessia was and is amazing. Helped with lambing."

"Hmm… really?" Caro frowns.

Ignoring her reaction, I continue, "Yes. She knew exactly what to do. In fact, she wants to return to Cornwall as soon as possible. I think she's more comfortable at the Hall."

"Why wouldn't she be? She's waited on hand and foot, and it's very rural."

"Actually, she's not waited on hand and foot," I snap. "And what do you mean by that?"

"Oh, for goodness' sake, Maxim. Give your hackles a rest. I think she's a little daunted by London life, that's all. And who wouldn't be? She does seem to attract a great deal of attention when she's here. It's not a surprise," Caroline mutters and begins to pack her portfolio away.

Rather than provoke an argument, I change the subject. "I'm going to sell Kit's car collection. Are there any that you'd like to keep?"

She pauses mid-packing as if considering the option, then shakes her head. "No. That was Kit's thing. Not mine."

"You're sure?"

She nods. "I should move out of the countess's rooms," she adds, a little sadly.

"There's no hurry. We've not moved from my room."

"Oh." She raises her eyebrows.

See, Alessia's not the mercenary little social-climbing, point-scorer you think, Caro!

"So, what's on the agenda while you're here?"

"I don't know how long we're going to stay. Alessia has

auditions at the RCM, RAM, Guildhall, and somewhere else. I can't remember."

"All of them!"

"Yes. She's talented. And she needs to be offered a place so I can secure her a visa. Otherwise, she'll have to return to Albania for a month or so. And neither of us want that."

Caroline rolls her eyes. "For heaven's sake. It's not like she's going to be sponging off the state. I don't know why it's so difficult."

I sigh. "Me neither. It's the Hostile Environment that our government thinks we need. It's extremely bloody irritating."

"Agreed." She grabs her portfolio and rounds the table, only to stop in her tracks as she spies Kit's journal on my desk.

Hell. I should have put it away.

She pales instantly. Her cheeks ashen. "You found it," she says in a small voice that speaks volumes.

"Yes. It was in a locked drawer in Kit's desk at the Hall."

She turns her face to mine, her eyes wide and fearful, and growing larger and darker as the seconds tick by—and we gaze at each other as the air is slowly sucked from the room by the weight of this small battered leather tome. By the weight of Kit's final written words.

"Say something," she whispers.

"What is there to say, Caro?" I shrug. This is none of my business.

"You've read it?"

I open my mouth and close it again.

"Maxim. Tell me!"

And I know she'll hound me until she has the truth.

"You did. I can tell. I can always read you."

Fuck. "The last entry."

She swallows. "What did it say?" Her words are barely audible.

There's a knock at the door, and Oliver opens it, radiating polite smiles and fucking good cheer as he ushers Alessia inside. My spirits soar as she walks into the room. My wife is the cavalry, saving me from a beyond-awkward conversation.

"Am I interrupting?" Alessia asks, not unkindly.

"No. Of course not." Delighted, I step toward her and kiss her lightly on her lips. Everyone else disappears. "How was it?"

She shrugs but smiles. "I don't know. We shall see. I like your office." She looks around me. "Hello, Caroline," she says sweetly.

"Alessia, darling. How are you?" Caroline seems to recover her fortitude and steps forward to give my wife a kiss on each cheek.

Oliver has left the room.

"Caroline was just showing Oliver and me the designs for the mansion block refurbishment I've been telling you about."

Alessia casts dark eyes at me and nods, but there's a question in her expression.

Fuck. She knows something's going down.

I haven't mentioned Kit's last written words to Alessia, partly because it's none of my business, let alone my wife's, and partly because I don't know what she'd think of me invading Kit's privacy. But mainly because Alessia's opinion of Caroline is tentative at best—I've worked that out for myself—and I don't want to damage it any further.

"I'd better go. Oh, I meant to tell you," Caroline says, her voice clipped, and she tosses her hair to one side, having reverted to her usual cool persona. "Your mother's finally been in touch."

Oh! "She has?"

"She wants to postpone Kit's memorial until the autumn."

"How do you feel about that?"

"I think it's a bit late. You know, it's a form of closure. A way to say a final goodbye." She looks away, probably to hide her emotion or her shame, I don't know.

"Yes, of course. We should talk to her. I wonder what Maryanne thinks?"

Caro nods. Her lips clamp together as if containing her grief. And I have to remember that Kit found out Caro was unfaithful—because she sure puts on a good show of the grieving widow.

"Is Rowena in London?" Alessia asks.

"She is."

Alessia looks from Caro to me. "You should talk to her. And maybe persuade her that…um…more soon. No. Sooner is better."

"She's coming over this evening. Maybe you'd like to join us for dinner," Caro offers.

"We'd like that very much," Alessia says without hesitation, taking hold of my hand so I can't object.

What?

Chapter Thirty-One

My wife has been quietly campaigning for me to reconcile with the Mothership since Rowena's midnight meltdown. Alessia thinks I haven't noticed, but for her to seize the moment to meet my mother with such enthusiasm is surprising, given how awful she's been to Alessia.

You should hear her side of Kit's story. Sometimes women find themselves in... difficult situations.

That she would volunteer to spend any time with the Mothership is either foolhardy or courageous.

Mate. Who are you kidding?

Alessia is beyond courageous.

She steps out of the spare bedroom to where I wait in the hall.

"Is this okay?" she asks, raising her chin, her dark eyes on me. She's dressed in her Jimmy Choos, elegant black trousers, and a cream silk blouse. Her hair is brushed and swept back in a chic fancy braid, and the pearls I bought her in Paris nestle at her ears. Her makeup is discreet, her perfume an expensive whisper of Chanel, and her engagement ring sparkles beneath the light from the chandelier.

She's every inch a peeress.

And for a split second, I'm transported back to a time when a timid young woman with the darkest of dark eyes clutched a broom and hesitantly told me her name in my hallway.

The headscarf.

The blue nylon housecoat.

The scuffed trainers.

A lump threatens to form in my throat.

My wife fucking rocks countessing.

I cough to clear my emotion. "You're perfect."

With a flick of her hand, she swats my compliment away, but I know from the lift of her lips that she's pleased. "*You* look perfect. Muchly."

"This old thing?" I grin and tug on the lapels of my Dior jacket. "Let's go and get this over with. You happy to walk in those heels?"

"Yes."

I help her into her jacket and set the alarm, and we leave the flat hand in hand.

Our time away in Cornwall has done the trick. There are no press to hound us when we leave the building, and it's a mild evening; the dusk air is still warmed by a gloriously bright day that heralded the coming spring.

"We should move to the new house," Alessia says as we approach what will be our home on Cheyne Walk.

"We should."

"I can organize that."

"Okay." I grin. "I'll leave it to you. We can move at anytime."

"The most important piece of furniture is the piano."

"We'll probably need to crane it out of the flat."

She stops outside the house. "A crane!"

"There are specialists. I think that's how we got it in there."

"O Zot!"

"Yeah. O Zot. All manner of shenanigans. I'd buy a new one, but I'm very fond of that piano."

"As am I," she says dreamily. "It has such a rich tone. You know, when I was cleaning your apartment, it was my escape. I used to play when you were out. It was wonderful."

I bring her hand to my lips and kiss her knuckles. "I'm glad you had an escape."

Reaching up, she cups my face. "In so many ways," she whispers, and her fingertips stroke the stubble on my cheek, stirring my desire.

Enough.

"Come. Let's get this over with before I decide to take you home and muss your makeup and ravish you."

She grins. "That would be fine. But we should see your mother."

I ring the doorbell at Trevelyan House, and Blake answers almost immediately.

"Good evening, Lord Trevethick."

"Blake."

"Lady Trevethick," he greets Alessia with a genial smile.

"Is my mother here?"

"Not yet, my lord."

"Good. Caroline in the drawing room?"

"Yes, indeed, with Lady Maryanne."

With Alessia's hand in mine, we head upstairs and along the open landing toward the drawing room. Before I open the door, I take a deep breath. I know Caroline will want to finish the conversation we started in my office.

Alessia mentally braces herself as Maxim opens the door. They enter to find Caroline in an animated conversation with Maryanne as they stand beside the bar cart holding drinks.

Three hefty candles, each with three wicks, burn brightly on the coffee table, and a fire blazes in the grate, giving the drawing room a welcome, warm glow.

"M.A." Maxim's voice caresses her nickname, betraying his fondness for his sister as he steps forward and kisses her cheek. "How was Seattle?"

"It was fabulous, Maxie." Maryanne hugs him and closes her eyes as she briefly holds him. Of course, they've not seen each other since their mother spilled her secrets in such an obnoxious fashion in Maxim's apartment.

Maryanne turns to Alessia and beams. "Alessia, darling. How are you? I hear you were quite the hit during lambing at the Hall." She hugs Alessia, long and hard, surprising her.

"Hi, Maryanne. Who have you been talking to at the Hall?"

"Gin and tonics for you two?" Caroline calls. "Hello again, Maxim," she says stiffly and offers her cheek, which he graces with a kiss.

Maryanne pulls back, her smile bright and sincere. "I have my sources. You look lovely."

"Thank you, as do you," Alessia responds. "And yes, please, Caroline."

Both women are impeccably dressed, as usual—Maryanne in a navy trouser suit, Caroline in a belted charcoal silk shirt dress— but this time, Alessia feels she is too.

Caroline busies herself with fixing drinks, and Maxim offers his help.

"You look happy, Alessia," Maryanne observes.

Alessia smiles. "So do you. You went to see your friend in Seattle?"

Maryanne barks with laughter. "He's more than a friend. I did. We had a great deal of fun, and I'm hoping you'll all get to meet Ethan at Easter."

"I look forward to that."

"Tell me about Cornwall. I miss it so." Maryanne gestures to one of the couches and Alessia perches on it while Maryanne sits beside her, all eyes and bright smiles as if she's genuinely pleased to see her and interested in what she has to say. Alessia relaxes a little and regales Maryanne with her exploits.

Caroline hands me a gin and tonic. "We were interrupted earlier. You never answered my question."

"Caro. I don't think this is the time or the place."

"Please," she whispers, her plea so heartfelt it confounds me. Sensing my weakness, she persists. "I *need* to know."

"Maxim!" Maryanne exclaims. "Tell me you didn't teach Alessia to drive in the Defender. What kind of sadist are you?"

I turn my attention to her and my wife, who's eyeing Caroline and me warily.

She knows something's going on.

"I did. And as ever, my wife did not let me down." I give Alessia a sweet, and what I hope is reassuring, smile.

"The Defender?" Caroline scoffs, eyeing me from beneath her lashes. "Really? You are a sadist."

"Alessia can drive that, so she can drive anything." I shrug and take a sip of my gin and tonic, pleased that both Caro and Maryanne are calling me out, albeit unnecessarily, on behalf of my wife.

Caroline's lips press into a hard line, and she moves to hand Alessia a drink, saving me from our awkward conversation about the contents of Kit's journal.

The door opens, and Rowena strides into the room. Stark in a flowing black jumpsuit, no doubt by Chanel, she halts as soon as she sets her myopic gaze on me.

"Hello, Mother," I greet her brightly and step forward to kiss her cheek. She remains utterly frozen, blinking into the distance like she's desperately trying to wish herself anywhere but here. Ignoring her reaction, I kiss her anyway, and as I do, it dawns on me that she's terrified.

My mother? Terrified?

I'm horrified. But, what upsets me more, is that I recognize that look because I've seen it before… on my wife.

Something twists and turns and breaks inside me.

And before I can stop myself, I gather Rowena's thin frame in my arms, holding her close as my heartbeat races. "It's okay," I whisper as she stands unyielding in my embrace. "It's okay. I've got you."

Breathing in her expensive perfume, I just hold her, probably for the first time in my life—I don't remember ever clutching her like this, even as a child—and I don't want to let go.

As we stand in the middle of the drawing room, my heart rate settles into a calmer rhythm, and I become aware that the conversation behind us has ceased and that all eyes are on us, though neither of us can see anyone.

Rowena does… nothing. Just stands there. In shock, probably, and I think she might have stopped breathing altogether, but finally, she shudders, and with a half sigh or silent sob, she raises her face to mine and kisses my cheek.

"My boy," she whispers and cups my face, her eyes brimming with tears.

"Oh, Mama," I mutter and kiss her forehead.

"I'm sorry," she says almost inaudibly.

"I know. Me too."

A lessia watches the mother-and-son exchange that unfolds before her, and tears prick her eyes. And even though she can't hear what they're saying, it's more than she could have hoped for…

She glances at her sisters-in-law. Maryanne is stunned into silence as she gapes at her mother and brother while Caroline stares at them, frowning in utter confusion. Finally, she scowls.

"What the hell is going on?" Caroline exclaims.

Y ou haven't told her?" Rowena asks me.

I shake my head. "No."

She nods, a trace of, dare I say, admiration teasing her lips. "You are just like your father. I think you are the best of him."

"That's the nicest thing you've ever said to me."

She half smiles, then rolls her eyes. "All these… feelings. This is frightfully bourgeois."

I chuckle. "I know."

She steps out of my embrace, taking the weight of my anger with her.

"Will somebody please explain what's happening here?" Caroline says.

"Caroline, darling. I think I have some explaining to do," Rowena says. "But first, Alessia."

A lessia's heart starts pumping as Maxim's mother faces her and raises her chin.

What is this?

"I owe you an apology."

Alessia's scalp tingles—she is not expecting this.

"What I said to you the last time we met was unforgivable. Heath had been interfering, as you know. But I brought him to heel. I didn't want him going to the press. Anyway, I hope you can find it within yourself to forgive me all the same."

Alessia rises from her seat and moves toward Rowena. "Of course," she says.

Rowena holds out a hand, and Alessia takes it, surprised at the chilliness of her mother-in-law's fingers. "You have a generous spirit, my dear. Don't lose that."

"My husband has lost one parent, and you have lost a child… Neither one of you needs to lose another."

Rowena blinks a couple of times, her surprise obvious. "Yes. That's exactly right." She squeezes Alessia's hand. "You've had quite the effect on my son."

"And he on me."

Maxim wraps his arm around Alessia's shoulders and kisses her temple.

"I hear great things from the Hall about you, my dear," Rowena adds kindly.

"Could someone please tell me what the fuck is going on?" Caroline snaps.

"Let me fix you a drink, Mother," Maxim says.

"Wine. Please, darling." She sits in one of the armchairs facing the fireplace, and Alessia takes a seat on the couch.

"Are you ready to hear this?" She's addressing her children.

"Yes," Maryanne and Maxim say simultaneously.

"Hear what?" Caroline asks, still bewildered.

Maryanne turns to Caroline. "Daddy was not Kit's father."

"What?" Caroline pales and looks from Maryanne to Maxim, but he's busy pouring wine.

"It's true," Rowena says, frowning at Maryanne, probably because she's just blurted out Rowena's secret so rudely.

"I'm just catching Caro up on events," Maryanne says in her defense.

Caroline's lips part, but it's not from surprise—more like recognition.

"I didn't mean to spring this on you, Caro darling. I thought I might be able to tell you privately. I didn't expect the rest of the family would be here. Apologies for that."

Caroline nods as if she understands… or she's in shock. Alessia's not sure.

I put a glass of chilled Chablis on the coffee table in front of my mother and take my place beside Alessia.

"Do you want to hear this?" Rowena is addressing Caroline.

"I do," Caro responds quietly.

"Okay. I'll keep this brief," she says in her clipped mid-Atlantic tone. She folds her hands in her lap and stares into the waning fire. "When I first came down to London, I was naive and stupid. I wasn't interested in taking the university place that I had secured; I wanted to have fun. My parents had been terribly strict, but they seemed to abandon all parental control once I moved out. I was lucky, I was living in Kensington with friends from school, and one of them had a job as a model. She dragged me along to her agency. They signed me up, and the rest, as they say… I became what was known as an It-girl." She says the final two words with disdain.

"It was the '80s. Greed was good. And I was greedy. I embraced the scene, parties, shoulder pads, big hair… and one day, I met a man who I thought was a good sort, a musician with a good head on his shoulders.

"Well, he was unattainable, and I became obsessed. But one night, after a great deal of alcohol… well, I attained him. I won't go into the sordid details, and he wanted nothing to do with me after that.

"Around the same time, I was doing a great deal of work with John, your father. As you know, he was such a talented photographer—at the peak of his career. He was the top pick for all the glossies… so we did many shoots together. And our relationship was…more than professional, shall we say. I knew he doted on me."

Rowena pauses and takes a sip of her drink.

"By the time I found out I was pregnant, the musician had disappeared. When I finally tracked him down, he told me that the child was my problem. And that was that.

"It was…" She frowns. "It was too late for me to…well… Your father took pity on me. He was good and kind like that. We married. He embraced Kit as his own. And it became our secret.

"Cameron guessed, of course." She glances at Alessia. "That's John's brother, Maxim's uncle. He was furious." She turns to Maryanne. "But your father loved me…" Her voice fades, and her eyes grow more luminous, and she stares into the fire. The crackle of the flames and the tick of the old Georgian clock accentuate the rapt silence.

She shakes her head as if erasing the memory. "Anyway, Kit's father moved to the U.S. and became a hugely successful entrepreneur, and very publicly gay, which probably explains his dismissal of me and my child. I never heard from him again, and I pushed him to the back of my mind. Until he died last year. It was on the news, and that's when I learned of his genetic condition." She pauses and takes a sip of wine. "That was a dark day.

"It coincided with Kit seeking help for his recurring headaches. So I encouraged him to find medical help without informing him about his biological father. Just after the new year, Kit told me he had an issue, and he wanted to tell you two." She glances at me and then at Maryanne. "And that's when I confessed to him." Her lower lip quivers, but she swallows and maintains her composure. "He was furious, of course. And afterwards, he went out on his motorbike—" Her voice cracks, and from inside her sleeve, she produces a cotton handkerchief.

"Well, we know the rest," I mutter gently.

"Our argument was the last exchange he had with anyone," she whispers. "He was so angry with me…" She sounds almost childlike.

The room falls silent again, the quiet only disrupted by the clock striking the half hour, startling Alessia. The sound galvanizes Caroline, who rises and comes to sit beside my mother, taking the other armchair and reaching for her hand. "He wasn't just angry with you. We both let him down," she murmurs, and I think only I can hear them.

Rowena casts her a sympathetic look. "I know," she says quietly.

"He told you?"

Rowena nods. "I am in no position to judge, darling. Kit could be… difficult."

Difficult? Kit?

Caroline glances at me and promptly averts her eyes.

What the hell is that about?

What other secrets has my family been keeping from me?

"It's time to give him a proper goodbye, Mama. For all our sakes," Maryanne pipes up.

"Yes," Caro and I say in unison.

"You're right," Rowena concedes and dabs the corners of each eye with her dainty handkerchief.

"Good," Caroline says. "We'll go ahead with his memorial service as planned."

There's a knock on the door, and Blake enters. "Dinner is served," he announces, seemingly oblivious as ever to the bombshells that have been dropped in this room. But I'm pleased to see him. All these secrets are making me hungry.

"You okay?" I ask Alessia.

"Yes. You?"

"I'm fine. Much better, in fact. You were right." I reach for her hand and we follow Caro out of the drawing room. "I needed to hear her story."

"You…um…reconciled before you heard her story."

"A wise young woman reminded me that Rowena's my one remaining parent."

Alessia's cheeks flush a lovely shade of pink, and she smiles at my compliment as we head downstairs into the dining room that has been lavishly set for dinner.

The grand mahogany table is a spectacle, laid with delicate white-and-gold china with matching gold cutlery and candelabras. Alessia gasps when she sees it. But she also spies the Yamaha ebony upright piano at one end of the room.

Caroline insists that Maxim sit at the head of the table. On either side of him, Caroline and his mother take their seats, with Maryanne beside Caro and Alessia sitting beside Rowena. Alessia is pleased not to be fazed by the layout of the impressive cutlery, and once again, she's grateful for the etiquette course.

Dinner is a convivial affair. It's like everyone has taken a deep breath and exhaled. Maxim is charming and inclusive. He talks at length to his mother about his plans for Cornwall: The distillery. Regenerative farming. And Maryanne and Rowena plague him with questions, and Maxim answers them with informed ease.

His mother seems like a different person. Like she's broken out of a cage and is feeling the sun on her face for the first time in a long while. Alessia is fascinated.

Maryanne talks more about Seattle and Ethan and her exploits there. Alessia speaks of her audition at the RCM and her auditions to come.

The only person who doesn't seem at ease is Caroline. She glances continually at Maxim as if trying to convey something.

Finally, during dessert, Caroline rises. Maxim automatically does too.

"Darling," she says to Maxim. "I need to speak to you and give you those items that belonged to Kit. Please. Can we do it now?"

Maxim's gaze slides to Alessia's, and his eyes are wide, with what—panic?

Why?

Alessia decides this is something between him and his ex-mistress. Nothing to do with her. So she gives him a reassuring smile and offers a slight shrug of her shoulder.

"Of course," he says to Caroline and follows her out of the room, leaving Alessia with her in-laws.

"Alessia, darling," Rowena says. "I've heard a great deal about your musical talent. I'd love to witness it. Would you do us the honor?"

"Of course. I'd love to." Alessia rises from the table and heads to the upright. She lifts the lid and tries the middle C. It has a rich, robust tone that echoes in pure gold through the room. "It's tuned," she says, almost to herself, and takes a seat on the stool.

With a sinking heart, I follow Caro into the dark shrine that was Kit's study. I've not been in here since he died. It's a little oppressive, with navy blue walls, large paintings, and a shelf crammed with his curios, photographs, and trophies. I think I detect a faint hint of his cologne, and a vision from a long-forgotten dream or nightmare pops unbidden into my head. He's leaning over me. *You've got this. This is what you were born to do.* And he's smiling his crooked, sincere smile that's reserved for those rare moments— well, I thought they were rare—when he'd fucked up.

I'm suddenly thrown.

Perhaps they weren't so rare where Caro was concerned.

Hell. I'd always looked up to Kit and envied him.

He got the girl. He got the title. He was gifted at his work in the City.

From the dining room, I hear the piano. The piano on which I learned to play.

Alessia.

She's playing *Clair de Lune*, and I remember the last time she played that, I did too—and what a life-affirming experience that was. It's calming, knowing she's close by, and it pulls me from my gloomy thoughts to the matter in hand. The last thing I want to do is betray his confidences. His journal was exactly that. It contains his private thoughts, and I don't want to intrude on those, and I don't want Caro to do the same.

I decide to grasp the bull by the horns. "I heard what you said to Rowena."

Caro leans against Kit's antique desk and crosses her arms. "You know, then."

I sigh. "I know that Kit knew you had been or were playing away."

Caro's gaze stays steady on mine. "What did he write in his journal?"

"He was angry with you and Rowena. That's all. That's the last entry. I don't think he meant to kill himself. He was just angry. Angry at the shitty hand he'd been dealt."

"Are you including me in that shitty hand?"

For fuck's sake.

I slump into one of the tartan armchairs facing his desk.

"I don't know, Caro. It wasn't me who wrote it. And I'm in no position to judge. Neither is Rowena, as she's said. Was it one person? Several people? That was between you and Kit and your conscience."

She peers down at her fingernails, then turns and slumps into the chair beside me. "I did love him."

"I know you did. What did Rowena mean about him being difficult?"

Caroline sits up straight and peers at her fingernails again. She sighs. "He was aloof and demanding. Controlling. Occasionally violent."

What the fuck!

"With you?" I ask, sitting up properly as shock reverberates through every cell in my body.

She nods and looks from her nails to the ceiling. "Not often."

"That's awful. Why didn't you tell us?"

"I couldn't. I was too ashamed. And to spite him, I sought companionship elsewhere. I didn't think he'd mind. He did."

"Oh, Caro, I'm so sorry."

"Maryanne noticed. She told your mother. I think Rowena had words with him."

She stops… and we listen to the faint strains of the piano that Alessia plays with such finesse, but all I can dwell on is that my family has been utterly shite, and I was completely unaware.

"I knew I'd made the wrong choice," she whispers.

"Caro. Don't. We're not going there. What's done is done."

"It was so hard for me, watching you aimlessly dipping your wick in anything with a short skirt and a pulse."

I make a face. "Like mother like son."

She has the grace to laugh.

"But not anymore," I add, relieved that she still has her sense of humor.

She rolls her eyes. "Yes. I've seen it. You light up like fucking Christmas when she walks into a room. It's nauseating."

"No, Caro. It's love."

"You were never like that with me."

"No."

"She's a lucky girl."

"I'm a lucky man."

"Are you going to give me the journal?"

"Do you really want to know what it says?"

"No. I just hope he didn't hate me."

"I never got the impression he hated you, Caro. You two had a fine time in Havana and Bequia last Christmas."

"We were making an effort. Don't get me wrong. There were good times too."

"Dwell on those, darling."

She nods sadly. "I try."

"We should get back."

"Yes." She rises, and I rise too. She leans over his desk and grasps a wooden box. "These are some of his things I thought you might like." She hands it to me.

"I'll check this out when I'm home."

"Okay."

With the box in one hand, I give her a one-armed hug. "I'm sorry, Caro."

"I know."

"And well done for not crying."

She laughs. "Let's get back to the family."

Family. Yes. My family. My fucked-up family.

Sheesh.

Thank God for Alessia.

Chapter Thirty-Two

We walk hand in hand back to the flat, with the wooden box tucked under my arm, as I refused Mrs. Blake's offer of a Waitrose bag.

"We survived the evening," I mutter to Alessia.

"It was… extra."

I laugh. "It was!"

"Your mother was kind to me over dinner."

"My mother has seen the error of her ways. She seemed like a different person at dinner after she'd aired all her dirty laundry to the family."

Alessia makes a strangled noise of disapproval.

"Sorry, was my mother's laundry an analogy too far?"

She shakes her head and laughs. "What did you discuss with Caroline?"

"Kit."

Alessia nods. "I worry because I think Caroline is still in love with you."

"I'm not so sure. Caroline and I were never a good match. We were good friends. Are good friends. And that's where she belongs. In the friend zone. She knows I only have eyes for you. I've never loved anyone like I love you."

Alessia grins. "I've never loved anyone but you."

"Not even the Arsehole?"

She laughs, horrified. "Especially not the Arsehole!"

"I wonder if he murdered those men. Your traffickers."

"I have wondered the same thing."

"Does he have that kind of... reach?"

"I don't know," Alessia says.

"It's best not to know."

"Yes. Like you say... I don't want to be mixed up in that world."

"No. But we should do something. To help women like Bleriana. I'm going to discuss it with Maryanne. In fact, you should join our board of trustees for the charitable trust. And we can find a charity that helps women like your friend."

"I would like that." She squeezes my hand, and we walk in companionable silence along the Embankment. Alessia is not one of those women that needs to fill all the spaces with chatter.

And I love her all the more for it.

"What's in the box?" she asks eventually.

"Some of Kit's things. I'll have a look tomorrow. Right now, I'm having to reevaluate my opinion of him."

"Why? Because he's only your half-brother?"

"No. That's not the reason. He'll always be my brother. It's because of how he treated Caro. And me, actually... He wasn't a kind man, and he had a dark side that he kept well hidden. But not so much from Caroline."

"Oh."

"Yeah. Caro and I talked about that too. But that's her story to tell, not mine."

We reach the building, where Alessia unlocks the front door, and we head inside.

"I will miss this place," I mutter as we wait for the lift.

"So will I. I found happiness here." Alessia leans up and kisses my cheek.

It's not enough. I snake my free arm around her waist and haul her against me, walking us into the lift when the doors open. "So did I. I found you." My lips meet hers, and I lean her into the wall as we kiss all the way to the sixth floor. Tongues and teeth and lips and love. It's all there—in our kiss. We're breathless when the doors open.

"Take me to bed, my lord," Alessia whispers, her sweet breath mingling with mine.

"You read my mind, my lady."

O nce I've switched off the alarm and placed the wooden box on the console table, my wife takes my hand and leads me into the bedroom. Her dark eyes on mine, she removes my jacket and places it on the sofa.

She stands beside it and removes her jacket, laying it on top of mine—keeping her dark eyes on me the whole time. Her fingers move to her blouse, and she starts to unbutton it as she watches me.

Oh. I can play this game.

I raise my hand, remove one cuff link and then the other, place them on the bedside table, and shake my cuffs loose.

Alessia licks her upper lip, and it might as well be my dick.

Fuck.

She peels off her shirt and lets it fall free onto the sofa, so she's in her lacy cream bra, her dusky nipples straining against the gossamer material. She stalks toward me, tall in her heels, and swats my fingers away where they've frozen at my shirt buttons while I gawk at her.

"Let me," she says, eyeing me from beneath her lashes.

"Be my guest," I whisper.

Who is this siren?

She gently tugs my shirt from my trousers and continues to unbutton it.

Bloody slowly.

Each button.

From the top. It's driving me crazy, my dick extending and hardening with each unfastening. When she's reached the bottom, with a flourish, she pulls my shirt apart, leans forward, and plants a soft, wet kiss on my chest.

Fuck this.

I clasp her face between my palms and bring her lips to mine.

Oh, baby.

Her lips taste sweet, and they're eager. Eager to please me. And it's hot as hell. Our tongues caress each other, consuming and stoking our desire as I walk her back toward our bed. She comes up for air, runs her hands across my shoulders, and pushes my shirt off, so it falls to the floor. She runs her fingers down my stomach, through my happy trail, to the waistband of my trousers.

My girl is impatient.

I like.

And as she undoes the button on my waistband, I'm breathless, my dick hot and heavy. Pining. For her.

A lessia wants to taste him.

All. Of. Him.

She lowers the zipper on his pants and slips her hand inside. He hisses with satisfaction when she palms his thick erection.

She steps back. "Take them off."

He grins in obvious delight that she's taking the lead. "As you wish, wife," he growls and slides off his shoes and socks, then removes his trousers and underwear in one swift move—so he's standing gloriously naked… and ready.

Very ready. For her.

"You're wearing too many clothes," he whispers and drops to his knees, gently unfastening her shoes and slipping them off. He gazes up at her and unzips her pants, removing them with a gentle tug, leaving her in her bra and panties.

Slowly, like a green-eyed panther, he rises to his feet and kisses her once more, his tongue wet and demanding. Alessia breaks free and moves them around so he's standing by the bed.

"You're still wearing too many clothes," he murmurs.

"Let's see what I can do about that."

She grins, and planting her hands on the warm skin of his chest, she pushes him onto the bed. He laughs as he falls, startled by her sudden move, but props himself up on his elbows to enjoy the floorshow. She stares down at him and takes a moment to appreciate the beauty that is her naked husband sprawled before her. From his broad shoulders to the smattering of hair at his chest and his tight, taut stomach, to the hair lining his belly that she wants to lick. He looks delectable, his skin still sporting a faded tan. And he's all hers.

His erection swells under her overt admiration.

Slowly, she shimmies out of her lace panties. Then, without taking her gaze off his glittering green eyes, she carefully removes her bra, one strap at a time.

"Tease," he mouths, his eyes growing darker with desire.

Alessia relishes the effect she has on him.

She drops her bra to the floor and runs her hands over her breasts, still pinning him with her gaze. His mouth drops open, slack with needy lust, and she cannot resist a sensual smile of triumph. He's panting when she crawls onto the bed, over and above his body. She grabs his wrists, holds them to the bed, beside his head, and peers down at him so they are almost nose to nose. "You are mine. I want you."

"Back at you, baby," Maxim breathes, and as she bends to taste his lips, she releases him.

His hands skim down her back, to her waist and then her backside, where he grabs and kneads her flesh with strong hands while they consume each other.

"Lady Trevethick, you have a fantastic arse," he whispers, and she grins, nipping his chin before trailing kisses down his sternum, his stomach, over his navel and belly. His breathing shallows, and he tenses with anticipation when she sheaths her hand around his rigid erection.

With her eyes on his, she runs her tongue around him before drawing him into her mouth.

He closes his eyes and falls back on the bed, his breath hissing between his teeth in sheer pleasure. Gently, he places a hand on her head as she takes him. Up. Down. Again. Her lips sheath her teeth while he eases himself farther into her mouth with a groan.

She's relentless.

Taking him. Higher.

"Enough," he breathes. "I want to come inside you." He's hoarse. With want.

Alessia moves to straddle him, guiding him inside her in one swift move.

"Ah!" she cries out, relishing the fullness of his invasion.

And she starts to move up and down, cradling her husband and picking up her rhythm, in perfect counterpoint to Maxim as he meets her rise and fall. She leans forward, resting her hands on his chest. His eyes blaze a fiery forest green, the pupils large and dark. Full of love. Full of lust. Full of need.

"I love you." Alessia's lips hover over his.

He jerks his hips up, craving more. "I want you." And he moves suddenly, surprising her and twisting them both, still linked, so he's on top of her—his weight pressing her into the mattress as he drives into her.

He folds his arms around her head, cocooning her as he moves with an intensity and passion that leaves Alessia breathless and near…near…

She cries out as she comes, and Maxim buries his head in the crook of her neck and follows, calling her name as he climaxes.

Alessia returns to earth, surprised at the speed and intensity of her orgasm. She holds him tight against her, loving that they are still intimately connected. Her heart overflows with emotion as she nuzzles his hair.

She cannot believe that this is her life now, as she lies with the man she loves.

Her loving husband.

Her reformed rake.

Will it always be like this?

This intense.

This passionate.

She hopes so… forever and ever. Feeling beyond replete, she takes Maxim's left hand and threads her fingers with his and raises his hand to her lips.

"This is the sexy thing… sexiest thing," she whispers, correcting herself.

"What? My hand?" Maxim grins, his eyes reflecting her love.

"No." She kisses the shining platinum ring. "This means you're mine."

"Always," he murmurs against the corner of her mouth. He tightens his arms around her and they lie together, entwined, skin against skin. "I just want to hold you. Until the end of time."

"Will that be long enough?" Alessia whispers and kisses his chest.

"Never…"

~

When Alessia wakes, she's alone. It's Saturday morning, and she's had a busy week. Lying back on the soft silk, she revels in the quiet but listens to see where Maxim might be—but the apartment is silent. She calls out his name, and there's no reply. Perhaps he's gone for a run or maybe to fence with Joe.

She smiles, remembering their evening. They'd been out with Tom, Henry, Caroline, and Joe to celebrate her acceptance into the Royal College of Music. Their evening had started at a new restaurant in Mayfair, where Maxim and Caroline knew the chef—the Mediterranean food was terrific—and they'd ended the night in the small hours at Maxim's club. It had been a relaxing, cheerful evening—a perfect way for Alessia and Maxim to decompress after the stress of Rowena's revelations earlier in the week and Alessia's taxing auditions.

Today she'll start packing up the apartment, as they hope to move within a week. She'll need to go shopping for food because her great-uncle and Bleriana are joining them for lunch tomorrow, and she wants to cook her favorite Albanian dish for them. She checks the time, and it's after ten. It's not like her to sleep in. She climbs out of bed and heads into the wet room.

Fifteen minutes later, dressed in tight jeans and a white T-shirt, she enters the hallway and notices the red light.

Oh.

Maxim is in his dark room. She's never known him to use it. The only time she's been in there was the first time he kissed her. Walking up to the door, she presses her ear to it and hears him humming tunelessly to himself and moving around inside. Tentatively she knocks on the door.

"Don't come in!" he shouts.

She smiles. She had no intention of going in. "Coffee?" she calls.

"Please. I should be finished in about five minutes."

"Have you had breakfast?"

"No."

She grins and heads into the kitchen, deciding that avocado on toast will be on the menu, one of Maxim's favorites. Maybe with some smoked salmon.

I have been waiting all week to develop my photographs from our time in Cornwall, and I'm thrilled with the results. I pin the last of the pictures to dry and admire my work.

It's my wife. Smiling. Beautiful. Tresyllian House is a stunning backdrop behind her. Next, Jensen and Healey gamboling up the lane, Alessia in the background, the evening light at magic hour. And the photograph is just that…magic. Alessia on the beach, staring out to sea.

Man, she's beautiful.

Then one of the deer on the horizon—this might be print-worthy, and it can be added to the collection of my prints we sell in the gallery in Trevethick.

But my favorite is the photograph I took in the lambing shed. Alessia's hair is escaping her braid, tendrils framing her beautiful face, and her eyes are shining with pure excitement—but it's her smile of joy, her smile at *me* that would light up the world if we let it, that I love. I grin back like an idiot at her infectious, intoxicating smile, pleased with my handiwork. I want this framed, and on every desk I own.

My stomach rumbles, and I switch off the red light and step out into the hallway.

I lean against the doorjamb and watch Alessia move gracefully through the kitchen as she makes breakfast.

Avocado on toast.

I approve.

Finally, she looks up and rewards me with that same smile that I'm blessed to have captured on film.

"Good morning, husband."

"Good morning, wife."

Alessia abandons the avocado mix she's spreading on toast, circles her arms around my waist, and offers me a brief kiss.

I run my nose along hers as I hold her. "I'm feeling very virtuous." I kiss her. "I've been for a run." I kiss her. "I've showered." I kiss her again. "And developed the film I had in my camera when we were in Cornwall. I can't wait to show you the prints. I feel I deserve my breakfast." I kiss the corner of her lips.

"You do and so much more," she whispers, her arms sliding over my chest as she peeks up at me from beneath her lashes with a coy, provocative look.

Oh… like that, is it?

My body responds, and I fold her more tightly in my embrace and continue to kiss her, tugging her lips gently with my teeth. Her hands are in my hair, pulling me closer as she slides her tongue into my mouth, challenging me with hers. Closing my eyes, I groan and deepen the kiss, tasting her sweet, sweet mouth, my tongue meeting her challenge. I move one hand to her nape, cradling her head, the other cupping a cheek of her well-formed, denim-clad arse. Her hands are in my hair, pulling me closer, and I turn and press her against the wall, pushing my hips to hers to find some friction for my hardening dick.

Fuck breakfast.

"God, what you do to me, my lady," I breathe against her jaw.

"What you do to me, my lord."

"Shall we skip—"

The doorbell rings twice, and I place my forehead against hers. "Fuck."

"Not right now, it would seem." Alessia giggles and wriggles out of my embrace to answer the intercom phone in the kitchen. "Hello?"

"Alessia! Good morning. Let me in!"

"It's Caroline," Alessia says.

Damned cockblocker.

"Hi. Okay!" Alessia answers with an apologetic smile at me.

I grin. "Rain check." I kiss her nose.

She glances at the front of my jeans. I laugh. "Yeah. Yeah. I'll deal with this."

Giggling, she leaves me to get a handle on myself and my erection while she opens the front door to welcome Caroline.

G ood morning, Alessia," Caroline says, giving her a quick hug and a kiss on each cheek in greeting. "I hope I'm not interrupting anything."

"No. Come in. We're about to have breakfast. Are you hungry?"

Caroline is wearing jeans, brown leather boots, and her tweed jacket over a cream cashmere sweater. She looks as elegant as ever, but Alessia is no longer intimidated by her, even though she's barefoot and in her softest, most worn jeans.

"Sounds great." Caroline smiles a genuine smile. Alessia reflects that Caroline has been much friendlier and more relaxed since dinner earlier in the week, and she wonders if what she and Maxim talked about after dinner is the reason.

"We are having avocado on toast."

"Yum. Hello, Maxim," Caroline says as they join Maxim in the kitchen.

"Caro." He kisses her upturned cheek. "Coffee?"

"Please."

"Sit," Alessia says, directing her to the kitchen table she's already laid for two.

"You two are so domestic. Are you getting any staff?"

Maxim glances at Alessia, and before she can say anything, "When we move, yes," he says.

Alessia frowns. She's not sure they need staff in London, but she doesn't contradict him, and she retrieves a place setting and arranges it on the table, followed by coffee cups and saucers.

"When do you move?" Caroline asks.

"End of this week."

"We are starting to pack today," Alessia says, principally to remind Maxim that he needs to think about what he wants to take. She pops another slice of sourdough bread into the toaster and continues to spread the avocado-and-smoked-salmon mix onto the toast that's done.

Caroline's forehead creases with doubt. "Isn't your removal company doing that?"

"Yes. But personal items. And we may have an opportunity to…what is the word. Declutter."

Caroline laughs while Maxim eyes Alessia with alarm.

"Good luck with that!" Caroline says as Maxim joins her at the table with a cafetiere full of strong coffee. "That smells good."

Alessia places breakfast in front of Caroline and Maxim and waits for the toaster to pop up with her slice of toast.

"Hmm… this looks great, Alessia. Thank you. And I have some good news for you two."

"Oh? What?" Maxim asks.

"I spoke to my father about Alessia and her visa."

Alessia's scalp prickles and Maxim's head jerks up. "Now that Alessia's been accepted into RCM, she can get a student visa… and we can go from there," he says.

"But Daddy will expedite indefinite leave. He just needs the forms."

"What?" Alessia breathes.

"He's a senior director at the Home Office. This is within his gift. I had dinner with him and the Stepsow on Thursday—oh, sorry, my stepmother—and told him that you needed to jump through all these ridiculous hoops. For God's sake—you're married to a peer of the realm. He agreed with me. That doesn't happen often. Anyway, he called me this morning, with a plan."

Caro, that's…" Words fail me. On the one hand, it would be great to stop worrying about Alessia's legal status in the UK. On the other hand, this feels like… cheating.

"Darling, title has its privileges." Caroline correctly interprets my frown. "Wealth too. Of course," she adds.

"It does," I mutter, and turn to my wife, who's spreading avocado and salmon on her toast.

"That's great. Thank you, Caroline," Alessia says with enthusiasm, and it's obvious she has no reservations at all.

"I'll talk to our immigration lawyer about it." *And also my wife.* I'm not sure I want to cheat our way to citizenship for Alessia. After all, deep down, that's how I feel about our wedding. We didn't follow the rules, which led to awkward press questions, and I don't want to end up in the press because we circumvented the visa system. I'd like to do this properly, but perhaps keep Caro's father in reserve.

"This is really tasty, Alessia," Caroline says. "No wonder you don't go out as much as you used to!"

Alessia joins them at the table. "Lime juice and ricotta. My secret ingredients."

The beauty of launching my wife at Dimitri Egonov's party is that we are plagued with invitations for social engagements. I mean, I used to get my fair share of invites, but now we're inundated. Everyone wants to meet my wife.

I put the correspondence aside. I'll go through it with Alessia when she returns from her shopping expedition. Tobias Strickland, young Bleriana, and now Caroline are joining us tomorrow for Sunday lunch, and she's out somewhere on the hunt for ingredients—to say she's excited about this is an understatement.

I have offered to take us out, but she wants to cook.

And far be it for me to get between an Albanian woman and her cooking.

I sit back in my chair and eye the wooden box Caroline gave me at the beginning of the week, standing unopened on my desk. I don't know what's stopping me.

Dude. Open the box.

Reaching for it, I set it in front of me and lift the hinged lid. Neatly coiled on the top of a scrap of blue velvet is Kit's old Iron Maiden belt. I laugh out loud—Caroline knows I loathed Kit's taste in music.

Petrol Head.

Metal Head.

He loved, loved, loved his heavy metal bands.

I pick up the weighty belt. The leather has seen better days. The buckle, on the other hand, is as fearsome as the day Kit acquired it. Made of pewter, it depicts a beast's head, with one red jeweled eye over a skull and crossbones, with *1980* and *1990* carved on small plaques on either side. Between the dates, EDDIE is engraved on a scroll. Kit was fourteen when he bought this, and it was his pride and joy. I remember at ten years old being so envious... Odd to think I spent so much of my early life envying my big brother.

I put it to one side, reach into the wooden box, and pull out another box—this one clad in green leather. It looks vaguely familiar... The crown on the front should be a clue, but I can't place it. Opening it up, I find my father's Rolex.

It's a gut punch.

Daddy.

I ease it out of the box. It's chunky. A manly man's watch made from stainless steel.

My dad's watch.

Rolex Oyster Cosmograph is written on the face above three dials.

The word Daytona appears in red above the third dial.

Fuck. I tear up examining it. I remember as a child—I used to fiddle with the crown and the two pushers while he wore it. I was fascinated by it and loved that he let me mess with it. He seemed to enjoy it. *Time is precious, my boy,* he used to say, and he was right.

I flip it over, and there's an inscription on the back.

> *Thank you.*
> *For everything.*
> *Always your Row.*

Whoa. I had no idea this was a present from my mother. He wore it every single day, I imagine, as a testament to her. I shake my head, knowing what I know now.

She was lucky.

He loved her very much.

He gave her respectability and a title, and her son an earldom. And on the back of this watch, there's only gratitude. She admitted she was obsessed with another man. A man who didn't want her or her child.

Maybe this was why I didn't want to open the wooden box. I knew there would be... *feelings.* I have to reconcile myself with the fact that my mother married for convenience, not love, and that my father didn't have the love of a good woman.

Like I do…

But he had her respect. So there's that. Maybe that was enough for him. I have to take comfort in that.

I place the Rolex back in its case and pull out another dark green velvet box.

Inside, nestled on velvet, are a pair of silver cuff links with the Trevethick coat of arms. These are very Kit, and I'm trying to remember if he had them made or if they were a gift. If they are a gift, they'll be from Caroline. I'm heartened that she's decided I should have them, and what's more, it's appropriate.

Finally, at the bottom of the wooden box, I find a silver-framed photograph of Kit, Maryanne, and myself as children. Kit stands proudly between us, taller than us because he's about twelve and Maryanne and I are seven and eight, respectively. My father took the photograph among the dunes on Trevethick beach in Cornwall. Kit's arms are draped possessively over us, and he's beaming with pride. He was always king of the castle. His blond curls shimmer in the Cornish sunlight that burnishes our tawny hair, and we stand in dark contrast to our golden elder brother. I remember our father encouraging us to smile, and he must have said something funny, because Maryanne and I are both laughing—even though we'd probably just been playing a game that Kit devised, where we were at his capricious mercy.

The light is wonderful. Hold still, progeny.

That was Dad's collective noun for the three of us.

And his love is clear to see in the frame.

I don't remember seeing this photograph anywhere in Kit's house, but it must have meant something to him if he had it framed. And that gives me a warm but melancholy feeling of homesickness.

Kit. Kit. Kit.

I'm so sorry.

I trace my finger over his image…

You bastard. You let your anger get the better of you.

A lump forms in my throat.

Even though you were sometimes an arsehole, I loved you and I miss you.

I hear the rattle of a key in the front door, and I abandon the box to help my wife.

Alessia shuts the door behind her using her foot, as she's laden with shopping bags—only to put them down as Maxim comes barreling toward her.

"Hey," she says as he wraps his arms around her and holds her tight. "What's wrong?" she asks, folding him in her arms.

"Nothing. I missed you. That's all." He holds her for several seconds, his nose buried in her hair.

"I am back. In one piece."

"I know. I know. I'm glad you're back."

I release her and remember that I have a duty to perform. "I need to show you something."

"Okay. Can I put the shopping away first?"

I laugh. "Of course. Let me help you."

"So this is the safe, which you know. But this is the number." I hand her a piece of paper. "Memorize that and eat it afterwards." I raise my brows.

She laughs. "Tasty."

We're in my walk-in closet, and since I found out that Kit didn't give Caro access to any of the safes, I thought I'd need to make sure my wife isn't ever put in that position. I twist the dial to the numbers: 11.14.2.63. Then I turn the handle and open it. Alessia peers inside, fascinated.

"See?"

"Yes. What's in there?"

Kit's journal. "Important documents. My birth certificate. Passport. You should give me yours. The jewelry you wore when we went to Egonov's, which I should take back to the bank."

"The bank?"

"Yes. The good stuff is stored there. We have a vault, and we should go and look. There might be something you like."

"Why are you showing me this?"

"If something happens to me."

Alessia eyes widen in alarm. "What's going to happen to you?"

I chuckle. "Nothing, I hope. I just think it's important for you to know where everything is. There's also one at Angwin and the Hall. And when we're there, I'll show you those. You need to know what's in them and where they are."

"Okay."

"Good." I grin, feeling… relieved.

"Now that we're in here. Are there any clothes in here that you'd like to donate to charity?"

"I like my clothes."

"Maxim, nobody needs this many clothes. I'll fetch a black plastic bag."

I sigh, examining my overstuffed wardrobe. Maybe Alessia has a point, but this wasn't how I wanted to spend the afternoon.

"There, I've filled one bag." I step out of my wardrobe, feeling inordinately pleased with myself.

Alessia looks up. She's on the floor beside my bedside drawers, with a cardboard box and a black plastic sack. She holds up a pair of handcuffs and swings them around her finger. "Yours?"

"Ah."

"Ah," she repeats and grins as I feel a fucking flush creep up my cheeks.

Why am I embarrassed?

I laugh, because I can't think what else to do, and sidle up to her.

"I thought you would have been through that drawer when you were cleaning."

"No. But I've seen these before. Once. And this ribbon was tied to the headboard." She holds up the ribbon.

Damn. That was to restrain Leticia and her talons.

"You know all my dirty secrets."

Alessia nimbly gets to her feet. "Do I?"

"Maybe not all of them." I step closer and stroke her cheek. "But we could make our own."

"Dirty secrets?" Her eyes light up and she skates her fingers down my chest to the waistband of my jeans. "How about the rain check?" She glances up at me through her lashes with her most come-hither look.

Fuck, yes.

Epilogue

February. The following year.
Cheyne Walk

"How is this?" Alessia steps out of her dressing room and slides her hands down the black satin of the long, body-skimming skirt she's wearing. She gazes intently at me—and I know she's looking for my approval.

She doesn't need my approval.

She's a fucking goddess.

"Wow."

"You like?"

The fitted bustier is leather and strappy, so I can see skin beneath the bodice before it meets the skirt. I motion with my finger that she do a twirl, and she laughs and obliges. The back is held together by three separate straps that are unfastened. "Would you like me to strap you into this stunning dress?"

Alessia giggles, and I suspect it's with nerves. "Please."

"You look sensational." I kiss the soft, fragrant skin of her naked shoulder. "Has your father seen this dress?"

"No. Is it too much?"

"No. It's perfect. You look like you could conquer the world in this."

"That's what I thought. It's Alaïa."

"It suits you."

"Caroline thought so. She's a djinn to shop with."

Deftly I strap my wife into her dress, and when she turns to face me, I notice she's wearing her gold cross, and Trevethick diamonds at her ears.

"I'm a very lucky man, Lady Trevethick. Now, let's go and shock your parents."

Alessia is thrilled that her parents are visiting for this special occasion. They're staying with us in Cheyne Walk, and they love it. Especially Alessia's mother, who has blossomed in Chelsea. Her English has improved, and she's beyond grateful to see her mother's brother, Toby, again.

We've settled into our new home. After a great deal of negotiation between Alessia and me, we have a cook-cum-housekeeper who likes to be called Cook, and whose husband lives with us and works part-time as a driver and a handyman.

And then there's Bleriana, who is staying with us for another two months. Alessia is delighted to have her with us.

Me, I'm not so sure.

But, while she's studying English, she's earning her keep by helping Cook around the house.

Like Alessia used to do.

I just haven't told Oliver because I know he'd want her on the payroll.

And Bleriana prefers cash.

She's still nervous around me, and that makes *me* nervous, but she's making progress with her therapy, so we're hopeful that Bleriana will, one day, be less anxious. Alessia has been instrumental in restoring Bleriana's relationship with her parents. She hopes to return to Albania and teach, but in the interim she's been helpful in setting up our charitable trust for women who have escaped trafficking. Personally, I think her skills will lend themselves to this line of work once her English improves.

Jak and Shpresa will leave tomorrow, and Alessia and I will be heading down to Cornwall. Our wedding anniversary is on Sunday, and I've booked the Hideout for the weekend where we can celebrate, just the two of us.

It's a surprise for my wife and I can't wait.

I have plans.

I follow her down the stairs to the drawing room on the first floor.

M y darling, you look beautiful," Shpresa says when Alessia enters the drawing room. She hugs her daughter. "I am so happy for you," she whispers against Alessia's ear, speaking in Albanian.

"Thank you, Mama. You look lovely too." Alessia kisses her cheek.

Alessia's father frowns and looks at Maxim. "You think this is acceptable?" He waves in Alessia's direction, and it's obvious he disapproves of her dress.

"She looks stunning," Maxim says, even though he's not understood a word her father has said. Maxim's eyes heat as he stares at her, and his lips lift, either amused by her father or with a wicked, salacious thought.

Alessia grins at him.

"Like I keep saying, my daughter is your problem," Jak mutters, and Alessia grasps her father's hand. He gives her a reluctant smile, and Alessia notices the ill-concealed pride reflected in his eyes. "Your husband doesn't seem to mind you are half-dressed." He shrugs and gives her a quick peck on her cheek.

"Baba, it's not up to my husband what I wear. It's up to me."

Maxim intervenes. "Are you ready? We have to go. The cars should be here."

The Trevelyan family have had a grand tier box on level one of the Albert Hall since it was built, or so I'm told. I usher in our guests, and I'm delighted to find Tom and Henry, glowing with newlywed happiness, in situ with Caroline, Joe, and Alessia's friend Tabitha. I introduce them all to Alessia's parents, and I'm pleased Bleriana is with us, as she can help translate for Jak.

Her English is definitely improving.

I offer champagne to everyone.

"I say, Trevethick, I bet you never envisaged this when you first met Alessia?" Tom says as we look down at the stage where the orchestra has started to assemble.

I laugh. "No. I did not. Who would have thought?"

"We're thrilled for her," Henry adds.

"Is she wearing the Alaïa?" Caroline interjects.

"She is. She looks sensational."

Caroline's smile is smug. "It was perfect. I'm so glad. She's going to rock this concert."

"Mate," says Joe.

"Yep. Who knew?" I swallow down my nerves. My wife is performing at the Royal Albert Hall.

From our box I survey the great hall as it fills with patrons and wonder if I ever foresaw this moment. I'm transported back to that day when I first heard her play.

Bach.

And I tiptoed up my hallway to peer around the drawing room door and spy on her.

Maybe I did foresee this. I knew then that her playing was concert standard, and since enrolling at the Royal College of Music, Alessia's skill and technique has grown exponentially.

She's a classical rock star.

She's also a draw for the press. Her rags-to-riches story is irresistible to tabloid editors—we're occasionally hounded by paparazzi on a slow news day. I suspect that's one reason why the seats below us are filling up and the Hall is almost sold out.

I shake my head in awe and wonder, and there's a knock on the box door. Joe opens it and welcomes my mother, who enters with Maryanne and Tobias.

"Hello, darling," she says, and offers me her cheek.

"Mother." I give her and Maryanne a quick peck, then shake Toby's hand, delighted to see him again. His palms are clammy, and I suspect he's nervous for his great-niece too.

Alessia is performing as part of the RCM's special program.

There are three other performers, but Alessia will be last— she's the highlight of the entire evening.

I can't wait.

But that's not the only reason I'm so nervous. I don't want her to be stressed in any way… but she's probably stressed right now. This morning—she told me she's pregnant. And I'm giddy with joy, but we have to keep it quiet for a few more weeks.

I'm going to be a father.

Me. A dad.

I'm fucking thrilled.

I take a gulp of champagne and blow out a breath, and in the distance, a bell rings.

The performance is about to begin.

AEDH WISHES FOR THE CLOTHS OF HEAVEN

Had I the heavens' embroidered cloths,
Enwrought with golden and silver light,
The blue and the dim and the dark cloths
Of night and light and the half-light,
I would spread the cloths under your feet:
But I, being poor, have only my dreams;
I have spread my dreams under your feet;
Tread softly because you tread on my dreams.

WILLIAM BUTLER YEATS, *THE WIND AMONG THE REEDS*
1865–1939

MUSIC OF *THE MISSUS*

CHAPTER FOUR
"Delicious"—Dafina Rexhepi

CHAPTER SIX
Piano Sonata No. 14, in C-Sharp Minor, Op. 27 No. 2, Movement
  Three (*Moonlight Sonata*)—Ludwig van Beethoven

CHAPTER SEVEN
"Vallja E Kukesit"—StrinGirls, Jeris
"Vallja E Rugoves Shota"—Valle
"Vallja E Kuksit"—Ilir Xhambazi

CHAPTER EIGHT
"Magnolia"—JJ Cale

CHAPTER NINE
"Only"—RY X

CHAPTER TEN
Violin Partita No. 3 in E Major, BWV 1006: I. Preludio—
    Johann Sebastian Bach (Arrangement for Piano by Sergei
    Rachmaninoff)

CHAPTER ELEVEN
"Lo-Fi House Is Dead"—Broosnica
"Only Love"—Ben Howard

CHAPTER TWELVE
"Claire de Lune"—Claude Debussy

CHAPTER SEVENTEEN
Fugue No. 15 in G Major, BWV 884— Johann Sebastian Bach

CHAPTER EIGHTEEN
"Runaway (feat. Candace Sosa)"—Armin van Buuren
Prelude No. 2 in C minor, BWV 847—Johann Sebastian Bach

CHAPTER TWENTY-FIVE
Cornfield Chase (from *Interstellar*)—Hans Zimmer

CHAPTER TWENTY-SEVEN
"North Country" (John Peel Session 1974)—Roy Harper

CHAPTER THIRTY
"Valle e Vogël"—Feim Ibrahimi
"Années de Pèlerinage, 3ème année, S. 163 IV, "Les jeux d'eaux
    à la Villa d'Este"—Franz Liszt
Piano Sonata No. 14, in C-Sharp Minor, Op. 27 No. 2, Movement
    Three (*Moonlight Sonata*)—Ludwig van Beethoven

CHAPTER THIRTY-ONE
"Claire de Lune"—Claude Debussy

ACKNOWLEDGMENTS

Writing *The Missus* would have been a lot more challenging without the help, advice, and support of the following lovely people, to whom I owe a huge debt of thanks:

My Albanian publisher, Manushaqe Bako of Dritan Editions, for her invaluable advice on Albanian wedding etiquette, and of course all her Albanian translations.

Kathleen Blandino for her web-mistress skills and for being a most trusted beta reader.

Ben Leonard, Chelsea Miller, Fergal Leonard, and Lee Woodford for explaining the tortuous labyrinth of visa applications for those who wish to live with their loved ones in the UK.

James Leonard for all the posh-boy terminology—okay yah?

Vicky Edwards for her advice on foreign marriages and UK law.

Chris Brewin for his hard-won insights into British police procedure.

My beloved "Major" for his expertise in music and DJ equipment.

My agent, Valerie Hoskins, for her constant emotional and moral support, her bad jokes, and her priceless insights on the challenges of farming in today's UK.

Kristie Taylor Beighley from Silk City, distillers of distinction, for her expert advice on creating fine spirits.

And my dear friend Ros Goode for all the tips about handling a Land Rover Defender!

Huge thanks to my talented editor Christa Désir, for buffing my grammar with great humor and finesse, and for the handholding.

To all my wonderful, industrious colleagues at Bloom Books and Sourcebooks—thank you for your hard work, professionalism, and for having my back.

Thank you to my author friends for your broad shoulders, the inspiration, and fun times—you know who you are… There are far too many of you to name, and I might miss someone off this extensive list and I'd be devastated if I did!

Thanks to the Ladies in the Bunker for your support, laughs, and hilarious memes.

Thanks to all the authors from the Author Conference on Clubhouse, from whom I've learned so much.

Massive thanks to the ladies of the *I Do Crew*—your support means everything to me.

And thank you to all those social media goddesses for their continued friendship, including Vanessa, Zoya, Emma, Philippa, Gitte, Nic, et al.

Thank you to my PA, Julie McQueen, for wrangling me and the Ladies in the Bunker.

As ever, thanks and much love to my husband, Niall Leonard, for tutting over my grammar, for listening (sometimes!), and for the constant supply of tea.

And to my boys, Major and Minor—thanks for being you! You both shine so brightly and bring me such joy. Love you, unconditionally, always.

And finally—to all my readers.
Thank you doesn't seem enough…
but thank you for reading.
Thank you for everything.

ABOUT THE AUTHOR

E L James is an incurable romantic and a self-confessed fangirl. After twenty-five years of working in television, she decided to pursue a childhood dream and write stories that readers could take to their hearts. The result was the controversial and sensuous romance *Fifty Shades of Grey* and its two sequels, *Fifty Shades Darker* and *Fifty Shades Freed*. In 2015, she published the #1 bestseller *Grey*, the story of *Fifty Shades of Grey* from the perspective of Christian Grey, and in 2017, the chart-topping *Darker*, the second part of the Fifty Shades story from Christian's point of view. She followed with the #1 *New York Times* bestseller *The Mister* in 2019. In 2021, she released the #1 *New York Times*, *USA Today*, *Wall Street Journal*, and international bestseller *Freed*, the third novel in the As Told by Christian trilogy. Her books have been published in fifty languages and have sold more than 165 million copies worldwide.

E L James has been recognized as one of *Time* magazine's Most Influential People in the World and *Publishers Weekly*'s Person of the Year. *Fifty Shades of Grey* stayed on the *New York Times* bestseller list for 133 consecutive weeks. *Fifty Shades Freed* won the Goodreads Choice Award (2012), and *Fifty Shades of Grey* was selected as one of the 100 Great Reads, as voted by readers, in PBS's The Great American Read (2018). *Darker* was longlisted for the 2019 International DUBLIN Literary Award.

She was a producer on each of the three Fifty Shades movies, which made more than a billion dollars at the box office. The third installment, *Fifty Shades Freed*, won the People's Choice Award for Drama in 2018.

E L James is blessed with two wonderful sons and lives with her husband, the novelist and screenwriter Niall Leonard, and their beloved dogs in the leafy suburbs of West London.